ALEX   DALE

In Shadows Deep

Copyright © 2024 by Alex Teasdale

All rights reserved. No part of this publication may be reproduced, stored or transmitted in any form or by any means, electronic, mechanical, photocopying, recording, scanning, or otherwise without written permission from the publisher. It is illegal to copy this book, post it to a website, or distribute it by any other means without permission.

This novel is entirely a work of fiction. The names, characters and incidents portrayed in it are the work of the author's imagination. Any resemblance to actual persons, living or dead, events or localities is entirely coincidental.

Alex Teasdale asserts the moral right to be identified as the author of this work.

Designations used by companies to distinguish their products are often claimed as trademarks. All brand names and product names used in this book and on its cover are trade names, service marks, trademarks and registered trademarks of their respective owners. The publishers and the book are not associated with any product or vendor mentioned in this book. None of the companies referenced within the book have endorsed the book.

First edition

ISBN: 9798325764264

This book was professionally typeset on Reedsy. Find out more at reedsy.com

To Laura
My muse and my flame.

In Shadows Deep
'Anon'

In shadows deep, where whispers talk,

I walk a path, alone I stalk,

A yearning deep within me lies,

to don her form beneath the skies...

1994

Prologue

Heavy rain lashed the windows on the small, shabby, terraced street. In the dimly lit living room of one of the middle houses, seven-year-old Lucas Miller sat frozen, clutching his stuffed lion tightly against his slight frame. Tears streamed down his face as he watched his dad, usually so strong and stoic, crumble into a chair, his body convulsing with howls of grief.

There was a chill that surrounded Lucas. Maybe the window was open, or maybe all the happiness had been sucked from the room, creating a gloomy vacuum. Lucas could hear his father whimpering and stared at him. Each sob echoed around the room, which right now felt like the entirety of his world. Nothing would be normal now, would it?

A group of police officers were gathered around the coffee table like moths, their stern faces creased with a painful sadness. However, they quickly tried to hide it every time one of them caught the eye of the small, vulnerable little child with the lion sitting in the armchair, almost engulfed by it. Lucas found their presence both comforting and unsettling and wasn't sure how to feel.

The police moths kept coming and going, but a relatively constant group always centred around the coffee table. He couldn't count them all; there seemed to be an endless stream, fluttering around his house, sifting through his things.

One officer, a particularly kind-hearted soul amidst the others, knelt beside Lucas, her gentle eyes trying to offer a glimmer of solace in the darkness that enveloped the room. She removed her hat and placed it under her arm, resting the other hand gently on his shoulder. She spoke softly, trying to comfort the young boy as best she could, and her words feebly offered some level of empathy and understanding.

'Lucas,' she began, her voice soothing and warm, 'I know this is incredibly difficult to understand, but we found something...'

'No, I'll tell him,' said his dad from across the room. The officer looked around and tried to give him a warm smile, but it faltered quickly.

'I don't mind. This is a tough time. Perhaps I should -' she said but was soon interrupted.

'No, I'm his father; it will come from me.' His eyes were red and swollen as he knelt before Lucas and tried to find the words to explain the unimaginable. His voice quivered as he looked into Lucas's big, blue, watery eyes. He still clutched the stuffed lion to his chest, pushing it against his racing little heart. He knew. His father didn't need to tell him, but Lucas let him anyway.

'Lucas, sweetheart. Mummy is... she isn't coming home.' Tears were rolling down his cheeks as he spoke. Lucas may have only been seven, but he was brilliant. He would watch the news and was already reading at a higher level than his age. There was no point in pretending. 'The police, they've, er... they've found her... body. In the canal. I'm so sorry,

Lucas, but she's not coming back.'

Lucas's heart sank, pushed down by the weight of those words on his bony shoulders. Even though he'd already known this, hearing it out loud had been heavier than he thought possible. His tears streamed uncontrollably, and something evil and nasty took hold and began gripping his little heart. He was feeling anger, genuine anger. He clung tighter to his stuffed lion, seeking some comfort and calmness in the familiarity of its soft fur and familiar scent.

The kind officer spoke, her voice tender as she tried to navigate the heart-breaking conversation.

'We'll do everything possible to find out what happened, Lucas. We're here for you and your dad. If you need to talk or if you're scared, please reach out to us. We'll do our best to help you through this.'

At that moment, amidst the anguish and devastation, Lucas found a glimmer of hope in the kindness of this officer. When she spoke, whatever gripped his heart loosened just a little. He nodded silently, the realisation that he would never see his mother again struggling to settle in. He leaned forward into his dad's chest, squashing the lion between them, and they hugged, not letting go for what seemed like hours.

2011

1

Sweat stung Ethan's eyes as he navigated the overgrown single track. This wasn't a mapped trail, just a deer path someone had mentioned in the online forum, promising an adrenaline rush with technical descents and hidden jumps. Ethan lived for those moments—the wind whipping through his hair, the rush of overcoming a treacherous section, the satisfying burn in his legs as he pushed his limits. He rounded a bend, tyres skidding on loose gravel, heart hammering in his chest. Ahead, the path narrowed drastically, barely wider than his handlebars. A thrill shot through him.

Suddenly, a flash of something bluish and solid jumped into his peripheral vision and startled him. He jerked the handlebars, tyres screaming in protest as he swerved to avoid a low-hanging branch. The bike skidded sideways on the uneven terrain, sending him tumbling off. Landing on a bed of pine needles with a grunt, Ethan cursed under his breath. The bike lay a few feet away, slightly bent at the front wheel.

He swore as he picked himself up and assessed his body,

1

wincing at the sting of gravel embedded in his palm. Nothing serious, he thought, rolling onto his stomach and pushing himself up. His bike was in a worse state than he was and they weren't cheap. Glancing back towards whatever it was he'd swerved for, a frown creased his forehead. It wasn't a branch—it was... something else.

Curiosity got the better of him and dampened his initial annoyance, so he pushed through the undergrowth and squinted at the object hanging limply from the thick oak branch overhead. As he drew closer, a sickening feeling bloomed in his stomach. It wasn't a piece of cloth, as he initially mistook it for. No, it was much worse. Bile rose in his throat as he recognised a pale, lifeless arm dangling at an unnatural angle, covered in mud and sticky dark blood.

His breath hitched. It was a woman. Her body hung upside down, her ankles bound with a thick rope secured to a sturdy branch. Revealing her haunted face, her long hair cascaded down like a dark waterfall. Her clothes were stained crimson, and there was a huge gash across her chest, leaving a dark hole where her heart would be. A pool of rich blood had collected at the base of the tree, soaking into the forest floor and matting the leaves together.

Every ounce of adrenaline began coursing through Ethan as time slowed and the world span. A cold, chilling fear took hold of him. This wasn't a prank, some morbid trail decoration. This was real. Someone was dead.

* * *

'For fuck's sake...' Lucas said, as he surveyed the scene of the crime with a grimace. His once-tidy flat now looked as though a small bomb had gone off in his wardrobe. Clothes, a chaotic jumble of colours and textures, lay scattered across the sofa like small body parts. A lone black sock mocked him from beneath the cushions, its partner nowhere to be seen. But it wasn't just socks that had fallen victim—his shoes, too, were missing. And he had a prime suspect.

A familiar pair of dark, soulful eyes peered at him from beneath the coffee table. Luna, a pint-sized black and white working cocker spaniel puppy, sat amidst the wreckage, her normally mischievous eyes wide with a false innocence so blatant it was almost offensive. While undeniably adorable and a champion cuddler, she possessed a notorious fondness for absconding with his footwear. Today wasn't the day for it, however.

'Alright, you little toerag.' A smile tugged at the corner of his lips despite his mock scowl. 'Where's the other one?'

Luna's tail thumped against the floor in a happy rhythm, clearly delighted at the game afoot. She had a mischievous glint in her eyes, which were bright with energy. When he first got her as a pup less than a year ago, he mistook the white membrane across her right eye for a lazy eye. It gave her a daft look, although he wouldn't change it. That being said, her cuteness couldn't excuse her criminal activities. She must be stopped.

The flat became a war zone as Lucas embarked on his daily sock retrieval mission. Clothes flew, pillows were wrestled aside, and Luna darted under furniture with the agility of a professional sock thief. The morning light streamed through the window, illuminating the new, sterile furniture and the

1

detritus of last week's house move. It wasn't much, but it was his, and the chaos held a certain endearing charm.

He crawled under the flimsy IKEA coffee table that he'd rebuilt last night, finally snagging the missing shoe with a triumphant cry. Luna sat at his feet, her head cocked in another display of faux innocence that would have won her an Oscar. Brushing off a layer of questionable-looking fluff, Lucas ruffled her ears. 'Alright, alright, you win this round.'

Her antics were a welcome distraction, a dash of silliness before a day that promised both apprehension and excitement. Today marked his first day with the West Yorkshire Police major crime team. A dream come true, some might say. They might also be wrong.

Lucas wasn't one for grand narratives. Sure, his mum's unsolved abduction case some seventeen years ago might have nudged him in this direction, but he wouldn't call it a crusade. No childhood trauma, no formative experiences with the cops other than a few bewildered weeks as a kid. His dad had shielded him from all that. Crime just fascinated him in a morbid, can't-look-away sort of way.

He stood, glimpsing himself in the mirror. Early twenties, decent build, a bit on the short side, but hey, you can't win them all. Short brown hair, eyes a little too close together (even he'd admit that), and a nose that looked like it had been rearranged at some point. Not conventionally handsome, maybe, but someone's type, he was sure. Just not anyone he'd met yet.

With a last kiss to the little white spot on Luna's head, he grabbed his keys and headed out the door. It was a rare warm day for England, even at the height of summer, and he was already regretting the jumper he'd hastily thrown on.

Outside, his pride and joy awaited—a slightly battered grey Volkswagen Golf GTI, a financial burden he wore with pride (and a touch of self-loathing). It was a bit much for a new recruit, a point his bank account regularly made, but damn, it was fast.

He fired up the engine, probably waking the entire street, and pulled away, a grin splitting his face. Sure, he was about to embark on a career enforcing the law, but that didn't mean he couldn't enjoy a little recreational speeding now and then.

2

He clicked his key fob and locked the car door with a satisfying thunk. Looking up at the Elland Road Headquarters, he tried to take it all in. People passing by would say it was a dull, possibly even ugly, building. The bland, standard brickwork and official police blue trim to the windows would not win any architectural awards. It was a building lost in the sea of newly formed glass office blocks and renovated buildings which scattered the city skyline.

Leeds was a massive city with a superficial shininess befitting the 'business capital of the year,' but a cold, dark underbelly lurked in the background. Petty crime rates were on the rise and well above the national average, with those offending getting younger and younger by the day. You were almost as likely to make millions in this city as you were to get mugged.

Lucas continued to stare at his new headquarters. It was nothing exciting unless, of course, you were starting a new job. Or you'd been knicked for something. He took a big breath and strode in, wearing a mask of self-confidence. After some direction from a somewhat grumpy bloke in reception, Lucas found his way to the Major Crime Unit on the third floor. He stepped into the bustling incident room, a nervous excitement coursing through his veins.

The room hummed with activity—detectives huddled in animated conversations, the indistinct murmur of phone calls, and the soft tap-tap of keyboards filling the air. It certainly gave the illusion that something productive was happening here. There were desks arranged around the outside of the room, little pods of four people to a table. They'd been placed in a way that allowed most people in the room to face the central aspect, where three huge boards had been set up. This was obviously where they placed the critical information for any active investigations. As he navigated through the maze of desks, his eyes searched for the face of Chloe Wilson, the Detective Sergeant he was scheduled to meet.

And there she was, a warm smile on her lips and a friendly glint in her eyes. Chloe stood by a desk, her thick, voluminous brown hair cascading over her shoulders in gentle waves, interspersed with subtle highlights that seemed to catch the light with every movement, giving it a warm, honeyed sheen. She turned and caught sight of him with her large brown eyes that became incredibly expressive as she cracked a large, friendly smile. It gave her an air of approachability that immediately put Lucas at ease. When he'd received the email explaining he'd be meeting DS Wilson, he'd immediately looked her up on Facebook, of course, so he knew what she looked like. Unfortunately, he also knew she'd been to Greece in 2009 with her young daughter, Rachel, and that she was currently single. Revealing this information would probably creep her out. Best not to mention that.

2

'Lucas, right?' she said, extending her hand in a welcoming gesture. 'I'm Chloe. It's nice to meet you. Find the place alright?'

Lucas shook her hand, which was warmer and softer than he'd expected. She had a pleasantly curvy figure, which she'd had no intention of trying to hide. The top two buttons of her blouse were undone, and her neatly pressed trousers were tight. Calm down, Lucas, he thought to himself. Don't shit where you eat.

'Good, good,' he replied as coolly as he could, his nerves fading ever so lightly with each passing moment. 'The bloke at the desk pointed me the right way. But just excited to be here, really.'

Chloe's smile widened, and she flicked her hair across to one side. 'That's the spirit! But I'm sure we'll break it soon enough. Let me show you around and introduce you to everyone.'

She guided Lucas through the room, pointing out various people of interest and explaining the somewhat dysfunctional-sounding team dynamics. She had very expressive hands, punctuating every word with animated gestures. Right now, she was pointing to a young but balding man with no neck who was sitting behind a desk that his knees didn't really fit under. His shirt was two sizes too big and was creased in a way that suggested it had spent the last week on his floor.

'This is DC Stephen Wright; he's the same rank as you. Crap, though, if I'm honest, you'll be better than him as long as you can hold a pen.'

'Oi, I'm dyspraxic, and you know that...'

'Right, and this is Paul.' She was now gesturing with one

of her delicate hands to an enormous man with little grey pools of sweat already creeping out from under his armpits. His glasses were thicker than the bottom of milk bottles, and he had wisps of grey hair, suggesting middle age was approaching. 'He has no sense of smell. Not sure if it makes him a worse copper or a better one, but he always brings food back from the canteen, so I guess we keep him around for the snacks.'

'DC Paul Carter,' he said as he waved back with a grin, followed by a thumbs up.

'Oh, sorry,' said Chloe to a plain-looking woman who had just pushed past her. Beige clothing and absolutely no charm. 'That was DS Stacy Schell. She should be more highly ranked than us, but they don't seem to want to promote her.'

'Cos she's piss poor at her job, ugly and unpleasant,' said dyspraxic Stephen with a shrug. 'Hopefully, you won't see much of her.' Lucas snorted as Chloe steered him away towards an empty desk opposite Paul. Her hand touched his shoulder, and his breath almost caught in his throat.

'We're a close-knit bunch here,' Chloe said as they approached the vacant desk. 'And this will be your spot. Make yourself at home, Lucas.'

Lucas saw the desk—a clean slate waiting to be filled with notes, case files, and the intricacies of investigations—or just scraps of paper and crisp packets. Either way, he was already feeling the seed of belonging being planted as he settled into the chair.

Just as Chloe sat beside him, a commanding voice cut through the room's chatter. 'Attention, everyone!' The detectives pivoted their heads to see Detective Inspector Patricia Carmichael striding into the room. She was about six feet in her tall heels, clearly an authoritative figure with an air of confidence that demanded respect. She had a commanding presence, her dark eyes sharp and piercing as they scanned the room. Her neat curls of black hair bobbed onto her shoulders, framing her youthful face. Her wrinkled neck gave the game away, though; she was older than she looked.

'We've got a nasty one today.' She began wiping scribbled notes from a whiteboard in the centre of the back wall. Everyone could see her from where they were sitting. Lucas leaned in slightly, his curiosity piqued. The room fell into a hushed silence; every gaze locked onto the DI as she wrote the word 'murder' on the board and turned to face them all.

'As per bloody usual, a member of the public has done our job for us. At about seven this morning, a mountain biker came across this up in Emmet Woods.' She held up an A4 picture that Lucas had to lean forward and squint at to see.

'She was found naked and hanging upside down from a tree by her ankles. Her throat has been cut, she has been stabbed god-knows how many times in the chest and her body had been completely drained of blood, pissed out onto the forest floor.' DI Carmichael gazed out at the group as she spoke. Lucas felt a shiver run down his spine, not fear, though. Excitement. 'Someone or something has mutilated her chest and parts of her face. Her clothes and jewellery were also taken,' DI Carmichael continued, her expression hardened. 'No identification on her, obviously. Based on the old bruises to her thighs and buttocks plus the circumstances and location, it's possible, maybe even probable, that she was involved in prostitution.' The room was filled with a heavy silence as the detectives absorbed the information.

DI Carmichael's voice snapped the room back into focus. 'We need to hit the ground running on this one,' she said, scanning the room with a purposeful stare. 'PC Johnson, I want you to work with the forensic analysis team and see what they find.' She pointed at the little chubby man, not much older than Lucas, who was nodding back at her with disinterest. 'Chloe, gather all the information we have on recent missing persons. And Paul, start digging into any local criminal activity related to prostitution. In fact, no, you stick to searching all local CCTV. Stephen, you find out what the local working girls know about this woman. We need to work out who she is as soon as possible.'

As she continued to assign roles, Lucas's heart raced with anticipation. He knew he was new to the team and eager to prove his worth. She rounded on him. 'You're new. DC Miller, is it? Think I've had an email about you.'

'Yes, M'am,' he replied keenly.

'You can quit that shit. We're not on TV. Call me boss, Pat, or DI Carmichael. I want you to accompany me to the autopsy,' she said, her gaze steady. 'Think of it as an initiation; I want to see what you're made of. If you think about puking, swallow it.'

Lucas met her gaze and nodded, his resolve unwavering. He wasn't going to wilt underneath her stare. This was his chance to demonstrate his commitment and ability.

'They've had all morning to cut her down and move the body, so it should be on the table in the next hour. Meet me in the morgue; it's on the basement floor of the LGI. She turned and walked back towards the whiteboard. 'Bring a pen!' she shouted over her shoulder.

'Have mine' Stephen said as he handed over a cheap biro,

and the team dispersed. Lucas and Chloe exchanged a brief look.

'Is she always like that?' he muttered.

Chloe leaned closer to Lucas, her hand on the arm of his chair, and her voice slightly hushed. 'She's tough, but fair. You'll learn a lot from her. Just give your best, and you'll do fine.' Lucas nodded, grateful for Chloe's guidance. 'Oh, and best have another coffee before the autopsy.'

2023

3

Lucas peered at himself in the rear-view mirror of the car. The last twelve years hadn't been kind to him, his face littered with crow's feet, loose skin and dark bags beneath his eyes. The stress of yet another desperate, ill-thought-out promotion had left lines of terrible experiences, worry and fatigue. His journey from the eager constable to the seasoned leader of the major crime unit had been marked by countless cases, each leaving its mark on him, physically and mentally.

'The Water's Edge Reaper' murders, however, were something that reached into the darkest corners of his soul, reminding him of the brutal nature of the job. These were the cases they'd get him with when all was said and done and his career was over. Why did you not catch this man? How could you fail? He couldn't blame staffing; this was one of the most well-funded cases in police history. He was in charge of the most prominent manhunt since the Yorkshire Ripper. Everyone was determined to find the links and similarities between this case and that one, even when they didn't exist.

One similarity that was emerging, however, was police incompetence. This case was also one of the most well-publicised in living memory, which did little to help. His face splashed across the tabloids with every new failure. The whispers of doubt that had accompanied his rise to DCI hadn't escaped his notice. Some believed that the years had worn away his edge, that he was not fit to lead such a high-stakes investigation. His most recent promotion, only a few weeks prior, was met with derision in some quarters. But Lucas had carried those doubts like weights on his shoulders, using them to fuel his determination to prove them wrong, although tonight, even he was having doubts.

As Lucas parked his brand new all-electric Volvo on the gravel carpark, a sense of grim familiarity settled over him. He turned off the lights and sat still for a few beats, flexing the fingers in his left hand open and closed. He tried to turn it palm up, but a shooting pain ricocheted up his arm and around his elbow. It was still fucked, so he reached into the glove compartment and took out a blister pack of pregabalin, popped one and swallowed it dry.

Grimacing, he looked at the worker ants, dressed in their little white forensic overalls, scurrying about collecting evidence. They were lit by those temporary tripod lights that were surprisingly bright and aggressive. He could drive off, you know? Who was going to stop him if he just drove away? He could go to Wales and see the beaches or drive to Scotland and get pissed on good whiskey and shortbread.

His fervent daydream bubble popped suddenly as his phone buzzed in the centre console, and the whole car started to ring. A name on the screen popped up—Emily West.

'Hiya' he said.

'You busy?' came the reply. A light and husky voice filled the car. Sexy husky, not smokes-twenty-fags a day husky.

3

'Err, sort of. No, go on, what's up?' he said, fiddling with a little piece of plastic that was loose around the radio volume control.

'Well, I was thinking you were coming round later, and it was getting late, so I thought I better call you to make sure you are OK, you know, you haven't been murdered or anything,' she said.

'No, I'm fine; I've just been called to another one. Sorry, I should have rung and let you know.'

'Another one?'

'Yes, sounds like him again.'

'Oh god, where?'

'Emmet Woods, down by Water's Edge. He's repeating himself. Look, I'm going to have to just get this done. Can we do tea tomorrow instead? If this one is as grim as it sounds, you'll probably be asked to assist Dr Cross with the autopsy in the morning anyway. So get an early night or something, and I'll see you there, OK? We can grab a coffee afterwards?' As he finished, the little piece of plastic came loose, and he flicked it away.

'Sure, that'd be nice,'

'Bye'

'See you tomorrow, handsome,' she said, and he closed the call.

Lucas climbed out of the car, zipped his jacket up and pulled his hood up to try to keep out the biting wind and slicing rain. The sound of wet gravel crunched underfoot as he made his way to the boundary.

A short copper carrying too much weight with a beard and a mullet stood with a clipboard looking at him. 'DCI Miller, good to see you.'

'Aye, you too, Constable. How are the kids?'

'Good, I think; I haven't had them for a few weeks. Ex-girlfriend took them on holiday last weekend. I'm told they enjoyed it.' he looked a little glum about this.

'Ah, glad they're doing well. Sorry you're not seeing them as much as you'd like, though, Johnson. At least being stood out here in the pissing rain will cheer you up.'

'Yup, just the tonic boss. Here, put these on. Sorry, it's a bit wet.' Lucas took the silly paper suit and shoe covers he held out for him.

'So, do we think this is another one of his, then? You know, 'The Water's Edge Reaper'. He had a big grin as he said it, which Lucas didn't think was very appropriate at all.

'Potentially, we don't know that yet,' he replied, not reciprocating the grin.

'It is the same bloke though, isn't it? It must be. We've been waiting for this, me and my mate have a bet going. He says it's Murray, sneakin' out of the nick, or that ginger bloke never actually topped himself. I don't, but this must be him; it fits the MO and everything, right?'

Lucas gave him a slightly withered look. 'Maybe, but we need to keep a level head, OK. Don't start speculating, it just clouds your judgement.'

'Sorry, sir.' His grin faded, and the rain continued to run down his face into his beard.

'Pass me the clipboard and point me to the SIO, please, mate,' said Lucas, and he did as he was told. Lucas headed into the woods, stepping on the little metal trays they put out to stop him from leaving footprints and contaminating the scene. They were wet and slippery, which made them slightly lethal. Someone was going to end up on their arse in the middle of this crime scene, he reckoned.

He stopped just before the tarpaulin tent that had been erected to keep everything as sterile as possible and to stop nosy journalists from getting grizzly photographs. He wafted a hand through the flap.

'Good to come in, lads?'

'Miller? Yeah, come in, don't slip in anything,' came the reply. Inside the tent were three men dressed like sperms in their white costumes.

'Sir, good to see you,' said the first of them, a man by the name of DC Michael Green. He was a good few years younger than Lucas and had the same boyish charm and looks that he'd seen in the mirror ten years ago. He was new to the team, but had already made an impression as a hardworking officer.

'You too, Green, and this must be DS Matthews.'

The two men shook hands; the detective sergeant was a tall, thin, pale man Lucas hoped had brains because there was undoubtedly no brawn. If he farted in this tent, it would probably send him spinning into the wind.

Huddled over something on the ground was the third man: Dr Daniel Cross, one of the forensic pathologists. Even hunched over, you could tell he was very tall and gangly. His hair was thinning, and he hadn't looked up at Lucas, but just stayed hunched.

'Are you taking a shit there, Dr Cross?' he said, smirking at DC Green.

'Very funny, DCI Miller, but no. I'm looking at this.'

He moved over to reveal a pale oval object covered in mud. It was about ten centimetres long, and it had a red-ragged edge. Lucas moved closer and dropped to his haunches alongside Dr Cross.

'What the fuck is that?' said Lucas.

'This,' said Dr Cross, pausing for dramatic effect and carefully wiping mud from the top of the object with a sterile brush. 'This is part of her face'.

Lucas stood up immediately. 'Her face?' he said, no longer feeling amused.

'Yeah, I think it's the left cheek with some of her lip. The rest of her is about twenty meters that way.' he gesticulated vaguely with his left hand.

'Right,' said Lucas. He stood there in silence, thinking.

'You alright, sir?' said DS Matthews.

'Just give me a moment,' He said, staring at the wet, muddy ground. He brought his head back up, and they looked at each other, unsure what to do. 'He normally just slashes and disfigures the face. This is the first time he's taken a whole chunk off. I need to see the rest of her,' said Lucas commandingly.

'OK, we'll walk with you; just follow in our footsteps.

'Dr Cross, can you give us a minute? We'll come back to... this in a moment, OK?'

'Sure, just don't tamper with anything, please, Lucas,' said Dr Cross, turning his attention back to the strip of flesh on the ground.

Lucas followed DS Matthews and DC Green in a single file, each standing on their footprint tray. It wasn't the easiest of tasks; the ground was rough and uneven. As he went, Lucas looked around, searching for something, anything. But it was dark, and the only light was the occasional flash from one of the tech team as they bagged and tagged something.

'What happened here, DS Matthews?'

3

'It seems she was running. We found blood spatter on the leaves over a three hundred-meter stretch, and then here,' he said, pointing with his index finger.

They arrived at a small clearing where a tarp had been erected, a large blue plastic sheet propped up by several branches and weighted down at the bottom.

'We found the body here. The killer's made no attempt to cover her,' said DC Green.

What do we know?' replied Lucas, hunching his shoulders up in a feeble attempt to ward off the rain. His little white suit was becoming increasingly see-through.

'Not a lot yet; we only arrived about an hour ago.' started DS Mathews. 'She's about thirty, white, no ID on her. There are some bruises on her arms and legs; it looks like a struggle. There are a few large lacerations on her abdomen. And obviously... well... her face.'

'What's he taken this time?'

'Not sure, but there are some really deep slashes to her abdomen. Cross has had her photographed and will get her moved shortly, I think. He'll go digging and find us something. There's not much else to see here. It's going to be a while before the report is in. I'm afraid it's all pretty routine until we have the results.'

'I see. When did this sort of stuff become routine, guys?' Lucas sighed. 'OK, so no sign of her clothes or jewellery then?'

'Not so far, no, I'll get the search team to check again, but it's unlikely; I think we would have found them.'

Lucas moved towards the tent and opened it to peer inside. The woman was still tied to the tree. She was sitting leaning forward, her legs stretched out in front, her arms hanging limp. Her hair was messy and covered the sight of her face, but the volume of blood that was splashed down her chest and wrapping her thigh hinted at the facial flaying. He moved into the tent and looked closely at the rope binding her hands. It was thin, brown, and surprisingly flimsy. It looked like a standard household washing line. The knot had been tied around the branch, and her hands and the skin underneath the rope were red and sore-looking. Abrasions and cuts indicated that she struggled. The rest of the women were barefoot and naked. Lucas counted about three or four huge lacerations to her abdomen, so deep he could see some of her intestines protruding slightly and evidence of bruising around her shoulders. He leaned forward and touched the cold flesh of her thigh with his gloved hand; the blood was tacky to the touch. No matter how many dead bodies he saw, he never quite got used to it. He moved away, opened the tent's flap and re-emerged to face the others.

'Who reported this?' he muttered grimly.

'Some kids. Came out to smoke weed or whatever.' said DS Mathews. 'I've got uniform questioning them, but it seems legit. They saw her from a distance and came over to see what it was but didn't touch anything and were pretty freaked out. The officer who took the call thought it sounded like a prank, but he called it in when they showed up and confirmed it was real. So that's quarter to seven. Forensics were here by eight, I think, and we were here soon after. She's been dead no more than twelve hours, probably less. You know what it's like to get a straight answer from the pathologists.'

'Right, so no witnesses, nothing? Just some kids?' said Lucas, scratching his soaked head.

'No, sorry, sir, nothing. It's a popular walking route, but

no one else was there. There was no sign of a struggle in the area we've found so far, but obviously we will keep looking,' continued DS Mathews.

'I see. Well, let me know as soon as you hear anything,' Said Lucas.

'Of course.' replied DS Mathews

'And have you put out an alert for her face yet?' said Lucas, looking around at the treetops. He froze. That was awkward, and they all cringed.

'Err...' came the noise from DC Green.

'Yeah, forget that. We'll wait to see what Dr Cross can do to get some ID. With any luck, she'll be on the database,' said Lucas, trying to regain control.

'Right, sir, we'll get on it.'

'Good. See you later.'

Lucas walked off into the dark, the sound of his crunching footsteps echoing in the distance. Dr Daniel Cross was still bent over the woman's strip of face, his hands covered in latex gloves. Lucas approached him and crouched down beside him.

'Any thoughts?' said Lucas

'Well, it looks like it's him again,' muttered Dr Cross, not looking up at Lucas. 'Her face has been mutilated, she's had her throat cut, and she has at some point been tied up with rope. Although I haven't got an official cause of death, it does look like the typical combination of repeated asphyxia followed by exsanguination. She has the petechia around her mouth.' He pointed at the strip of skin on the floor, and Lucas noticed some little red spots around the bottom. He also noticed where her lip was for the first time and became hot and nauseated.

'What's he taken this time?'

'Stomach, I think. I'll tell you more tomorrow.

'Right. So PM in the AM then?' he said, trying once again to regain his composure.

'Yeah, I'll get that sorted. Will you be coming to watch and learn this time, or will you be flirting with our mortuary assistants?' said Dr Cross with a sly grin.

'Probably flirt,' he replied, grinning back.

Lucas stood up again and walked back towards the car park. As he passed through the crime scene tape and peeled his paper suit off, he looked around, searching for something, anything, that might be out of place, but the scene was just a mess. He could feel the eyes of the growing huddle of journalists and onlookers burning in to his back. It was nine-thirty in the evening, wet and cold. What the hell possessed these ghouls to come visit a crime scene like this?

He recognised a few of them, including a tall, withered-looking man, a few years older than Lucas. He had a well-receded hairline and a face so smug it was a battle not to kick his head every time he looked at you. His name was Simon Davies, a crime reporter for the local rag, the Yorkshire Post. Complete arsehole, in Lucas's most valued opinion. He was fighting his way to the front of the mob and got just close enough to be heard shouting,

'DCI Miller! A word, please?' Lucas ignored him and turned to Sergeant Andrew Johnson, who was still standing by the tape, shivering.

'Make sure you get the details of all this lot,' he said. 'And if Davies asks for a statement, tell him he's a bellend.' He climbed further up the hill and got to his car, but someone was leaning against it. Simon Davies, the reporter, had obviously sprinted up to cut him off.

'What do you want, Simon? You know you're not getting anything this early into an investigation,' snapped Lucas.

'We're twelve years in DCI, that's not early,' he said with a horrible, greasy voice and a smug, onanistic expression.

'You're assuming that this is linked to some previous cases, which it may not be,' replied Lucas, who steered Simon Davies out of the way and got into the driver's seat of his car.

'Certainly seems that way, given one of her organs is gone again,' came the reply. How did he know that already, Lucas thought? Hopefully, the kids who found her had said something, not one of his officers. He started the engine and leaned out of the window.

'Go away, Simon. You'll get an official statement tomorrow.'

'Just a word now, for our avid readers?' replied Simon Davies, exaggeratedly fluttering his eyelashes.

'You want a word? It's four letters and begins with a C,' and with that, Lucas drove off, missing the reporter's foot by an inch. He picked up his phone whilst driving and tapped out a text.

'We were right. It's him. We've found another one. See you tomorrow x.'

2011

4

Lucas was in the bowels of the Leeds General Infirmary, waiting for the autopsy to begin. It was a dark, windowless room, illuminated with greenish fluorescent lighting and white tiled walls. The air inside was heavy, tainted by an unavoidable acrid scent of formaldehyde and a faint whiff of something organic. A sparsely furnished room lay before him with a metal gurney, stainless steel table, and plastic chairs dotted throughout. The dead body on the gurney was small and emaciated. Lucas stood by, his gaze fixed on the table where the lifeless body lay and beside him stood his new boss, DI Carmichael, a formidable figure who was irritatingly taller than him and significantly more imposing.

'So, Miller,' she began, her voice as sharp as the gleaming steel tools on the table. 'What brought you to this unit? As far as I understand, you should be in South Yorkshire. Shit, I know, but we all do our time. Transfers like yours usually come with some baggage.' Her questions cut through the sterile air and hovered over the victim's body.

Lucas tried to meet her gaze with determination and cautious respect. 'No baggage, ma'am. Just a desire to work on something that matters. And I'm from Leeds, I live here. It was more convenient.' Even Lucas could tell his voice betrayed him. There was more to tell. DI Carmichael's eyebrows arched, scepticism etched into her expression.

'I told you not to use Ma'am. Start listening.' There was an awkward pause. 'Something that matters, huh? Sounds like bullshit to me. You're on the fast-track programme. They allowed the transfer because you're clever, and we pay clever people well.'

'OK, I find it more interesting than the other branches of police work. Is that a problem?'

She smiled at him. 'Now we're getting somewhere. Honesty might get you in trouble elsewhere, but it will get you far with me.' she paused, eyeing him up with her piercing gaze. 'Keep talking.'

He hesitated, unsure how far he wanted to take this conversation. He'd only just met this woman, so telling her about his mother seemed premature, as did telling her about his father.

'You got a girlfriend? A boyfriend? What makes DC Miller tick, I wonder?'

Dr Cross had just emerged from the changing rooms like the slender man. He was wearing a white jumpsuit with a pointless plastic apron tied over the top. Over-large brown gloves covered his hands, and his feet were in matching Wellington boots. His whole attire was a blend of practicality and professionalism.

Lucas hesitated. 'I have a dog, Luna. She keeps me grounded.' He paused, weighing his words. 'As for a partner, not looking for one.'

'Do you have fun, DC Miller?' said DI Carmichael, her tone probing. But before he could answer, Dr Cross, whose face was now covered by a plastic visor, began talking loudly, his voice echoing from the thick walls.

'OK folks, let's get started.' He picked up a very sharp-looking scalpel, rested it against the sternum of the corpse for a few seconds, and then slid it down her torso in one clean sweep. There was no blood, which took Lucas by surprise. It just peeled away, like when you cut the skin on pork.

Lucas was transfixed by the procedure and watched as the pathologist expertly sliced through the skin, creating a sizeable Y-shaped incision across her front and releasing the layers of fat and muscle below. Lucas had to steady himself on the table. He felt dizzy and sick; he hadn't expected it to be so... violent. This was something else entirely. He was transfixed. It was horrifying to watch. But he couldn't look away, even if he tried. He felt compelled to learn. To understand. The way she looked up close, how she was built, how she was made.

It was the first time he had ever seen a dead body being dissected. In fact, it was the first time he had ever seen a dead body at all. It differed from the television; it was real. The sight of a corpse is nothing compared to the smell. The room smelt of death; all the formaldehyde in the world cannot mask the smell of death.

'Fun, DC Miller. Are you having fun?' DI Carmichael said, leaning towards his ear.

'Not really, if I'm honest,' he muttered back.

'What would you rather be doing, then?' She said again, and Lucas realised she was chewing something. He stared at the little pack of chewing gum in her hand, slightly incredulous. She held it out to him.

'Have one? I always get hungry at these things. I'm not

allowed to eat; chewing gum is the best I'll get away with,' she smiled. 'You'll get used to it.'

The sound of a circular saw suddenly erupted in the room, making Lucas jump. Dr Cross carefully placed it across the sternum of the little body, in the line he'd already made before pushing down and cutting deeply. As he sliced into the torso and peeled the ribs apart, he released a puff of foul-smelling air from the cavity. Lucas had to sit down.

The autopsy continued for what felt like hours until Dr Cross stopped suddenly and had a somewhat panicked-looking conversation with his assistant. Lucas's ears twitched. What had they found?

The pathologist moved back to the little body and began rummaging in her chest cavity. The way his arm just disappeared inside her sent the room spinning again for Lucas. He pulled something from the depths and examined it without sharing his discovery with the group. Finally, he made his way from the table over to Lucas and DI Carmichael. He was standing in front of them, the little body behind him whilst an assistant put the various organs and detritus into a black bin liner.

'Right; you'll want to listen closely. The victim is an unidentified female; she's of small stature, five foot two and weighs only fifty-seven kilograms, probably in her late teens or early twenties. Possibly younger. She's malnourished, with bruising on her arms consistent with having been restrained. There's also blunt force trauma to the body here and here. These marks are from penetrating trauma, though, as she has three cuts to the abdomen of varying depths and another two to the left side of her chest. No hesitation marks. The tracks of these head down, but the lower wounds have upward facing paths. I suspect she was initially stabbed by someone sweeping up, but when she hit the floor, he could straddle her and stab her downwards. This was likely done just before death, but unfortunately, I don't believe it to be the actual cause of death. They've missed pretty much every structure of importance.'

Lucas shifted his feet from side to side. It was getting hot in this room, and he could feel his back beginning to run with sweat. The mortuary assistant was now ramming the bin liner of organs back into the little woman's abdomen with a frightening level of aggression.

'They probably would have been fatal if she'd been left alone, but she wasn't. In fact, she was subsequently tied up by her ankles. The ligature marks show she was alive when this happened. Equally, the eleven-centimetre cut across her neck was evidently made whilst her heart was pumping. It's a right-to-left incision, and it's deep. They've severed the right anterior and internal jugular veins, the right carotid artery, as well as the left anterior jugular vein. Her larynx is exposed down to the glottis. The hyoid bone is also fractured in multiple places, implying a significant amount of force was applied to her throat. She was asphyxiated. Strangled. Based on the pattern of petechia around the mouth and eyes, I think it was probably prolonged, but again, not fatal. They kept her alive until they chose to kill her.'

At this announcement, Lucas flinched and had to look away. What sort of person would do that? Dr Cross continued his voice monotone and professional as he listed the heinous crimes that had befallen the unnamed women. 'The remaining disfigurement to the face occurred after death rather than during the assault on her neck. It was probably done as a last-ditch attempt to make identification harder.' He paused and looked directly at DI Carmichael, who stared back. She had a surprisingly soft expression whenever he looked at her. Pause over, he continued. 'There is evidence of recent sexual activity, unclear if that was consensual or not. But there is semen in the vagina. There are fibroids in her uterus and evidence of scarring, consistent with her having had an abortion in the past.'

'Great,' said Carmichael, 'that might help with identification.'

'Possibly, but I haven't got to the best bit yet. She was interfered with post-mortem. These cuts to the chest were made sometime later, and I know why. He has removed her heart. In its place, they've left this.'

He held up a small glass vial with something brown curled up inside. Dr Cross carefully opened the vial and removed, it became apparent, was a small piece of paper. He unfurled it while Lucas and DI Carmichael watched on with bated breath, utterly transfixed by this discovery.

'It's a poem,' said Dr Cross, confused. He turned the paper around so the others could see the curled, calligraphic writing that slithered across it.

Beneath the moon's lamenting gaze, the heart beats slow, in shadowed haze,
Its crimson tides of love and dread, where secrets dark and light have bled.

'What the fuck is this supposed to mean?' said Carmichael, chewing her gum more and more furiously.

Dr Cross looked again at Lucas and DI Carmichael before he

began removing his gloves and visor. 'I have no idea. It's not something I've come across in practice. I've seen something similar with cult crimes, especially in the USA, but not here. I think this woman meant something to whoever killed her.'

'We need to work out who she is first,' muttered Carmichael.

'I can't find any identifying marks on her body; she has no tattoos, and her hands and legs are free of birthmarks. I'd say she was probably local. Her hair was in surprisingly good condition, given how emaciated she was. There's enough here to be consistent with the theory that she was a young, sexually active woman. I can't say if she's a working girl, but nothing here suggests she wasn't.

Lucas realised he'd been holding his breath and exhaled loudly. Dr Cross looked at him directly for the first time.

'You're new. You can look her over if you wish. As long as Pat is supervising.'

'I'd rather not, Dr Cross,' replied Lucas stiffly.

'Suit yourself. The body is being taken down for storage. There's nothing more I can tell you. You'll want a DNA profile; we'll take samples and pass them to the lab. I'll pass the poem to the lab as well. Otherwise, we're done here.' He turned to the DI and smiled. Lucas thought it was probably as warm as he ever looked; he was a dour-looking bloke who Lucas suspected darkened any room he entered.

However, he seemed to have the opposite effect on DI Carmichael when he said, 'Good to see you, Pat.'

She giggled like a little girl, blushed and said, 'You too, Dan. You're looking tanned, have you been away?' The man was ghostly white, thought Lucas. If this was him tanned, he must be translucent the rest of the time.

'Been to see my dad in Tenby. Picked the right weekend, got the weather for it.' He nodded his head towards Lucas and turned back to DI Carmichael.

'You got a new pet? Anything else we can do for you?'

DI Carmichael stepped towards the door and giggled again. 'Fresh constable for the slaughter. No thanks, Dan. I think we've got everything we need for now. See you soon.'

'I hope so,' Dr Cross said as he made his way out, but Lucas caught his arm.

'I have a few questions.'

'I don't think so,' he replied, raising his eyebrows at Lucas' sudden request. 'Pat asked the questions, and she said we're done. I offered you the chance a minute ago. You saw a dead body; there's nothing more to see. Remember, if you feel sick, there's a bin right by the door. You won't have to go too far.'

'It's just...' Lucas began, his voice cracking under the pressure of being on the spot, 'there are two types of bruising. It's clear that she was tied up, but it doesn't look like it was in one go. She looks like she was moved and tied up multiple times.'

Dr Cross looked at the young detective with a curious expression. 'The bruising would have come from a struggle before the girl was killed. He likely grabbed her round the ankles to keep her still whilst he tied.'

'But it doesn't look like it,' pushed Lucas. The doctor paused for a second, considering his response.

'You're keen. I get it. I am not always right, but I do not pretend to be. But you really need to think before you speak. It is too easy to make assumptions about these cases.' He looked at Lucas's face. 'I know this is your first murder, boy, but this is not a game. You need to understand that.' He paused and put his hands on his hips. 'I'm sorry. I am tired.' He removed his plastic visor and ran his hands through his thinning hair.

As he walked out the door, Lucas could hear him muttering under his breath, 'dickhead.'

Lucas turned to see DI Carmichael, hands on hips, looking at him.

'The fuck was that about? I was just beginning to like you. Come on.' She walked to the large, shiny metal door.

Lucas followed the DI, trying to catch up. He was having trouble with the heat, and the room's smell was making him nauseated. They got into the lift, heading up towards the main concourse. The doors had only just closed when she rounded on him.

'I need to trust you, Miller. You're inexperienced. I can't help you if you piss off other people, least of all my staff.'

'I'm sorry,' he replied, his voice low, feeling the weight of her disappointment in him.

'Yeah. I know you are. Just keep it in your pants next time.'

The doors opened, and he followed the DI into the bustle of the hospital proper.

'You've got a reputation for being ambitious, based on your academy results and your prelim stuff,' she remarked, her gaze piercing. 'Transferring to the major crime unit as soon as possible, on the fast track program—Is reaching my position your goal?'

Lucas met her gaze head-on. 'Yeah,' he replied firmly.

DI Carmichael's expression remained impassive. 'You've got a long way to go then.' And walked away, leaving Lucas alone beside a sickly-looking man with a fairly infective-sounding cough. Lucas dodged the spittle and began his journey back to the station. That was not really how that was supposed to go.

He arrived back at the station and approached his desk, where a flurry of papers awaited his attention. However, as he sifted through the documents, he noticed something that struck him. He seemed to be the only one in the room genuinely stressed about the case. Around him, the others moved with a degree of detachment, as if they were merely checking off another item on a long list of tasks.

Frowning, Lucas turned to DI Chloe Wilson, who was clicking through the missing people's reports on the computer.

'Is it just me,' he began, his voice low, 'or does it seem like nobody else is taking this as seriously as they should?'

Chloe's gaze met his, sympathy and understanding in her eyes. She leaned in slightly, her voice a mere whisper.

'Carmichael cares, and of course, I care, but you see, Lucas, the odds of catching the killer of a sex worker are slim. People are jaded. If we don't get lucky in the first few days, this will get parked for something bigger.'

Lucas considered this, not wanting to agree, but feeling she was right. This wasn't just his case. He had to make the best of what he had. He needed to get this right.

He could feel a growing unease, a feeling that perhaps he was too keen and that his eagerness to prove himself would alienate people. He drummed his fingers on the desk for a moment and sighed. This would be a long shift.

5

Lucas arrived at his desk the following day, and Chloe was already there. As he approached, he'd seen the back of her head; her long brown hair was tied in a messy ponytail today, matching her pale brown top.

'We got anything in?' he said, raising his voice enough to be heard by the others in the room. 'What's on the board?'

DI Carmichael turned towards him, eyes locked on his like a hawk, startling him a bit. He hadn't realised she was there.

'We have nothing new on our unidentified female. No name, ID, or dental records yet, but they might arrive later. We're going to need to find a way to ID her soon. Perhaps if you were on time, you'd know this.'

'Sorry, I was, er... parking. They haven't given me a space yet,' He said. This was a lie. In truth, he'd had to check on his father, who lived about fifteen minutes from the station in the wrong direction. This was the real reason he'd requested the transfer to Leeds. In the years that followed the murder of his mother, he'd slowly lost a father as well. Lucas often said he'd found Christ but in the catholic sense of the word. The blood of Christ; two bottles a day. He was still functional and held down a menial job in the local supermarket, but

Lucas knew it was only a matter of time before he would lose that.

'You will not get a parking space while remaining a DC, so best work on changing that. It would help if we could match her with some prostitutes. That would be a good place to start. We also need to work out what the toss that poem means.'

He'd gone cherry red, and Chloe leaned over to him, whispering in his ear, 'I know you think we don't care about finding this girl, but we will do our jobs properly.' she winked. Going even more red, Lucas caught himself grinning as she settled back in her chair before sitting down himself.

He'd been assigned to three different cases and was about to chase up an alibi for a man called Hàoyú Zhang, who owned a small cleaning business called 'Sparkling Panda'. Mr Zhang had been accused of pushing his wife down his garden steps, but claimed to have been having an affair with a member of his staff in a hotel across the city at the time. Once he'd done this, he'd need to visit a primary school and collect statements from some teachers about one of the support staff who'd been discovered with a phenomenal amount of indecent images of children on his computer.

However, his first job in this case was to log in the CCTV footage from the area around the path leading to Emmet Woods and then down to the area called 'Water's Edge' where the body had been found. Chloe was working on the murdered girl as well, so he had more of a vested interest in working on this one as a priority.

As it was a rural area, there wasn't much to go on, but a local off-licence and a grotty-looking barber had provided some grainy footage of the road and cycle path nearby. He

5

checked the dates and times of the recordings, made sure the cameras were working, and then began the tedious process of working through them, looking for any sign of a man who was trying to dispose of a body.

A couple of hours passed, and he was still staring at the screens, frustrated by the lack of anything useful.

'You got anything?' he said to Chloe, Paul, and Stephen.

The two blokes shrugged and, in unison, said, 'fuck all, mate, you?' Lucas looked down at the little tally he was keeping on his notepad.

'Two cocker spaniels like mine, three border collies, a couple of sausage dogs and something white and fluffy, possibly a Bichon Frise. Lots of people walk their dogs down here, but nobody is disposing of a body.'

Chloe piped up and said, 'Couple of maybes over here? Want to check them out with me?' she said, clearly directing her question at Lucas. He smiled, nodded and slid his wheelie chair over to her desk.

'Two girls that I think could be a match for the body. Obviously, photographs are fairly useless, given what he did to the face, but we've got a girl, Amy Savage, aged nineteen, who vanished about three weeks ago. She was homeless, slept rough, and had been seen in the red-light district and reported missing, bizarrely, by a regular punter who was missing his weekly bit of strange. They didn't give a name, but if she looks likely, we can try to track the phone that was used. Let's talk to her parents, see if they have anything more to say.'

'Sounds like there's something in that. And the other one?'

'The other one is different. She's a young girl, just turned sixteen last month, called Jessica Murray. She was a pupil at St Anne's, the local girls' grammar school, but her family says she ran away. We have found no evidence to suggest that this is true. She was reported missing three days ago. I'm not sure if she's a match for the body; the last photo we have of her, she looks too big, but I think we should keep an eye on her. See what you think when we see a more recent photo. Her dad owns a garage and has been threatening to pull every CCTV camera in the city. According to the file, there are no images of her leaving the school and no images of her on any cameras in the town centre. You recognise her from your hunt through the CCTV recordings?'

She showed him a school photo of a young girl with a round face, long brown hair, and a pleasant smile. She wore a dark blue blazer over a grey uniform adorned with the St Anne's crest.

Lucas shook his head. 'No, sorry. I didn't see anyone who looked like her.'

'Yeah, me neither. But if she's run away, then she could be in trouble. Apparently, she was a bit of a rebel but was doing well academically. Her grades were pretty good, considering she was struggling. I think she might have been trying to escape from something. Her father has a temper, apparently. Done time for GBH. Beat the shit out of a lad for supporting Manchester United.' She glanced sideways at Lucas.

'Actually, that seems fairly reasonable,' and she grinned, looking pretty when she smiled, he noticed. 'Gut instinct, but maybe he could have something to do with it?'

'Do we want to be careful what we say to him, then?' Lucas asked, feeling slightly uneasy.

Chloe nodded. 'Yes. Absolutely. He's a nasty piece of work, so let me do the talking.'

5

'No, I'll do the talking, you should – '

'I can look after myself, Miller,' she said firmly. 'I'm Detective Sargent, you're Detective Constable. Not to pull rank, but I've been at this longer than you. Being fast-tracked means you've passed exams, not that you're good. You'll still need to prove that.'

Lucas smirked back at her, 'Fair enough won't take long. So why's he threatening the CCTV companies?'

'I think he thinks the police aren't doing enough to find her. Which we're probably not in fairness. Right, I've got the addresses; let's go. Amy first, and then little Jessica.'

2023

6

DCI Lucas Miller entered the police station through a set of double doors, which automatically slid open as he approached. He closed his sopping wet umbrella, leaving a small puddle on the shiny floor, swiped his key card lazily and passed through the gate, which had swung open. The hallway down to the incident room was brightly lit and decorated with various phallic-looking modern art pieces, none of which made any sense to him. It made the whole environment feel sleek, futuristic, and like a Scandinavian sex museum.

As Lucas made his way down, he passed several other officers, who deliberately ignored him. This wasn't the first time this had occurred, and he knew that most of the station still judged him for what had happened a few years earlier. Lucas didn't care; he was used to it and had become accustomed to working alone. He thought it was easier for him that way without worrying about the politics and backstabbing that seemed to be part and parcel of being a detective.

As he reached the door of the incident room, he turned and peered through the window. A small group of detectives and junior staff had gathered around the collection of whiteboards which adorned the far wall. Lucas could see they had already put up some photos of the woman tied to the tree last night. Gruesome as it was, he was pleased they had shown even a bit of initiative.

He pushed open the door, using his right hand to avoid the pain in his left, and walked in, his footsteps echoing loudly on the polished floor. The group turned and watched him as he approached, their eyes boring into him with curiosity and disdain. Lucas didn't care. He was used to their stares and their whispers.

'Alright, everyone,' he said, pulling up a chair and sitting at the front of the room. 'Let's get started. What have we got?' The group looked around at each other, unsure who should speak first. 'I'll tell you then,' he pointed at the picture they'd blue-tacked to the board. 'Another unknown woman, early thirties, probably. Another one with a missing organ. The stomach, as predicted, most likely. Another murder with no fucking evidence left behind. Assuming we're linking everything, this is the eleventh woman to die at the hands of this prick, the second in the last twelve months, and we still know jack shit about him.'

The group nodded silently, their faces grim. Some of them, like Lucas, had been working on the case for years, but were still no closer to identifying the killer. It was frustrating as hell, and they all felt the rot of defeat settling in.

'We have to keep trying,' Lucas said determinedly. 'We've got to keep searching, keep digging, keep looking for any small clue that could help us identify this bastard. He's out there, and we're going to catch him. I promise you that.'

The group nodded again, but Lucas could tell they weren't

convinced this time. They'd heard his stereotypical Hollywood speech before, and they couldn't give a toss anymore. They looked tired and demoralised, and he couldn't blame them. He felt the same way. But he couldn't give up, not yet. He had to keep going; he had to find this killer before anyone else died.

'Look, guys,' he said, standing up and walking to the board. 'We've all been working ourselves into early graves for this case. We've interviewed hundreds of suspects, examined thousands of pieces of evidence, and come up empty-handed every time.' There was an awkward pause. It hung in the air for a few seconds, and he knew why. 'But we can't stop now. We can't let this prick win. So let's keep at it.' He looked around at the group, expecting them to be inspired by his speech, but they just looked back at him with blank faces. Lucas sighed. He knew he was wasting his breath. They all hated him, and he couldn't blame them. 'Mayor, I need you to contact missing persons again and see where we are with this one.'

A little chubby Asian man answered, looking mildly pissed off. His name was Sadiq Khan, so obviously, he was known as mayor. 'Why do I have to ring -

'Because DI Wilson won't talk to me, you know that, Sadiq, ' snapped Lucas

'Well, this is childish, just apolo-'

'Ring her. Now.' DI Sadiq 'Mayor' Khan glared at Lucas, his face flushed.

'Fine,' he picked up the phone and sat sulking on the edge of the desk as Lucas turned to the rest of the group.

'Does anyone have anything of any value?'

DS Kimberly Sterling put her hand up. She was a slim

woman, roughly the same age as Lucas. Undeniably pretty with light brown hair to her shoulders, very fair skin and a large, engaging smile. Her eyes were unusually widely spaced but far from detracting from her, adding something unique that held your attention. Lucas looked at her mouth, maybe a little longer than he should have done, certainly long enough to notice that her teeth seemed the same shape. It just worked. Lucas didn't know DS Sterling all that well; she'd recently just returned to work after a year off on the sick. Cancer maybe? Although looking at her right now, it was impossible to tell what an awful year she must have had.

'Go ahead, Kim, ' Lucas said eventually, nodding at her.

'I've been trying to get hold of a new criminal profiler to cut down the number of suspects we've got, ' she said a little too quickly and with a very subtle accent. He couldn't place it, although he was sure he'd been told where she was from at some point. She was nervous, but that was understandable, given she'd only been back a few weeks. A groan from the group.

'This isn't 'Wire in the Blood' Kim, no Robson Green is going to burst through that door and clairvoyant this shit,' said DS Mathews

'Yeah, but even a shitty profiler is better than the one we have,' she snapped back. 'I'm already sick of this fucking place.' She leant back in her chair, took a small handheld electric fan out from her desk, and began blowing at her face.

Lucas sighed. He knew how she felt. 'Okay, let's just concentrate on what we can do, not what we can't do'. The group nodded silently. It was going to be a long day.

'Kim, who were you thinking of?' said Lucas.

DS Kim Sterling continued to fan herself as she replied.

She had gone a bit pink and clammy, he'd noticed. 'There's a guy called Professor Hawthorne who a friend of mine worked with in London. He's a bit of an oddball or a dick, depending on who you ask. He's good at what he does, apparently.'

'Okay, fine, let's bring him in,' said Lucas. 'We've got nothing to lose. In the meantime, we'll continue to work on our own leads.'

As Lucas turned to leave, he heard someone mutter, 'Yeah, like we've got any.' He ignored it. Chief Constable Patricia Carmichael wouldn't have accepted this nonsense when she was running the ship. She would have whipped them all into shape. But she had moved up in the world, and they were left with the ineffective DCI Lucas Miller. Sadiq returned from his phone call looking grumpy.

'Two things. Firstly, Missing Persons says no luck yet. They're still going through the database.'

'Keep them on it, Mayor. We need to identify this woman so we can start investigating,' replied Lucas.

'They've got the same response as always, though. It'll take time.'

'I don't have time,'

'Sometimes I think DI Wilson just drags her heels in with you, sir,' Sadiq replied, rolling his eyes.

'She's better than that. Let me know if you hear anything else from them. And secondly? What was the second thing you wanted to say?' said Lucas.

'Bloody Simon Davies on the phone again asking for an exclusive. I told him to get rodded, but I thought you ought to know if you see 'police tell journalist to 'get rodded'' in the paper tomorrow.

'Vampires, cheers Sadiq'

He left the room, heading back to his office to plan his next move. As he walked, he couldn't help but feel like he was failing. He was supposed to be a top-rate detective, but he hadn't even been able to find one lead in all this time. Maybe Dr Cross would find something more beneficial for him.

7

It was cold, oh so cold. Lucas put his hands out and touched the wall nearby, which was made entirely of newspaper. He couldn't read a single word of it, though, because his eyes would not focus. Or maybe it wasn't written in a human language. The newspaper wall rippled, and a faint echo rang out around him. Lucas looked up and realised he was in an eerie giant box made entirely of newspaper, and he suddenly became painfully aware of its unnatural essence. He could see the edges of the box, up high and out of reach. They were burning slowly, but the smoke emanating from the embers was flowing downward, back into the flames, which seemed to produce no heat. Shadows danced at the periphery of his vision, and the air was thick with an unsettling silence. The world around him was desolate and void, painted in monochromatic hues of despair.

What was that over there? A lake? He set off to find it, and each step he took echoed as if he were walking through an endless void. The ambience was punctuated by soft whispers and the feeling of unseen eyes watching him, heightening the sense of dread that clawed at his psyche. As he ventured further, the surreal newspaper landscape began to warp, and the ground beneath him began pulsating like the heartbeat of the nightmare itself.

Given how slowly he'd been walking, he reached the lake more quickly than he expected. It wasn't really a lake, but something much worse. It was so grotesque that it defied all logic and reason. Before him lay a colossal fingerprint, but not of ink or dust; this macabre creation was composed of the twisted, bloodied bodies of women, each arranged in a meticulous, chilling pattern, dark red and sticky with blood. They were squirming, grasping at their faces and the dim, empty cavities where their eyes should be sitting. The screams that appeared on their faces were silent. The air reeked of iron and death, the sight overwhelming Lucas with horror and disbelief. At the centre of this ghastly spiralling fingerprint sat a giant, bloodshot eyeball, its iris a haunting shade of dull blue. The eye, unnervingly lifelike, darted around frantically as if searching for something—or someone.

As Lucas stared in abject horror, the eye suddenly stilled, its gaze locking onto his. Time seemed to freeze, the connection between them electric and terrifying. In that gaze, Lucas felt an inexplicable recognition, a reflection of the darkness he'd been chasing in his waking hours. The eye held a silent accusation, a mirror to the soul of the killer he sought. It was a moment of surreal understanding, a twisted communion in this nightmarish realm. And then it blinked.

Lucas awoke with a start, his heart pounding, sweat drenching his skin. The surrounding room was safe and familiar, yet the echo of the nightmare lingered, its images etched onto his retinas. The alarm clock read 05:54. As he sat in the dark, disoriented and trying to steady his breath, an ominous and overbearing feeling of guilt washed over him.

'Fuck this,' he muttered to himself as he grabbed the blister pack next to his bed and got up to take a cold shower.

* * *

He'd shifted the thought of his latest nightmare as he stood by himself, rattling off a quick text.

'I'm outside the back entrance.'

Ping, the reply was almost immediate,

'*2 secs x.*'

He waited, his hands in his pockets, enjoying the cool, fresh air. You could smell that it had been raining last night, and it was strangely comforting. He was round the back of the hospital, in a clearing between ugly grey buildings. The dull sound of city traffic filtered through and drifted around him as he waited. The pain in that left forearm was dissipating already, and it had hardly been five minutes since he'd taken another pill from that blister pack.

The back door to the mortuary opened, and a woman strode out, at least five years younger than Lucas. Emily West had a strong, athletic figure, with toned arms that stuck aggressively from her tight, sleeveless black and white dress. Her caramel complexion was a pleasant contrast to the drab surroundings and was improved further by her beaming grin as she came over to Lucas. Her eyes were small, dark and piercing. They were set into an angular but pretty face framed by her dark, sleek hair, which had been slicked down. She was a bit of a head-turner, but she knew it. She smiled at him and waved as he walked towards her. They kissed, and he embraced her firmly.

'Hi, Em. How's the day going?' he said, smiling as best he could.

'As well as can be expected, given the state of these bodies. You did a number on that woman last night.' She replied, grinning. Her accent was softer and hinted of snobbery, which Lucas subconsciously always ignored. Lucas winced.

'Hey, nothing to do with me; I find them; I don't put them there.'

She looked down over her glasses at him. 'Oh, I don't know, mind, you look the type. Your eyes are too close together. Plus, you're a naughty boy. You should have been at the autopsy earlier.'

'Yeah, I'm sorry about that. Dr Cross annoyed with me?' he said, not looking nearly as guilty as he should. Dr Cross could go fuck himself, in his humble opinion.

'Huh, yeah, Dan's pretty hacked off you weren't there. I smoothed things over for you. Don't worry. Also, there was nothing ground-breaking to report. It was the stomach and you've got another poem. We've taken some DNA from this latest victim. It's a start.'

'She needs to be on the system, but even then, we've identified nine of the victims so far, and where's it gotten us?' said Lucas, who didn't share her optimism.

'Well, you got that one to court; I know you didn't—' she started, but Lucas immediately cut her off.

'No, I'm not talking about that, Em.'

'Oh.'

'It's just, I need some answers, clues, anything,'

'I know. Dan feels the same way. I think he's got a few ideas.'

'Well, let's see what the creeps got.'

'Hey! Play nice, alright. I don't know why two don't get on; you've got a lot in common, you know,' Said Emily before turning and opening the back door. 'Come on, then. He's waiting for you.'

'We get on fine, Em; we're just not best buds,'

They walked into Dr Cross' mortuary office to find him sitting behind his desk. Em left him at the door, where he found Dr Cross fiddling in one of his desk drawers before he spotted Lucas. He looked up, rolled his eyes, and then returned to whatever he was doing.

'You know, as DCI, you really ought to attend these autopsies,' he said, more than a hint of irritation in his voice.

'They're all the same, seen one, seen them all,' replied Lucas, pulling out a chair from the other side of the desk. He didn't like this office; it was a little shrine to the ego of Daniel Cross. His medical degree from Cardiff University hung on the wall above a bookcase dedicated to all the grim books he'd published, mostly on post-mortem identification, and his specialist subject: cult murder. Dr Cross stopped what he was doing and booted up the computer.

'I like you, Lucas, for some unknown reason. But the level of ignorance you possess is staggering, if I'm honest. Do you have this much disregard for my colleagues?' he said.

'Yes, you will be pleased to note I also fail to attend Dr Stevens and Dr Valenti's autopsies on the rare occasion I'm asked to attend them. But go on, please, please, please, prove me wrong. What have we found with this one which we haven't found with the others?' said Lucas.

Dr Cross put his hands up in exasperation. 'It is not always about finding something new; repetition links the cases. Her stomach was removed, we guessed that, but she was also killed slowly, over a prolonged period, with repeated asphyxiation and ultimately by blood loss. She was stripped naked, her clothes and jewellery taken. It's the same MO and the same signature.'

'They're the same thing,' smirked Lucas.

'They're not actually; the modus operandi is how the killer commits the crime. He abducts, he asphyxiates, and he uses a knife to cut their throats. Taking their eyes serves no purpose; it is an extra. Garnish. Their signature, if you will.'

'Dunno. They sound the same to me. Right, so was the poem correct?' said Lucas. Dr Cross picked up a photograph from his desk and showed it to Lucas. It depicted the familiar little strip of brown paper with the swirly writing across it.

'The stomach's cauldron, boiling, churns, where fire of hunger ever burns,
Its acid touch, a witch's brew, conjuring desires of you.'

'Great. Anyway, we know all this. Anything we can use to narrow down our search? Any mistakes this time?' said Lucas, casually scratching a mark on Dr Cross's desk.

'Well, I found something new. There were a few fibres on the body which looked out of place. They're from a synthetic fabric, maybe a carpet or something similar,' said Dr Cross, who was typing something into the computer.

'Alright, good. We can start looking into carpet manufacturers and distributors in the area,'

'You can, but this fibre is quite common at first glance and could have come from anywhere.'

'Fine. Any other ideas?'

'She was found tied to a tree as you saw; the rope used to tie her there was also fairly generic and could have been purchased anywhere.' Lucas sighed and stood up, ambling over to the bookshelf whilst Dr Cross continued. 'It's the same with the nails used to pin her hands together. Both items were easily obtainable. We can trace them to the manufacturer, but these things are universal. I imagine you'll never be able to prove who bought them,' said Dr Cross.

Lucas sighed again, fiddling with *'The Manson Murders: A Deep Dive in the World of Cult Crime by Dr Daniel Cross'*.

'You don't think this is some sort of cult thing, do you?' he asked, knowing perfectly well what the response would be.

'No, I do not, as you bloody well know, Lucas. I have explained this many times before. Now, put my things back.

Lucas slid the book back into its place. 'This guy is smart. He doesn't leave any evidence behind.' He was getting frustrated. They had the same conversation every time. No evidence was left behind, the horrible mutilation of the body, and they got nowhere. Whenever they got a lead, it was always from somewhere else.

'He's a psychopath who enjoys killing and torturing women. He's not that smart, DCI. I am sure your keen mind will catch him eventually.' Lucas ignored the sarcasm in his voice.

'Well, he's done it eleven times without getting caught. He must have something going for him,' Lucas replied. Dr Cross shook his head.

'You're giving him too much credit. He's just another murderer, not a criminal mastermind. It's not hard to kill someone and get away with it.'

Lucas nodded. He knew that was true, unfortunately. There were countless unsolved murders in the country, and many of them were probably committed by people who had never even been suspects.

'Alright, I'll keep looking into this carpet fibre. Maybe we can find something to link it to a specific brand or location.'

'Good. Let me know if you find anything.' Lucas turned to leave. He had a feeling they wouldn't find anything useful. This case was going nowhere.

'Oh, and Detective? If you had attended this morning, you might have been able to tell your team all of this. Stop you from sounding quite so lost up there. Just a thought.' Dr Cross smiled smugly and returned to typing on his computer. Lucas rolled his eyes and left the room without lingering. He was getting sick of this case. And he was getting sick of Dr Cross and his smug attitude. He wasn't doing anything at all.

But then again, neither was Lucas.

2011

8

'So, tell us about Amy,' Chloe said as she sat on the couch opposite Mr and Mrs Savage. Mrs Savage looked like she'd been crying; her eyes were red, and her make-up was everywhere, although this might be the case most of the time. Neither she nor her husband were well kept. Her hair was greasy and tangled, and she had a yellowish hue to her waxy skin. His thin grey hair was dangling down in front of his deeply bagged eyes, but he made no effort to move it, which irritated Lucas. They looked like they were struggling. Their home was small, dirty and filled with old furniture and a strong odour of smoke. Lucas looked at the coffee table, which was littered with cigarette packets, some empty, some half open, some unopened. It gave Lucas a very uncomfortable feeling in his stomach.

'Not much to tell,' Mrs Savage replied, her eyes never leaving the floor. 'Amy was a good girl, but she had problems.'

'Like?'

'Drugs. Nothing hard, just weed and stuff. She was always high; I couldn't talk to her when she was, so we stopped trying. Then, one day, she was gone. Took some clothes and vanished. We thought she'd come back, but she didn't.'

8

'When did she disappear? How long has it been?' asked Chloe, glancing at Lucas.

'It's been a few weeks. I don't know how long. She wasn't here a lot anyway, so it wasn't obvious until we realised she hadn't come home for a while,' replied Mrs Savage. Chloe paused and put her hands on her lap, adopting disarming body language. Lucas was quietly impressed.

'This is a tough question, but were you aware of what she was doing?'

'You mean she was shagging for money? Yeah. We knew. Makes us terrible parents, right? How are you supposed to control a kid like that?' She looked up at the two detectives, her eyes filled with tears. 'You have kids?'

'No, I don't' said Lucas

'Yeah. I've got a little girl,' said Chloe. Mrs Savage sat back and looked at the ceiling, her eyes still welling up.

'It's a tough world out there, Detective. You do your best for them and try to keep them safe, but they grow up, and they're not kids anymore. You can't protect them all the time, and they need to find their own way in the world. Some do a better job than others and maybe we were shit, but please don't say we don't care. Because we do.'

There was a silence that hung in the room; Chloe was writing, and the Savages were fidgeting nervously. Just as Lucas felt he'd have to break the silence, Mr Savage spoke.

'Guess you want a DNA or whatever? I hope it's not her.'

* * *

They left the house, and the DNA sample was stored safely in an evidence bag. Lucas clicked the door behind him and went after Chloe, who had already reached the garden gate. When he reached her, she had been accosted by a tall man with thinning hair. He was probably only about five years older than Lucas, although he looked a lot older. He wore a light pink shirt, green chinos, and a red lanyard around his neck. Lucas inspected the badge on the end with a beady eye. It said 'press' with a name too small to read.

'Any news on the identification of the body, DS Wilson?' said the man in a nondescript accent, although it wasn't local.

'Fuck off, Davies, ' she snapped back, physically lurching in his direction.

'Woah, calm it, love; I'm only asking on behalf of the nation,' he replied, smirking.

'You write for the local fish wrapper, hardly the voice of the nation. And care to explain what you're doing outside this lady's house?' she continued. Lucas was now next to Chloe, so he asked,

'Who is this guy?'

The tall man stuck out a giant hand with long, slender fingers, and Lucas took it instinctively.

'Simon Davies, crime correspondent for the Yorkshire Post. You must be new. We've not met before.'

'He's a snake, Lucas,' said Chloe, shooting Mr Davies a filthy look. 'I don't trust many journalists, certainly not this weasel.'

'That's harsh. We're just trying to get to the truth of the matter. Like you do,' said Simon Davies in a tone that was supposed to sound innocent.

'I'll tell you the truth. The body hasn't been identified yet. There's no news because there is nothing to report. The press conference is at 4 pm. If you want a story, be there,' said Chloe as she pushed past him, Lucas in tow.

'Nice to meet you,' said Simon Davies, winking at Lucas as they left. No sooner had they got into the car than Chloe launched into an extended twenty-minute TED Talk as they drove across the city, detailing in great depth every object she'd like to insert into Simon Davies' many orifices. The woman was a force to be reckoned with, and Lucas was sure he did not want to get on the wrong side of her. She may have been a very good-looking woman, but her description of her police-issue shoes being lodged in Davies' colon made Lucas slightly nauseated. The woman had one hell of an imagination on her.

9

Chloe had finally calmed down enough to breathe, although her messy ponytail was now even more chaotic, and some strands of her hair had escaped, making her look slightly wild. Lucas had received an email detailing another case he'd been assigned. A simple home invasion robbery, it seemed, but Chloe hadn't been given the same case, so he wasn't all that bothered.

They were headed towards Jessica Murray's house, and the conversation with the Savages left them somewhat pensive. However, the meeting with the journalist Simon Davies still appeared more troubling for Chloe.

'He's slimy, and I just don't like him. He seems to have a knack for being in the right place at the right time, and he's made a bit of a career out of it,' She said.

'Just journalists for you. More interested in the story than the people behind it,' replied Lucas, keen to move on from this conversation. Chloe sensed his reluctance and grunted, glanced at her sat nav and turned the car down a side street.

'I'm not sure if Amy matches our body,' Chloe said, changing the subject, her gaze fixed on the road in front of her.

'She's a possible match for the age range. She could be

tied up with this somehow,'

'Yeah. I don't know; I'm not sure I'm buying that personally. Speaking to the punter who reported her missing would be good.'

They pulled into the driveway of a large detached house, which stood a few paces back from the street, nestled within a neatly kept front yard. A low, welcoming picket fence covered in climbing ivy delineated its boundary. The garden was a mix of perfectly aligned flower beds and a well-manicured lawn. A brand new large black Range Rover sat on the drive. Jacob Murray might be rough, but he'd married well. His father-in-law had left them a significant amount of money when he died. The complete set-up reeked of new-money.

'I wonder why she ran away,' said Lucas as they exited the car and walked to the front door. It was black, with a large central knocker shaped like a lion.

'Lions are my favourite animal,' said Lucas, instinctively. Chloe just looked at him blankly as she knocked on the door. It was opened by a middle-aged woman in a white blouse and black trousers. She looked like she'd been crying, just like Mrs Savage.

'Mrs Murray,' said Chloe, flashing her ID badge like they do on TV. 'I'm Detective Wilson, and this is DC Miller. Can we come in?'

Her eyes widened slightly when she heard they were police, but she said, 'Of course,' sniffled and turned, leading them to the front room.

Lucas couldn't help but notice how different the two homes were. The Savages had been struggling to make ends meet, whilst the Murrays lived in a large house in the suburbs with a nice car in the drive.

'How is your husband, Mrs Murray?' Chloe asked.

'Please, call me Catherine. He's doing okay. He's distraught, of course. We both are.' She didn't know what to do with her hands, as she kept moving them from her side to her lap and back again.

'When was the last time you saw Jessica?' Chloe spoke with a softness, which clearly resonated with Catherine Murray, as she was physically looking less tense as the conversation progressed.

'It would have been just before she left for school. I went to work, and she was still here when I left. I didn't realise until I came back that she had left. It was only when the school called to say she hadn't turned up. I tried to call her mobile, but she didn't answer.

'Was she behaving normally that day?'

'Yes, as far as I could tell. She seemed okay, but I think she was keeping things from me. I feel like I should have done more, but I just didn't know what.' she shrugged meekly, and her bottom lip began to wobble. She pulled a little tissue from the underside of her shirt cuff to wipe her eyes.

'What do you mean?' said Lucas, slightly too abruptly, earning him a laser-like stare from Chloe. Not that he minded, not with those brown eyes. After a bit of sniffing, Catherine composed herself and said,

'She was a teenage girl; they keep their secrets. I thought she was okay; maybe she was struggling with something. I'm her mother, and I should have known.'

'There was no way you could have known, Mrs Murray,' said Chloe, regaining control of the dialogue. 'This is not your fault. And there's every chance she is fine and might turn up soon. You need to stay positive for yourself and your husband. Try to focus on the good times. What was she like?'

Chloe was very good at this in all fairness, she was a very empathetic person. Lucas found it quite inspiring and kept his mouth shut for a bit.

'She was always smiling; she was a happy girl, always full of life. Jess loved dancing and swimming, and she was good at them. She wanted to be a teacher.' She looked at them, tears welling in her eyes. 'If I think she's dead, that's it. That's all I'll remember. I have to keep hope; I can't give up on her, not yet' Catherine stood up at this and turned to the window.

'Did she have a boyfriend?'

'I don't think so, but I wouldn't have known if she did. She never mentioned a boy, but I don't think she would have told me if there was someone. She was always so close with her father,' said Catherine, not breaking eye contact with a squirrel who was scurrying around the back garden.

'Did she have any problems with the other girls at school? Any friends that you were aware of?'

'She was pretty popular, but she was best friends with Grace. They've known each other for years.'

'Can we get her details?'

As Mrs Murray wrote the name and number of her daughter's friend, Lucas looked up at the ceiling. Had he just heard a creak? However, his attention was suddenly drawn back to the room because Chloe had embarked on some personal questions.

'If there were another way of asking this or getting this information, I would use it, but unfortunately, I really have to ask. Do you know if she was sexually active?' Catherine

Murray sighed, shaking her head and focusing again on something in the back garden. Just for a fleeting moment, Lucas got the impression she was hiding something.

'No. I mean, I don't know. She kept herself to herself, like I said. She was so young. I wanted her to focus on her studies.'

'We need to get a DNA sample from you, Mrs Murray, ' Chloe said, battling on. Whatever had bothered Lucas about Catherine's demeanour had not registered with Chloe.

'Of course. Whatever it takes to find her. She's my baby. Can I give you this as well, please?' She handed Chloe a little picture of Jessica from a party she'd attended. It looked pretty recent. 'She looks happy in that picture. Can you use that on the TV, please, if you need to?'

'Of course, ' said Chloe softly. 'That's a lovely necklace she's got on.'

'Yeah, it's a locket. Belonged to my mum, and then me, and now Jess. She doesn't take it off. Well, she hadn't; she hadn't worn it in about a month, actually. I was worried she'd lost it, but she said she hadn't. It's not in her room, I've looked. She probably had it on when she went missing.'

There was a definite creak on the stairs this time, and Lucas almost broke his neck as he looked up so quickly. Someone was listening in on the conversation. The culprit knew they'd been rumbled because they heard another creak, followed by some thumps, and the door crashed open. Mr Murray was standing in the doorway. An enormous lump of a man with no neck and massive arms littered with tattoos. He was red in the face, and a large, unhealthy-looking blood vessel swelled on the right of his neck. His pock-marked skin suggested steroid abuse, and his abnormally flared nostrils hinted at powder-based substance abuse. The monstrous wreck of a man pointed aggressively at Lucas, who didn't flinch. People like this didn't scare him.

'Fucking Nora, I see you've finally turned up then,' spat Jacob Murray as he sat down, pushing Catherine Murray out of the way, legs spread with a dominating pose. 'That body you found. Is it her then? After ignoring her for weeks, have you let my daughter die? Is that what you've come round to tell us? Eh!'

'We're still investigating,' Chloe replied.

'Shut it, you, I'm talking to him,' snarled Mr Murray.

'Wind your neck in, mate; that's a senior officer you're verbally abusing,' said Lucas, firmly and without hesitation. 'We're still investigating. No one has been identified yet. We have some questions for you, though.'

'Oh yeah, going to blame me, are you?'

'Not unless you did it.'

'Fuck off. So what do you want us for?'

'We want to take a DNA sample from you both. It's just to rule you out,' said Chloe, jumping in ahead of Lucas, but this only earned her a wide-eyed, manic stare from Mr Murray. Lucas was quickly beginning to realise the bloke was high on something.

'You always let this bitch speak for you?'

'It's called respect,' said Lucas.

'Yeah, yeah, whatever,' he said, reaching for a cigarette. 'You can have mine later. I'll drop it off at the station. Don't worry, I won't skip town.'

'Why not just provide one now? Something to hide?'

'Like what? Why not fuck off and find my daughter? It seems I'm the only one who's been out looking for her.'

Lucas made to reply, but he stopped when Chloe put her

hand on his knee. She gave him a look which suggested she thought getting involved in an argument here was futile. Instead, Chloe nodded, turning to look at Mrs Murray, who was staring at the floor, her eyes wet with tears. But Mr Murray had different ideas.

'Are you going to pin it on me, then? Because you can try, but there's nothing in it.'

'Why would you suggest that?' asked Chloe, but Mr Murray just ignored her, so Lucas repeated it.

'She asked you a question. Why would you suggest that?'

'She's always telling lies,' said Murry, pointing at his wife, who was cowering by the window, obviously terrified of this gorilla of a man. 'About me and the kids. It's all bullshit, though. She wants attention.'

'That's not true, I don't...I don't think this is helping,' Mrs Murray said, her voice barely a whisper.

'It's fine,' said Lucas, trying to defuse the situation. 'We just need a sample from you. No one is accusing anyone of anything.'

Mr Murray looked at them both with suspicion. 'I fucking hate the police. Sent me down for jack shit. You can have mine tomorrow; I've got to go to work. Now piss off.' He stood up, flexed his obscenely juiced muscles and pointed towards the door. Lucas didn't shift, but Chloe took the lead and steered him from the room whilst he maintained the hundred-yard death stare with Mr Murray. As they walked back to the car, Chloe sighed.

'He seems like an arse-hole.'

'Yeah. That's an understatement. I don't know how the wife puts up with it. Must be tough.'

'She's probably used to it. Not that it excuses it. You

need to keep a cooler head, though; I don't want you getting decked, not on my watch.'

'I'd like to have seen him try. I've grown up with dickheads like that, trying to bully me about my mum. Doesn't work. Fucking hate bullies.'

'Your mum?'

'Another time,' said Lucas, still bouncing from foot to foot. 'So, where to now?' Chloe checked her watch. It was half-six in the evening, and the sun was beginning to set. Her reddish hair was very suited to this light, thought Lucas.

'We've done what we can today. Fancy a drink?' His heart skipped a little beat, and he smiled, probably more goofy than he wanted to.

'Sounds good,' He replied, trying to sound cool. Chloe flashed him a glorious smile, her heart-shaped eyes lighting up as they entered the car. However, she couldn't help herself, muttering,

'He was massive. He'd have ripped your sodding head off...'

2023

10

The following day, Lucas returned to the police station tired, even more apathetic, and once again completely soaked from the rain, which seemed to be just relentless at the moment. His tiny Cocker Spaniel, Luna, was struggling to sleep at night. She was old, and the arthritis was getting to her. As he flexed his left hand a few times, Lucas thought he might know how she felt. These days, the only way she'd settle at night was to share the bed with him, which was cute but not conducive to a good night's sleep. He kept waking to find either her hot little breath on his face or a rogue paw wedged in his bum crack.

As he walked into the incident room with squelching shoes, he was surprised to see DI Chloe Wilson sitting in his chair, eating a croissant and accompanied by a uniformed, tall, young black lady he'd never seen before. He stopped in the doorway, unsure of what to say.

'Morning,' he said stiffly, stepping into the room.

Chloe ignored him and continued looking out the window as she chewed. Her accomplice acknowledged him with a glance and then stared awkwardly at the floor. Chloe was wearing a black blouse and pencil skirt, which only highlighted the honeycomb brown of her hair tightly formed in a bun at the back of her head. She looked stern but, unfortunately for Lucas, still attractive.

Once she'd swallowed, she muttered 'Morning,' barely making eye contact with him, focussing on her croissant. 'We need to talk.'

'About what?' he asked, sitting across from her. She looked up somewhat abruptly and fixed him with a glare.

'About this case. We have a woman who might match your latest victim. Bianca Dumitrescu, twenty-nine, was reported missing this morning by her husband. She's been on the game for six months; they can't pay their bills, apparently. The physical description matches the pitiful description DS Khan sent over to my team. DC Adams here has the details.' Right on cue, the uniformed officer produced a file from her side and handed it to Lucas.

'Okay, that's good. Have we got DNA from her?' said Lucas, avoiding the unnecessary jibe about his team.

'Not yet. I'm sending someone over to collect it this morning. You should accompany them and interview the husband.'

'Good. Yeah, I'll send someone,' said Lucas, sitting in his chair, swinging nervously from side to side. There was an awkward silence. Lucas could feel the tension in the air between them. He knew they needed to address it.

'How are you then? How's Rachel?'

'We're fine,' came the curt reply. However, after a momentary pause, she softened briefly, adding, 'I was sorry to hear about your dad.'

Lucas went a little pink. 'He's well looked after, thanks. Listen,' he said, leaning forward slightly. 'I know you're still mad at me. I understand.'

Chloe scoffed. She was chewing the croissant with menace and spoke with her mouthful, carelessly spitting flakes across at Lucas. 'Mad? I'm not mad, Detective. I never have been. I was disappointed. But it was a year ago now; I'm past it.' Lucas nodded. He deserved that.

'I know, I fucked up. But I've learnt from it. I won't make the same mistake again.' There was another awkward silence. Chloe considered her thoughts.

'Rumour has it, you're already screwing that poor little mortuary assistant. Bit young for you, isn't she?'

'What? No. She's just a friend.' The rush of blood to his ears might have given the game away.

Chloe gave him a withering look. 'A friend you text constantly and meet in secret. It sounds like something's going on.'

'Nothing is going on. I promise you that. Meeting in secret? What are you talking about?' The heat was rising in his neck. He wasn't a good liar.

The withered look became more sceptical. 'Even the walls have ears, Lucas. I would say it was good to see you. But it wasn't.'

She got up from his chair, brushed some crumbs off her chest onto his desk and walked out with DC Adams trailing in just behind. She didn't look back.

'She's still got the hots for you, that one,' said Sadiq 'Mayor' Khan from behind his desk.

'What the fuck gave you that impression, DC Khan?'

'She could have rung me back. Instead, she came to eat a croissant at your desk. She's keen.'

Lucas shook his head and walked back to his desk. 'That's

not true. She's just wanted to see how badly this is going.'

There wasn't time to think about Chloe anymore; he had work to do. He clicked his fingers and pointed at a startled red-headed woman a few desks back.

'DS Stone, take DC Khan and speak to the family of Mrs Dumitrescu. Keep it light; she will be hard to identify without DNA or fingerprints. Maybe leave the gory details out, just in case.'

2011

11

It was a cool evening, not much breeze, but the patio heater overhead kept them warm. They were on the terrace of a posh bar called '*The Gilded Goblet*,' which provided a romantic view of the city skyline and looked very picturesque in the summer evening hue. Lucas sipped his beer, glancing over at Chloe, staring off into the distance whilst holding some hideously expensive gin cocktail he'd bought her. The multicoloured sparkles of the city lights were reflecting off her hazel eyes as she looked out over the balcony. Her skin was flawless, thought Lucas, as his mind started drifting.

'Tricky first case,' said Chloe, suddenly snapping Lucas back from wherever his mind was going.

'Yeah, tough one to start on. But what do you reckon? Do you think either of those girls is ours?' He'd rather not talk about work, but it was clearly where Chloe's mind was currently focused. She sighed and turned back to him.

'I don't know. There's no evidence linking them to the body we found other than the age range,' she said, stirring the tiny straw in her drink.

'The picture of Jessica is fairly similar to the body, I thought. Similar facial structure, perhaps, although it's hard to tell after all the damage that was done. And her dad seems like an absolute piece of work,'

'Yeah. But we can't jump to conclusions. We need to find out what happened to her, what she was doing?'

'True. It's frustrating though.'

They sat silently for a while, sipping their drinks and watching the city lights twinkle. Chloe took a very long sip from her straw; her lips pursed around the edge, and her cheeks sucked in. Lucas was getting warm, and then she made eye contact with him. Christ. He wanted to say something funny and insightful but had nothing.

'You okay?' he asked, trying desperately not to look flushed, or worse.

'Yeah, I'm fine. I was just thinking about Jessica and Amy. I have a daughter of my own, so I can't imagine what it's like to lose a child,' said Chloe, moving the conversation swiftly back to more serious matters. Was she flirting or not?

'I'm not going to be much help; I can't even imagine what it must be like to have a child,' he tried to laugh, and she gave him a casual smirk. Perhaps she found it funny, or maybe it was just pity. 'But of course, no, it must be awful. It doesn't bear thinking about. I'd like to meet your daughter one day. How old is she?'

'Oh, Rachel, she's just turned four, actually. Starting in school shortly. She's great, can be a bit of a terror, but I think she gets that from her father,' She said, a big smirk on her face as she reminisced about something. Lucas shifted slightly, suddenly very uncomfortable in his seat.

'Ah right, yeah, he still around then?' he left the question dangling.

'Sort of. He's a better dad than he was a boyfriend, anyway.

She's with him tonight, hence...' she tilted her drink to acknowledge it.

'But you two are... you know?'

'Over? Yeah, god, yeah. I mean, we still fuck from time to time, but—' she suddenly burst into laughter at the look on Lucas's face. He'd gone slightly ashen, and the look of disappointment on his face must have been blindingly obvious. 'I'm only messing; he's long gone. I only see him to pick Rachel up, etc. Don't worry, I'm very single.' She took another suspiciously long sip from her straw.

'Ahh, good. Just didn't want to get beaten up by some muscled ex of yours,' he said, trying to style this out.

'Why does it matter? We're only co-workers anyway?' she said, but there was a very mischievous way in which she stared at him, mouth clamped around the straw yet again. It was a good job that Lucas was wearing loose trousers.

'Well, err... Yeah. I know.' This was about to get awkward and not the romantic conversation he was going for, so to diffuse the situation, he blurted,

'So, what's your favourite colour?'

'What do you mean?' She snorted, giving him a quizzical look.

'I mean, what's your favourite colour? What colour do you think of when you think of me?' She raised an eyebrow.

'You're kidding, right? Miller, you don't have a chance with me.'

He grinned in a show of false confidence. 'Why not?'

She shook her head. 'Because I don't date people from work. It's too messy.'

'Okay, fair enough. But you never know. Maybe one day, I'll win you over.' She laughed loudly enough for people on a neighbouring table to notice, causing Lucas to cringe slightly.

'Yeah, I doubt it.'

Lucas shrugged. 'Never say never, Chloe. That's all I'm asking.'

She sighed. 'OK, I won't rule it out, but you're going to have a hell of a time trying to change my mind, no matter how cute you are. One measly single cocktail isn't going to be enough for you.' She winked at him. He smirked back, and they both laughed.

'I'd better get some more drinks then,' he said, grinning.

12

'Urrgh'

Lucas was frustrated, running his fingers through his hair as he leaned back in his chair. He also had a slight headache from the drinks last night, which wasn't helping anything. Chloe sat at the desk across from him, biting her lip as she read over the notes from their investigation. She'd had four gins and was completely unaffected. Nothing had happened; he'd ordered her a taxi, and she'd gone with a smile and a gentle hug. It was sweet in reality. She looked up at him; her features crinkled with concern.

'We'll find something,' she said.

'Maybe, maybe not'

'Don't give up hope yet; we've only just got this case. It'll come together; I know it will.'

Lucas sighed, looking at the board of evidence that was spread in front of him. Young female, probably abducted, definitely killed. Horribly so as well. Repeated strangulation and removal of her heart. That poem rammed into her chest, taunting them. He wondered, as he had throughout his training, what the evidence board would have shown when they were investigating his mother's death. They'd never found the person who did it, and although the case was technically still open, he knew they never would. The not knowing was almost the worst bit; there was no closure. Everyone had been investigated, and for a long time, even he wondered if it could have been his dad, but he'd quickly pushed that thought to the side. His mother would never have married someone like that. Although that was what they always said. But his dad had always been so kind to him. Lucas knew it wasn't him, but he'd still been essentially ostracised from their village at the time and that had led to the inevitable drink problem, which was only getting worse, even now seventeen years later.

'Why do you think he took the heart?' asked Lucas out loud to anyone listening.

'Maybe he's just a freak,' said Stephen.

'Yeah, but why? I mean, it's gruesome and disgusting. The level of violence suggests anger, but the precision would require calmness. There is a reason. I need to think,' he said, tapping his head. 'Any luck with the rope, Paul?'

Lucas was staring out the window towards the bulk of the sprawling city. In the distance, a large red crane was shifting something inconceivably heavy across a building site. From this side of the building, he could also just about see Elland Road Stadium, home of Leeds United Football Club. He'd supported them since birth and experienced the highs and lows of the last two decades. Last season, they'd been promoted back to the Championship and had a half-decent season, so of course, the city was dreaming of returning to the Premier League this time.

'Sir?' said Paul.

'What?' said Lucas, returning to reality.

'You asked me a question; I said forensics on the rope is limited. No prints or anything, just a lot of the victim's DNA. Same from the note and vial. Fibres from the rope match the fibres underneath her fingernails, though. So she desperately struggled to undo the knots before... you know.'

'Aye, Dr Cross said that would likely be the case. He's a bit of a prick, isn't he?' said Lucas, hoping for a murmur of confirmation from the group. Instead, a few of them jumped to his defence.

'Na, you just don't know him yet,' said Stephen. 'he usually gets a few rounds at the Christmas party in fairness.'

'He can be full of it, but he's a more useful pathologist than the other two, Cooper or Bates. At least he tells you something useful; Bates can be genuinely obstructive,' said Paul.

'Plus, he is strangely sexy,' said Chloe with a giggle, and Lucas's heart plummeted in his chest, but with that, the phone suddenly rang, and Stephen leaned across to answer it. After listening for a few seconds, he leaned around his computer, a phone pressed against his shoulder.

'Boss.' Lucas and Chloe both looked up at him. 'Oh, err... DS Wilson, boss.'

'Go on,' said Chloe as Lucas shifted his eyes back to the computer, and his cheeks went a lovely salmon colour.

'It's Simon from the lab; they want to discuss the DNA with you. They've got a match.'

Chloe jumped up from her chair and practically sprinted to the other side of the desk. She snatched the phone from Stephen and essentially shouted down the phone;

'DS Wilson, what the story?' There was a brief pause, and Lucas looked at Chloe, who was giving him a concerned stare back. He could just about make out Simon's squeaky voice, replying,

'It's Simon; I have a match on the DNA sample from the girl in the forest. It's Jessica Murray.'

'Ah, great work. It was incredibly helpful. Thanks!' She made to put the phone down, but was stopped by a strangled yelp from the other end of the line. She put it back to her ear.

'DS Wilson, wait, there's more,' He continued, and she could hear him nervously licking his dry lips down the phone

'Go on?'

'We also got a match for some of the semen found inside her.'

'Right,' He was acting as if he was announcing the Oscar for the best picture or something.

'Well... It belongs to Jacob Murray.'

13

DI Carmichael was pacing around her office, her high heels clacking on the vinyl flooring. Her arms were crossed, and her brow was creased with stress. Lucas and Chloe sat on the chairs by the large, overly formal captain's desk in the corner. It didn't fit with the rest of the modern furniture in here. She had a bright yellow IKEA sofa along the window, some metal shelves in the corner covered in police investigation textbooks and a smattering of peculiar surreal art on the walls. One picture depicted a forest floor covered in broken clocks and multicoloured spiders, which made absolutely no sense to Lucas. They both kept turning their heads at increasingly awkward angles, attempting to face their rapidly moving boss.

'So you're telling me that some of the semen found on Jessica Murray belonged to her father?' she repeated, for what must have been the fourth time.

'Yeah, that's correct,' said Chloe. 'No further DNA matches yet for any of the other material we've found, though.'

'I see'. Carmichael paused by the window, looking out over the city skyline. The sky was a hazy pink as the sun dipped low over the horizon, the light hitting the buildings and casting long shadows onto the streets.

'What do we do now?' Chloe asked, breaking the silence.

'We bring Murray in, and we interview him. He will have to come up with something pretty interesting to wriggle off this hook.'

'Should we inform the family?' Lucas asked, looking at Carmichael's back.

'We can inform them we've found Jessica. Don't tell them about the semen yet, though. I want to interview him first.'

'We can't just bring him in without notifying his wife. It's not right. What if she tries to contact him while we're questioning him?' Chloe looked at her boss with concern. She knew Murray was a scumbag, but he was also a father, and it wasn't right to keep his family in the dark.

'I'll deal with that. I can conjure up an excuse in no time. You two get him in immediately.' She replied.

Lucas and Chloe exchanged glances. Chloe wasn't sure; Lucas, however, wanted to pull the bloke in by his bollocks. It made more sense now why the bastard hadn't wanted to cooperate when they tried to take a DNA sample. He had something to hide.

'Why did he even provide a sample if he knew this would happen?' asked Carmichael

'He didn't; we're still waiting for his sample. We didn't need it. He was on the system from when he did his time,' replied Lucas.

'Then why didn't Jessica's DNA flag sooner, paternal link and all that? Oh, right? He's not the father?'

'No, but I'm not sure he knows that'.

'Right, well, keep it to yourselves for now.'

A phone started to screech and Carmichael turned to answer it as they left the office. The pair headed downstairs and back towards the car, hoping they could pull in Murray before the end of the day.

As they made their way down the station staircase, Lucas's phone vibrated, the screen lighting up with a familiar name that made him stiffen – 'Dad'. He glanced at Chloe, who was lost in thought, checking some emails on her phone. With a subtle movement, Lucas silenced the phone and slipped it into his coat pocket. But it buzzed again, insistent.

Sighing, Lucas excused himself with a muted, 'Personal call, gotta take this,' before stepping into a corridor just off the staircase.

'Dad?' Lucas answered, his voice betraying none of the reluctance he felt. The line crackled with the sound of laboured breathing and the unmistakable clinking of bottles in the background.

'Lu... Lucas? Is that you? I... I can't find the...' His father's voice was slurred, the sentences trailing off into mumbles. Lucas's jaw clenched as he listened, the familiar cocktail of embarrassment and concern churning in his stomach.

'Yeah, Dad, it's me. What can't you find?' he asked, his voice low, eyes darting back down the corridor to where Chloe was waiting, hopefully just out of earshot.

'The remote... for the telly. It's gone. Stolen?' His father's voice wavered, a blend of confusion and misplaced nostalgia seeping through the drunken slur.

'It's okay, Dad. It'll turn up. You should get some rest, okay? I'll swing by tomorrow, alright?'

'Mmm... okay, son. Be safe, yeah?' The line went dead, leaving Lucas staring at the phone, the silence suddenly heavy in his ears. He let out a breath he didn't realise he'd been holding and slipped the phone back into his pocket.

As Lucas re-joined her on the staircase, he met Chloe's curious look with a shrug, as if to say, 'Nothing important,' but internally, he made a note to visit his father after they dealt with Jacob Murray.

Right now, however, duty called, and he couldn't afford distractions.

2023

14

Lucas was sitting at his desk, head in his hands. A newspaper lay next to him, folded so that it hid the front page, although he'd already seen it. The headline read '*When Are We Due Another? The Water's Edge Reaper at Large*' by Simon Davies. It had the usual picture of himself and Detective Superintendent Carmichael looking incompetent attached to it. There was also a little timeline, which made for grim reading, but in all fairness, thought Lucas, it effectively highlighted the problem.

Timeline of Murders

2011

- September 12th: *Jessica Murray is found murdered in a wooded area. She has been stabbed multiple times, and her body is mutilated.*

2012

- *January 8th: Amber Smith is found murdered in the park behind her house. She has been strangled and stabbed, and her body is hidden from public view.*

2013

- *May 3rd: Rhian Morris is found murdered in a gravel carpark. She has been strangled again, with multiple stab wounds, and a rumour circulates that her ears have been removed.*

2014

- *April 24th: Sabina Barbu is found dumped near an abandoned quarry close to her home. She has been strangled and beaten, and her body has been left to the environment.*

2015

- *January 16th: Vicky Turner is found murdered behind a Tesco superstore in Bradford. She has been strangled, stabbed and mutilated.*

- *August 6th: Amrita Kaur is found murdered in her back garden. She has been strangled, and strong rumours suggest her eyes have been taken.*

2016

- *May 27th:* Sophia Sidorova is discovered dead in her tent after the Leeds Music Festival. She has been strangled and beaten.

2020

- *August 13th:* Hannah George is found murdered outside 'The Potted Plant' garden centre where she worked. Strangled and stabbed, she heralds the return of the Water's Edge Reaper.

2021

- *February 9th:* Grace Morton is found murdered in a farmer's field. She has been strangled, beaten and mutilated.

2022

- *October 10th:* Rebecca King is found murdered in her car. She has been stabbed multiple times.

2023

- *November 17th:* The body of an unidentified female is discovered in Emmet Woods. Discovered by local children, *eyewitness reports that this bears the hallmarks of yet another Reaper slaying.*

It really was unpleasant. Of course, it skipped a considerable amount of detail and half of the details it included were incorrect, but that wasn't the point. The public would read this and understandably be sceptical as to what he and his team were actually doing.

As he sat there, his head in his hands, contemplating where to go next, his mind wandered. Every day that he failed to catch this man, more women were at risk, and more of them would die. He thought about his mother and how he'd worked so hard to get this job, to stop that from happening to anyone else. He'd suffered a tremendous psychological burden to help others, but he was failing, and he was getting flayed for it. Who would be the next person who he failed?

* * *

She stands on the dimly lit street corner, a flicker of defiance in her gaze as she assesses the vehicles that slow down beside her. She will tell herself that this was not the life she chose, that she was forced into it. But she'd be lying; she chose this. Not because she enjoys it, far from it. The clients made her skin crawl and made her sick to her stomach. But she had opportunities to get out and failed to take them. Dangerously low self-worth? A self-destructive nature, perhaps? Either way, she had nobody else to blame.

14

A chill dribbles down her exposed spine. A backless top wasn't ideal on a night like this. Nor were the shorts. She'd been doing this for a few years, and the nerves never left her.

She was taking a colossal risk every time she took to the streets of Holbeck, but what choice did she have, really? Ever since the 'managed approach' legal red-light district had been closed down by the council, they had been left exposed. A killer was on the loose; it was all over the papers and dominated the conversation between the working girls. She could take her business online, of course. *'OnlyFans'* and other websites where she could self-promote would provide a safer alternative. If she was prettier anyway. Who would want to see her on the internet? Her unique selling point was that you could physically do what you wanted to her. At least, that's what she believed. Years and years of mental insult would surely drive your self-worth into the dirt.

The hum of an engine works its way around the corner, headlights dimmed as it approaches the curb. It's a compact car, black and looked about twenty years old. A window rolls down, and a man leans forward. Good hairline, beady little eyes and an unpleasant face.

'How much you taking, love?' His voice is gruff, his tone impatient.

'Thirty. Gets you a quarter an hour, babe. Fifty if you want me for half an hour.'

He huffs, but reaches into his drink holder and pulls out the money. She grabs it and tucks it away before sliding into the front seat. The engine revs and the car jerks as it pulls away from the curb.

He is silent as they drive, and she is thankful for it. It takes two minutes for them to pull into a secluded car park, where he parks. Her make-up is already smudged from the previous client, but he doesn't care.

'Start sucking.'

From across the car park, they watch. Silent. Complete darkness. They can see her in his car, her little head bobs up in time in rhythm. Should take little time with technique like that. A few minutes pass, and her head is back up. They are arguing; she is shouting, and he is gesticulating. Suddenly, he slaps her forcefully and across the face. She opens the car door and steps out into the blackness. They followed.

'Fucking arsehole! I said not in my mouth!' she slams the door, every muscle fibre twitching in her thin, wiry little arm was trying to break his window. He drives off, almost taking her foot off as he does so.

She is alone in bleakness. She can't see, but she can hear. Someone is close. A presence. She feels a hand on her shoulder and jumps. It's them. A smile crosses her face, a smile of relief. They had seen what had happened and were going to help her. This was it, her out. She had found her way out. She turns to face them, to thank them.

But she sees a face, a face she doesn't recognise. A face she doesn't know. A fist flies out, her head flies backwards, and she crumples.

She wakes tied up and in darkness. Out of the gloom, they step. She glimpses them, carrying a blade, glowing hot as if it had been heated. They grab her hair and searing pain suddenly shoots through her like a Catherine wheel. Her eye is on fire; hot blood and fluid pour down her face, across her chin and down her throat, stretching wide and screaming. She can't move; fear, pain, and the rope are all holding her

14

in place. They hold her hair, pulling it so hard she can feel it ripping from her scalp. The knife is down past her eye, deep within her skull. She can feel it moving; it is tearing and slicing.

They are laughing.
They are watching.
The blade is cutting.
Her scream is silenced.
She can't breathe.
She can't fight.
She can't even cry.
Her eye is lost.
She is blind.
The world around her fades slowly and softly.
Then... nothing.

2011

15

Shocking Arrest in Local Murder Case: Suspect Apprehended in Grisly Crime
By Simon Davies, Crime Correspondent

The community is in shock after the murder of a young girl whose body was found mutilated in the woods on Monday. The girl, who has not yet been named, was discovered by a dog walker in the Water's Edge region of Emmet Woods, close to where the victim is believed to have lived.

Police have arrested a 42-year-old local man in connection with the murder. Although police have released no details at present, pending further investigation and notification of the victim's family, the man is known to the victim and is believed to be her father.

'This is a senseless tragedy,' said Detective Chief Inspector Patricia Carmichael. 'Our hearts go out to the victim's family and friends during this difficult time. We will release more details in due course. However, I would ask all those in the media and online to refrain from speculation.'

Neighbours and residents have said that the community is now living in fear.

'It's horrifying to think that something like this could happen so close to home,' said one resident who wished to remain anonymous, as many gathered near the crime scene, offering condolences and support to one another during this difficult time.

'I'm afraid to let my children play outside,' said Stacey Smith, who owns a local hair salon, 'Full Volume'. 'I don't know who could do something like this.'

Police are asking anyone with information about the case to contact them immediately.

DI Carmichael slammed the paper down on her desk, causing ripples to form in her cup of tea, which was steaming by her brand-new computer. How on earth did the press get hold of this so soon? They'd only arrested him a couple of hours ago, for crying out loud. This must have gone to the press last night!

She took a deep breath and stepped out of her office. She looked around and caught sight of Murray's wife, Catherine, in the corridor, standing with two officers doing their best to calm her down.

'It's just not possible!' Catherine said, tears streaming down her face. 'He loves Jess; he would never hurt her. She must have just wandered off or something.'

The bloody media, thought Carmichael, evidently someone had not kept it to themselves. Carmichael approached and placed a hand on the distraught woman's arm.

'Mrs Murray, why don't you come to my office? We have some important things to discuss.' Catherine nodded, her eyes red and swollen, and allowed Carmichael to lead her away from the two officers who had failed in their task. She had instructed them to tell Murray they wanted to follow up on his statement.

Once inside Carmichael's office, the DI took a deep breath and gestured to a chair in the centre of the room. Catherine Murray sat down and wiped away the tears streaming down her face. Carmichael could tell that the poor woman had no idea what was truly coming. She could sense that her husband had not told her the truth.

'Catherine, I have something that I need to tell you, but you must understand that this is very sensitive information.'

'Okay. What is it? Why have you arrested Jacob?' Catherine's voice trembled, and she was shivering.

Carmichael hesitated; she did not want to be the one to tell this woman her husband was a suspected sex offender, but someone had to be the one.

'There isn't an easy way to tell you this...'

2023

16

The DNA evidence was a match two days later. Mr Dumitrescu was in tatters. The screams of agony which reverberated around the station when he arrived were incredibly hard to listen to.

'If he was that arsed about her, why pimp her out?' said DI Khan, biting into an apple as the screams continued in the background.

They were all gathered in the incident room, surrounding the large boards which displayed the case's timeline. The white noise of rain continued to strike the large office windows. Despite only being 11 am, the lights in the office were on because it was so grey and overcast outside.

'Sometimes you need money. They're not all prudish, you know,' came the swift response from DS Kim Sterling. She sat at her desk with her feet on a stool and a very warm-looking fleece jumper on.

'Nothing prudish about not wanting some bloke rattling your wife. They'd lost their savings. They weren't struggling for money that much. She could have gotten a job at McDonald's or something, but no. He puts her on the streets, and she gets murdered by some sicko' spat DI Khan through bits of half-chewed apple.

'Well, we can't change it. What we can do is catch the wanker,' replied Lucas, who was massaging the scar on his arm and flexing his fingers around a little stress ball his physio had given him a few months back when he'd still been attending his sessions.

'Well, we still need to manage that. He's been doing this for years. I mean, shit, how many women have there been? It's like a fucking game to him.'

'It's not a game to him; it's serious. He's a murderer, and he needs to be caught. So get your head in the game, DI Khan,' snapped Lucas, somewhat losing his temper and falling back on his Americanism inspirational tripe that he sometimes spouted. He hated it even coming out of his mouth, but he didn't know what else to say.

'Yes, sir,' said Khan, who had just realised he was about to cross a line he didn't want to cross.

'And stop swearing so much. You'll give the newbies a poor impression,'

'Yes, sir. Sorry, sir,'

Over the next few days, the team was marginally more productive. Having a new name to work towards had given them a new sense of purpose. It was a wave Lucas wanted his team to ride as long as possible.

They were looking into people that Bianca Dumitrescu might have known. Difficult, given what she did. They'd hardly advertised on social media, and, of course, people who had used their service weren't exactly forthcoming either.

What was helpful, though, was that in order to keep her 'safe,' Mr Dumitrescu had insisted that she work from their flat, which had a video-enabled doorbell. This allowed him to film most of the clients his wife had. He hadn't mentioned this to the police before, as he was afraid of being charged with voyeurism. However, now that his wife was confirmed as being dead, he had agreed to hand over the footage.

The team was excited. They had a chance of catching this guy. If he were in the video, then they would have him.

Lucas stood over DC Green's shoulder, watching him scan through the tapes. They'd immediately gone to the last dated entry, 19th September 2023. There was very little on the tape, just Bianca occasionally coming out and pacing around on the path, looking cold and having a fag, whilst trees swayed in the breeze at a million miles an hour behind her.

On this night, she wore a shimmering sequin top, denim shorts and pink high heels. She was small in stature, although she had a bit of a gut on her, which poked out occasionally from under the shiny top. Her hair was big and seductive, but the amount of hair spray she must have used to keep her hair like that, it was little wonder she hadn't just ignited on the cigarette.

Occasionally, a car would drive up, she would exit the house, lean in through the window, they'd talk briefly, and she'd get in, and they'd drive away. Part of the deal was that clients wouldn't enter their marital home. Suppose there had to be some boundaries to all of this. Instead, she offered a more casual, 'suck and fuck in the car' style service, apparently.

These romantic exchanges through a car window had happened three times now, and she had returned within thirty minutes each time. The latest car pulled up, a dark Peugeot 106. They couldn't make out the registration plate, but it was an old model. The late 90s, the early 2000s, perhaps? A tall, slender, light-haired man was there. You couldn't really make out his face in great detail, but it looked cramped, and his eyes were like little piss-holes.

She leaned in through the window, they talked, and then she got in. The tape kept going at double speed. The ticker in the corner said fifteen minutes had passed. Then thirty. Then, an hour. She didn't come back. This was it. They finally had a suspect.

'That's him, that's the fucker. I knew he'd be in there. Well done, Miller.'

'Thank you, Mayor. But we need to confirm who that actually is first; we can't just arrest anyone tall and blonde. We need a name and some evidence. Let's not jump the gun here. We've been in this position before,' said Lucas calmly. Inside, he had that little fizz they all got when the chase was on; you had a lead and were following it. He often thought it must be the same for a hound when it smelled the fox, not that he agreed with that sort of thing.

'Of course, sir. But I bet you anything it's him,' Sadiq Khan turned away excitedly, put his hands on his waist and opened up his jacket as he did so.

'Very brave of you, Sadiq. What are you betting? Fifty quid? How about a go in your car?' said DC Green, but DI Khan ignored him.

'Let's make sure before we say anything. I want a name and an address,' said Lucas.

'Yes, sir'

'That car is pretty clear, looks like an old Peugeot. DC Green, run the partial plate and see if we get any old bangers to come up.'

'Right, boss'

16

An hour later, they had a name. There were fourteen cars with the partial plate they'd pulled, but only one was an old Peugeot. It was found to be registered by a man called Peter Roper.

'This is the guy. He's our man,' repeated DI Khan excitedly. DI Khan had only joined the team a few years ago, and he was still fresh regarding this investigation.

Lucas had been here before, a few times. Suspects only seemed to bring trouble and no resolution. He was jaded, but he tried to allow himself to get marginally excited.

'We still need to prove it. Find out everything you can about this man. I want a report on my desk in the morning. We'll pay him a brief visit first thing.'

17

'Ouch, ya fuck!' Lucas had just spilt hot coffee on his lap. He was moving the mountain of paperwork across the desk to make room for the brand-spanking new folder that had just been presented to him.

'Thanks, Kim'

'No problem, sir.' She flashed him a winning smile, noticing the large coffee stain on his crotch. 'Do you want me to get you a cloth as well?' her smile had taken on a slightly wicked slant.

'Please,' he said desperately.

'No worries, I'm not drying it for you though, dirty sod,' she cackled as she left the room, leaving Lucas slightly flustered.

He started sifting through the highly detailed dossier DS Sterling had provided. Peter Roper lived in a small bungalow outside the main bulk of the city in Greater Leeds. A rather large metropolitan shit hole called Morley. Sometimes used to film the long-running ITV soap Emmerdale, this place quickly became a hot spot for petty crime and drugs. None of this was included in the tourism brochure.

Peter Roper was a sixty-two-year-old unemployed former

electrician. He was divorced and had one son, who he rarely saw. He'd been through the courts multiple times a while ago but appeared to have just given up in the last ten years. It was hard to tell from the records, but he seemed to be a relatively quiet person. There have not been too many issues with the police, not even a parking ticket for the last decade. His only interaction was when he reported his van missing in 2007 and again in 2019 when he'd been found drunk on the side of the road, receiving a caution only. He appeared to have stopped working a few years back when his small business, VoltEdge Electricals, had folded. He'd owed a lot of money and had been declared bankrupt only a few months ago. An initial background check confirmed that he'd been registered as living in Leeds for the last fifteen years, so he could be present for all the murders. With no true interactions with the police, there were no fingerprints or DNA on file, which might account for the fact he'd not turned up before today. Something was niggling at Lucas, though. This all sounded pathetic and not the profile of a clever, sophisticated serial killer who harvested organs and left poetic clues for the police. That said, the information was helpful, so Lucas got up, scrubbed a bit more from his suspicious crotch stain, and went to inform Superintendent Carmichael.

The superintendent was in a good mood. Lucas could tell as soon as he walked in. The news of the CCTV footage must have reached her already.

'This is excellent work, DCI Miller. But don't get too carried away. We might have a link to this case, but you have a long way to go to link him to the previous eleven.'

'Of course, Super,' he said, slightly irritated that she was stating the obvious. Lucas knew he did too much as a DCI, he had done as a DI as well. He couldn't help getting involved in proper police work, it was in his nature. Carmichael, on the other hand, had taken a giant step backwards from the frontline, but seemed comfortable to take the credit for the investigation moving on again. Not that Lucas felt he deserved all the credit, either; most of this was just blind luck, just waiting for a mistake.

'I'll send the team over this afternoon. I've applied for a warrant but can't see it being refused, so we'll search the place. Hopefully, we'll find something. If not, we'll bring him in for questioning regardless, and we'll see how he fairs under pressure,' continued Lucas.

'Yes, good work, Lucas. I want a good, clean arrest. No slip-ups, no fuck ups. No mistakes. Is that clear?' she wagged her increasingly bony finger at him, and he noticed again how her hands aged her far more than her face did. The last ten years had taken the shine off Pat Carmichael, but she still made every attempt to polish herself. She was clearly dying her hair, and her make-up remained expensive. She was in very good shape, although she'd perhaps become more unhealthy and underweight in the last few years, undoubtedly because of stress.

'I don't need to remind you; this one has no second chances. We make a mess of this, and I cannot, and will not, put my neck out for you again. Clear?'

'Yes, boss,' he said, wondering how this had become a lecture. He found that this often happened since his fuck up a few years back. Someone would give him well-earned recognition for something positive, only to remember they weren't supposed to like him. Carmichael was usually better than that; she'd stuck by him, but there was still an undercurrent, even with her.

'Good. You're dismissed.'

Lucas left her office and returned to his desk. He sat down and let out a long sigh. He was tired and frustrated. The last few months had been trying for him and the team. They'd all been under tremendous pressure from above. This was their big break. He felt they had a chance of catching this guy. This was the man who had haunted the streets of Leeds for years. He had murdered countless women, and now, finally, they had him. The parallels with the infamous Yorkshire Ripper, Peter Sutcliffe, were pretty obvious. Journalists were having a field day; the name 'Reaper' even sounded similar, but Lucas was adamant that the mistakes in that case wouldn't be repeated on this. So far, he was failing. But, finally, they had another name. The only thing was, the more he read, the more he felt that something wasn't quite right. Peter Roper seemed like an ordinary man. His life, so far, had been unremarkable, from a violence and crime perspective at least. He looked up again and stared out of the window. He thought about what it must be like to be estranged from your children, stuck in a dead-end job you didn't enjoy. Could he understand why he'd been paying for sex? Yes, probably. It was not something Lucas would do, but he could understand it, even if it was just on an animalistic level. But murder? That was different, and serial murders were a whole new ball game. Something didn't fit.

18

The next day, he was up early. It was an important day. There was a knock at his door, and Luna attempted to bark menacingly. She failed, and a soft 'woof' just evaporated from her little grey snout. Lucas answered it and found DS Sterling waiting at his doorstep, takeaway coffee and Gregg's sausage roll in hand.

'Good morning, sir. I got you some breakfast.'

'Thanks, Kim. You're too good to me' he smiled as he grabbed his shoes, leaving the door ajar so they could still talk.

'No, sir. I just wanted to make sure you were up and ready.' He chuckled as he struggled to get his right shoe on. He should have just undone the laces, but he was halfway in now and kept wiggling the heel until his foot finally slipped in. 'Thanks for coming with me; your report was so detailed. I thought you'd be keen to meet the man in person.'

'Absolutely. It's nice to get back into the swing of things.'

Lucas nodded and smiled. He finished getting ready, and the two left in his car. It wasn't long before Lucas began overheating as DS Sterling seemed to like the heating on full blast.

'Kim, do you know anything about the previous cases?'

'Of course, I've been off with cancer, not living under a rock,' She replied, tutting. 'Eleven, well now twelve, women brutally murdered over the course of a decade. The new ripper, or 'The Water's Edge Reaper' or whatever the press is calling it these days. National manhunt dominates the front pages almost daily. There are very few leads and lots of dead ends. Police incompetency, possible corruption...' She paused. Lucas kept his eyes on the road and just grunted. She continued, waving her arms around animatedly as she spoke. She was putting on a fake 1980s high-pitched TV voice. Not a terrible impression, thought Lucas.

'Women fear this man. Is it safe to go out at night alone? Will the girl's night out still be a thing in a few years, or should we only be moved under the watchful gaze of our protective men?'

'You don't think women should fear him?' asked Lucas

'Of course, take sensible precautions. Don't go wandering around at night, and Christ knows how desperate you'd have to be these days to work the streets. But to suggest that the answer to this is to place your trust in a man seems a bit... silly to me. Given it's a supposedly a bloke who's killing us.'

'I think that's a fair point, Kim, but not everyone is as battle-hardened as you clearly are.'

'Cancer couldn't have me, and some creepy-crawly pervert sure as shit isn't going to.' She puffed her chest out in her thick autumn jumper, police lanyard falling around her neck. Despite her spindly, noodle-like arms, he certainly wouldn't mess with her, thought Lucas. After a few seconds, in which DS Kim Sterling took some deep breaths, she started again.

'I've started to go through the case files again. Some of

them pre-date my time on the force, and obviously, I was off sick for a year. But I was fairly well involved in numbers six and seven, Amrita Kaur and Sophia Sidorova. I just thought a fresh pair of eyes might be useful.'

'A fair idea. You can bring this profiler mate of yours in as well. See what he thinks. I know Carmichael isn't a fan, but frankly, I'll take all the help we can get. Given everything you've just said, what sort of monster are you expecting Roper to be?'

'I don't know,' she replied pensively.

'That report was the most detailed report I've received in ten years, and you did it in an evening. You have an opinion, and I want to hear it,' he said encouragingly.

'He doesn't sound that bad,' she said slowly, unsure of the response she might receive.

'No? Have you ever met a murderer?'

'No, but he sounds sad. He sounds like a sad old man paying for the company of a woman.'

'A fair point. Just remember, Peter Sutcliffe was described as charming, as was Ted Bundy. Harold Shipman was a GP and pillar of the community. They're normal people doing very abnormal things. Keep your mind open, please. Your report hasn't convinced me either way. We need to find hard evidence.'

'Or not find it?' she muttered.

'Yeah, or that,' replied Lucas.

The rest of the drive was more enjoyable. They put the radio on and listened to some of the latest hits. DS Sterling seemed to get excited about any song that was being played, whilst Lucas just enjoyed her company. It was certainly better than watching the dilapidated streets of Morley, West

18

Yorkshire, creep past the window. The occasional business was holding its own, but most of the shops on the high street had been left bare following the pandemic.

They arrived at Roper's place, just outside a particularly grimy council estate. It was a small, run-down semi-detached house with a pebble-dash exterior and a rusting metal roof. They pulled outside, and Lucas turned the engine off, paused, and got out. The uniformed officers pulled up their cars behind him and got out as well, standing guard at the entrance to the drive. Lucas straightened his jacket and put his hands in his pockets in a way that made him feel quite cool. He started walking towards the house, with DS Sterling trailing just behind. It was a chilly morning, but thankfully, it was not raining as it had been non-stop for the past fortnight. The wind blew around him, and the grass swayed in the breeze. The clouds were dark and heavy, and there were a lot of them, he thought.

'Right, DS Sterling. This is it,' he said and knocked on the door. No one came. They waited. He knocked again. Nothing.

'Let's go round the back.' He signalled to the uniformed officers, and a couple left their posts at the front of the property. They all walked around the side of the house, where a path led to the back garden. It was overgrown, and the grass reached their knees. It looked like it had been a while since anyone had been there. Lucas pushed open the gate, and it creaked in protest. The back garden was almost as overgrown as the front. The grass was knee-high, as were the nettles, rose bushes and brambles. There was a shed, which was a little more tidy than the rest of the garden. It was old and falling apart, but it looked like it was well looked after. The wood was painted a dark green colour, and it seemed sturdy despite its age. There was a window with a small latch that was frosted so that no one could look inside. There was a small padlock on the door that was firmly closed. Lucas stepped towards the shed and tried the door. It was locked.

'Oi! The fuck you doing in my garden?' Roper's head was sticking out the top-floor window. He didn't look happy.

'Sorry, Mr Roper. We're from the police. I'm DCI Lucas Miller. This is DS Kimberly Sterling, and these are my henchmen. Could we come in?'

'What do you want? I haven't done anything!'

'We just have some questions for you, sir. It's about Bianca Dumitrescu.'

'Who?'

'Can we come in, please?' He took an envelope from his jacket pocket and flashed it at Roper.

'We have a warrant, but we don't need to break any doors down if you open them.'

'Fine, fine, wait.' His head popped back in through the window. A minute later, Lucas heard the front door open. He and DS Sterling walked around to the front door. Peter Roper was waiting for them.

'Come in, come in,' he said quickly, glancing round to make sure the neighbours weren't watching, which they probably were.

The house was small, with walls that were white and peeling. Old floorboards creaked underfoot and the whole place was rather cold and empty. The air was still and quiet, and as they walked into the living room, Lucas could see why. The entire room was bare except for a small table in the centre that had a single wooden chair pushed up next to it.

18

There was a bed in the corner, which was unmade and had some suspicious stains across it. On the floor by the head of the bed, next to a few clothes strewn across the floor, sat a two-litre bottle of what Lucas hoped was cider. There was a door leading to the kitchen and a second door leading to the bathroom. Lopsided pictures adorned the walls of some of Roper's family, including one of his ex-wife. She had a kind face, and his son looked very young in this picture, so it must have been old.

'Do you want to sit down?' he offered the chair to DS Sterling, but she politely refused with a hand gesture.

'No, thank you, we'll stand. You can take the seat, though,' she said, and he obliged without thinking.

'So, what do you want?' he asked nervously. He was tall and gangly, with blonde hair. It was nicotine-stained yellow at the front, as were his teeth. The nasty little eyes on the video were watery and pathetic up close. He had a nervous tick that meant he scratched his chin when uncomfortable. Lucas looked him directly in the eye and began.

'Where were you on the night of Sunday, 19th September this year?'

'Huh? What am I under arrest for?' he replied, startled.

'You're not under arrest at the moment. We're going to ask some questions, and then we'll see, said Lucas flatly.

'Err, right? What date again?'

'Sunday'

'I don't know'

'Sunday the 19th of September, Mr Roper. The Sunday just gone. Four days ago.'

'I was here, I think. Probably at home. I don't really go out much.'

'Well, we'll have to check with your neighbours then.'

'Go ahead' As he said this, he sank back into his little wooden chair and folded his arms like a petulant child.

'Mr Roper, are you familiar with the name Bianca Dumitrescu?'

'No'

'Do you know her husband, Mr Borka Dumitrescu?'

'No'

'Have you ever used prostitutes?' This got him scratching his chin vigorously. He looked down at the floor and licked his lips.

'Why do you wanna know that?' he said after a slightly awkward pause.

'Did you visit one on Sunday?' Again, he looked down at the ground. Lucas pressed on, sensing he might have an opening here.

'Well, yeah, but...' He gestured around the room. 'How else am I going to get laid? I don't exactly have a lot going for me at the moment. And I didn't know it was a crime officer. I thought it was legal now, what with those red-light areas.'

'It is legal, although those red-light districts were closed a few years ago,' said Lucas, scribbling something on his notepad.

'Ah, right, then why are you here?' said Peter, increasingly agitated and confused. DS Sterling opened her little folder and presented him with a nice, normal picture of Bianca Dumitrescu. She was grinning broadly, showing quite a significant amount of upper gum. Mr Roper was not smiling. Given how violently he was now scraping at it, he was about to rip his chin apart.

'This lady was found dead on Monday. Someone removed

18

her stomach. The last person to have seen her alive would appear to be you. We have you on video,' said Lucas matter-of-factly.

Mr Roper was drip white, and you could see the dark blue blood in his veins through his translucent skin. He stared at the picture. Then he looked up at the two officers and wobbled slightly. Suddenly, his eyes rolled back in his head, and he lost all core strength. He slipped off the chair and dropped like a stone, smashing into the table well before either Lucas, Kim or the officers by the door could catch him.

'Bollocks!'

2011

19

Three floors down from DI Carmichael's office was interview room three, which was currently occupied by four people. Lucas and Chloe sat opposite the aggressive bulk of Jacob Murray and his slimy little solicitor, Vincent Sharp. Jacob Murray was flexing his muscles, which might have been intimidating if he didn't also have a pot belly which was poking out from under his overly tight T-shirt and noticeably smaller legs. The bloke looked like a toffee apple. Typical new money, thought Lucas.

However, the solicitor, Vincent Sharp, looked like he'd been rung from a mechanic's rag; he was that oily. He must have been at least fifty, but his hair was dyed jet black and was slicked back over his domed head. There were tiny little pricks on his forehead, too, from where he'd recently had some Botox injections. He looked the part, but was well-renowned for being totally fucking useless.

'So, let me get this straight. You did not see or speak to your daughter on the day that she was reported missing?' Lucas said, raising an eyebrow at Murray. They'd agreed that Lucas would conduct this interview, given that he'd refused to speak to Chloe in the house. Carmichael was on the other side of the two-way mirror and had pre-prepared Lucas with several questions. Nobody was that keen for the new DC to dive in balls deep and interview a suspect so soon, so Lucas was eager to take this unusual opportunity.

'Nope. Can I go now? I got kids of my own, and they need picking up. Their mum will kill me if I don't pick 'em up.'

'Care has been arranged for your children, don't worry,' said Chloe, and he turned to look at her. She could see the cogs winding in his head and the urge to shout something abusive to her, forming at his mouth. But he didn't; he said nothing and turned back to Lucas.

'Jacob Murray, you need to be aware of something. This will be hard to hear, and there is no easy way of putting it. So I prefer just to say it.' Lucas paused. Hit them with the warning shot, and then deliver the bad news. If he was innocent, this would be awful to hear. If he was guilty, he'd know the game was up. Either way, it was bad news. 'The body we found in the woods is your daughter. DNA testing has proven it.'

Jacob Murray just sat there in the chair opposite, hardly blinking. He said nothing. He just stared. Lucas could feel his knuckles tightening, rage flooding up his neck. Murray didn't care, not one bit. He looked down, and Lucas wondered if he was capable of shame or guilt.

'You know that means that she died in those woods? Do you know why?' Murray shrugged, looking back up. He glanced at his solicitor, who remained silently greasy as if he'd been told to keep his mouth shut. 'Your daughter was murdered. But she wasn't just killed; she was tortured and mutilated.' There was an audible silence. He just stared back, unblinking and emotionless, the complete opposite of the absolute fury a few days ago.

Lucas had expected a response, but Murray had gone completely quiet and motionless, as if waiting for someone else to speak. Lucas pressed on, pushing aside his anger.

'Mr Murray, if you were involved in her death in any way, you need to tell us. The sooner you confess, the better it will be for you. It will also help the rest of your family to know what happened to her. Did you argue?' Murray didn't move a muscle.

'We can protect you. Just tell us what you were doing the night she went missing.'

'I didn't kill her,' he said simply.

'OK, then what happened?'

'No. I can't tell you anything, alright? You'll make something up and bang me up anyway.' Murray leaned back in his chair and stared at his hands, which were folded on the table. He was refusing to say anything more. Lucas had been hoping for a confession, but Murray gave them nothing.

Lucas licked his lips. They were dry and cracked. Fuck this, he thought, we're going off-piste.

'The heart beats slow, in shadowed haze, beneath the moon's lamenting gaze. Its crimson tides of love and dread, where secrets dark and light have bled.'

'What the fuck you on about? That a poem? You some sort of poof mate?' snarled Murray.

'Mean anything to you, Jacob?'

'Naa, I don't read poems.'

'That poem was on a piece of paper that we found inside your daughter. In her chest, where her heart should have been. Why did you put it there?' Lucas had done it. He noticed Murray suddenly look paler.

'I... I didn't put no poem inside her. I didn't kill her,' he said, but more uncomfortable than he'd been up to this point.

'OK, Jacob. Let me tell you something else we found inside, Jessica. We found semen inside your daughter.' Murray continued to stare back, but there was a flicker behind his eyes, fear perhaps. Lucas could see Chloe shifting nervously in the seat next to him, and somehow, he felt Carmichael tense up behind the mirror. She'd warned him about this.

'It was yours.'

Vincent Sharp sat forward abruptly, and the greasy fucker nearly slipped off the chair as he snapped his head round to face Murray. Before anyone else could react, Murray lunged at Lucas suddenly, grabbing his collar and screaming.

'She was a dirty, fucking little whore! I caught her with one of them fucking kids!'

'That's enough!' Chloe and the solicitor were both up from their chairs and grabbing Murray by the shoulders, pulling him away from Lucas. A burly PC with a mullet, who had been standing by the door, dived in to help as well. Between himself and Chloe, they managed to hold him down long enough for Murray to come to his senses, as few as they were. He went slack in the officer's grasp and fell back into his chair. Lucas's shirt was ripped, and his neck stung where Murray's nails had scratched him.

Vincent Sharp stood up and put his arm on his client's shoulder. He leaned over and whispered in his ear. Murray shook his head. He didn't seem to be interested in speaking any more.

Lucas was furious. He had hoped Murray would confess. But the man seemed resigned to silence now. He was also a little worried about how much trouble that little stunt would get him into with Carmichael.

'Do you think I hurt my daughter?' he said without looking up.

'What?' Lucas was incredulous. He could hardly believe what Murray was implying. 'What are you talking about? The DNA evidence proves you had sexual intercourse with her.'

Murray was staring straight at Lucas, his face blank and his eyes empty. 'You think I don't know what you're doing? You're trying to fuck with me head. It ain't working, though.'

'Mr Murray, this is the evidence, plain and simple. The evidence says that you were in physical contact with your daughter shortly before she died. Do you want to tell us why you never came forward, or do we need to keep looking at you?' Lucas had to control his rage. He couldn't show any more anger. It might tip Murray over the edge and make him even less cooperative. Murray didn't say a word.

'Fine. Interview suspended at fourteen twenty-three. We will be back.'

2023

20

Police Incompetence and Public Fear as Water's Edge Reaper Strikes Again

By Simon Davies, Senior Crime Correspondent

The discovery of the body of another woman believed to be the eleventh victim of the 'Water's Edge Reaper' has sparked renewed public outrage and calls for action from the police.

The victim, who has been named locally as Bianca Dumitrescu (36), was found by the Water's Edge area of Emmet Woods, only a few 100 meters from where she lived and only a stone's throw from where the body of Jessica Murray was discovered in 2011. Both bodies were mutilated and left uncovered.

The 'Water's Edge Reaper' has been terrorising the community for the past 12 years, and police have been unable to catch them. Many believe that the police are incompetent and that they are not doing enough to protect the public.

'I'm terrified to go out at night,' said one local resident. 'I don't know if I will be the next victim.'

'The police need to do more to catch this killer,' said another resident. 'They're not doing enough to protect us.'

The police have defended their handling of the case, saying that they are doing everything they can to apprehend the perpetrator; however, they have admitted that they are frustrated by their lack of progress.

'We are working tirelessly to catch this individual,' said a police spokesperson. 'We understand the public's frustration, but ask for their patience and support.'

The 'Water's Edge Reaper' has become a symbol of the fear and insecurity that many people feel in the community. These crimes have had a devastating impact on the victims' families and friends, and they have left the community reeling.

The police are under increasing pressure to catch the culprit and know that they need to do more to regain the public's trust.

Detective Superintendent Carmichael was looking as irritated as it was possible to look. They were in her office, and she was hovering by the window, her shoulders hunched and her face screwed up with frustration.

'How badly did Roper hurt himself? Are we sure it was just a faint?' she said.

'Yeah, docs looked him over. Got an ECG and some bloods and everything,' said Lucas.

'We're too good to these people. Did we squeeze anything out of him?'

'Yeah, we managed to interview him obviously,' Lucas said, trying to sound positive, even if he wasn't.

'Yeah, and? Anything?'

'No. He admitted to using the services of Bianca Dumitrescu, but denied killing her. He says she asked to be dropped off nearer some shops up the road. Wanted some mints or something for her breath.'

20

'This shop presumably has CCTV?'

'It does, but it hasn't been turned on for a month. It still runs on tapes, and the owner didn't have the money to buy more.'

'Fuck's sake, tapes? Do they even still make those? So, despite that, are there any witnesses to what happened at the shop? Did she make it as far as getting mints?' Carmichael stopped hunching at this and moved her hands to her hips, looking even more commanding than usual.

'Shopkeeper remembers her, got there about ten forty-five-ish. He says she's been in a few times. I think he fancied her, if I'm honest. She got some mints, some fags and left. There's a pub about a hundred yards up the road, towards her house; we're asking if anyone there saw her. She'll have been going past around last orders,' Said Lucas, desperately trying not to sound like they were losing their lead.

'Great, that's something. Any links to the others?'

'He had solid alibis for six of them, nothing for two, and then some slightly shaky ones for the rest.'

'Gut feeling?'

'Not him boss'

'Shit, well, let's not completely discount him until – '

DS Sterling suddenly burst through the door, looking flustered. She looked at Lucas for a second before switching to Detective Superintendent Carmichael.

'Sir! Ma'am! We have another one! Just been called in a few minutes ago.'

'Another body? Where?' said Carmichael, immediately reaching for her jacket without hesitation.

DS Sterling gulped. 'The hospital. This one's alive.'

2012

21

Lucas fiddled with the dials on his car radio, turning the volume up. Traffic was terrible today, but he'd given himself plenty of time to get to the courts. It had been a little over a year since the small, emaciated body of Jessica Murray had been discovered in the woods. It had taken them less than a week to make an arrest. The father, it was always the father. Discovering his semen inside his daughter was about as conclusive evidence as you could get that he had raped her. He'd never really denied it. But he had denied murdering her.

The bloke was tapped in the head, thought Lucas, but there was something... something niggling at the back of Lucas's brain. The problem was that the semen was the only evidence they had. There were no blood-stained trousers, no muddy boots, no suspicious fibres, and there was none of her DNA in the boot of his car. They couldn't link him to the poem they'd found inside her chest, and Lucas wasn't even sure the bloke could read, let alone write that. They'd never even found the murder weapon. No witnesses and no smoking gun.

Lucas shook his head to clear his thoughts. It was a

frustrating drive to get to Leeds Crown Court, especially during rush hour, and the courts were in the city centre, so there wasn't a faster way of getting there. Despite only being three weeks until Christmas, it wasn't as bitterly cold as it might have been. He'd have been comfortable in the car if it weren't for the horribly low sun penetrating the cabin underneath the visor, causing him to squint hard. He turned the radio up. It was some pretentiously sad song he wasn't interested in listening to, sung by some jumped-up celebrities aiming for the Christmas number one. It was probably for charity, he guessed, and it did at least drown out that niggling feeling.

Conveniently, the Crown, County, and Magistrates courts were all essentially part of the same complex, so he knew where to go. This was the first proper conviction he was going to be a part of, for a murder at least. He'd had some smaller ones in between, but nothing of this magnitude. He'd been a key witness or the arresting officer in three armed robberies, a nasty sexual assault and a relatively brutal domestic abuse case. Not bad for a year and a half on the job. This was the big one, however. It had made the national press, not just the local rag.

He pulled into the multi-story round the corner, paid an excessive amount for inner city parking, and then strode down to the courts. Chloe was already waiting for him alongside DI Carmichael. His boss looked suitably irritated as she always did, but this was just a prickly demeanour she wore to ward off trouble. She was actually a great person to work for, he'd discovered. Although, today, with those knee-high boots and dressed in all black, she looked like a dominatrix. It wouldn't have surprised him in the slightest to find out she liked to kick men in the bollocks as a hobby.

Chloe spotted him as he approached and flashed a wonderful smile in his direction. She'd done her hair up all fancy, wearing her best make-up and a professional-looking suit. Lucas had made no secret of the fact he fancied her. She'd said early on that she didn't want a relationship at work, and he'd always respected those boundaries. There were moments when he thought she'd changed her mind, but no, they remained 'just friends,' which was fair enough.

'Morning,' he said to them both. He got a smile from Chloe and a grunt from his boss.

'Morning,' said Chloe. 'Ready to get our man?'

'Sure, I'm quite excited, if I'm honest.'

The court was packed, and the press was hanging out of every corner of the place. A few television cameras were dotted amongst the crowd. The father had become something of a cause célèbre. It was an easy target for people with an axe to grind, a way to show the world just how much society had failed.

Lucas, Carmichael, and Chloe were shown through to the viewing gallery of Court Room one, where they took their seats on the polished wooden benches that lined the room. Lucas looked down over the balcony at the room below. He saw the sleek, glass-panelled witness box standing adjacent to the judge's imposing raised dais and, in the centre, a long mahogany table stretched across the wall. The various legal people furiously flicked through notes at the last minute, scrutinising documents and conferring with one another. There were surprisingly large flat-screen TVs on the walls, presumably ready to display evidence when required, and a large red digital clock silently ticking away the seconds over where the judge would be sitting.

A few minutes passed, and then a hushed silence spread around the room. The jury was brought in first, followed by the defendant, Jacob Murray. He was placed at a table next to his lawyer. It was not the same greasy weasel that had sat in the interview room over a year ago, but a much more professional-looking woman. Murray had lost weight; even in his suit, you could tell he wasn't as muscled as he used to be. It's hard to get the steroids in the nick, perhaps. He glanced at the gallery, and his eyes locked with Lucas's, who felt his heart skip a beat. There was something there that wasn't quite right. The man seemed almost at peace. It was an odd thing to think, but it was true. He certainly didn't look like a man on his way to prison for murder.

'I'm still not sure he's guilty,' Lucas whispered to Chloe, who gave him a strange look.

'He's as guilty as sin, we found his... you know,' she hissed back.

'Yes, but...' Lucas paused. 'I don't know. We're missing something. I'm still not sure he killed her.'

'The CPS don't agree, and it's too late, anyway.'

'I know.' said Lucas, but the tone of doubt was unmistakable.

'Would you two shut the fuck up?' Carmichael was glaring across at them like an irritable ostrich. They sat back in their seats quickly like scalded children.

The judge entered the room, and the proceedings began. After an hour of legal jargon and pointless back and forth between the prosecution and defence, the first witness was called. It was the pathologist. He'd done the initial examinations on the body and then left it to the forensics team. Dr Cross made his way to the stand and waited patiently for the questioning to begin.

'Dr Daniel Cross. You conducted the initial examination of Jessica Murray's body. Is that correct?'

'Myself and others, yes.' He drawled, his privately educated voice thick with privilege thought Lucas.

'And others, Dr Cross? Can you explain the process, please?'

'There were several forensic scientists who secured the scene and made an initial assessment of the body. Then, I arrived and made my own assessment of the scene and the body before supervising its safe removal and transport back to the morgue. Once they have arrived in the morgue, one of our forensically trained histopathologists will typically perform an autopsy within a day or so. Either myself, Dr Cooper or Dr Humber. In this instance, it was my assistant, Mrs Lansbury and me. All of this is in the report I provided.'

'I see. And what did you find?'

Dr Cross launched into a very detailed description of her injuries. Each incision made and every bruise he had found. When he talked about how her heart was missing and the poem in the bottle, Lucas had heard enough. He didn't need to hear it all again; he'd studied the pictures to know it in more detail than he'd ever be able to forget. He looked at Chloe and Carmichael. Both of them were paying rapt attention to the doctor. Jacob Murray had his head bowed and was staring at the floor. He didn't want to hear any of this, and Lucas couldn't blame him.

'And can you explain to the court what your findings led you to conclude?'

'That she died from exsanguination leading to hypovolemia and ultimately myocardial infarction because of reduced cardiac preload. Admittedly difficult to confirm without the heart,' he said matter-of-factly, as if this was obvious. Turning slightly to the jury, he continued. 'Blood loss. Injuries to the major vessels in her neck will probably have made death swift; the preceding injuries will have been excruciating. The heart was removed after death, so will not have increased her suffering.'

'Thank you. That is all from the prosecution, your honour.' The man with the silly wig sat down, only to be replaced by a woman with an equally ridiculous wig, who was Murray's solicitor for the defence.

'Dr Cross, thank you for painting such a vivid picture. Now tell me, is it possible to tell exactly when the semen sample was deposited?'

'That is a question better suited for my forensic scientist colleagues.'

'I am asking you.'

'Well, you shouldn't be. I am not the expert witness in this regard, but as far as I am aware, no, it is not. It was dry, and the only other samples we found were older than a week. It could have been deposited any time in the previous two weeks, but no more than that. But you should not take my word for it.'

'And you testified earlier that the bruises you found were not consistent with sexual abuse?'

'No, I said the bruises I found could be suggestive of a lack of consent. Of course, I cannot tell you categorically that they were left as a result of a rape or sexual abuse. But they were certainly consistent with such an event.'

'So it is possible that the sample was left sometime before

the murder?'

'Yes, but...'

'No buts Doctor, yes or no?'

'Yes.' He made no attempt to hide his dislike of the lawyer. Not many people got away with being rude to Dr Cross.

'No further questions, your honour.'

Lucas looked over at Chloe and Carmichael. 'What was that all about?' he asked.

'She's trying to muddy the waters. Make us doubt his guilt,' Carmichael said.

'Well, I already do. This whole thing doesn't add up. I know the guy is sick in the head, but he just doesn't seem like a killer to me.'

'Don't worry, Lucas, you'll see plenty worse than this before you're done. Now shut up.,' hissed Carmichael.

Lucas tried to turn his attention back to the floor, but failed. He got up and tried to sneak out but kicked two members of the press by accident as he did so; luckily, one of them was Simon Davies, who he'd grown to dislike immeasurably. Muttering his apologies, he ran for the door, ignoring the stifled shouts that followed him. He needed some fresh air, so took a long walk around the block and called his father. He sounded like he'd been drinking; of course, he had. This made him feel no better. He knew they had the wrong guy. He could feel it.

After half an hour, he walked back into the court and sat beside Chloe and Carmichael. They looked at him and then at each other, then turned their attention back to the floor.

'What did I miss?' Lucas whispered.

'Nothing really, they're just calling witnesses now. Some psychologist has given a character assessment of the accused.'

'And?'

'It was not positive. I think they called him a cunt in Latin,' said Carmichael.

Lucas sighed and sat back in his seat. He wanted to scream. Something was missing here, and he didn't know what.

Before too long, the court rested for the day. Lucas got up and stretched. The sun shone through the large glass windows that ran along the length of the courtroom, casting the room in a golden light. It might have been quite beautiful if he wasn't so pissed off.

'I'm going for another walk,' he said to Chloe. 'See you tomorrow?' She gave him a brief nod and smiled.

'OK, I'll see you tomorrow. Try to get some sleep tonight.'

'I'll try.'

Lucas left the courthouse deep in thought. The press were hanging around outside, but they weren't interested in an insignificant little detective constable. Despite having a fairly significant role in the capture and arrest of Jacob Murray, there was no escape from the fact that he was still at the bottom of the food chain. Only really DS Wilson and DI Carmichael had acknowledged his fairly integral role in all of this.

He strode away from the press and headed to his car, where he stayed there for a moment, thinking. He couldn't get rid of the feeling that Jacob Murray was innocent of murder. But how could he prove it? And did he need to prove it? He hardly wanted the bloke free. Raping your daughter was arguably worse than anything else he could think of.

He needed a shower, a shit and a beer, not necessarily in that order or at the same time.

21

Despite his doubts, over the next week, it was becoming increasingly apparent that Jacob Murray was going down for murder, whether he'd committed it or not. The prosecution was very persuasive, and whichever way you cut it, the man had undoubtedly raped his daughter. So how much of a stretch was it to see that he'd murdered her as well? When the guilty verdict was eventually read out, even the niggling thing at the back of Lucas's mind cheered. The bloke could rot. The biggest worry that Lucas had, which everyone else seemed to be missing, was if he hadn't killed Jessica, someone else had.

And they might do it again.

2023

22

The roads were pretty quiet as Lucas, DSI Carmichael, and DI Khan powered towards the Leeds General Infirmary, where they arrived after about a quarter of an hour. The car ride was quiet, as they were all deep in thought. It was nice to see Carmichael out of her office. It had been a few years since she'd bothered to do any field work. Not that she needed to. Now she was a pen-pushing DSI.

'So, this one's alive then?' said Lucas as he drove into the mortuary car park. Why pay for parking when he was already allowed to park there?

'Yes, but in what sort of state? We don't know yet. I mean, shit, we have enough dead girls without having to deal with a living one,' said DI Khan from the back seat.

'Fair point,' said Carmichael. 'What do we think happened here? Dare I ask, but does she still have her eyes?'

'I don't know about her eyes yet, but it sounds as though she survived an attack by our man. It's unclear whether he got interrupted or she forced him off and escaped. Either way, she got free,' said DI Khan.

'My understanding is that a member of the public found her when he was taking the bins out early in the morning and called an ambulance. They only linked it to our case once she was in the hospital,' said Lucas.

'She must be so scared,' said Carmichael, staring out the window.

'Of who?' said DI Khan

'Whoever did it to her, you bellend,' snapped Lucas.

They were silent the rest of the way to the hospital. They parked the car and ran up to the intensive care unit, where one of the more senior consultants appeared. She introduced herself as Dr Shazad. She was in her late forties, spoke with a soft South Indian accent, and quietly oozed competence, which was always reassuring in a doctor. Her black hair was tied up, and she wore a set of pale blue scrubs with a black stethoscope around her neck.

'Doctor, I'm DSI Carmichael. This is DCI Lucas Miller and DI Sadiq Khan. Thanks for seeing us; I know you must be busy. What can you tell us about the condition of the patient?'

Lucas loved watching Carmichael interacting with people she deemed cleverer than her because she always made a little extra effort to be more professional and eloquent. It was sweet, really.

'Of course, but you won't like what I have to say,' said Dr Shazad, placing her hands together apologetically.

'Is she dead?' said Carmichael quickly.

'No, much worse,' replied Dr Shazad. What could be worse than death?

The doctor led them around the corner to one of the quiet 'family' rooms. Pleasant pictures on the wall and soft, squishy chairs. What a lovely little place to be told your relatives are dead or dying. They were accompanied by a nurse and a plump, very distressed-looking PC with an eighties mullet. This was PC Andrew Johnson, whom Lucas had encountered a few times. He was first on the scene and the poor chap who'd brought her in.

'Right, we couldn't give you detailed information over the phone,' explained Dr Shazad. 'I have never seen anything like this in my career.' The two detectives waited with bated breath for whatever she was about to say. 'The pain this girl is in, I simply cannot imagine.'

'What have they done to her?'

'Everything. She has been stabbed in the abdomen at least four times; she is currently undergoing an emergency laparotomy with the general surgeons—no doubt they'll resect something. CT polytrauma suggests a bowel perforation, but no liver or splenic lacerations, some small mercy. She's got some laryngeal and tracheal injuries, sharp and blunt, which are life-changing; she's going to get a tracheostomy. Hopefully, it will only be short term, but there's a significant risk that it'll be permanent. There are several fairly large wounds to her arms and legs where I think she has struggled, but worst of all, this man appears to have also attempted to remove her eyeballs from her skull. One of them is partially intact; the surgeons will look at it, but from my limited experience with ophthalmology, I don't think they'll recover sight. Communication is limited as she has also suffered some barotrauma to her ears, which is the only thing I'm confident she will recover from. These are some of the worst injuries I've ever seen in twenty-five years.' She took a deep breath and paused. 'The amount of pain doesn't bear thinking about.'

'Jesus fucking Christ,' said DI Khan, verbalising what

everyone else was thinking.

'That is not even the last of it,' said Dr Shazad grimly.

'What?' gasped PC Johnson from the corner.

'There is an object currently penetrating her vagina; we think it has gone through her cervix and into her bladder. We do not truly know how far it goes until after surgery. She has been sexually assaulted, though; I can tell you that for certain.'

'With what?'

'We don't know. It doesn't appear to be a knife. It's not big enough, and it's the wrong shape. Looking at the images, it might be a pen, but we'll let you know when we have retrieved it.' Everyone stood there in stunned silence. They couldn't even imagine the hell that this woman had been through.

'Do we have any idea who she is?' said Lucas.

'Yes, she was found with her wallet close by,' blurted PC Johnson, causing Lucas to jump slightly.

'Pardon?'

'Her wallet. It was with her when we found her.'

'But he's never done that before? Left ID?'

'He's never left one alive before either, Lucas; maybe he was interrupted on this one,' Said DI Khan.

The PC reached into his pocket and pulled out his phone. He flicked through until he found what he was looking for—a picture of a driving licence, which he handed to DSI Carmichael.

'They've taken the original to the lab, but here you are. Amelia Watson, born 14th of February, year 2000.'

Lucas felt his heart skip a beat and a shooting pain jolt through his left forearm. What did he say? Lucas took the

22

phone from DCI Carmichael and looked closely at the green provisional driver's licence. The little black-and-white picture showed a thin, practically emaciated blonde girl with enormous, bulbous eyes staring back. Fuck. This wasn't good. He could feel the redness and the heat building behind his neck; his mouth was drying out, and his arm was pulsing.

'Right, so who the hell is she then?'

'Dunno, boss,' said Lucas. But he did. This wouldn't end well.

23

Dr Shazad had gone to get updates on Amelia's condition from theatre, PC Johnson had to return to his post and DI Khan had returned to the crime scene to interview witnesses, leaving Lucas in silence. Detective Superintendent Carmichael was also in the room, but she was on the phone with DI Chloe Wilson about missing persons, and Lucas was trying not to earwig.

'Yeah, Amelia Watson. No, A for alpha, yeah, that's right. Anything? Right, OK, well look, if you hear anything, we need to know A-S-A-P. Ring DCI Miller. Uh uh, fine, ring me then.' She hung up.

'Anything?' said Lucas.

'No, she's not been reported missing. We've sent officers around to the address on the driver's licence, but it's an old one. Parents used to own it but moved out two years ago, and she's not updated it,'

'I'll show her picture to some girls in Holbeck and the surrounding area.' Holbeck used to be the 'managed approach' area in Leeds, where street workers could sell their wares without fear of prosecution. Essentially, the red-light district. It was scrapped a few years back, what with the

'Water's Edge Reaper' on the loose, but in Lucas's opinion, this made it even harder to keep track of what was happening.

'Good idea. But that's not a job for a DCI; get Khan or someone to do that.'

'It's OK, I'll do – '

'No, you need to be pulling the strings. Khan will do that. Or that new DC, Sterling or whatever she's called.'

'DS Sterling isn't new. She's been here for a few years. She just had time off because of breast cancer.'

'Really? She doesn't look like she has cancer,' said Carmichael.

'Had. She's been given the initial all-clear, I think. What does someone with cancer look like, anyway?'

'Don't start. You know what I meant. Look, the point is you're above all that now. Get the others to do the donkey work. Oh, and get her picture circulated. I'll ring the press office, we'll have to make a statement, and we'll have to keep this under control. The last thing we need is the press turning up here to get a look at the poor girl. You know what that leach Davies is like. He'll already be printing the details as we speak.'

'Yes, boss,' nodded Lucas, a sickly feeling forming in his stomach.

'Fuck sake,' Carmichael suddenly shouted into the void.

'Yep,' agreed Lucas flatly.

They left the hospital and walked down the steps to the car park. It was cold, and the air was still, but Lucas could see snow clouds beginning to form on the horizon. He sighed as the phone in his pocket buzzed. He took it out and glanced at a text from Em.

We are still on for tonight, handsome? xx

He didn't reply. His heart was pounding, his head was thumping, and his palms were sweating. The pain in his left forearm was building up and becoming sharp and intense. He tried flexing his fingers and massaging the deep, thick scar from the elbow, but it didn't work. Turning away from Carmichael, he reached into his jacket pocket, retrieved his blister, and took another pregabalin. He needed to think this through. Why would they work out the connection? She might not survive the surgery, so why would she mention him? It was in her interests to keep quiet, too. But if she did... he was fucked. He needed to get control of the situation, and quickly.

24

Once again, the rain cascaded down as Lucas ran back into the station from the car park. He was sopping wet as he made a bee-line for his desk, sitting down heavily with a squelch as he put his head in his hands, running them through his thinning, and slowly greying hair. He took a deep breath and sensed DS Sterling loitering nearby. She was hopping from foot to foot like she needed a piss.

'Can I help you, Kim?' said Lucas, with a slight hint of frustration, which wasn't intended.

'Yes, well, no. But, er, well...'

'Spit it out.'

'Are you OK, sir? Only you seem a bit off. And well, I'm worried. And I wanted to know if I could help?'

'I'm fine, Kim. I'm just dealing with some personal stuff, that's all. But thank you for asking.' He softened his tone. There was no need to be rude. It made a change that someone cared about how he was feeling.

'Of course, Lucas. I'm mean, sir. If you want to talk about anything, well, I'm here.' She smiled at him, almost nervously.

'I know Kim. I appreciate it,' he smiled back, but it might

have looked more like a grimace, given his mood.

'OK,' She gave him another warm smile, turned and left. A little hint of her perfume lingered. It was nice and comforting. Lucas had no idea why he didn't tell her what was happening. He should have done and felt terrible lying to her, but he had to protect himself. If she knew, he could lose everything. He didn't want to, but he couldn't disobey a direct order from Carmichael, so he picked up the phone and rang DI Khan. He'd have to think of another way.

'DI Khan'

'Mayor Khan, I need a favour,' said Lucas,

'Of course you do,' came the withered reply.

'Can you take a trip to Holbeck? See if you can find anyone who knows the girl, see if they can ID her or tell us where she lives. Maybe give them a picture of her driving licence? But be careful, don't make it obvious. We're trying to keep this one out of the public eye.'

'That's probably more suitable for a DS, boss,' he said back, clearly nettled.

'Aye, well, Superintendent Carmichael wanted me to ask you. So there we are.'

'Ah, fine. Right, I'll get onto it shortly then.'

Lucas put the phone down and checked his watch, an expensive Longines diver, that had been a gift from Chloe a few years back. He had an hour or so to kill, so he picked up the phone and checked on Amelia Watson, hoping she might be out of theatre. However, the staff nurse who answered told him she was still having surgery.

'She's got the tracheostomy in now, and the general surgeons have finished their bit. She's ended up with a fairly substantial resection and an ileostomy. They couldn't save the eye, so they've taken what's left.'

'Any news on the object found in her... you know?' said Lucas, sinking into his chair.

'Not yet. They've removed it, but nobody has confirmed to me what it is. One of the junior docs has seen the scan and thinks it might be a pen or something. God knows how, but he rammed it through her cervix and forced it through the uterus into the bladder. They've repaired it, or at least attempted to.'

'OK, thanks for letting me know.'

'No problem.' He hung up the phone and sat back in his chair. Christ. This girl had been through hell and back. He was making things worse, and he knew it.

DI Khan returned to the station at 5 pm with a lead on Amelia Watson. There were a couple of girls who recognised her from the picture; one knew where she lived. She had apparently been on the game for at least a few years, which was a long time round here. Lucas already knew that bit, of course.

The clock ticked past 8 pm, and Lucas realised he had sat at his desk for two hours. He owed Amelia, so he had a plan, which he had been preparing for mentally all day. Begrudgingly, he slowly left his chair and made his way over to Carmichael's office, knocked on the door, and waited. She was on the phone, but he heard her pause.

'Come in!' She flapped a hand at a chair as he entered, but Lucas remained standing.

'Yeah, alright, keep your knickers on, Dan. Yeah, I know you're a doctor as well; I've told them all of this. OK. Having a pop at me won't help you. Just wait, leave it with me, and I'll get it sorted. Yeah.' She'd gone ever so slightly pink and swivelled her chair around so she wasn't directly facing Lucas. 'OK, well maybe tomorrow night you could come over? That'd be nice. I'm looking forward to it.' She looked slightly flustered as she lifted the phone off her ear and hung up.

'All OK?' asked Lucas

'Yes, fine.' She was still pink. He knew she fancied the pathologist. Why she was trying to be coy was anyone's guess. 'It was Dan. The hospital didn't let Dr Cooper in to examine Amelia Watson from a forensic perspective. They've scrubbed the shit out of her in theatre — evidence down the swanny. Dan tried to push it, but they're having none of it. I'm not sure how I'll be any more persuasive.'

'Trying to save her life though,' he retorted

'Well, yeah, I get that. Just got to keep him happy.' She nodded at her phone. 'Anyway, what do you want? Why aren't you sitting down?'

'I know Amelia Watson,' he said bluntly.

'Pardon,' she said, looking slightly startled.

'The victim, I know her,' He repeated, trying to look calm. She checked her watch dramatically,

'And it's taken you, what, twelve hours to come and tell me this? What the fuck is going on, Lucas? In what capacity do you know her? She was already beginning to boil, and she was getting increasingly animated with every word.

'I don't know her very well,' he said hurriedly, stepping back from her.

'That's not what I asked. How do you know a prostitute?' demanded Carmichael, the venom rising in her voice. Lucas didn't say anything. He just looked down, trying to pick his next words carefully.

24

'Oh, for fuck's sake, Lucas! You have to be kidding me? If you've fucked a victim, I'll...'

'No, it's not that, don't worry!' he interrupted.

'Then what is it? Christ, all fucking mighty, please make this good.' She stood up and leant over the desk menacingly.

'I've been using her as a mole. She gives me information on what's happening on the streets with the girls, and I turn a blind eye to what she does. I didn't tell you, as I'm not supposed to have unofficial informants. I've been working with her for a few years.'

'We all ignore prostitutes Lucas, why does this have to be such a big secret?' she said, and she wasn't softening. Her arms remained folded, and her eyes narrowed.

'She's in deeper than that. Drugs mainly,' he said, trying to look casual as he shrugged.

'We're not the drugs squad.'

'I know. That's why I ignore that side of things. But she's into some heavy stuff, is all, so I just wanted to let you know in case you got any calls from the drugs unit,' he finished, somewhat meekly.

She looked him up and down. A little twitch in her shoulders suggested she'd relaxed a little.

'It's lucky we can trust you to pick your battles, DCI Miller, and that's the only reason I'm going to keep my mouth shut and look the other way on this one. As far as anyone else is concerned, at least. But between you and me, I'm absolutely pissing raging.'

'Thank you, boss,' he said, a wave of relief flooding him.

'But, because we're doing that, I'm going to ask, have you thought about all the repercussions here, Lucas? Have you?' He was silent. 'I have put my neck out to promote you. Twice.

Do not *ever* pull this shit again. Get out. I will be grumpy with you for at least a few days. Catch this prick if you want to get back in my good books. Go on, fuck off.'

She wafted a hand at him, and he sped out of the office as quickly as he could, without protest, and closed her door behind him. He paused, his heart thumping. That went well. He may be in her bad books, but that was better than the alternative. It was a good job he hadn't actually told her the truth.

2013

25

The Christmas party was in full swing for the West Yorkshire Police-Leeds branch. Drinks were flowing; music was blaring, and everyone was letting their hair down. Well-deserved, most would say, after a tough few years, although there were rumblings in the press suggesting not everyone thought the police should be allowed to celebrate. Luckily, the people-that-be disagreed, and they'd spent a decent amount of money on hiring out *The Queen's Hotel* in the city centre. It needed a bit of a refurb, but it was certainly a nice place to be.

Newly promoted, DS Lucas Miller sat in the corner, drinking a beer and watching everyone else have a good time through wavy, hazy eyes. He'd had more than a few drinks and was nearly finished by a round of tequila shots with DCI Hayward's team. That shit, sickly feeling was building in his stomach and his social battery was just about running dry. He wanted to go home, but his taxi was booked for 1 am, and it wasn't even midnight yet. There was absolutely no chance of him getting a room at the hotel either, not at those prices.

'You seem lonely,' said Chloe, sliding into a seat beside him. She looked particularly exciting tonight, thought Lucas. Even through his spinning vision, he noted how her golden brown hair cascaded down her shoulders in loose, flowing waves, and the subtle highlights glistened in the party lights. She was giving him an intense stare with her large sparkling brown eyes, and her lips were slightly parted, coloured a festive shade of deep red. She was wearing a deep emerald green dress, hugging her curves perfectly. The sequins sparkled and shimmed as she moved, and a subtle slit down the side revealed a hint of her toned legs.

'Nah, I'm fine, just drunk,' Lucas said, holding up his pint glass, sloshing a bit for good measure. He put on his best smile. It wasn't difficult to smile at Chloe. What was more difficult was to maintain eye contact. Do not look at her chest.

'You look like you've had enough,' she said with a chuckle.

'I'm fine, Chloe. Promise. Just a bit pissed.' He smiled at her again. As lovely as she was, and maybe it was just the drink talking, but he was finding this pretty difficult. It's difficult when you like someone, and they know it, but you know they're not interested in taking anything further. It was almost painful to sit here, knowing he wanted something she didn't.

'OK, I'm going to get another drink. Want anything?'

'Nah, I'm alright, thanks.'

Chloe stood up and made her way to the bar, leaving Lucas sitting alone. He watched her weave through the crowd and sighed. He'd fancied her from the moment they'd met, but he was tired of this game of cat and mouse. If she didn't want him, then she didn't want him — end of story. In fact, he needed to tell her this. Now. That would be a good idea. But don't stare at her tits.

He stood up and headed to the bar. He stood next to Chloe

and leaned on the bar. She smiled at him.

'What's up?' she said over the thumping music.

'I just needed some air.'

'I don't think it's very airy here. I mean, there's people everywhere. You're more likely to get drunk in here.'

'Oh, yeah, well, I wanted to talk to you.'

'About what?'

'About us. About us not being together.'

'Oh. Right. OK.' She folded some of her hair behind her ear as he said this but maintained intense eye contact, and for a moment, he thought he saw disappointment in her eyes. But it was gone almost as soon as it came, and she was smiling now, almost expectantly. Christ, she looked good in that dress. Don't stare at her breasts.

'Yeah,' he said. 'I know I'm drunk, and I know it's not fair. You have excellent reasons, and I respect them. But I'm struggling, Chloe. I keep waiting for something which won't happen. You either fancy me or you don't. It's as simple as that, and I know you don't. Which is fine. I wouldn't either. So I'm gonna go home, sleep and not keep punishing myself. I'm sorry.' he stumbled backwards slightly. 'You look really hot in that dress, though. Just so you know.' He swayed backwards again. She reached out and held his forearm, her touch sending an electric shock through him.

'You've got a long wait for your taxi, Lucas. Why not come back to mine and get a cab in the morning? Plus, you're drunk; someone might take advantage of you.' Lucas looked at her. She was smiling again, but there was something about the smile which warmed him.

'I can get a taxi off the street, don't need to wait long, really.'

'Please?' she said, fluttering her eyelids and pressing her cleavage together slightly as she leant forward. Do not look, Lucas.

'You sure?' he asked before catching himself and saying, 'No, that sounds coun.. county... err..'

'Counterintuitive?' she suggested.

'Yeah. That.'

'Look, come back. I'm sure. I've also been thinking, and I think we need this chat. But we should have it somewhere we can hear each other' She took him by the hand, and he followed her out of the pub and pretty much straight into a taxi. He felt a bit like this was happening to someone else, and he wasn't actually sure where this was going. He felt comfortable with Chloe, though, who was holding his hand, and their shoulders were touching.

His mind was racing with a hundred possibilities of what all this meant, but equally, he'd spent two years fancying this woman, so it might also just be her being friendly and caring. He'd just told her he liked her, though, and he didn't think she was cruel enough to lead him on so soon. He didn't doubt she liked him, but whether she fancied him. That was another question entirely. She paid for the taxi and led him up the stairs to her flat. She got him a glass of water, and he downed it.

'You alright?' she asked.

'Yeah,' he said. 'Just.. you know... Confused, I think.'

'I can tell,' she said with a cute little laugh that made her breasts wobble. Don't look.

'I should go home,' Lucas whispered. 'I've put you in an awkward position and don't want you to feel you have to do anything you don't want.'

'No, you can stay. Why are you whispering?' she giggled.

'I, I don't want to wake Rachel,' he said, continuing to whisper.

She laughed again. 'How irresponsible a parent do you think I am? She's at her dad's tonight. We have the place to ourselves.'

Lucas looked down at her for a long moment. She really was quite a bit shorter than he was. His heart was pounding in his chest.

'Oh,' he said simply, no longer whispering. 'You look wonderful tonight Chloe, just in case nobody had told you.'

'Three people told me, actually,' she said, smirking, 'But I was hoping you were the one to notice me. Given all you've done is stare at my tits for the last half an hour, can I assume you like the dress?'

Lucas's mouth was dry, but he cracked an apologetically guilty smile. 'I always notice you, Chloe.'

With that, she leaned over, stood on her tiptoes and kissed him. Her lips were soft and sweet. The kiss was tender. He pulled her closer to him, his hands running across her back, and he felt her heart beating through her chest. He broke the kiss and looked into her eyes. They were shining in the dim light. She was gorgeous; he thought.

Don't fuck this up.

26

There was a horrible shrill screeching coming from the bedside table. His head was pounding, and his mouth was drier than the Sahara desert. The wailing continued. A slender, freckled arm reached across Lucas's chest and picked up the shrieking object.

'Hel... hello?' said Chloe, her mouth clearly as dry as his. A squeaky voice was on the other end of the phone, and he couldn't quite make out what was being said.

'Yeah, OK. I'll be there shortly. Yeah, text me the address. Thanks.' She put the phone down and buried her head in his shoulder. 'That was Carmichael. She's been called out and wants me to join her. Sounds like another nasty one.'

'I'll come with you,' he said, keen to keep this moment going for as long as he could.

'You don't need to. Enjoy your day off.'

'No, I'm fine; we can get some coffee and breakfast on the way if you like?'

He rolled over and looked her in the eyes. They were as beautiful as ever, shining in the morning light. Her hair, thick and opulent, flowed around her shoulders like a river of honey. He smiled at her, and she smiled back. He leaned forward and kissed her softly on the lips. She kissed him back. They lay there for a few moments, enjoying each other's company. She lifted the bed sheets and had a little peek.

'Oh, hello. Don't bother pointing that thing at me. We've got to go!' she said, getting out of bed and cackling to herself.

Lucas watched her, his nether regions frustrated, as she got dressed. She was stunning, and he couldn't believe that after two years of wanting it, he was finally sharing a bed with Chloe Wilson.

'Are you going to stay in bed all day? Thought you were buying me breakfast,' she asked as she threw his boxers at him.

'Just admiring the view,' he said with a grin, catching the boxers before they smacked him in the face.

She laughed and left the room. Lucas got up, his head pounding. He showered and dressed as quickly as possible, putting on the well-fitted shirt and chinos from the previous night. He sniffed the armpits. Not too foul. He'd get away with it, but he desperately needed coffee. And painkillers. Lots of them. He followed Chloe out of the bedroom and down the stairs, where she was waiting for him by the door. They walked out the door into the crisp morning air. It was cold, and it stung Lucas's face. He shivered slightly. He wasn't dressed warm enough, but it would do for the short walk to the car. Unusually, she drove, as he wasn't convinced he was under the limit just yet.

They arrived at the crime scene, where they found two uniformed police officers standing guard, keeping the press and public at bay. One of them had a ridiculous ginger mullet that hadn't been in fashion for thirty years.

They were on a major stretch of road on the city's outskirts, towards the airport. It wasn't exactly rural, but it had some trees, at least. Lucas was taking a huge bite from a sausage and bacon sandwich as the mulleted officer waved Lucas and Chloe through whilst they silently giggled to each other at its ridiculousness.

When they saw Carmichael's car parked in the lay-by, they made a beeline for it. Carmichael was sitting in the car, a look of deep concentration on her face. Lucas knocked on the window, and she jumped. She looked out at him and beckoned him closer as she wound the window down. He leaned his head in, acutely aware that his hot breath might still smell.

'You scared the shit out of me, Miller,' she said, irritated. 'What the toss are you doing here?'

'I was with Chloe and got dragged along.'

'Well, I guess you are a DS as well now, as of last week.' She looked him up and down, then at Chloe, and smirked. 'Weren't you wearing that shirt last night, DS Miller?' He looked down at himself. Bollocks. He could feel the heat rising in his ears.

'I, er. Well...'

'It's OK, Miller; the team has been waiting for you two to shag for ages now. I thought she'd hold out for longer personally, but I guess I have higher standards than DS Wilson.' She flashed a smile at Chloe and gave her a big, exaggerated wink. Chloe blushed almost as hard as Lucas and began furiously fidgeting with her coat.

'So, what've we got?' Lucas said, trying to change the subject as quickly as he could.

'Council workers have been sent to sweep the road, clean the lay-bys, etc., and found that.' She wafted a hand down the slope by the side of the road. Lucas could see the top of their telltale white tents just peering over the lip.

'Right. And what exactly is that?'

'I want you both to have a look. I know what I think, but I want your opinions as well. Oh, and you'll want this.' She handed Chloe a little round metal tin of *'Odour balm'*. 'She's been there for a while.'

Lucas nodded and followed Chloe to the little plastic table with the gloves and paper suits. He picked a set for himself and one for Chloe before they walked down the slope, where they found themselves at the edge of a sort of gravel car park. Dr Cross emerged from the little white tent, followed by a man with a large camera.

'Detectives,' he said, nodding at the pair of them. 'Needless to say, don't touch anything in there, please. We've not completed everything. Dr Cooper tells me one of her cases was recently contaminated by a smelly little detective constable; I don't want the same on one of mine.'

'Yeah, no worries, Doc. You may not have heard, but I'm a detective sergeant now,' said Lucas, puffing his chest out.

'Congratulations,' Dr Cross replied, a very subtle note of sarcasm in his voice. 'But all the same, don't touch anything. You're also wearing DS Wilson's deodorant, I notice. Naughty, naughty.' He gave a large, wicked grin and departed.

Lucas, who'd gone pink again, muttered to Chloe, 'Haven't seen him smiling in ages, prick.'

They opened the tent flap and stood just inside. A young woman, probably no older than eighteen, was lying in the middle of the tent on the gravel surface. Most of her clothes were missing, but the small white vest that remained was

26

torn and bloodied, and she had multiple moderate wounds to her torso and one huge gash underneath her rib cage, which was lifted up like a clamshell. Flies and maggots were moving in the black cavity in her chest. Her skin was mottled with a green hue, and she'd started to bloat quite severely. Her face was hideously distorted and bulbous, and he could see her tongue was swollen and protruding from her mouth. There was a rope around her left ankle, which was swollen to where it almost engulfed the knot. Her legs were covered with dark red scratch marks and bruises, and he could see the same on her arms. The smell was terrible. It was thick and cloying, coating the back of Lucas's throat and making him gag. He put a couple of lumps of the *odour balm* under his nose and breathed deeply through his mouth. The smell was still there, but less overpowering. Lucas stood for a few moments, taking in the horror before him. The girl was just a kid, really. He looked at Chloe, who had pushed past him and was now kneeling beside the girl and looking at her wounds. She looked up at him, and he could see the sadness in her eyes. She shook her head and looked back down at the girl.

Lucas took one last glance before he stepped back out of the tent, and took a deep breath of the cold, fresh air. It helped clear his head, but the image of the body was burnt into his mind. This was not the way to deal with a hangover. Dr Cross was talking to a forensic scientist and looked over at him.

'Are you alright, Detective? You look pale.'

'Yeah.' He continued to gulp in some of the slightly fresher air. 'Anything you can tell me?'

'Not beyond the obvious. It's a female; she's young and has probably been here at least a week or two. It's been cold recently, which will have preserved her, so to be in this state, probably closer to two. There is no form of identification that we can see. We've taken fingerprints and DNA, etc. We've not found any clothes other than the top she's wearing. No jewellery or anything, but she wore rings; I can see the staining on her fingers. That wound under the rib cage intrigues me; I'll let you know more when I have it. In the meantime, if you wouldn't mind?' He wafted his hand at Lucas, who was happy to be dismissed. He and Chloe walked back up the hill to Carmichael, who patiently awaited them.

'Well?' she asked.

'I've seen that scene before.'

'That's what I thought.'

'Copycat?' said Chloe

'Possibly. I'm going to go back to the office. There are some files on my desk I want to look through. Why don't you and Miller get some treats for the team?' She forced a tenner into her hands. 'This is going to be a tricky one.'

27

Lucas chucked two packets of Tangfastics and a box of Quality Street on the central desk in the enquiry room. The team was fairly pensive; they'd heard the basic gist of what had happened, and nobody was best pleased. Especially given that most of them were even more hungover than Lucas.

'But Murray is inside?' said dyspraxic Stephen, just missing his mouth with a cherry Tangfastic.

'It could be a copycat?' said Paul, already sweating profusely even though it was barely 10 am. He definitely had some underlying health condition, thought Lucas.

'Or a coincidence?' added Chloe.

DI Carmichael was leaning against the board, deep in thought. 'Yeah, it could be anything. But the MO is similar.'

'How similar?'

'On the face of it, very similar. We'll wait for the autopsy report from the creeps below. I think we need to be open to the possibility that this might be the same person who killed Jessica Murray,' said Carmichael.

'But like I said, that was her dad. And he's in the nick?' repeated Stephen, puzzled.

'Yes, well, his conviction was never that convincing, Stephen. We know that,' Lucas spoke up for the first time. 'That's why we need to work on finding out everything we can about our new unidentified woman. Her friends, family, boyfriend, anything. Someone will be missing her, and someone will know something.' The team all nodded and set to work.

'Are you going to the autopsy, boss?' Lucas said.

'No, I'm going to pass on this one. I'll meet Dan for a coffee and report afterwards. We must keep the press away from this until we know more, so I will speak to the chief inspector.'

'Do you want me to go?' he hoped the answer would be no.

'I'm not sure about Dr Cooper or the others, but Dan can handle an autopsy by himself. We'll get his report this afternoon and go from there. I want you to worry about getting an ID. Start with the lost and found box.'

Lucas sighed, returned to his desk, loaded the missing person database, and began sifting through. At least he was sitting opposite Chloe and could catch her eye now and again. Hours passed, and he wasn't getting anywhere, obviously, as they had nothing to go on. There were one hundred and sixty-two missing girls between the ages of sixteen and twenty-five currently in the North of England, and there was a reasonable probability theirs wasn't even reported as missing.

He'd been wasting his time for a few hours more before the double doors opened, and Dr Cross strode in, imperious and pompous.

'What the fuck are you doing up top, Dr Cross?' said Lucas without thinking.

'Pardon, detective?' his eyes flashed towards Lucas, who shrivelled up quickly, like a snail's eyestalk.

'No, sorry, I meant, normally we come to you to get the report,' he bluffed. Dr Cross looked at Lucas with mild disdain.

'Well, today is an exception. I need to speak to Pat. Where is she? She is not answering her phone.'

'DI Carmichael's going to the chief. She was sorting out the publicity side of things.'

'Right,' he took out his mobile phone and rang her again.

'No, she's with the chief, don't ring -'

'Hello, yeah Pat, it's Dan. Yeah, your team said. No, it's pretty urgent, actually. It's probably better if we do it in the office. You'll have many questions, and I think your team will need to be fully informed. OK. OK. Yes, of course, no problem.' He hung up and, without saying a word, sat down at Chloe's desk and started playing on his phone. Chloe, standing only a meter away, beside the evidence boards, said nothing.

'Errr... Are you going to fill us in, Dr Cross?' said Lucas.

'Of course. When your senior, DI Carmichael, is here.'

'Prick,' muttered Lucas under his breath as he caught the eyes of Stephen, Paul and even Stacy, who he'd forgotten was even there given she was so bloody useless. They all held the same sentiment.

Fifteen awkward minutes passed before DI Carmichael arrived, looking stressed.

'Some absolute weapon at the Yorkshire Post has already started asking questions, linking this to bloody Jess Murray. How the hell do they always seem to know?'

'Maybe they're the killer boss,' smirked Paul

'Not this one. He couldn't kill a fly with his spindly little arms. I think he's working with that streak of piss Davies. Either way, an absolute pain in my hairy arse. Right, Dan, go, go, tell me what's so important.'

Dr Cross stood up and took a pen from beside the whiteboard. He wrote a somewhat gruesome shopping list;

1. *Asphyxiated*
2. *Between 2 and 5 stab wounds to the abdomen with an abnormally long knife*
3. *Tied by the ankles with rope*
4. *Body left semi-hidden*
5. *Clothes removed, and all jewellery taken*
6. *Organ removed*

'This could be the report of Jessica Murray'. He left a dramatic pause. 'It could also be the report of our unidentified female from the lay-by. Having completed the autopsy, I can confirm her right lung has been removed. Not professionally; it's been torn out, and this was in her chest.' He took out an A4 photograph from inside his jacket and showed it to Carmichael.

'Fuck me,' she groaned, and Lucas stood up to look over her shoulder. The photo was of a note, very similar to the one that they'd found inside Jessica Murray.

The lungs do lie, in caverns deep, breathing whispers of a sigh, Their rise and fall, a ghostly dance, in life's fragile, fleeting trance.

27

'So they're definitely the same bloke?' said Lucas. 'Or a copycat?'

'Almost certainly the work of the same man. You did not release the details of the heart, the note, or the rope to the public. A copycat is unlikely. This girl was not raped or sexually assaulted. That is the only difference. But Mr Murray never denied that part.'

'Fuck.' muttered Carmichael.

'Quite. But it gets worse. Dr Cooper has just reminded me that this could also be the report for Amber Smith, a twenty-three-year-old, murdered eighteen months ago, just outside Bradford. She'd had her spleen removed. It was being investigated by a different team. I don't know how we missed it. You have a third.' He didn't need to pause for dramatic effect here. Everyone was stunned.

'Double fuck.'

2023

28

It was very late. Close to midnight, in fact. As he walked back to his car underneath the yellow glow of the street lamps, Lucas looked at his phone and saw the text from Em asking about plans for the night. Shit, he'd forgotten to reply! He decided to call her, apologise and explain why he'd not managed to get in touch. She was half asleep when she answered and sounded groggy and mildly irritated.

'Look, I should have rung ahead and explained, but we were called to another victim.'

'Yeah, I know Lucas. Dan told me this one is alive, right? Mental,' she said, yawning loudly.

'Yeah, she's in a bit of a state, thou–Dan?' he said, a little more accusatory than intended.

'Cross. Dr Dan Cross, my boss. He rang to ask if I can go to the hospital tomorrow and try to collect some evidence, what little the surgeons have left us at least.'

'Ah, yeah, of course,' said Lucas, but something squirmed in his belly. There was something odd about her tone today. He'd blatantly pissed her off. They'd have to do their night-in some other time, he explained; it was part and parcel of the job. She said she understood and everything was

OK. He promised to ring her the following day and arrange something, although he wasn't so keen if she would be in a mood with him.

When he finally got back to his house, he was exhausted. Mentally and physically. He wondered if the events of these last twelve years were finally catching up with him. As he spotted himself in the mirror, he realised they already had. His gaunt face, scrawny arms and grey receding hairline made him look older than his thirty-five years. The heavy bags beneath his eyes meant he needed sleep. Maybe a glass of water, though, before bed. He reached up to the top shelf of his cupboard to grab a cup but wasn't paying attention, and a small glass came tumbling out and shattered on the worktop. Lucas had tried to catch it, but only grabbed a large shard of glass that sliced through his palm.

'Ow! Fuck's sake!' he yelled, startling Luna, who was snuffled up in her basket. She came to see him, tail wagging, as he looked down at the nasty, diagonal slice across his hand. It was bleeding profusely, so he grabbed a tea towel and wrapped it up before trying to find an old first aid kit. Eventually, he had it wrapped in a bandage, and he'd taken a paracetamol for the pain. The time had now gone 1 am; so much for his early night.

He collapsed into his bed with the warm body of his ageing spaniel lying next to him and was out for the count almost instantly. But sleep wasn't easy.

He was back in the box, lined with illegible newsprint. Footsteps echoed loudly in his ears as he once more made the trudge across to the gigantic, pulsating fingerprint. The whole thing was squirming and slithering as the flayed women arched their way through its creases, and thick red blood dripped onto the print below. The colossal bloodshot eye searched the landscape, and the hairs on his neck stood to attention. Heart rate quickening, awaiting the inevitable...

* * *

As soon as his alarm went off, he was awake. Bleary-eyed and slow-moving, the thought of the coffee downstairs, in powerful espresso form, was all that could motivate him. This was another awful day. Another day of hell for Amelia Watson. Another dreadful day of pain. He picked up the phone and dialled DS Sterling. She'd been promoted in his phone log to 'frequent numbers,' just below '*DCI Carmichael*' but above '*Emily West*'.

'Hello?' said the pleasant, kind voice of DS Kim Sterling.

'Hiya, you are in the office yet?'

'No, I'm stuck in traffic, but can I help?'

'I was thinking of taking a look at where Amelia Watson was found. Fancy picking me up and coming along for the ride?'

'Oh, yeah, of course! That'd be fun. Well, not fun, but yeah. Great!'

'Great,' he said, swallowing a little pill from his blister pack and taking a sip of his silly little espresso in its silly little mug, 'I'll be ready in five mins. Get here when you can.'

'On it, Boss, ' She said excitedly before hanging up.

Lucas put his phone down and rubbed the bridge of his nose, the bandaged palm of his hand and finally, the tense shooting pain in his forearm, which he knew would dissipate shortly. He already had a large scar down that arm. Adding a new one to the palm wouldn't make much difference. It wasn't bleeding, at least.

He had another sip of coffee and finished it as DS Sterling turned up. Her black trousers and shirt looked quite professional, but the black leather jacket gave her a distinctly cool edge. She beamed at him as he greeted her, and he got in the passenger seat of her car. Getting in and out of her car was an ordeal as she owned a grey Audi TT, which was low and impractical. The fact it had just started raining heavily again didn't help. The car was her 'fuck it' purchase post-cancer.

Once he'd explained the slightly dramatic-looking bandage on his hand and she had fiddled with the sat nav on her phone, they set off. Where Amelia Watson was found was only a five-minute car ride away from an area of woodland known as *'The Billing'*. Situated in a small village on the outskirts of Leeds, it was some way from the Holbeck red-light zone. Riding with Kim was an enjoyable experience. She was giggly and extremely talkative when she got going.

'Forensics have sealed it off, obviously, but we're still waiting for their report. Carmichael said the complete report has been delayed because our pathologists and forensic team still haven't been able to examine Amelia, but that will hopefully be this afternoon. Rumour has it that surgeons and doctors took swabs and stuff for us, but I think we're worried they've taken the wrong ones or something.' As she stopped for breath, Lucas noticed that she repeatedly rubbed the outside of her left leg as she said all this.

'You alright?'

'Huh? Oh, my leg? Yeah, I'm still getting immunotherapy injections every few weeks for my... er... cancer,' she said as she went a little pink around the cheeks.

'Are you okay? Should you be back at work?'

'Yeah, yeah, it's an excellent distraction. I need it. I was going mad cooped up at home like a chicken.'

'Good, so long as you're sure.'

'No, I'm OK. Pretty much any way. But thanks.' She took her eyes off the road for a split second to give him a warm smile of appreciation.

'It's OK, just talk to me if you're ever not OK. Not just as a boss, but as a friend, OK?'

She'd gone from a light pink blush to a full tomato red. She kept her eyes firmly on the road this time, not looking over at Lucas.

'You're the only one who still asks how I am.'

'Oh. Everyone else cares; I think they don't know what to say.'

There was a silence between them. Not an awkward silence, but a full, heavy silence that seemed to pull them closer together. He turned, looked at her, and then back out of the windscreen. This might be dangerous ground he was treading, but he felt safe with her. She'd take his inquisitiveness the way it was meant.

'Sorry, it's probably annoying. The elephant in the room and all that. The big C.' she mumbled.

'No, not at all. I'd like to hear more about it if you want to talk?' he said. 'What happened? One minute, you were part of the team, and then next, you were just... gone.'

'It was breast cancer, caught early. Aggressive, but I got aggressive back,' she paused. 'Needed chemo and surgery, obviously, hence the year off. Silver lining though. I didn't lose my hair, and I got some brand new tits!' A sheepish grin ran across her face. This caught Lucas entirely off guard, and he laughed and snorted loudly, which made them both laugh more. He punched her gently on the shoulder.

'Can't say I've noticed.'

'Oh, I bet you have, you perv!'

'I am still your boss, mind,' teased Lucas.

'Oh yeah shit, sorry boss,' and she made a show of shutting her mouth and looking embarrassed. They both laughed hard.

Lucas had started to forget about the potential mess he was in, and the feeling of dread over a potentially very long day evaporated.

'In all seriousness, you don't look like you had cancer. I assumed you would have lost all your hair if I'm honest.'

'Thanks! I used the cold cap; it's like this freezing swimming cap thing they put on your head when you're having chemo. Fucking horrible, but at least I'm not bald,' she said, grinning and running her fingers through the shorter, browner hair she now possessed. Lucas could tell she was reminiscing about her dyed blonde hair that had flowed down to the small of her back.

'It just strips you of everything it means to be a woman. My hair, my fertility, my tits. I don't know, it's changed me, I think,' she said, a bit more grimly.

Not entirely sure what to say, Lucas just rested his hand over hers, which was on the gear stick, and squeezed it. That seemed to be enough.

29

They arrived at the small pebble car park, next to a local Sunday league football pitch, to find a moderate forensic presence. SOCO were all still there milling about in their white plastic suits and ridiculous little foot covers, like the ones you see at the swimming pool for parents still wearing shoes by the pool. Everything was sealed off with blue and white cordon tape and surrounded by a halo of the local press, obviously hoping they might get some snippet of information. He doubted Amelia Watson would be ID'd by the press just yet, which was a slight relief. Most of them had been in the business long enough not to let slip details of victims, simply referring to them as 'a woman'. They'd been given that explicit instruction from DCI Carmichael. Although he would be a fool to believe they wouldn't speculate, especially with the human personification of thrush that was Simon Davies floating around.

   They parked up and hopped out. Lucas introduced himself to the supervising SOCO Officer, whom he'd met several times before. She didn't know who the hell he was, though. She was a plain woman in her late 30s called Sharon, who had curly blonde hair, thick black-rimmed glasses, sharp cheekbones and slightly bucked teeth.

'What's a DCI doing at one of our scenes? Don't trust DI Kumar, eh?' Her accent was scouse and quite jarring.

'Listen' He took her to one side and lowered his voice. 'Firstly, it's DI Khan, not Kumar. Secondly, I trust all my officers implicitly, but the more eyes on this scene, the better. Now, please walk me through it.'

He expected some resistance from her, as if it was her scene and her rules. But she responded pretty well to his prickly demeanour and softened a little. She grimaced as she began her description of what had happened there.

'Well, sir, we've —

She was interrupted by a loud bit of commotion from the entrance to the scene. A man in a long jacket and driving gloves was trying to get through the barrier, but wasn't being let through by the rather burley officers guarding the perimeter of the scene. They were aggressively discussing what might happen to him if he didn't just leave. It looked like it might involve their truncheons and his arsehole, based on Lucas's interpretation of the hand gestures. Interested to see what was happening, Lucas left Sharon and Kim together and jogged over to the agitation.

'What is going on here?' said Lucas with some authority as he arrived at the perimeter tape.

An angry PC replied, 'This man claims to be a professor of crime or some shit and wants to come onto the scene. I told him, no, he's not on the list. He won't leave, so I was explaining how I'm about –'

'You got ID?' asked Lucas, interrupting the PC before he heard something graphic he might need to report.

'Of course,' said the gentleman. He must have been at least six foot five and wore expensive-looking heeled boots the size of canoes. His entire head was hairless, as smooth as an egg, with tiny little eyebrows which sat above some incredibly blue eyes, the only feature he could see. That being said, he had a jawline that Superman would be proud of, and underneath that jacket, there were plenty of muscles. He pulled out a neat leather wallet and brandished it at Lucas. A driving licence for Professor Oliver Hawthorne was sitting within it.

'OK, let him in,' said Lucas finally.

'But sir, he's not – ' protested the PC desperately.

'Well, add him. And let him in. He's here to help. We've been expecting him.'

'Oh. Right, yes sir,'

'Thank you, gentlemen,' said Professor Hawthorne smugly as Lucas led him to DS Sterling, who was still standing with forensic Sharon. When they saw the Professor, SOCO Sharon went pink, and DS Sterling bit her lip and swept some of her hair behind her ear, which slightly irritated Lucas. He spoke to the professor from the corner of his mouth, only to say, 'You better help this operation, not hinder it.' Rather than reply, Professor Hawthorne merely smiled at him benignly.

'Right, Sharon, sorry, you were saying?' said Lucas.

'Who the fucks this?' she had returned to a normal colour and became prickly once more.

'DS Sterling's suggestion. Professor Hawthorne is a criminal profiler from London. Here to help.'

'Right, well. You might be a handsome bastard, but you look a right cunt in those boots,' said Sharon directly to

Professor Hawthorne, who raised a thin eyebrow before Sharon launched into her monologue.

'Not a huge amount to report yet, but more than we usually get at these 'Reaper' scenes, so we're going through it twice. Your victim was found crying out from beside this post here.' She pointed to a concrete pillar that supported the boundary of the football pitch. It was messy and covered in weeds. 'Victim's blood is all over the place, but there are also some spatters that don't fit the scene. We'll get them tested, but I think they may be from the perpetrator. Or from you,' she pointed to his bandaged hand, which Lucas withdrew instinctively.

'DNA profile isn't much use without a target, though,' said Kim with some trepidation. 'We've yet to pick up any significant DNA from previous scenes.'

'True, but this proves he's made a mistake here. This isn't some power play. He's not kept her alive for fun. He's fucked up. That's important; it's the first time we've had an advantage over him,' said Lucas. Professor Hawthorne wasn't saying anything, merely observing from his great height.

'Exactly,' said Sharon before continuing. 'There are also some partial footprints in the mud around where she was found. We've made a cast and will get them properly analysed, but eye-balling it, they're size ten boots, possibly a generic brand, possibly something more unique. We'll have to wait and see. Depending on the depth and cadence of his stride, we might also get an estimated weight and height range for you.'

'This is great work, guys,' said Lucas, clapping his hands together, forgetting about his cut for a split second. The pain gave him a swift reminder.

'That everything?' interjected Kim.

'Nope, DS Sterton.' said Sharon, ignoring the irritated look on Kim's face. 'Come over here'

She led them towards a small, dark alleyway just behind the boundary of the football pitch. It was hidden, almost invisible.

'I've sent some lads in. There are a few syringes, empty packets, and wrappers. They're taking samples and doing the usual. There is not much else yet. The site is used for drug dealing, and it seems pretty regular, so hopefully, we'll find someone who was here last night. It's a good place for a drop. They might have seen something.'

'Excellent, thanks. Once you've bagged and tagged everything for me, can I get a full report, please?'

'What, like every other time? Obviously, you'll get a report, sir,' she spat. What a strange woman, thought Lucas. Everyone was so bloody hostile to him. Except for Kim, she at least seemed to rate him as DCI.

'Right, thanks. Have you found the assailant's weapon or weapons yet? Asked Lucas bluntly, not looking at Sharon as he said it.

'Huh? No, we've not. He didn't have a chance to use them before he was interrupted. Based on a preliminary analysis of the spatter pattern by the post, most of her injuries were inflicted elsewhere. I don't think he's done much to her here other than beat her to a pulp. It's all drip pattern, no arterial spray. You can trace those drips back to that space there. Tire tracks suggest an SUV or something, but it's a generic seventeen-inch wheel. The standard wheelbase is consistent with a few manufacturers.

Tyres are manufactured by Goodyear, though, and they aren't cheap. So it may be a fairly nice, sporty SUV. Just a guess, though.'

'Hmm,' said Lucas. 'He usually inflicts some cuts and certainly the fatal wounds at the scene. I think he must have been interrupted by something. He may well have had to react quickly and chosen to throw any tools he had?'

'Well, be my guest if you want to scour the area. Just don't contaminate anything, or I'll personally chop your dick off.' and with that, she marched off to shout at some more junior members of the team.

Kim and Professor Hawthorne were deep in conversation when Lucas turned his attention back to them.

'Right you, any thoughts so far?' said Lucas to the Professor.

'Some.' Now, he was being more direct, and it was clear he had a BBC southern accent. He was going to struggle to fit in with that around here.

'Are you okay with me trying winthropping?'

'What the fuck is that? Can you do that in public, or will I need to do you for indecency?'

'It's an under-used technique based on geographical profiling,' he replied, ignoring Lucas's joke and talking like he had swallowed the textbook. 'There are several theories, such as rational choice theory and crime geometry, but basically, I'll get inside the head of the killer and predict where they might hide their tools. And then we look there.'

'So you're going to imagine you're the killer and hope that leads you to something?'

'Essentially, yes, but with a lot more science,' he said, beaming.

29

'Be my guest, mate, knock yourself out. Run it past Little Miss Cheerful over there because I'm not hanging about whilst you get into character or whatever you do.' Lucas rolled his eyes and left, taking a slightly embarrassed-looking DS Sterling with him.

Professor Hawthorne stood on the grass, surveying the scene with piercing blue eyes. Kim and Lucas headed back over to the football pitch together and waded back to the car, feeling slightly more optimistic. Finally, the killer had made a mistake.

30

'He didn't sound so weird on the phone. Plus, he's got an excellent reputation in the Met,' protested DS Sterling.

'Don't stress, Kim, he'll either be shit, and nobody remembers him, or he's excellent. Either way, not your fault.'

They got into the car, and she drove them back to the station, taking the scenic route. At first, Lucas thought she didn't know her way around the sprawling city, but when she stopped off at a bakery she liked, to get them some lunch, he began to think she was doing it deliberately. She was chattering away, barely pausing for breath, as he sat back and enjoyed her company. They returned to the station in good spirits and walked through the doors together.

'Thought I was DI on this case now?' said Sadiq 'Mayor' Khan from behind a computer, a strong note of bitterness emanating from his voice.

'You are, which is why I trusted you to chase the forensics from Amelia's house and start hunting out potential kidnap sites.'

'Right, yes, well, of course you can trust me. I've done all that; we're ready for a briefing. I just thought...'

'Just thought what, DS Khan?' said Lucas, putting his

keys and wallet down on the desk with a bit of a thunk. The bandage from his hand had slipped, and it was bleeding again.

'Is your hand OK?' said DI Khan,

'Yeah, just a cut,' replied Lucas, wrapping it back in the bandage tightly and stuffing it in his pocket. 'So, what did you just think, DI Khan?'

'That you might take me, your DI, rather than... you know,' he nodded at DS Sterling, who was staring him out with her large, widely spaced eyes.

'It's all hands on deck, Khan. If you've got a problem with that, you can take it up with DSI Carmichael,' said Kim with some firm bite.

'Well, no. That's fine. I'll do some paperwork and leave you two to it then,' he sulked.

'No need, DI Khan, we must keep everyone in the loop. Gather the troops, and we'll have a quick end-of-the-day brainstorm. Including DSI Carmichael, please,' said Lucas.

'Ah, yes, alright then,' he turned and clicked his fingers at DS Richards and DC Stenson, who panicked and started gathering bits of paper together.

Kim and Lucas exchanged glances and smiled at one another. They took off their coats and sat at their desks almost in unison. He wanted to consolidate the team's thoughts before the close of play. He felt like they'd made some progress for the first time in a long time.

Detective Superintendent Carmichael came rolling in five minutes later, looking mildly annoyed. She still had the same purposeful stride of years gone by, but her shoulders were more hunched and her features thinner.

'Right, what's up? Thought you were leading this now,

Miller?'

'I am, but I thought you'd want to oversee...' She grunted, waved a bony hand at him and sat down. Lucas went a little pink but continued.

'Right, where are we with our victim, Amelia Watson?'

DS Richards, a timid-looking redhead covered in little freckles, spoke; her voice was quite soft and difficult to pick up. 'Out of surgery seemed to go well, apparently. It's too early to tell how she's going to respond mentally, but they reckon she can hear what's going on despite the trauma to her ears. She's been permanently blinded, though. Forensics examined her this afternoon. Not sure what they've found yet?'

'Not much, unfortunately,' piped up DC Stenson, a short but stocky young black man in the corner. Lucas had noticed him going about his work effectively; he'd go far, he thought. 'I just got off the phone to that mortuary girl, the pretty one –'

'Em,' said Lucas instinctively.

'Yeah, that's the one,' continued DC Stenson. Nobody saw DS Sterling's shoulders drop slightly.

'She's covered in cuts and stuff. They've swabbed them, but I reckon the surgeons might have wiped away a lot of useful stuff. There was some material the doctors got from under her fingernails, which might be promising. From their descriptions of the wounds, Cross thinks it's likely that the same blade was used as was used on the others, but it's hard to tell. The object pulled out of her... her, well... her. It was a pen. A 'Sonnet' model Parker fountain pen, with gold trim, and very nice.'

'Rare and traceable?' asked DI Khan.

'Doubt it, I've got one of them at home, I think,' said Lucas.

'Maybe it was you, then?' said Carmichael, with a sly grin sliding across her face. 'Always thought you looked the type'

'He's right, unfortunately; I've already checked with the UK Parker offices. They sell hundreds of these every year, and that model has been in circulation for ten years. They're nice pens, but not glamorous enough to get individual codes.'

'Fuck, so unlikely to get much from this?'

'Not if we pull DNA, which we might do from under the lid.'

'OK, right, so moving on then? Anything from the house?' said Lucas.

DC Carter stood up and started talking, his voice quivering because everyone was looking at him. He was a young lad with a shiny product in his hair and greasy skin covered in spots.

'Yes, we found some stuff of interest. There was a little diary or notebook in a drawer in the bedroom. She's been using it to write about some of her clients. Most of it is rubbish, like if they're weird or particularly nice, tip well, etc. Some stuff about who enjoys being tied up and who likes costumes and this sort of thing' He was going pink as he waffled. Lucas coughed and made a motion with his hand for him to get to the point. 'So anyway, I think one of her clients is a copper.'

There was a slightly stunned silence. Lucas froze, his insides became knotted, and he had the urge to be violently sick.

'Why do you think that?' said Carmichael, leaning forward.

'This client likes to brag, apparently. He's told her that he's involved in the Water's Edge Reaper investigation, says he's really important.'

'Most likely bullshit,' scoffed DI Khan.

'Well yeah, that's what I thought, but look,' he handed Lucas and DI Khan an A4 sheet of paper with a photograph of a page from Amelia's diary on it. Lucas recognised the handwriting but kept his face neutral. There was her entry about the client, but underneath it, there was a cramped footnote which read;

'Apparently it was me mate Biancs who was done gutted she was lush'

A little sad face and a heart had been drawn next to it.

'She's dated that 19th of September. We didn't release Bianca Dumitrescu's name to the press until the 22nd. So whoever told her that probably did have access to the investigation.'

'Fucking nora,' hissed Carmichael, making to stand up, but suddenly, the doors to the inquiry room burst open, and in strode the imposing Professor Hawthorne, closely followed by SOCO Sharon. Everyone turned to look just as Sharon held aloft a long plastic evidence bag. Lucas strained to see what was in it, but as they got closer, it became obvious. The bag contained two items. A small glass vial with the familiar curled-up brown paper and a very long, very sharp-looking knife.

'Your man is a genius,' proclaimed Sharon, 'his wind thripping or whatever it was!'

'Winthropping' corrected Professor Hawthorne.

'Whatever. He found this rammed into a hedge about forty meters from where she was found. I don't know how we missed it.'

'Because you weren't looking properly,' he said matter-of-factly.

'Oi you, I'm blowing your trumpet here.'

Lucas forgot about Amelia's diary briefly and was beaming at Sharon. This was it; everything was slotting into place, and now they had the murder weapon! The net would start closing on this guy. He could feel it.

'Brilliant work! Does the note say what I think it does?'

The eyes, twin orbs of night and day, see the world in shades of grey.
Reflecting back the soul's own light, piercing through the darkest night.

Sharon concluded. It sounded less romantic and poet in the harsh Liverpool accent. Lucas nodded. It was word for word what they expected.

'Right, let's get this back to the lab, and then we can start putting together a plan of attack. I'm hoping that the weapon has fingerprints or DNA on it. It's also quite unusual, so this may be infinitely more traceable than some of the other stuff he's left us.'

'Sorry, sorry,' said Carmichael, who was now standing. 'Like, thank you for finding the knife, but er... who the pissing hell are you?'

'Oh yeah, shit,' said Lucas, 'This is Professor Hawthorne. He's a criminal profiler from the Metropolitan down south. He's been lent to us to help.'

'Who said we needed help?'

'We did,' replied Professor Hawthorne, rather unhelpfully,

thought Lucas. 'You've been chasing this person for over twelve years. You should have asked for help sooner. It's becoming a little embarrassing.'

'Oh,' said Carmichael. She wasn't used to having someone talk back to her, certainly not so calm and self-assured.

'I want access to the lot. I want to build my own timeline, re-examine the evidence and see if a fresh pair of eyes can't move this along,' continued Professor Hawthorne.

'But...'

'I'll get the chief superintendent to ring you. He's a friend of mine. He'll tell you how things are going to work. I need to be fully appraised, and then you can all come and ask me questions.'

Carmichael looked aghast. The cogs in her head desperately tried to combat her need for diplomacy with her guttural urge to call the man a cunt.

'Fine!' she hissed and stormed off.

'Well,' said DS Sterling, 'I can't believe that worked.'

'I can,' said Professor Hawthorne, his voice quiet, but he had a smug look on his face.

'Thanks again for helping out,' said Lucas, extending his hand and giving the professor a firm handshake. 'And you too, Sharon. Thanks!

'All in a day's work. You'll have a report on your desk before 8 am tomorrow, ' she said in her thick accent.

'Fantastic,' said Lucas. They had a lead, a possibly bent copper, and a murder weapon. One by one, people left the room, leaving Lucas, Kim, and the three DCs to tidy up. It was 6:30 pm, not that late, but late enough that none of them wanted to stay. They'd agreed that this was the most positive day they'd had for years, and they could wait until morning

30

to plan their next move.

To the pub then.

2014

31

The sun was setting, casting a golden hue over the local park as Chloe, Lucas, and Luna made their way along the winding paths. The air was filled with the sound of children playing in the distance, the occasional bark of other dogs, and the serene rustling of leaves in the gentle breeze. It was the perfect evening for a walk. With Luna's leash gently held in Lucas's hand, they meandered through the sprawling expanse of their local park; the little dog trotted ahead, her nose to the ground, tail wagging with uncontained excitement. With its towering trees and manicured paths, the park offered a perfect escape, a place where thoughts and conversations flowed as freely as the gentle breeze.

'You know,' Lucas said, glancing sideways at Chloe, 'I told you right from the start it was going to be the uncle who did it. It's always a family member, and the dad was too obvious.'

'Oh, look at me, DS Miller, working out the plot of an ITV drama,' laughed Chloe, imitating Lucas in a ridiculously high-pitched voice.

'Ah, shut it, you. Have you caught that rapist yet?'

'DNA came back yesterday, and it's the brother. Sick people.'

'I told you it was always the family,' chuckled Lucas grimly.

'But well done, another one solved. You must be up for promotion soon; your exams have been done for a while now. Have you spoken to anyone about it?'

'No, I haven't talked to the boss yet,' Chloe admitted, watching Luna chase after a nearby goose. 'I've been so caught up with cases, and honestly, I'm not even sure if I'm ready for more responsibility.'

Lucas gave her a look of disbelief. 'Are you kidding? You're the most dedicated detective I know. If anyone deserves that promotion, it's you.'

Chloe smiled and squeezed his hand. 'Thanks Lucas, I appreciate – oh, nice!'

Luna suddenly decided it was the perfect time to relieve herself beside an especially luscious bush. Her back curled like a little question mark as she took a shit, maintaining eye contact with Lucas the entire time.

'Ah, duty calls,' Lucas said, watching Luna finish her business.

'Rock, paper, scissors for it?' laughed Chloe.

'Of course, straight shot or best of three?'

'Straight shot.'

They stood face to face, hands ready. 'three, two, one, go!' they chanted in unison. Chloe revealed a flat palm, which she used to cover Lucas's fist, throwing her hands up in victory.

'Ha! It looks like it's your turn to do the honours,' she teased, handing him a small pink bag from the roll.

Lucas grumbled but squatted down and picked up the turd, tying the bag securely. 'Christ, what have we been feeding you? This thing's the same length as her!'

With Luna's brief interruption taken care of, they continued their walk, the sky now painted in hues of pink and orange. The park seemed to glow under the twilight sky as they passed an elderly couple sitting on a bench, feeding the swans. Lucas stopped momentarily and sat on a bench, pulling Chloe beside him. They watched Luna trotting around the pond's edge, jumping at her reflection in the water.

'If she ends up in that water, she isn't getting in my car,' said Chloe.

'Try and stop her,' replied Lucas, staring out into the distance as his arm found its way around her shoulders. They sat in comfortable silence, watching as the sky deepened to a velvety blue, the first stars beginning to twinkle. The surrounding park quietened, the families and children making their way home, leaving behind a still peace.

'Lucas,' said Chloe quietly, her voice barely above a whisper, 'there's something I need to tell you.' Lucas turned to face her, his expression one of gentle inquiry. Chloe took a moment, gathering her thoughts, her heart throbbing in her chest.

'I'm pregnant,' she finally said, the words tumbling out in a rush of emotion.

Lucas's reaction was immediate. His eyes widened in surprise, a myriad of emotions flashing across his face before settling on a look of profound joy. 'Chloe, that's... that's incredible!' he exclaimed, reaching across the bench to envelop her in a warm, reassuring embrace. Chloe melted into his arms, a sense of relief washing over her. She had been nervous about his reaction, but the love and support in his eyes told her everything she needed to know.

'I was so worried about telling you. We haven't ever talked about this; I didn't know how you'd react,' she admitted, her voice muffled against his chest.

'Chloe, nothing in this world could make me happier,' Lucas said, pulling back to look into her eyes. 'It is mine, right?'

'Of course it bloody is!' said Chloe, laughing, 'but it's another reason I haven't spoken about a promotion. I didn't know if you'd want to keep it?'

'Keep it? Of course, I want to keep it, as long as you do. I think Rachel will want a little brother or sister, and I certainly want to be a dad!'

They sat on that park bench for hours, chatting away, and not even once did they think about the four dead girls: Jess, Amber, Rhian and Sabina. Right now, why should they?

32

Lucas's hands clenched the steering wheel as he navigated the rain-slicked streets of Leeds once more. It was his day off, but the case that had consumed his life for the past few years left no room for rest. Of course, he'd been allocated other cases, all the sergeants had. His current active investigations included a couple of open and closed domestic abuse deaths and a mugging gone wrong. However, the case being dubbed 'The Water's Edge Reaper' was the one that consumed him. The brutality of it, the media, the fact it was women, like his mother. He was desperate to be the one that solved it.

The soft hum of the tyre on the tarmac starkly contrasted his chaotic thoughts, but the familiar route to the central library provided a sense of mechanical calmness. The library had become his second home recently, his escape into the world of gothic poetry that seemed so entwined with the grim reality of this case.

The notes that the killer was leaving fascinated him. What was their purpose? Was it just to taunt the police, or did it mean something to the victims? They'd scoured the internet for references to the couplets, but nothing had turned up. They'd also consulted a literary expert who didn't recognise it. Most people felt they were the killer's own musings, but Lucas was different, so he'd been spending much of his free time searching old gothic books in the library's records to find something that only he thought would be there. The poetic pieces were fragments of a larger puzzle that Lucas was determined to solve.

As he drove, the car's radio crackled, the evening news breaking through the patter of raindrops on the roof. 'Another body was discovered last Tuesday,' the broadcaster's voice was solemn, 'marking the fourth victim in what appears to be a series of brutal killings shaking the local community. Could this, in fact, be the return of the Yorkshire Ripper?'

Parking his car in the central library's shadowed multistorey, he ran a hand through his damp hair, steeling himself for another long night among ancient tomes and dark tales. The grand building loomed before him, its towering pillars and stone gargoyles standing guard over centuries of knowledge.

He pushed through the heavy wooden doors, the scent of old books and leather binding immediately enveloping him. The main hall was quiet, the usual library hush felt especially heavy tonight. Lucas acknowledged the librarian with a nod, his face now a familiar fixture in the labyrinth of shelves. He found the helpful records keeper, whom he'd once again arranged to meet.

'Thanks again for doing this,' said Lucas.

'Nice to have someone take an interest,' replied the ever-so-thin lady helping him. She took him down into the basement, where the oldest and rarest books were kept. He was only allowed down here because DI Carmichael had written him a note, like a schoolchild.

Hours passed as he combed through the delicate books on the shelves before him, a list in hand that had grown longer with each visit. The titles blurred together — *'Verses of the Macabre,' 'Odes to Nightfall,'* and *'Whispers from the Grave.'* His eyes ached from scanning the fine print, and the weight of sleeplessness bore down on him like the tomes surrounding him.

His mind started to wander, the lines of poetry he had memorised mingling with the reality of the gruesome scenes he had witnessed. The heart, the lungs, the spleen, the liver — organs taken, messages left behind. What did it mean? Why these organs? Why these words?

Something caught his eye just as fatigue threatened to close his heavy eyelids. It was not the ornate binding or the title that drew him in, but the peculiar placement on the shelf. The book was slightly ajar, as if it had been hastily returned to its nook without care for the order. It had been years since anyone else had been down here, apparently.

Lucas reached for the book, taking it gently from the shelf. It had significantly less dust than others he'd handled tonight. It was bound in faded grey leather, the title barely visible, *'Laments of the Spectral Muse'.* His fingers trembled slightly as he opened the cover, the spine creaking like a door in an abandoned house. The pages were fragile and as faded as the outside had been. There were hundreds of poems in this book, each headed with a graphic and terrifying illustration. Lucas flicked through it for a few minutes, absorbed by some of the imagery's appalling brutality.

There. Page one hundred and thirty-one, an illustration of a man lying on his back, covered from head to foot in body parts which had been placed on top of him in their rough anatomical position. Beneath it was a poem titled *'In Shadows Deep'*.

In shadows deep, where whispers talk, I walk a path, alone I stalk,
A yearning deep within me lies, to don her form beneath the skies.

Her heart beats slow, in shadowed haze, beneath the moon's lamenting gaze,
Its crimson tides of love and dread, where secrets dark and light have bled.

Her spleen, an organ oft forgot, harbours anger, hatches plot,
In shadows deep, it bides its time, a keeper of the body's grime

Her lungs do lie, in caverns deep, breathing whispers of a sigh,
Their rise and fall, a ghostly dance, in life's fragile, fleeting trance.

Her liver toils in silent gloom, purging poison from its room,
A guardian in the night so deep, cleansing sins while others sleep.

Her colon, a labyrinthine cave, where shadows dwell and whispers rave,
A passage dark, where secrets hide, in its depths, they silently bide.

Her kidneys, in their silent lair, draw poisons out with utmost

care,
A pair of shadows, cleansing deep, where secrets of the blood they keep.

Her bladder, a keeper of the deep, holds the waters where dreams may seep,
A vessel for the liquid night, releasing tales by moonlight's right.

Her gallbladder, a bitter store, of resentments held in core,
A pouch of shadows, filled with bile, releasing pain, mile after mile.

Her appendix, a relic of the past, in the body's shadow vast,
A ghostly organ, silent, still, harbouring secrets, it might likely kill.

Her thyroid, a butterfly in shadow's hold, whispers secrets, bold and old,
Its wings flutter with every breath, in the dance of life and death.

Her pancreas, in hidden lair, balances the essence rare,
A silent alchemist at night, turning death to life, dark to light.

Her uterus, a cradle of night, where creation stirs in moonlight's blight,
A sacred chamber, veiled in mist, where life's first dawn and twilight kissed.

Her ovaries, twin moons in dark embrace, hold the seeds of time and space,
In their depths, the future sleeps, in the silence, destiny creeps.

The stomach's cauldron, boiling, churns, where fire of hunger ever burns,
Its acid touch, a witch's brew, conjuring desires of you.

Her eyes, twin orbs of night and day, see the world in shades of grey,
Reflecting back the soul's own light, piercing through the darkest night.

Her tongue, a serpent in its cave, tasting sweetness that we crave,
Yet in its folds, a poison lies, speaking truths and speaking lies.

Her brain, an enigma wrapped in shade, where memories flicker and fears invade, A labyrinth of thoughts, endlessly deep, cradling secrets it must keep

Her spine, a tower in the night, holding the body upright,
A pillar of bones, whispering tales, of burdens borne and strength prevails.

Her skin, a tapestry of night, shrouds the body from the light,
A barrier to the world outside, where secrets dark and demons hide.

Her hair, a veil of silken thread, drapes the living and the dead,
A crown of shadows, softly spun, under the pale and waning sun.

Her teeth, a graveyard's gleaming white, biting through the shroud of night,
They tear apart the veil of fear, in the silent scream, we hear.

Her nails, like claws of beasts untold, scratch the surface, bold and cold,
Marking time on prison walls, in the castle's darkened halls.

Her breasts, twin guardians of life, nurturing amidst strife,
In their curve, a solace found, where warmth and comfort abound.

Through these verses, dark and deep, her body's secrets I do keep,
In every organ, tale, and rhyme, lies the echo of her time.

His breath hitched as his eyes frantically moved down the verses. Lucas felt a chill run down his spine as realisation dawned on him. Each couplet matched the notes found with the victims. But there were more — so much more — verses that filled the gaps and completed the story that the killer was telling. This wasn't going to end soon. He'd only just got going.

The pattern was there, hidden within the scribblings of a Victorian mind long passed. The killer was using the poem not just as a signature but as a map, a guide to something darker and more profound than Lucas had feared.

Lucas took as many photographs of the book as possible, knowing the answers he sought were within these pages. It was a breakthrough, and the night suddenly seemed a little less dark.

33

Lucas's heart raced as he clutched the photographs of the gothic poem, his mind ablaze with the realisation that he might finally have the key to unlocking the mystery of the so-called 'Water's Edge Reaper'. The night felt brighter as the darkness retreated in the face of his newfound hope. He could barely contain his excitement as he imagined sharing this breakthrough with Chloe and the rest of the team.

He'd driven home as quickly as possible and barely remembered the journey, as his mind had been elsewhere. As he approached their home, the light pouring from the bedroom window cut through the night, guiding him back.

'Chloe! I found it!' he shouted as he crashed through the front door and bounded up the steps. 'You're going to have kittens when you read it. It's creepy as fuck, and there are at least twenty verses to the sodding thing,'

Chloe hadn't replied, but he knew she was in the bedroom, so he opened the door without bothering to knock. His face fell, and his excitement turned to concern as he found Chloe, not getting changed or reading a book as he'd expected, but curled up on their bed, her body shaking with sobs. He froze in the doorway and a thick with a sense of despair washed over him.

'Chloe?' Lucas's voice was tentative, his excitement replaced with worry. He approached the bed slowly, setting aside the photographs. The breakthrough had suddenly become irrelevant.

Chloe looked up with profound anguish, her eyes red and swollen from crying. The sight of her in such pain struck Lucas like a physical blow, his heart twisting in his chest.

'What happened? Are you okay?' he said.

'I lost the baby,' she whispered, the words barely audible but heavy with grief.

For a moment, Lucas stood frozen, the significance of her words sinking in. The joy of his discovery evaporated, replaced by a deep, aching empathy for the woman he loved. He sat beside her on the bed, clutching her in his arms, trying to offer comfort through his presence. Words seemed trivial in the face of such loss, but he felt compelled to speak.

'I'm so sorry, Chloe.'

'I... I failed,' she sobbed.

'What? No, don't be silly!' he said, clutching her tighter still.

'I'm so sorry, Lucas'

'Shush, shush, stop apologising. This isn't your fault,' he said, kissing her forehead, which was damp with tears that had rolled up as she lay on the bed.

They sat in silence, only the sound of Chloe's soft crying and Lucas' occasional whisper of comfort. He wanted to fix this, to make her pain go away, but he knew some wounds were beyond the reach of simple solutions. Luna had come up from her bed and lie across Chloe's stomach gently. She knew. He could see it in her eyes.

After a while, Chloe's sobs subsided, and she looked up at Lucas, her eyes searching his. 'I thought we were ready for this. I was so excited.'

Lucas held her gaze, his own eyes glistening with unshed tears. 'We were, and we are. This doesn't change how much I love you or how much I wanted this, too.'

The bedroom had become claustrophobic, filled with unsaid dreams and plans for a future that suddenly seemed uncertain. Lucas wanted to bring back the light to Chloe's eyes, to find some way to ease her pain. In his desire to help, he thought of mentioning the breakthrough with the case, hoping to distract her and give her something else to focus on.

'I found something tonight, Chloe. I found the poem. Maybe we could look at it together,' Lucas said, gently trying to steer the conversation towards something that might momentarily lift her spirits.

But his words, meant to comfort, seemed to have the opposite effect. Chloe pulled away slightly, her expression shifting. 'Is that all you can think about right now? The fucking reaper case?' Her voice was tinged with disbelief and hurt.

Lucas's heart sank. 'No, of course not. I just thought — '

'What? That I'd forget about our loss because of some poem?' Chloe's words were sharp, reflecting her pain rather than anger at him.

Lucas felt a sudden chasm opening between them. This had backfired miserably. 'I didn't mean it like that. I'm just trying to be here for you in any way I can.'

Chloe turned away, her shoulders shaking as she cried again. Lucas felt helpless, his words inadequate to bridge

33

the gap his mistake had widened. He reached out, touching her shoulder gently. 'I'm sorry, Chloe. I'm so, so sorry.'

For a few moments, they sat in more silence as Lucas tried desperately to think of anything he could do or say that might fix this. But there wasn't. They'd both lost something precious, and it wouldn't just heal over. Slowly, Chloe turned back to face him, her eyes meeting his. The hurt was still there, but so was the love, and they both started crying this time. The floodgates opened by their shared sorrow and the release of tension from their argument. This time, Lucas didn't try to offer solutions or distractions. He simply held her, and they cried together, mourning their loss and the brief distance that had grown between them.

2016

34

The familiar BBC chime sounded out around Lucas's flat, and the TV screen faded in, showing the familiar backdrop of Yorkshire's picturesque countryside edited to form some tacky artistic intro screen. The words *'Look North'* appeared before a serious-faced female news anchor faded into view.

'Good evening, and thank you for joining us—tonight's top story. We bring you a chilling report that has sent shockwaves across Yorkshire and echoes a dark chapter from four decades ago. A serial killer, dubbed by some as 'The Water's Edge Reaper,' is terrorising the region, leaving a trail of fear and sorrow in their wake, and the police seem to be no closer to finding the culprit. Jenny Moore reports.'

She faded out only to be replaced by some stock footage of the Yorkshire Dales, serene and untouched by the horrors that had unfolded over the last three and a half years. As the Dales fade out, the piercing dark eye of the Yorkshire Ripper, Peter Sutcliffe, loomed large across the screen, a black-and-white, monotone image of evil. A clear, irritatingly posh BBC accent provided the loud and obtrusive voiceover.

'The Water's Edge Reaper,' a moniker reminiscent of the infamous 'Yorkshire Ripper,' has struck terror into the hearts of residents across Yorkshire. So far, at least six women have fallen victim to this reign of terror. Their names are etched in our hearts: Jessica Murray, Amber Smith, Rhian Morris, Sabina Barbu, Vicky Turner, and Amrita Kaur.' Images of the victims, their faces vibrant with life, flashed across the screen, followed by more sombre images from their candlelit memorials.

'These crimes show a brutality that is hauntingly reminiscent of the dark days when Peter Sutcliffe roamed these same streets. The 'Waters Edge Reaper' abducts his victims, subjecting them to unimaginable horrors before ending their lives in what sources have described as a 'truly gruesome' manner.' The screen shifted to grainy security footage of darkened streets and eerie alleyways.

'The modus operandi and sheer brutality of these killings have sent shockwaves through the region, leaving residents living in fear, with many remembering how life changed during Sutcliffe's heyday some forty years ago.' A swift camera cut and the screen showed a recent press conference. The sound of frantic camera clicks surrounded DI Carmichael and DCI Woodbridge, who sat before a sea of reporters.

'As the investigation continues, the pressure on DCI Woodbridge, formerly of the Metropolitan police and lead investigator, is reaching unprecedented levels. He faces increasing scrutiny and growing frustration among the public, leading to calls for him to step down from a role he has held for a little under two years.'

Although the image on the screen showed a tense exchange between Carmichael and a reporter, there was no sound, meaning you couldn't actually hear the sensible and diplomatic answer she was giving. The smug-looking anchor reappeared, joined by a second person, but not one that Lucas recognised.

'To help us understand the gravity of this situation, we've invited Dr Emily Stevens, a renowned criminologist, to provide insight into the case.' Dr Stevens appeared on the screen, her expression irritating and highly slapable. Lucas thought she must be fresh out of some red-brick university, with no clue about the reality of a murder enquiry.

She began, 'Thank you for having me on the show, and I must say, it's a fascinating case. There are a lot of parallels between the Yorkshire Ripper in terms of the brutality of the crimes, how the killer is targeting women and the modus operandi. It's all very similar and worth inspecting. It's very rare to see such a brutal serial killer emerge in modern times, with DNA evidence and highly sophisticated forensic techniques. This individual must be meticulous and intelligent to evade detection for so long.'

Lucas rolled his eyes as he continued watching. Typical of the BBC to take someone so new to the game and give her a platform to spout inane shite. Linking this to the Yorkshire Ripper was sensationalism; Lucas thought the parallels were superficial. Highlighting that the killer avoided capture by being clever and careful was hardly insightful.

The news report switched back to the anchor in the studio. 'Dr Stevens, do you think we are, in fact, dealing with a copycat killer, someone who is trying to emulate the Yorkshire Ripper?'

'I don't believe so. But I think we are dealing with the same level of evil. This is a highly organised individual with an extreme hatred of women. He is extremely dangerous and poses a significant threat to the community.'

'And do you believe the police are currently doing enough to protect the women in our community?'

'That's a tough question to answer, but they are doing a good job, given the circumstances. They've got some excellent officers working on the case and are doing everything they can to catch this individual. However, mistakes such as the wrongful conviction of Jacob Murray will not look good to the public. The fact this killer is still out there, wreaking havoc on our communities, will only further erode the trust of the public in the police force.'

Lucas scoffed out loud, startling Luna, who was curled up in a doughnut shape on his lap. Jacob Murray raped his daughter; he just didn't murder her, and Lucas had said as much right from the very start. His murder conviction may have been overturned, but he was still serving another seven years for her rape. They didn't at least give them credit for that.

'Thank you, Doctor, for your insights. For more on this story, we will bring you a special report with our Crime Correspondent, Tom Doyle, who is travelling in the Yorkshire Dales and will provide an exclusive first-hand account of the investigation and the effect this has on the local communities. We will speak to experts on the subject to explore what lessons can be learned from the Yorkshire Ripper case and how this might help in the hunt for 'The Water's Edge Reaper'.

And now to other news, Prime Minister David Cameron is facing mounting pressure from MPs following revelations regarding his family tax affairs in the leaked Panama papers...'

Lucas switched off the TV and sat in silence for a moment.

34

He sighed. The media could be such a nuisance, but Dr Stevens was correct about one thing. The fact the killer was still out there and the lack of progress in the investigation was becoming an increasing source of concern. They knew the killer would strike again; there were eighteen more verses to '*In Shadows Deep.*' This could go on for years.

The case was getting more complex and more brutal by the day. He didn't know how much longer they could continue to turn a blind eye to the fact that they had so little to go off. Each crime scene gave the impression of being a disorganised mess, but when you analysed them, they were so unbelievably clean and bereft of evidence it was hard to fathom. All the victims had been snatched quickly, unseen and with minimal fuss. They'd been tortured somewhere else, a location as yet unknown, before being killed and dumped in public areas, away from witnesses and CCTV. The killer could harvest whatever organ he chose, leave the couplet and vanish. They had no fingerprints; they had no strange fibres, no footprints. Everyone they'd interviewed - family members and local weirdos - had a watertight alibi. The items that had been stolen from the victims had never been found, nor had the money in their pockets or wallets. It was almost like the killer could just reach into thin air and grab their victims, then return them when he'd finished. They were taunting them.

He shook his head. There was no such thing as magic. This guy was just exceptionally good at hiding his tracks. Or exceptionally lucky. But there was no such thing as luck. It was a statistical improbability that someone could evade detection for so long. There must be something they're missing. He made a mental note to review the files again for what good it might do.

Reaching for his laptop, he opened it up, wondering if he should have been in the office instead of hiding away at home. He could have made himself useful and helped the team with some legwork, but he was too tired, too worn out by everything that had happened. He felt he needed to take a step back to recharge his batteries, which had been running on empty for so long. His thoughts drifted to the victims. Six women, all savagely murdered, their bodies discarded like trash. He thought of their families and the grief and pain they must be going through.

A loud banging on the front door brought him back to the present, causing Luna to bark loudly. Lucas opened the door to see Chloe struggling to get a large box inside.

'Woah, let me help you with that.'

'Thanks, ' she gasped, and he took the other end of the box. Together, they manoeuvred it into the living room. Luna was barking excitedly, chasing around their feet and jumping up at their legs with her tongue flopping everywhere.

'What's all this then?' said Lucas.

'It's the party decorations; Kate said I could borrow some of them, remember?'

'Oh, yeah,' he said, clicking his fingers. Chloe started emptying the contents of the box onto the floor. 'You can't just stand there. Come and help me.

'Yes, boss,' said Lucas, with a mock salute. 'Shall I get Rachel as well? She might want to get involved?'

'Yeah, please,' she said, pulling out some bunting that had no end, like a magician's handkerchief.

Lucas strode up the stairs and knocked on a bedroom door. It had been about eight months since he'd moved in with

Chloe and her daughter Rachel. It had taken some getting used to sharing a space with two other people. Well, three other people. He came as a package with Luna, of course. Chloe's daughter was a troublesome child, but he liked her. She was that slightly complicated age of seven, going on eight. She was a full human he could interact with, but she had a real temper. Plus, she was well aware he wasn't her dad. From what little Lucas had seen of him, though, that wasn't a bad thing.

The decision to move into Chloe's had been tough. She owned a lovely new building with enough space for all of them, whereas Lucas's flat had hardly been big enough for him and the dog. It was his space, however. It had fetched a decent price, meaning they'd had enough spare cash to get a holiday a few months ago — two weeks in Spain. Sun, sea, sand and a lot of repeatedly reviewing the case notes.

He opened the door and walked into the bright pink room. 'Rachel, mum's here with the decorations for Saturday. She wants your help, deciding what you want?'

Rachel was wearing a yellow t-shirt and blue dungarees, lying on her front watching something on the iPad. She looked like a minion. As Lucas stood in the doorway, she looked up from the screen and grinned. 'Okay.'

'Come on then,' Lucas ushered her out of the room and walked her down the stairs.

They joined Chloe in the living room, where she had already assembled the pieces of a cake stand and inflated several balloons with a large number eight on them.

Luna was still running around excitedly, occasionally leaping up to steal one of the party hats. Chloe was having a great time, teasing her by wiggling the bunting across the floor, so Luna had to jump on her back legs and try slamming her paws down to stomp on it. Her long spaniel ears flapped about ridiculously. Lucas watched the two of them playing from the doorway, loving how Chloe giggled. His girls.

'Rachel, can you hold this bit steady while I screw it in?' said Chloe as Rachel and Lucas entered the room.

'Okay,' she squealed with excitement, seeing all the decorations.

'Lucas, can you sort the lights out?'

'Yes, ma'am,' he said, giving another mock salute. He picked up the tangled mess of fairy lights and set about unraveling them.

They spent the next couple of hours decorating the house, making it look fun and to Rachel's specifications. Lucas also organised a playlist full of rubbish, tacky boy bands that he couldn't stand. Once they were finished, they stood back to admire their handiwork.

'It looks amazing,' said Lucas, beaming down at Rachel and putting his arm around her.

'Thank you, both of you,' said Chloe.

Rachel's face glowed proudly. 'We should have a movie night,' she said.

'That's a great idea,' said Lucas. 'What do you think, mum?'

'Sure, why not?' came the garbled reply, as Chloe had just popped a handful of crisps into her mouth.

'Can we watch *'Despicable Me'*?' asked Rachel, looking slightly ridiculous in her dungarees.

Lucas and Chloe exchanged glances before Chloe answered. 'Yes, I don't see why not.'

'Yay!'

34

Lucas wasn't truly watching; he never got this sort of American animated stuff. He'd have picked something hideously violent, *'Arnie Shags the Wolfman'* or something equally ridiculous. But he knew his place, and they spent the rest of the evening watching little yellow creatures and eating popcorn.

After the film ended, he helped Rachel brush her teeth and tucked her into bed, a job which didn't take long as she was asleep within minutes. He closed her bedroom door quietly and walked back downstairs to find Chloe asleep on the sofa. Her head lolled to the side with Luna up against her, a tiny pink belly and an abundance of nipples on show. Both snored softly, so he covered them with a blanket and crept off to the bed. This case had been a shit show, but at least it had led him to Chloe, he thought. It was a nice thought, and he tried to cling to it for as long as possible before he drifted away to an uncomfortable sleep.

35

The following day, dawn broke on a bright but especially cold spring morning. Lucas was woken by the sounds of Chloe and Rachel getting ready for school. Rolling over, he tried to go back to sleep, but his mind wouldn't let him and ruminated over the case again. He didn't have Chloe's ability to switch off when he came home. Eventually he bit the bullet and got out of bed, scratching his head and yawning; he might as well get up and wash.

After scuttling naked across the hallway, he turned on the shower, stared into space, and waited for it to heat up before stepping under the steaming water. He washed his smelly bits with shower gel, letting the water cascade over his face and body, and stood there for a few minutes, just enjoying the feeling of the water on his skin. Finally, he stepped out of the shower, dried himself off, and wrapped a towel around his waist. The reflection in the mirror stared back, noting the dark circles under his eyes and the beginnings of stubble on his chin. He was proud of his thick shoulders and deep chest, but his motivation for the gym was waning. He needed to get some more sleep.

Leaving the bathroom, he headed for his bedroom to pull

on some clean clothes. He rubbed his temples, feeling a headache coming on, possibly a migraine. He wondered if he should call in sick today, knowing he wouldn't be useful to the team. But he also knew he needed to be there. He couldn't leave them to deal with this alone.

He drove Chloe to the Elland Road station via the school, where they dropped off Rachel. The school was in a lovely part of the city, affluent and respectable. Unfortunately, you had to get there by going through a council estate rougher than a badger's arse. Lucas was being a snob; it was probably fine, full of salt-of-the-earth people just struggling. But the fact every other house had a white good in the front garden stopped him from letting Rachel walk to school.

As soon as they arrived at the station, he could tell something had happened. There was a palpable atmosphere of excitement and tension.

'What the hell is going on?' he asked.

'No idea,' said Chloe, and they headed for the incident room, where the team was buzzing with activity.

'What's happening?'

'DCI Woodbridge is gone,' replied DC Peters with a half smirk.

'What?' gasped Lucas.

'He's got the sack, just heard.' He'd assumed that heads would roll but that it would be DI Carmichaels that would be first on the block, as she was really the one leading the investigation. But then again, he was sure she would have had something up her sleeve to cover her arse, and DCI Woodbridge was shit. They'd airlifted him from the Metropolitan police two years ago when the case was hotting up. He'd achieved the grand total of fuck all in his time, and

Carmichael had been as diplomatic as ever. She'd made it crystal clear she didn't want him there.

'And get this. They've just called DI Carmichael in as well!'

Ah, maybe not then. That didn't bode well, and he liked her. She might have been prickly, but he felt she had your back. Plus, he didn't think that the pace of the investigation was her fault; they just had nothing to go on and no luck at all.

The team milled around, trying to figure out what was happening. The door opened, and DI Carmichael entered the room. She looked pale and drawn, as if she'd been through quite an ordeal. Lucas wasn't surprised. With the way things had been going, she probably had been. She looked around the room, taking in the faces of her team.

'I have some news for you. I've been relieved of my position,' she said quickly and dramatically, shrugging her shoulders and staring at the ground. The room erupted in a chorus of protests and disbelief. Carmichael held up her hand with a maintained sense of authority.

'However.' She paused for effect. 'I have also been promoted to Detective Chief Inspector, effective immediately.' She allowed herself a sly smirk. There was a moment of stunned silence, then a round of applause. Lucas clapped along with the others, feeling a mixture of relief and surprise. Despite the recent shit show, he thought she genuinely deserved this promotion, but the optics of promoting within a failing team didn't seem great. It certainly didn't seem to be something that would fly with the public, not if the news report he'd watched last night was anything to go by.

The new DCI Carmichael held up her hand for silence again. 'I appreciate your support, but we have work to do. This creep has been prowling our streets for too long, and this is the time we need to get our shit together and act. Right, DS Miller, a word, please.'

'Yes, Detective Chief Inspector,' said Lucas, beaming and nodding at her. He followed her out of the incident room and into her office. She'd regained her mojo and was walking with more purpose already.

'What the hell is happening?' he asked as soon as the door was closed.

'The powers that be have decided that it's time for a fresh approach to this investigation,' she said, sitting on the edge of her desk and fixing him with a powerful stare.

Lucas felt a surge of mild anger. 'And they think that a total restructuring of the team will help? This is a complete mess. Woodbridge was shit mind.'

'Indeed. And I intend to be significantly less shit. But I need a right-hand man, and I have been tasked with hiring my replacement' She fixed him with a telling stare. It took Lucas a few seconds to twig, but then...

'Me?'

'Yes. It's not ideal, but I need someone I can trust to lead the team.'

'But I'm not even a DI?' he asked, confused.

'They're going to promote you to acting DI. Effective immediately. You'll need to pass your exams in a few months if you want to keep it permanently. Consider it a trial period. Probation.'

'This is madness. I'm not ready for this,' he said, slightly panicked. Of course, he was honoured, but it was quick. 'What about DS Wilson, boss? She's already passed her exams?'

'I wouldn't ask you if I didn't think you could handle it,' she replied firmly. 'DS Wilson's time will come. I believe in your talent, and my first choice would be you. I know you're shagging her, but don't pass up this opportunity, Lucas.'

'I don't know what to say'

'You say yes. We need a fresh approach, and you know the case as well as anyone. I'm sure as shit not inviting some ponce from the Met up here, so don't let me down. I have had to argue a bit to get you this position.'

'I'm not sure this is what they want, though, and I don't think the public will be all that impressed—promoting a junior from within,' he said, moving over to sit on the chair in front of her desk. His legs were feeling a little wobbly.

There was a knock at the door. They both turned round to see a shy-looking DC Sterling holding a piece of paper. She was cute, thought Lucas, with her enormous eyes and long blonde hair down to the small of her back.

'Sorry, sorry. Er... sorry to interrupt, but I think I've found something you'll want to see,' she said.

'Not now, constable, show me later.'

'I, oh, err, yes, OK!' she scuttled off, and Carmichael rounded on Lucas again.

'Look, I'm not going to force you to take this job, but I think you'd be a good fit, and I'd like to think I've earned your loyalty.' A knowing look appeared on her well-made-up face.

''You have...' he said.

'You were also the only one who expressed your doubts about Murray a few years back. It wasn't a popular opinion to defend a bloke who raped his own daughter, but you were right. We should have listened to you sooner. That's the leadership I want from you. The ability to call it as you see it and do the right thing.'

'Thanks, I'll do my best,' he replied.

'You'd better. I won't hold your hand through this mind. You're on your own.' she wagged a finger at him.

'I understand.'

'Good, now get back to your team and try to look a bit happier. You're the new man in charge. But don't forget, I'm in charge, really.'

36

Lucas returned to the incident room, pride filling his chest. But as he edged closer to the room, the feeling dissipated, and a fresh wave of emotions began to creep through. He took a deep breath and addressed his team.

'Listen up, people, I have some news for you' his voice quivered slightly, so he cleared his throat. The team stopped what they were doing and looked at him expectantly.

'I'm now your new boss' he spread his arms wide as if he were the new messiah and prophet who promised to solve this case. There was a chorus of surprised gasps and murmurs. Lucas held up his hand for quiet.

'I've been asked to step up and replace Carmichael as DI and take the lead of the ground team for the Reaper case. Nothing changes, though, guys. But we should get a bit more freedom to investigate this properly.'

There was another muted round of applause, and Lucas sat down at his desk, taking a deep breath as he did so. He had a feeling that this was going to be a long day. He glanced at Chloe, who gave him an encouraging smile, although she didn't hold his stare.

'Everything OK?' he asked, reaching across to squeeze her hand.

'Yeah, of course, why wouldn't it be?' She reciprocated the squeeze, but there was a delay, and she removed her hand quickly. Odd.

'I don't know, you just look a little off?' he said.

'No, I just didn't sleep well on the sofa. Your dog has no concept of personal space. But yeah, anyway, congratulations. It's great that they chose you. I'm not surprised; I knew you'd get the gig. This must be the quickest promotion from DC to DI for years. Very impressive, Lucas, even for a fast-tracked officer.' Once again, she gave a forced smile, which might fool others, but not Lucas. He'd sensed that Chloe was a little put-out, that he'd been given the promotion instead of her, even though she'd been on the force longer than him. It was difficult to blame her, in all honesty; if the boot were on the other foot, he'd be pissed off as well.

'Well, I'm sure it won't last; it's only acting, anyway. I've still got to pass my exams. I'm sure they'll send someone else in soon.'

'Yeah, of course. I'll be glad when this is all over. I'm ready for a break,' said Chloe, without looking at him.

'Me too.' Somehow, this had taken the shine off a promotion he should have been celebrating.

He thought for a moment, rapping his knuckles on the desk. They needed a team briefing, but a large-scale team briefing. Everyone should be there. He sent out a cluster of emails and waited.

Within the hour, everyone at his disposal was huddled in the inquiry room. Not just constables, PCs and other low-level minions. But also, there were a few forensics from the lab, the data analyst, and the media team. Christ, even Dr Cross, Dr Cooper and one of the mortuary assistants had slithered up from the hospital to join them, looking suitably irritated.

Lucas got up and walked, with as much authority as he could manage, to the central whiteboard. This had pictures of all six women spread across a timeline. We need to think outside the box; he thought.

'Right.' he said, turning to face the entire team. 'I know we've tried this before, but I want to try again. We're chasing this bloke, and he's always one step ahead of us. We need to even the odds. All these women are between sixteen and thirty-two; they're all from a lower socio-economic status, and four of them are known to have been working as prostitutes. They're all brunette, they're all petite, and all under five-foot-four. That's very broad, but it's still a pattern. So, what other patterns do we see? What about their addresses, workplaces, social life? And please, dear god, we need to work out what these bloody poems mean!'

The team was quiet momentarily, then DC Sterling piped up, raising a slender pale arm. The soft, unassumingly pretty DC who had interrupted them earlier went pink as soon as she spoke.

'I've been looking at the victimology, trying to establish any links between them. There is one thing, but I don't know how to explain it. It might be nothing, but...'

'Go on,' urged Lucas encouragingly.

'They're all connected to the internet, well, they're all active on social media. Instagram, Facebook, Vine, you name it, they've got a profile.'

'But doesn't everyone these days?' said dyspraxic Steven through a mouthful of chocolate biscuit.

'Yes, but I've gone through each of their accounts and followers. They all have Twitter, and they have one thing in common. They're all followed by a user called @HeLaCF10. There's no profile picture, and they've never tweeted themselves. They only follow the *BBC*, *Guardian*, *Daily Mail* and about twenty people, six of which are our victims.'

Lucas beamed at her. 'This is brilliant. How did you find this?'

'I was doing some digging into the victim's lives, and I came across it. I've been going through their accounts, and it was a bit of a weird coincidence,' she said, shrugging meekly.

'Well done, good find, possibly great find. DC Sterling, I want you to review everything you can find on this user. See if there are any more links. I want to know who this person is, where he is, what he's doing now, and what he did yesterday. I want to know the precise time he's going to take a shit tomorrow. DC Hancock, I want you to check out the other fourteen people this freak is following. I need to know they're safe. If they are, we need to keep them that way, so we need a plan of action to contact them.'

There was a buzz of activity now around the room. Suddenly, the world felt a bit more positive.

'Perhaps, with the idea that he's internet savvy, I could look at re-profiling the killer?' said a voice beside him, and the room turned to see who had spoken. Lucas looked over at Simon Ross, their criminal profiler. He'd been a soggy tissue during the entire investigation, and Lucas wondered why on earth they paid him to sit around being pointless.

'Yeah, sure, that would be great if you think you could shed more light on what he might do next,' said Lucas, keen not to engage with the bloke.

'Do you think I could speak to your pathologists to get an insight into how aggressive his crimes might be?' he asked oddly. Lucas was probably showing his irritation. This should have been done a long time ago.

Before Lucas could respond, Dr Cross's voice boomed out from a desk dead centre of the room, 'I can assure you, Mr Ross, that the killer can be very aggressive. Stabbing a woman's abdomen is seldom done calmly. Nor is it a sane man who makes the decision to tear out a heart or a spleen or gut someone of their colon. It does not strike me as a whim. But if you want to examine my notes or pick my brains, I'll oblige. I'm sure Dr Cooper will do the same. As will any other pathologist who's worked here these last five years. How does that sound?' It sounded bloody terrifying the way he said it. If Lucas had been showing some irritation, that was nothing compared to the seething menace that was seeping from Dr Cross.

Despite wanting to watch Dr Cross continue to shred the poor profiler further, Lucas dismissed the team and made good his escape before it got any more awkward. He left the room as quickly as he could without looking like he was running away and walked straight into Chloe, who had clearly tried to escape without catching him.

'You OK?' he asked her again, probably for the tenth time.

'Yeah, fine. I was thinking about the case. That was an excellent speech. You looked authoritative.'

'Thanks. I think it's good to have the entire team involved.'

'I agree,' she replied, somewhat flatly again. Oh boy, how long was this going to last?

36

'When we get the reports back from Sterling and Hancock, I want you to go through them with me, please. I need you; you're smarter than I am, and you know it.' He gave her an encouraging look and stroked her arm.

She smiled. 'It's true, you're not exactly the sharpest tool in the shed, so I'll help you.' She grinned at him. 'I'm going to head out for a bit; I'll be back later, OK?'

'Sure, see you later.'

She left and didn't look back. He shrugged it off and went back to his desk where there was a pile of paperwork and phone calls to make. He looked at his watch and sighed. It was already 3 pm… being a Detective Inspector was bloody stressful.

2023

37

Interview room three was unpleasant, ominous, and claustrophobic. It was also too hot, but this was at Lucas's request. He'd placed his waistcoat over the back of his chair, which was the most comfortable in the room by some distance, and rolled his sleeves up. However, PC Andrew Johnson was very uncomfortable in his small plastic chair that was digging into his sides. Though plain, the chairs in this room were imprinted with countless individuals who had been questioned within these walls. They were symbols of authority and vulnerability, depending on which side of the table one occupied.

The walls were painted an oppressive and dull shade of institutional grey, their surfaces marred by imperfections that hinted at a history of wear and tear. Harsh fluorescent lights buzzed overhead, casting stark shadows that seemed to dance around them in the otherwise murky gloom. Although the heating was on full blast, the room's ambience was intentionally cold and unwelcoming, everything designed to unnerve its occupants.

The room's centrepiece was a sturdy, well-worn table that bore many scars from past interrogations. Its surface, scratched and stained, told stories of old encounters with suspects, witnesses, and detectives alike. Lucas had caused one big dent many years earlier when he'd riled Jacob Murray to such a degree that he'd launched himself across the table at the detective.

Lucas sat on one side of the table, his gaze steady and determined, ready to pierce through the veil of lies. PC Andrew Johnson sat with a palpable tension, his eyes darting around nervously, avoiding the piercing aggression which was oozing out of Lucas. He was a fairly stout little man with a bright ginger retro mullet.

A soft electrical hum leaked from the ever-watchful presence of a ceiling-mounted camera which loomed overhead, capturing every word and gesture with big-brother-like menace. A small green LED light blinked steadily on an audio recorder in the corner of the desk. As time slithered forward, the room seemed to close in around them.

The door behind Lucas opened, and Detective Superintendent Carmichael walked in. If Lucas seemed menacing, that was nothing compared to how venomous she looked today. Behind her was PC Johnson's solicitor, a meek-looking man who'd clearly had a recent hair transplant, which hadn't worked. He reminded Lucas of one of Luna's chewed tennis balls. He was in an overly large pin-striped suit and still had a little smear of shaving cream behind his left ear. Carmichael sat next to Lucas and looked straight at PC Johnson, who was joined on his side by the meek solicitor.

Nobody said a word for a few moments. Lucas, not breaking eye contact for a second, leaned across and clicked the record button on the audio recorder so the tiny green LED turned red. PC Johnson licked his lips. Lucas stared at him for a few more stressful seconds before he finally spoke. It was so sudden that PC Johnson and his solicitor jumped slightly.

'DCI Miller and Detective Superintendent Carmichael on the 9th of November 2023 at 07:12 am. Present also are PC Andrew Johnson and his solicitor, Benjamin James. State your name for the tape,' he pointed at Johnson.

'Er... PC Andrew Johnson'

'You too,' said Carmichael at the meek man.

'Benjamin James, solicitor representing Mr Johnson'

'Now.' Lucas paused again and looked as closely into PC Johnson's eyes as possible. 'Do you enjoy poetry, constable?'

'No, I hate it. Well, not hate it. I don't understand it, I –' Lucas cut him off.

'I want you, very carefully, to tell me where you were on the evening of the 4th of October this year.' PC Johnson swallowed and perspired. He opened his mouth, but no words came out. Lucas continued to stare at him, his face a mixture of anger, confusion, and disbelief. 'Well? I don't have all day,' He snapped.

'I don't, I don't know. I'd have to check,' stuttered PC Johnson.

'You don't know? Really?'

'Really?' he said desperately. 'I don't even know what day of the week it was.'

'It was a Wednesday. You weren't at work. I'll give you that bit for free.'

'Right. Er... I don't know. Please, Lucas, we're friends; I didn't...'

'We're colleagues,' said Lucas curtly, 'and you'll address me as DCI Miller.'

233

'Yes, sorry sir,' said a sheepish PC Johnson. DSI Carmichael still hadn't said a word, and she just brooded next to Lucas with a palpable menace. Nobody liked a dirty copper, least of all Patricia Carmichael.

'Come on, you're a terrible liar, PC Johnson. Tell me where you were,' continued Lucas.

'I, er… I think I stayed in…Yes! I did. I was at home watching the Leeds match on TV. Won one nil against Queens Park Rangers, a goal from…'

'Alone?' interrupted Lucas. He'd watched the match as well, and it was Crysencio Summerville who'd scored.

'Ah, well. Yeah.'

'So you have no way of proving that?'

'Er…'

Lucas sighed. He opened a manila folder on the desk before him and extracted an A4 photograph of Amelia Watson, which he turned and slid over to PC Johnson.

'Who is this?'

'It's that girl we just found. The one in the hospital. I picked her up after an emergency call came through.'

'Exactly.' He took out another picture; this one was taken by our pathologist yesterday from the hospital. She was intubated, with what looked like a hundred tubes sticking out of her. Her face was puffy and bruised, with large cuts which had been stitched together. Her eyes were covered with white eye patches.

'This is what she looks like this morning,' he continued.

'Fucking Christ, I don't need to see that. I… I know, I mean, I've heard. I've seen. That's awful, it is, but I don't know anything. Why would I? I'm trying to help,' protested PC Johnson.

'Are you sure about that? I'm not so sure personally,' said Lucas to Carmichael, but she didn't reply; she just stared at PC Johnson.

'Why are you asking me all these questions?' he said, eyes wide with fear. Lucas smiled at him, more than a hint of menace in his eyes.

'Can you not think of a reason?' He let the question hang momentarily, seeing that PC Johnson was battling with something in his head.

'Er...' He continued to lick his lips, which were dry and flaky, in the furnace of interview room three. 'Well... I guess because... I err...' He looked around, hoping someone would help him. His lawyer looked about as useful as a knitted condom, so Lucas obliged.

'Paid her for sex two nights before she went missing?' he suggested

'Er, yes, ' said the PC, who was a very unusual shade of purple, his fidgeting eyes now fixed on the floor.

'We have CCTV footage of you and her in a bar by her flat on the 2nd of October at 20:28 and leaving again at 21:31. You withdrew one hundred pounds in cash shortly beforehand. Your internet history shows you visiting numerous escort websites the night in question and your phone records show you rang her for two minutes at 19:12 before she texted you her address. Plus, we have recovered sixteen condoms from the bin in her room. How much do you want to bet we find your vile, congealed DNA at the end of one?'

'OK, hang on now,' piped up Mr James for the first time, 'You can't –' but Lucas interrupted and dismissed him with one wave of the hand, and he shrunk timidly back into his chair. Carmichael still hadn't said a word; she just kept staring at PC Johnson.

'We have a footprint which matches your size at the scene; witnesses reported a commotion around the time she was found and someone driving away at speed in a Volvo SUV, like yours.'

'Look, OK. I did visit her that night, but it was consensual. I didn't harm her, I swear. It was two nights before she went missing. I didn't do anything.'

'Consensual, you say? That's not what the evidence suggests. As I have already said, we have a witness who saw your car in the area when Amelia Watson was found battered and traumatised. What were you doing there?'

'It wasn't my car. I wasn't there when they found her. I was on duty; that's why I was the first officer on the scene!' He was getting a little more frenetic now and was waving his hands about as he talked.

'Look, your alibi is shaky at best. We need to know the truth here. Tell me everything, and maybe we can help you,' said Lucas, speaking quickly to encourage a sense of urgency.

'I am doing!' he yelled, fear pulsing through him. Lucas took the opportunity for another pause. He'd been taught the importance of silence in an interview like this. People wanted to fill the awkward silence, so they kept speaking. But not Johnson; he was holding his nerve surprisingly well despite initial appearances.

Lucas popped the silence. 'What was the nature of your encounter on the 2nd of October, then?'

'Look, I didn't rape her. We had sex, and I paid her for it. It was all very boring and vanilla. I'm not into weird stuff. I'm telling you. We had a normal session, nothing weird or violent—just a normal shag. And when I left, she was alive and well and not cut to pieces or anything. She was fine.' His eyes flicked quickly between Lucas and Carmichael.

'And you have no idea who did that to her?' asked Lucas.

'None.'

'You didn't want to mention shagging the victim earlier before we got you in for questioning?'

'No, because... well, because I'm a police officer, and that would have made me look bad,' said PC Johnson, faltering.

'You didn't think being a suspect in the murder of a prostitute was going to make you look bad?'

'No, because I didn't do it. I didn't think that was an issue.'

Lucas shook his head. 'I can't even begin to tell you how many times we've heard that line. You'd be surprised.

'No, no. I didn't kill her. I didn't, I promise.'

'Ahh, well, if you promise. We should probably release you, right?'

'Look –

There was a sharp, desperate knock at the door. Lucas turned, and DS Kim Sterling put her head through the door, looking slightly mad.

'Can I have a word, please, sir?'

He nodded at her and then turned back to the table, 'Right, well, let's pause the interview at 07:37. I'll be back in a few minutes.'

Lucas left the room, leaving Carmichael, PC Johnson, and Mr James to stew. Carmichael still hadn't said a word. In all honesty, Lucas wasn't even sure she was breathing. She'd been so silent, which made him uncomfortable; god knows what it was doing to PC Johnson. The click of him closing the door firmly behind him echoed slightly in the dank interview room.

'Did you do it?' asked Carmichael directly and, suddenly, causing PC Johnson to let out a short but audible squeal.

'No. no. Look, I didn't do it!' he repeated, looking exceptionally desperate now. Carmichael just grunted at him.

The door sprang open, and Lucas marched back with anger and purpose. He clicked the recorder again and said,

'Interview terminated at 07.38.' He gestured to another officer, who had just re-entered the room. 'Take him to a cell somewhere now. You best get thinking. You'll need another fourteen alibis, ' he said, pointing at PC Johnson threateningly. The officer obliged in handcuffing PC Johnson and escorting him swiftly from the room, his solicitor in tow, making some hollow threat of police brutality.

'What the fuck is going on, Miller?' said Carmichael, her voice raised and the arteries in her thin neck pulsing rapidly.

'It's Amelia Watson, boss. She's awake.'

2016

38

The next few days were a blur for the new DI Lucas Miller. He was paraded in front of the local media and dragged from pillar to post by his team. However, he seemed to have inspired them, as everyone was grafting hard. If they weren't working on something new, they were revisiting something old and ensuring nothing had been overlooked.

DC Sterling had put together a dossier on the other potential targets that @HeLaCF10 followed, all of whom matched the victim profile. They'd all been warned to be careful, and a small group of constables were tasked with tailing them. They were going to stop him, somehow.

Lucas and Chloe worked on the reports that came in from the team. It was hard going, but they seemed to have done a pretty thorough job. All new potential targets were known sex workers or young women living alone and in poverty. There didn't appear to be any other connection. There were no mutual friends, no places of work, no common interests. They simply matched the demographic. The killer had a type, and he found his targets online.

Lucas was reviewing the latest reports in his office when he heard a knock at the door.

'Come in,' he said, without looking up.

'Sir' said DC Hancock, walking into his office. He was carrying a pile of papers.

'Just wanted to give you these, sir; they're all the background checks on the next potential victims. It seems like they're all safe. I even called a few of them personally, and they've all said they're fine. There's no one stalking them or anything. I've left you a note in the file, but I thought you'd want to know first-hand.'

'Thank you,' Lucas said whilst stifling a yawn. He was glad that this part was over. He had worried they would be too late for one of them.

'What next, sir?'

'I want to have a briefing at ten. You can tell the rest of the team about your findings.'

'Yes sir, will do,' said DC Hancock smartly before turning and leaving. Lucas put his head in his hands and took a deep breath. This job was fucking stressful. He was starting to think that maybe he wasn't cut out for it after all. He got up, walked to the window, looked down at the car park, and sighed loudly.

'What are you doing?' came a voice, which caused Lucas to jump violently. He hadn't noticed that Chloe had come into the room.

'Fucking hell Chloe, you scared the shit out of me! How long have you been there?'

'Not long. I wanted to ask you something...'

'Yeah?'

'Do you fancy grabbing a coffee or something? She looked oddly awkward. It had been like this for the last week. Living with her had become strange, and he felt like he was walking on eggshells, especially when the subject of his recent promotion came up.

They walked to a small coffee shop near the police station. It was run by an ex-cop who had been shot in the stomach during a raid on a drug den. He was permanently disabled and could no longer work in the force. But he knew most of the team at the station, the coffee was good and it was quiet. Chloe went to order while Lucas sat at a table and took out his phone. She returned two minutes later with coffee to go and sat down across from him, looking serious.

'You OK?'

'I'm not sure.' She was fidgeting and looked nervous.

'Is there something wrong?'

'No, no, I don't think so,' she mumbled, and Lucas pulled a face.

'Come on, what is it?'

'Look, I'm a bit hurt, actually. You might have put my name forward when DCI Carmichael was looking for a new DI. I have been at this longer than you and I've sort of earned it,' she said, a bit too quickly and garbled.

'I did, actually, but she caught me off guard if I'm honest,' said Lucas, the dawning of realisation occurring in his head. 'She said she'd rather have me, and I said yes because I panicked. I'm sorry, I didn't realise you felt that way. I thought you'd be happy where you are?'

'I am, but I also want to progress. I've been working my arse off for years, and I just thought it might be nice to get a bit more respect.' Even though she was babbling, she was keeping her voice down, so it wasn't easy to understand. Something was bubbling under the surface; he could feel it.

'I respect you, Chloe, I do. I... I don't know. She didn't

really give me the option. She forced it on me. You should probably speak to her about why she wanted me?' But that wasn't the right thing to say, apparently. She stood up and slammed her coffee on the table, spilling the hot, brown contents everywhere.

'I can't believe you're being such a wanker about this. Do you think I haven't spoken to her about it?' she said, much more loudly.

'I didn't know you'd spoken to her about it. She didn't mention it, and I didn't think you wanted it.'

'Well, you've just proved to me that you're an idiot then!' she said, leaving Lucas stunned. They'd never argued like this before.

'Chloe, I'm sorry, I didn't know. I put your name forward, but I would have rejected her offer if I'd known. It's not too late. I could speak to her?'

'Don't bother!' She stormed off, leaving her coffee half-finished or half-spilt. Lucas was shocked. He couldn't believe they'd had their first proper argument, and in public, too. He went after her, but she was already driving away.

'What the hell is going on?'

Lucas took the long walk back to the office, feeling depressed. He really liked Chloe, and an uncomfortable feeling of guilt was squirming in the pit of his stomach, making him slightly angry with himself. He decided the best thing to do would be to get back to work, and then he could try to smooth things over when they got home.

* * *

A few hours later, he was sitting at his desk, trying to make sense of a report, when someone knocked on his door again. DC Sterling popped her little head in, smiled and said, 'Are we having that briefing then, boss?'

'Fuck, yeah, sorry. Two seconds!' Lucas had forgotten all about the briefing; he'd been so distracted by Chloe. He made his way back into the inquiry room and addressed the team.

'Right, so, as you know, we've been investigating the potential next targets of our killer. DC Hancock has some good news. All the women that @HeLaCF10 is following are safe. All of them are accounted for. None of them have reported any unusual behaviour. They're all fine, but we want to keep it that way. As a show to the public, we will patrol the streets of the red-light districts in Leeds, York and Sheffield. We've warned the media to stay off the killer's back; we don't need him getting nervous and running off somewhere.'

There was an indistinct murmur from the team as they digested this information.

'DC Sterling, can you tell me what you've learned about this Twitter handle?' She got up, her long blonde hair flowing behind her. She looked nervous as she spoke to the assembled officers, and Lucas could see that her shoulders were slightly higher than usual, as she was tense.

'Well, um, DC Hancocks went through all the @HeLaCF10 followers, and they only follow young women who fit the victim profile, as we know, including all the victims. I think it's clear this person, whoever it is, is using social media to find potential targets. It also seems like he's quite tech-savvy; he knows how to cover his tracks. He doesn't use any other social media platforms, just Twitter, and he's been logging in using a sophisticated VPN. We can't trace where the account was set up or logged in from. We're looking into the possibility that the username is a code or an acronym for something, but we haven't figured out what yet. I've also sent a message to Twitter, asking them to take the account down, but they won't. They've said it's against their principles.'

'What a load of bollocks. A serial killer is using this account,' Lucas said. He was getting tired and cranky. 'We'll leave it for now, but I want us to keep –'

The office phone rang. The nearest PC, a chubby little man called Andrew Johnson with a shit mullet, answered it.

Lucas continued, 'Any luck with monitoring the chat rooms? Some Victorian poetry freak might know something about all this?'

'Sir!' shouted PC Johnson.

'Not now, constable,' said Lucas, looking around at the group, hoping someone was still going to answer his question.

'Please, sir!' interrupted PC Johnson again. 'They've found another body.'

39

'This is fucking ace!' screamed Leah, her head spinning, the world moving in a trance-like state of drug-fuelled haze.

The festival grounds were alive with energy, pulsating beats from The Main Stage as the *Red Hot Chilli Peppers* blasted out *'Californication'* to the thousands of people before them.

'Dream of Californicaaaaaation!'

'Dream of Californicaaaaaation!'

The beats from the giant speakers set the rhythm for thousands of bodies moving in unison. Leah's heart raced as she soaked in the atmosphere, the air thick with the scent of sweat, beer, and the earthy aroma of cannabis. Multicoloured lights cut through the night sky, illuminating faces painted with a neon glow, glitter sparkling under the moonlight.

With his lanky frame, Ojo was throwing some wild shapes to her right, moving with a grace that belied his size, his silhouette a blur of motion among the sea of dancers. The ground beneath their feet vibrated with the bass, a tangible presence that Leah felt in her bones, driving her forward, deeper into the night's embrace. She looked to her right, and Danny had his tongue so far down Jess's throat that she assumed he was licking her arsehole.

'Get back to the fucking tent if you're gonna shag!' said Leah, just about maintaining her balance. Sophia would have loved this; why did she have to throw a whitey and flake out on them? She always did this. She went too hard too soon and ended up bailing before the night was done. Her loss, though, thought Leah.

As the set drew to a close, the group, breathless and exhilarated, made their way through the throng of people, laughter and snippets of conversations swirling around them like confetti. The path to the camping area was a winding trail of fairy lights, guiding weary revellers back to their temporary homes.

Their campsite, a small clearing amidst a sea of tents, welcomed them with open arms. The air here was cooler, the noise from The Main Stage a distant echo. Leah's gaze swept over the familiar setup—the cluster of tents huddled together like mushrooms, the makeshift flagpole with its brightly coloured bandanas fluttering in the breeze, like the north star, leading them through the chaotic landscape of the festival.

As they approached, Leah's footsteps slowed, a sense of unease creeping into her exhilarated state. The flap of Sophia's tent was open, swaying gently in the night air. Why was it open?

'Sophia, you in there?' Leah's mouth was dry, and her heart was racing. But that might have been the drugs.

There was no response from the tent, and suddenly, the silence drowned out the laughter and music that had filled the air back towards the stages.

With a glance at her friends, Leah stepped forward, her hand shaking. The tent's interior was bathed in the soft glow of a lantern outside, revealing a scene that stopped Leah in her tracks.

Blood. Blood was everywhere, and Sophia lay motionless in the middle of the red pool, her face pale and waxy. Her hair was tangled with blood and sweat, and her stomach was torn open, her guts spread out across the tent. Leah looked into Sophia's eyes, which seemed to stare both at her and through her, their black and empty gaze haunting in the half-light.

She screamed.

2023

40

The car's engine rumbled with a guttural growl as they wound through the labyrinth of thoroughfares that made up the sprawling city of Leeds. Drenched in the cool, grey light of early morning, the streets glinted with jeopardy as they drove from the Elland Road Police Station to the Leeds General Infirmary. It wouldn't be a long drive, a quarter of an hour at most, through Holbeck and across the River Aire. The city's pulse was beating quickly, with scattered commuters and early risers venturing onto the streets. The car, a basic but sturdy Peugeot, moved with purpose through the city's arteries, the tyres humming softly against the asphalt.

As they navigated the winding roads, the car's headlights pierced through the early morning mist, creating a halo of light that danced on the wet pavement. Occasional raindrops spattered against the windshield, but the weather was bearable overall. Lucas's thoughts were focused on the upcoming interview with Amelia Watson. Carmichael, sitting beside him, was equally contemplative, although there was a stiffness to her which unsettled him. Their shared silence spoke volumes.

'You seem annoyed?' said Lucas, breaking the tension.

'Not annoyed. I'm confused.' She said, not looking at him.

40

'What about boss?'

'You.'

'Me? What the hell have I done?' he said, startled, stealing his gaze off the road for a second to look at her. She still wasn't looking back.

'I thought you would have learned your lesson about going in so aggressively on a suspect. Given your track record, I'm struggling with the fact I've got to have this conversation with you again.'

'What is that supposed to mean?'

'You know bloody well what, and don't pretend you don't!' said Carmichael, raising her voice. There was an awkward silence. 'I'm not buying PC whatever-the-fuck he's called back there as a killer. No, I don't see it,' she said, shaking her head.

'But boss, he's been shagging her. His car was in the area and the footprint -

'Lucas, don't be thick. That evidence is shit, and you know it,' she interrupted. 'You didn't need to go in so hard on him back there. Showing him the girl in the hospital is a dodgy move.'

'You were there. You could have stopped me?'

'I didn't see the need to humiliate you in the interview room or spoil the tape. I'm nice like that.'

'But - ' he started, but she cut him off again.

'How'd you hurt your hand, Lucas? You've admitted to knowing her. The footprint was a size eight walking boot, like that one you've got on now. Fuck, you even drive a Volvo SUV now, don't you? Was it you? Bet you own a Parker pen, don't you? How did you really cut your hand, DCI Miller? Great, so in three sentences, it's become you who we should suspect!'

'You're being ridiculous,'

'Yes, I am. But it wasn't hard now, was it? Point made,' she said, folding her arms like a child. 'I don't think he did it. I really don't.'

'Well, I hope for your sake you're right,' muttered Lucas like a scolded child.

'Yeah, well, I'm pretty good at this detective lark. A sight better than you, not least given I'm more senior.'

'Is that right?' scoffed Lucas, although he instantly regretted his sudden surge of confidence.

'Yes, it is. Don't get too big for your boots, son. And you best remember who got you promoted.'

'I haven't forgotten, believe me.' Lucas's eyes glinted with anger and resentment, his jaw clenched tight. They spent the remainder of the journey in an uncomfortable silence.

It was bustling with activity when they pulled into the Leeds General Infirmary car park. Lucas counted twelve ambulances outside, attempting to drop off patients into an already overfilled and understaffed hospital. The usual array of visitors and staff milled about the entrances, swimming in a sea of patients, half of whom were standing with a drip stand in one hand and a cigarette in the other.

Lucas and Carmichael strode confidently towards the main entrance, their shoes clacking on the polished tile floor. They were still unhappy with one another but had silently and professionally agreed to be civil whilst on duty. The reception area was equally busy, with nurses and doctors scurrying about, trying to get where they needed to be. The pair made their way towards the reception desk, weaving through the throngs of people. Lucas flashed his badge at the young man sitting behind the desk, who directed them through the hospital to the Intensive Care Unit. A somewhat aggressive nurse met them at the entrance to the unit and made them wait until the consultant was available.

'How long will that be?' said Lucas

'No idea. She has to finish the ward round; we're at capacity today. I'd guess about half an hour from now, but it depends on what happens. You must wait in the quiet room round the corner.'

Carmichael and Lucas made their way to the quiet room, a small, nondescript room furnished with a few cheap chairs and a water cooler. There were a few pictures of butterflies and daffodils on the wall, but otherwise, the room was empty. Most people who'd sat in here would receive dreadful news, thought Lucas.

He sat down and leaned his head against the wall, letting out a deep sigh. Carmichael stood, looking out the window at the view of the hospital car park. The minutes crawled by, and the pair exchanged little more than a glance. Lucas spent most of the time massaging his arm. With the rush to leave the station in such a hurry, he'd forgotten to grab his blister pack of pregabalin. He was nearly out anyway; he'd have to stop by his dad's after work and pick some more up. After more than three-quarters of an hour, there was a knock on the door, and the aggressive nurse barked that they could go in.

'Thank you,' said Lucas. He stood up and smoothed out his waistcoat. 'You ready?'

'Of course. Are you OK? You look like shit.'

'Yeah, just warm is all,' he lied. He'd gone pale, and the nerves had kicked in again. What if Amelia blurted something out? Fuck, he was suddenly regretting not having his pills even more now.

The pair exited the quiet room and went down the corridor towards the ICU proper. Lucas's heart was pounding, and he could feel his hands getting clammy, and the pain in his forearm was intensifying rapidly. He was nervous, and it showed. With sweaty palms, which he wiped on his trousers, they approached the doors and he took a deep breath. He wasn't sure what Amelia would be like, but it was what she might say which scared him.

At the entrance, they were asked to wear surgical masks, gloves, and these silly little plastic aprons. A vague reminder that COVID-19 had existed not that long ago. The doors swung open, and the sterile smell of the ICU wafted out. The place was a bustling hive of activity. There were at least fifteen bays that Lucas could count, each one home to a human entangled in tubes, pipes, and wires. These connected to a confusing array of machines, screens and ventilators, none of which made any sense to Lucas. They meant something to the nurses and doctors hurrying around as they kept fiddling with the dials and squeezing medications in the patient's veins. The atmosphere was one of controlled chaos, with the hum of voices punctuated by the beeping of those machines.

Lucas and Carmichael were greeted by the friendly face of Dr Shazad, who led them to Amelia's bedside. Bay number six was guarded by a very smiley little Filipino nurse, who introduced himself as Alberto.

The only suggestion that Amelia Watson was awake was that she was sitting up. She had neat white ovals of gauze covering the holes where her eyes used to be. Around the left angle of her jaw, a large dressing extended up behind her ear. Had he begun peeling her face off before he was interrupted? She had a small, white, curved tube sticking out the front of her neck, just above the sternum. It had little plastic wings which had been stitched into place. Her head turned and vaguely followed their approach, but her face remained expressionless. Lucas was taken aback by her appearance. She looked frail, her skin pale and clammy, not at all the vibrant, frankly feral young woman he'd known briefly these last five years. The coloured bruises on her face stood out in stark contrast to her skin, and her hair was matted and greasy. She looked like she'd been through the wringer, and Lucas could feel the guilt washing over him.

'Hello, Amelia,' Lucas said in the gentlest voice he could manage. She didn't respond.

'How are you doing? You gave us all a bit of a fright,' shouted Carmichael abruptly from behind him. She licked her lips and then tried to speak, but a raspy rush of air just leaked from the tube in her neck.

'Is she able to talk?' Lucas asked Dr Shazad.

'Oh yeah, we need to get a speaking valve. Hang on.' One nurse went to the trolly by her bed to fetch it. 'She's got a tracheostomy. She's breathing on her own, which is a good sign, but her throat is damaged, so we've put a tube in as a temporary measure until the swelling to her throat above it has settled down.' The nurse returned and attached a kind of bung to the end of the tube.

'You'll have to hold it for her, Tracey,' instructed Dr Shazad to a lady in green scrubs. She turned to the nurse and pointed to a little bag of fluid hanging up next to the bed, 'Might as well restart the antibiotics whilst these guys are here.' She did as she was told and began fiddling with something in Amelia's arm.

'She's weak, guys; you'll only have a few minutes, really. This can't be a formal interview or anything. She's still fairly heavily medicated, so I don't think you'll get anything you can use in court. Just thought she might give you something, so you're not twiddling your thumbs,' said Dr Shazad in her soothing, soft accent.

'Thanks.' said Lucas, before turning his attention back to Amelia. He crouched beside her so his head was level with hers and gently took her hand. He spoke fast so as not to give her a chance to reply until he'd said everything.

'Amelia, it's DCI Lucas Miller. Do you remember me?' he paused briefly before adding, 'I'm with Detective Superintendent Carmichael and Dr Shazad. You're not in trouble; we're here to find out who did this to you.'

She opened her mouth slightly and tried to say something. Lucas's throat constricted so much he might need a tracheostomy of his own. Please don't say anything stupid. The green lady pushed the little valve on the tracheostomy gently, and then a soft, strained and wispy voice spoke.

'Mil... Miller?'

'Yeah, Amelia, it's me.' He was sweating. Fuck, it was warm in the ICU unit. Surely Carmichael could tell he was nervous? But he continued.

'Do you remember what happened, Amelia? Who did this to you?'

'P...pu...punter,' she gasped.

'OK? Good, great. Do you know their name?'

'N... no. Not a real one.' She liked her lips and shifted slightly in her bed. 'T... Thomas.'

'OK, that's really helpful.' He thought for a split second.

He needed to ask simple, direct questions.

'Young, middle age or old?'

'Middle.'

'Tall or short?'

'Tall, very... very tall.'

'Great, well done. What colour hair?'

'Balding.'

'OK, any scars? Any tattoos?'

'I... can't... breathe.'

'Pardon?'

The machines around the bedside started beeping aggressively. Amelia's lips had turned a deep blue, and Dr Shazad was suddenly pushing past him to get to the bedside. 'Take the valve off. Put her back on the vent now!' Amelia slowly slumped back in the bed and had lost all muscular tone.

'What's happening?' asked Lucas, confused.

'She's going into respiratory arrest!' she barked at Lucas whilst staring at a monitor. She then ignored them entirely and focused all her efforts on Amelia. 'Someone check that tube isn't blocked and get the arrest team here now.'

'No blockage on suction, inner tubes clean'

'SATS are only 79%... 76% and dropping. CO_2 is rising; we're not venting properly. Sinus Tachycardia. If that tube isn't blocked, this has got to be lung-based. I think she's had a massive pulmonary embolus. We need to consider thrombolysing now.'

Everyone was moving around with such speed. At first, Lucas thought it was chaos, but as he observed, he realised everyone had a job and was doing it. It was incredibly synchronised. Nobody was useless, and there was complete trust in each member of the team.

The beeping machine was going haywire now. A little blue number, which had been moving between 96% and 100% when they arrived, was now flashing red and reading 45%. He didn't know what that meant, but assumed it wasn't good.

'Right, I've lost a pulse. She's in PEA.' The ECG monitor she was staring at showed a beating mass of lines that concerned Dr Shazad, as she acted immediately. 'We're starting CPR. Tom, you're on chest, Barbs, you swap in with him; Cassie, where the hell is that de-fib?' The bed was suddenly plunged back, making Amelia completely flat. They ripped her top open, exposing everything and placed large white wired pads across her chest over her heart. This was not a time for dignity. A large bloke in blue put his hands firmly in the centre of Amelia's chest, his arms extended, and he began putting his full weight down through her ribs. He was so much bigger than she was, and suddenly, there was an audible crack as he broke her ribs straight down the centre. He didn't stop—steady, rhythmical compressions. Lucas could see her chest was now deep and concave, with flecks of bright red blood being ejected from her tracheostomy into the ventilation tube. Her whole body was now grey and becoming mottled whilst she flopped like a rag-doll. This lasted for two full minutes as Lucas and Carmichael watched in horror and awe.

'Rhythm check,' said Dr Shazad loudly. Suddenly, there was a pause. Everyone stopped, staring at the ECG monitor above the bed. Silence, waiting for Dr Shazad to make a call. 'Sinus bradycardia. Pulse?'

'No central pulse,' shouted the person nearest her head.

'PEA, back on the chest.' The compressions started again, and more cracking, more rag-doll flopping ensued. Lucas and Carmichael just watched on in abject terror.

'1 milligram of adrenaline going in now,' shouted a nurse, and a lady in green by a whiteboard wrote it down in shorthand.

Compressions continued, and the little red number now read 36%. The ECG remained a mess of violently bouncing lines, and the monitor remained unchanged.

'Stop compressions!'

'Any change? Pulse?'

'No pulse, fuck, she's flipped into VF, resuming CPR. She needs a shock!

'Charging!' shouted a junior doctor operating a machine to the right of Amelia. He was standing to attention, his finger poised over a large button. 'Shock ready, stand clear!'

Again, everyone stopped and moved a meter back from Amelia.

'Shocking.' He pressed the button. Lucas could smell the sweat and the burning. Amelia's whole body tensed up, almost off the bed, and then flopped back down again.

'Still in VF, resume compressions.' The man resumed his compressions, and Dr Shazad emerged next to Amelia's limp grey arm with a syringe.

'I'm going to thrombolyse.' She injected the solution through the big green cannula in Amelia's arm. Compressions continued, and the foul smell of sweat and blood became almost too much. Lucas stepped back.

'Off the chest. Charging. Clear!' Everyone jumped away again, and Amelia was shocked again—still, nothing.

'Still in VF. Resume CPR.'

They were running out of options, but Lucas wasn't paying attention. He was feeling very light-headed, and his vision started getting fuzzy. It was sweltering, and his clothes felt uncomfortably close to his skin. He was sweating profusely and was now having great difficulty breathing himself. The room was spinning, and his head was aching. Christ, he needed his pregabalin right now; he couldn't cope with this.

'Lucas, are you alright?' Carmichael's face was blurry, and she sounded like she was speaking from underwater.

He had to sit down in the corner whilst the resuscitation attempt continued. His thoughts flew back to when his grandfather had died. He'd been in and out of the hospital with pneumonia. It was his own fault; he was a lifelong smoker and had never taken his health seriously. On the last admission, a young doctor had discussed the possibility of a *'Do not attempt resuscitation order'* with them. She'd explained how unpleasant it was, how the chance of survival was so impossibly small and how cruel it would have been to subject Grandad to it. They'd argued, of course. They weren't about to give up on him. It was explained that they weren't giving up, they would still give antibiotics and the like, they just wouldn't do this to him if his heart stopped. They'd let him go peacefully, with dignity. The doctors signed the form, anyway. It was a medical decision, not a family decision. He'd been hurt and upset, but right now, he couldn't be more grateful. He was big enough to admit he didn't have a clue. You see CPR on TV, and it looks so simple, so miraculous. The brutal reality in front of him was anything but. If those ribs that had so ferociously cracked belonged to his grandfather, if that blood in the ventilation tube belonged to his grandfather, if the burning smell were from his grandfather, he'd be yelling at them to stop. Let him die. Please.

He was suddenly aware of a woman crouching beside him and Carmichael kneeling beside her.

'You alright? You don't look great.'

'It's hot,' he said thickly. He was sweating and could feel the blood draining from his face.

'You've gone awfully pale'

'It's just hot. I think I'm dehydrated.'

The alarms from the machine were creating an almighty cacophony of noise. They'd been at this for at least thirty minutes now.

'Fuck, asystole again.'

'Cycle twelve, back on the chest?'

'No. She's gone, I'm calling it. We can't do anything more,' said Dr Shazad. Everyone stopped what they had been doing and looked down at Amelia's lifeless form. She was grey, her lips blue. No breath. No heartbeat. Nothing. 'Anyone disagree?' Silence.

'Time of death, 12:17 pm'

41

Lucas stepped out of the stark white hospital, the image of Amelia's lifeless body haunting him. He could see her cold grey body scorched into his retina. The fluorescent lights of the hospital corridor seemed to flicker in his mind's eye, casting shadows over his thoughts. His arm throbbed, a relentless, pulsating pain that mirrored his racing heart. It wasn't just physical pain; it was a manifestation of the stress that clung to him like a second skin. Each step he took away from the hospital felt heavy, laden with a mix of relief and a deep-seated unease that settled in his stomach. He could barely focus as DSI Carmichael drove them back to the station, and he didn't even step inside once they arrived. He made an excuse and left immediately, but he didn't go home.

Instead, Lucas navigated the dilapidated and desolate city streets towards his father's warden-controlled flat, his mind racing with conflicting emotions. The chilly winter air and bullet-like rain did little to ease the tightness in his chest. Memories flooded back—the news of his mother's murder, his father's downward spiral into alcoholism, and the chasm it created between them. He remembered the echo of his father's voice, once solid and reassuring, now often slurred and distant. Lucas's footsteps echoed on the pavement, as they did in his nightmares, as he headed back to a man he barely recognised as his father.

The flat, nestled in a neglected corner of the city, was as grim as ever. He only came back once a month, if he did at all. Frankly, why the hell should he? He hesitated at the door, taking a moment to brace himself.

Inside, the air was stale, thick with the scent of unwashed linen and old alcohol. His father sat hunched on a worn-out sofa, and his eyes were cloudy and vacant. Tremors shook his hands as he reached for a glass, unsteady and uncertain. The TV flickered in the background, casting a ghostly glow on his father's face, deepening the lines of age and ruin. Lucas observed his surroundings, and a slight pang of pity momentarily flickered through him. Lucas cleared his throat, breaking the silence.

'Dad, it's me,'

His father looked up, squinting as if trying to place the face before him. 'Lucas?' His voice was a hoarse whisper, a shadow of its former strength. 'Come for your annual visit?'

The conversation was stilted, strained by years of distance and disappointment. Lucas struggled to find words that wouldn't betray his true intent for visiting. He asked perfunctory questions about his father's health, each answer more disheartening than the last. Inwardly, Lucas battled with guilt. He was here under the guise of concern, but his eyes darted to the medicine cabinet. The knowledge of what he planned to do weighed heavily on him, yet his desperation for the pregabalin overshadowed his conscience. Also, it was his father's fault he even needed the bloody pregabalin.

Lucas seized his chance as his father turned momentarily

to the flickering TV. He quietly rummaged through the medicine cabinet, his fingers closing around the familiar box of medicine. He took a couple of strips and left the rest, as they'd stop giving it to his father if he kept losing it. The act was swift, almost mechanical. Lucas felt a surge of relief mixed with a nauseating sense of betrayal. He tucked the blister packs away, hidden from sight, his heart pounding in his ears.

With a hurried goodbye, Lucas left the flat. The dreary afternoon air felt colder now, biting at his skin. As he walked away, the burden of what he had done settled in as usual. The drugs in his pocket were a temporary solution, a fleeting escape from his problems. But the look in his father's eyes, that mix of confusion and faint recognition, would be more challenging to escape.

* * *

'So I was like, really? Him? Tasha could do so much better than Mike, don't you think?'

'Huh?' said Lucas, struggling to remain engaged in Ems's conversation.

'Tasha, she's pretty. Mike's well... not,' Em continued, somewhat oblivious to the fact that Lucas was glazing over.

'Yeah, might be a nice bloke, though,' he said flippantly, not fully engaging.

'Well, yeah, but she's twenty-four; she's not after a nice bloke yet,' she said in a way that suggested it should have been obvious.

'Seems daft to me,' he muttered.

Lucas didn't give a fuck if he was honest. Em had come round after he'd explained how shit his day had been, ostensibly to make him feel better, but she wasn't doing an excellent job of it. Why they were talking about some girl from the mortuary reception desk that he'd never met before when he'd just witnessed someone die in front of him, he wasn't quite sure. He'd been feeling the age gap between him and Em more recently. The idea of a bendy twenty-five-year-old with caramel skin and long dark hair seemed appealing at first, but right now, a more emotionally intelligent woman his own age would be just perfect. Preferably still bendy, though, he thought.

'Anyway, I said to her, why are you wasting your time with Mike? You're too good for him, and then she just kind of stormed off.'

'Did she say why?' he said, now scraping little bits of dirt out from under his fingernails with a penknife. It was much more engaging.

'Apparently, it's none of my business. She thinks I'm jealous, which is ridiculous. He's not my type. He's way too old.'

'How old?'

'I dunno, like thirty-eight? Thirty-nine?'

'That's not very old.'

'Yeah, but I've never gone for guys older than me.'

'I'm thirty-four?' said Lucas flatly, looking up at her.

'But you're different,' she said, turning to him and putting her arms around his neck.

'Am I? How?'

'Because... well, you're just... you. I don't know,'

'Is this an age thing or an older guy thing?'

'I don't know'

'I mean, is it that you don't like older guys, or are you worried you're not as mature as them? Is it an ego thing?' probed Lucas, removing Ems's hands from his shoulders and moving over to the sink. The large cut on his hand was healing well, but was still incredibly sore. His arm was feeling much better, though.

'I guess I always thought older men would want a woman who was, y'know, more grown up,' said Em, looking at the back of his head. Lucas didn't respond, but honestly, he didn't need to; Em was off talking to herself or the wall again. Luna was lying on the floor, splayed out like she'd been dropped from a great height. Her little grey snout snuffled occasionally, and her pink belly rose and fell softly. She'd listen to him, and she'd comfort him. It was amazing, he thought, looking at the little dog on the floor, that they'd never had a proper two-way conversation. They communicated alright, but never a conversation, and yet he thought she probably knew him best. She was the one who was there all the time.

In fairness to Em, she was a pretty superb cook. The pasta Bolognese she'd made was tasty and drastically improved his mood, but it was all for nothing when they had their big argument. Given the day's events, Lucas wasn't exactly in the mood for anything more physical tonight, which upset Em. This was then compounded by the fact he tried to bring Luna to bed with him for a cuddle, despite *'knowing'* that Em couldn't sleep with her in the bed. He was going to give in and take the dog back downstairs, but with one look into those huge brown orbs, he knew where his heart was.

'It's me or the bloody dog, Lucas!' shouted Em, pointing at the door.

'Oh, don't be so fucking daft, Em, it's one night,' he scoffed. 'I saw a woman die this morning, and I just want a cuddle with Luna.'

'It's the principle!' She was growing more petulant. Her angular facial features became harsh and aggressive when angry, which didn't suit her. 'You've seen lots of dead bodies. Why is this one any different?'

'I watched her die, Em; how are you not getting this? Right, look, perhaps you should go tonight. We'll sort this out in the morning?' said Lucas, trying to remain calm.

'Oh, so you're chucking me out? You're choosing the dog over me?' she shrieked, tears welling in her eyes.

'I'm not chucking you out! I just want the dog in the bed tonight because I've had a rough-'

'So yeah, the dog. Over me. Great.' She grabbed her bag off the floor.

'Oh, grow up.'

'I grow up? You're the one desperate for cuddles with some stupid-'

'Don't you even fucking think about finishing that sentence! Luna was here before you, and she will bloody well be here after you!'

'No, she fucking won't! Look at her; she'll be dead in a month,' spat Em, who immediately regretted the words as they fell from her mouth.

'Out! Now! Get out of my fucking house!' Lucas was seeing red. He'd lost his composure completely.

'OK, look, I'm so-' she said, backtracking, but it was too late. She'd done it.

'Out!' he yelled at the top of his voice, which boomed around his apartment. Em looked startled. She hadn't imagined he'd genuinely kick her out. She was so used to getting her way. He didn't back down. Picking her bag off the floor and her keys off the table, he thrust them into her hands and marched her to the front door. He opened it and stood there, like a doorman, waiting for Em to leave. She was crying as she made her way out the front door.

She turned and said, 'I'm sorry, I shouldn't have said that about Luna.'

'No. You shouldn't. We'll talk tomorrow, but I've not got the head for it now. Text me when you're home safe,' said Lucas, seething but somehow maintaining some composure.

She left, and he closed the door, resting his head against the cool PVC. A softness ran against his calf, and he looked down to see Luna grinning up at him, her thin tail wagging as fast as it could. He reached down and scratched her behind the ear. She leaned into it and let out a soft sigh. He scooped her up and held her in his arms like a furry baby. There was no resistance; she sat there comfortably, and he kissed the white spot on her forehead.

'Come on. Don't look at me like that. Of course, I was always going to choose you.'

2016

42

The question on the public's lips was 'who?'. Who had just been murdered? Who was the killer? Who would be next? At this point, perspective comes into play. If you were Lucas and the rest of the Water's Edge Reaper Task Force, learning the identification of this seventh victim was reasonably straightforward. Unfortunately, if you were the father of Sophia Sidorova, there was nothing remotely easy about being informed that they'd just discovered the defiled and mutilated corpse of your daughter in her tent. She and a group of friends had been attending the famous 'Leeds Festival' held in Bramham Park this past weekend. The weather had held out, and they'd enjoyed music from bands such as Biffy Clyro, The 1975, and her personal favourite, Imagine Dragons. Unfortunately, it wasn't yet clear if she had been murdered before, during, or after they'd performed their headline set.

Lucas was behind the wheel as he hated being driven, and the team was quiet. Nobody could believe what was happening.

'Fuck,' said Chloe out of the blue whilst deep in thought.

'You can say that again,' Lucas said.

42

'Fuck.' They both laughed grimly. She was still a little off with him, but this latest setback had made her forget about it for the time being.

Again, perspective. A young girl was dead, and her best friend would forever have to live with the memory of the mutilated corpse she'd discovered in her tent. Added to that, her murderer and the murderer of six others was still at large.

DC Hancock searched the internet on an iPad in the back of the car. 'If this girl, Sophia, is another Reaper case, boss, she's not being followed by our guy. As far as I can tell, she doesn't even have Twitter.'

'Check for other socials; she has something, surely. That's how he selects them. I can feel it,'

'It's just not here, boss.'

'Check Instagram, check Snapchat, check Facebook, fuck it, check Myspace and Bebo if they still exist. I want everything. If he's got her on something, I want to know what.'

'Yes, boss.'

'What was it you were saying?' Lucas asked after a few moments.

'Huh?' replied Chloe

'Back at the office, you were telling everyone about the Twitter handle @whatever-the-fuck-it-is'

'I wasn't. It was DC Sterling.' she said coolly, tightening her ponytail more firmly than could have been comfortable. 'But as it happens, I have been trying to find out what the handle refers to.'

'And?' he said, ignoring his mix-up and hoping he hadn't just taken them two steps backwards.

'I still need to figure it out. It doesn't appear to mean anything. I think he must have just hammered the keyboard when creating it.'

'OK, keep on it. What else do you have?'

'Nothing much. They're good at covering their tracks. I've spoken to Darren in Digital Forensics, and they can't pinpoint their IP address, and the phone numbers on the accounts are unregistered pay-as-you-go burners. Feels like we're heading down a dead end again.'

'No, we're being *led* down to a dead end. Someone's taking the piss out of us,' said Lucas grimly as he took a left and pulled into the park entrance.

An irritatingly handsome young man with an orange jacket pointed them up the drive and into the car park. There was rubbish everywhere, and sheets of newspaper were floating about in the breeze. Random bits of tent were caught against fence posts, and there was very little intact grass to note, just sludge. A few of the festival marquees were still visible across the muddy plains, but they were being dismantled at that very moment by somewhat shaken-looking staff. Only a day earlier, the place had been filled with thousands of young adults drinking, taking drugs, and, frankly, having a great time. Now it was filled with police officers, the press, and a forensic team.

'Let's go.' Lucas sighed. They got out of the car, put on the disposable white suits and headed over to where the body had been found, just up the hill. A small group of officers were standing in front of a taped-off area, talking amongst themselves, and they didn't notice Lucas and the team as they arrived. Lucas had to cough to get their attention.

'Oh, shit, sorry, sir. Didn't see you there,' said the first officer, a young woman who looked very nervous.

'It's alright, I'm not a ghost. Have we had any of the

pathologists down yet?'

'Yes, sir, they're just over there.'

She pointed towards a small orange tent, barely big enough for one person, which Lucas knew from the brief had housed three teenagers over the last weekend. Cosy.

The body of Sophia Sidorova had been pulled from the tent and was lying next to its entrance on a tarpaulin sheet. Lucas and Chloe saw three figures bending over the body, also dressed in white plastic coveralls and gloves.

'I'll get started then, shall I?' said Chloe glumly.

'Sure, I'll join you in a minute; I just want to take a look around first,' replied Lucas. He turned and surveyed the surroundings. It was barren and exposed, but yesterday, when they suspected this had happened, the whole place would have been teeming with people and tents. It might have been the perfect camouflage. There would be little chance of them securing anything like footprints or even properly defining the boundaries of the crime scene. It was too vast, and too much footfall had occurred, even in this short space of time. He looked over the crest of the hill where he could see them taking down The Main Stage and hoped that Sophia had at least got to see her favourite band play.

Lucas wandered back over to Chloe and DC Hancock, who were talking to the people in white suits. The grass was soft and wet, and it was difficult not to slip in the thick brown dirt. The white suits made it tricky to discern who was who, but the lanky figure of Dr Cross, leaning down over a victim, was becoming all too familiar now. Lucas realised that the slightly plumper and more feminine figure next to him was that of Dr Cooper, a pathologist with whom he much preferred to work. As he approached, Dr Cross looked up, his face obscured by a mask.

'I think you know what I'm going to say,' he drawled.

'Fucking hell. He's done it again?' said Lucas sarcastically.

'It looks that way. The usual similarities.' He was pointed down at the pale, waxy body of the young girl who had been pulled from the tent and was sprawled out across an enormous sheet of blue tarpaulin. She was bigger than the previous victims, certainly not fat, but noticeably more curvy than his usual type. She was naked, apart from a single sock on her right foot and her festival bracelet, which was still strapped to her left wrist. Lividity has caused her back to turn purple, but she was too fresh to begin bloating. She did almost look as if she was sleeping, or at least she would have done had it not been for the dry blood she was caked in and the gigantic open wound across her lower abdomen. He'd been expecting it for months.

The gaping black hole carved into her belly was so unsettling. It had been commented on frequently before about how he could even view the bodies of these young women, given what had happened to his mother, but he maintained it was different. He'd never seen his mother's body, only heard about it, so that helped. In truth, he suspected there was something wrong with him, a screw loose, but the way these bodies made him feel... well, they didn't make him feel, not anymore.

Dr Cooper spoke, lifting the mask from her face to reveal her soft, round features. 'Hi Lucas, Hi Chloe. Good to see you both.'

'Same wounds?' asked Chloe, rubbing some odour balm under her nostrils after receiving a waft of something rancid from the tent.

42

'She's been tortured, just like the rest, albeit briefly in this case. She was repeatedly strangled and stabbed at least four times in the abdomen. Her bladder is gone; I can see through the wound. Blood loss is significant.' An assistant, who had continued photographing the body whilst Dr Cooper spoke, reached across and opened the tent so Lucas could see inside. The unmistakable stench of iron and warm blood hit him like a train, catching the back of his throat.

'Give me some of that,' he said, reaching out for Chloe's *Odour Balm*. It was quite literally a bloodbath, as it had pooled in the centre, where a divot was in the ground.

'The ligature mark around the neck is thinner than usual, so I suspect it's a different rope he's used. We'll know more once we get her back to the morgue,' continued Dr Cooper.

'How long has she been here?' said Chloe, looking into the bleak distance, her long hair rippling in the breeze.

'Fresh. Killed overnight. No more than twelve hours, I reckon. She's fairly stiff.' Dr Cross tugged on one of her arms to confirm.

'Is there always this much blood?' whimpered DC Hancock, who hadn't said a word until this point.

Lucas was about to answer, but stopped. He was right; there wasn't typically this much blood.

'No. There isn't,' he said after a few seconds. 'He usually takes them and tortures them over a few hours somewhere else before bringing them to the disposal site and finishing them off there. He's not done that this time.'

'He hasn't,' said Dr Cooper as Dr Cross squatted down and started doing something to the body. 'The whole attack took place in that tent. This wasn't even inside the wound this time, but just thrown at her, I think.' She held up the familiar small glass vial soaked in blood. She opened up and unfurled the paper with her gloved hands, although Lucas didn't need her to. He knew what was written on it, in that swirly writing, before she read it aloud.

The bladder, a keeper of the deep, holds the waters where dreams may seep,
A vessel for the liquid night, releasing tales by moonlight's right.

Lucas and Chloe turned away and started looking around. The tent was on the edge of the field, at most twenty yards to the wall and woodland beyond. Lucas was trying to see the path leading away from the body in his mind's eye.

'If he'd planned this, he could have taken her into the woods. I think this was spontaneous. Do you think he couldn't risk taking her out of the tent in case he was seen?' Lucas said out loud to nobody in particular. Chloe was looking down at the woodland as well.

'I wonder if he was hiding in there, waiting for someone to be left alone. It could have been any girl, in any tent this side of the field,' she said, speaking slowly and carefully. 'It's incredibly risky. He doesn't normally take chances like this. Why has he broken his pattern, do you think?'

'Maybe we've forced him to? If he knows about our discovery of his Twitter profile but is desperate to kill again, this might have just been opportunistic.'

'I don't think you just pass a massive music festival. Do you think he was attending? He might have been working here?' said Dr Cooper, trying to be helpful. Lucas had a strange feeling. The woods, the tents, the girl. Something was off.

42

'This is the first time I've been to one of these scenes and felt like it was random. It's almost too random, deliberately so. Like I said earlier, someone is fucking with us. I feel like it's been staged,' he said pensively.

'Staged?' said DC Hancock

'It's brazen, different enough that we might start looking elsewhere. But it's eye-catching. He knew she'd be discovered quickly in the tent, so he's not dragged this one out. I don't think he's enjoyed this one as much. I think he's been forced into another murder. This is for our benefit. Everything is so... deliberately chaotic,' mused Lucas, patrolling the tent and the tarpaulin with Sophia's body sprawled across it.

'I see what you mean,' said Chloe, 'but it might be a premature leap. Vicky Turner was killed behind the big Tesco; that scene wasn't too dissimilar to this. Blood everywhere, the body tied to a bin. Not exactly subtle.'

'No, but she'd still been taken and tortured off-site. Even if it had only been for a few hours. This is staged. I don't know what it is, but something about this isn't right. It's too conveniently different.'

Dr Cross finished whatever he'd been doing to Sophia and stood up, nodding at Dr Cooper.

'We're going to take her to the morgue. We'll have some more news for you in the morning once we've done the autopsy. I'll let you know as soon as possible if anything important comes up. Although now you're *acting* DI, it might be prudent actually to attend the autopsy?' he said, a condescending stare directed at Lucas.

'Yes, well. Maybe,' said Lucas dismissively. Dr Cross puffed his cheeks out, looked mildly more irritated than usual and headed back towards the forensic truck nearby with Dr Cooper. Lucas and Chloe turned in the sloppy earth and ambled back to the car, neither of them talking, whilst DC Hancock followed, looking green.

Lucas was getting a thrill from this one. It was different, and it might hold clues vital to the case. His mind was racing, and he thought about the fields, the tent, the blood, the knife, the killer. The only thing that didn't cross his mind was how the father of Sophia Sidorova must be feeling right now.

43

As they reached the car, Lucas's hand paused on the door handle, and he looked around at the fields surrounding them. Hundreds of people were here; surely someone had seen or heard something? They'd had unprecedented bad luck with witnesses in this case.

'Who found the body?'

'They did,' said DC Hancock, pointing across the mud to a police car about fifty yards away. A uniformed officer stood handing out little cups of tea to two very shaken-looking people, one male and one female. The male was dressed in shorts and a T-shirt, as opposed to the girl, who was wearing tight leather trousers, wellies and an oversized white shirt caked in mud and blood. Both of them were covered by a standard police issue comforting blanket. Stupid thing to be wearing at a festival, thought Lucas, who headed across the field, trying not to slip on the wet ground.

'Hello, I'm Detective Inspector Lucas Miller.' The couple looked up, dazed. Both had obviously been crying.

'Sophia is dead,' said the young man, more of as a statement than a question.

'Yes, I'm so sorry. What are your names?' said Lucas.

'I'm Danny; this is Leah. I still can't believe it.'

'Me either. We all came here together. She's one of my best friends; we were at university together,' said Leah. Her voice cracking, and Lucas could see that she was about to cry again.

'I'm very sorry. This must be very difficult, but it would be a big help if you could tell me what happened?'

'We didn't do anything, if that's what you mean. I swear. I had no idea,' said Danny.

'No, I know you didn't. But it will help us find out what happened here if we get a full picture of how the weekend went.'

'Right. Well, we came here on Friday morning. There was me, clearly and er... Leah, two others called Ojo and Jess and Sophia as well. It's been a good festival, with lots of drinking out in the arena each night. You know,' he shrugged as he finished, clearly bereft of ideas.

'Did you have a tent?' asked Chloe, who had just appeared beside Lucas, startling him a little. 'Sorry, I'm Detective Wilson,' she added.

'Yeah, but we only used it for sleeping. The three girls were in one, and me and Ojo shared another.'

'When did you last see Sophia?' said Lucas

'Last night. She left about halfway through the Chilli Peppers set and said she was unwell. We didn't go with her, because she told us not to. When we got back about half four in the morning, I went to see if she was alright and... and...' he just raised an arm softly and gesticulated at the tent in the distance, tears forming in his eyes.

'Thank you. I appreciate how hard this must be. Had she taken anything?' said Chloe. Danny and Leah glanced at each other, and he hesitated.

'Yes,' said Leah. 'She'd taken pills. We all brought our own stuff for the weekend, but Sophia bought some here.'

'Proper creepy bloke him,' muttered Danny.

'What do you mean by that?' said Chloe.

'Oh, I just mean, the guy she bought them off had been hanging around our tents all weekend, trying to sell stuff. He was odd; he only really wanted to sell it to the girls because Ojo tried to get some, and he wouldn't sell it.' Danny said, going pink. 'Don't judge us, please; everyone here's doing it.'

'Don't worry, a few pills are not our concern here,' said Lucas. 'But I want to know more about this bloke. What did he look like?'

'He was older, like forties or something, and he worked here, or at least he had one of the high-vis vests on. He was about as tall as you, I think?' said Leah, looking over at Danny, who was probably about six-foot-two. 'And he had bright red hair,' she added as an afterthought.

Lucas could feel his pulse quicken. There was something in this. He could feel it.

'That's great. When you say hanging about, where did you see him?'

'Oh, he moved in between the tents, you know, just kept appearing,' said Danny.

'Actually, no, I saw him watching us from over there,' said Leah, pointing to the little woodland that Lucas had noticed earlier. 'He went there to smoke. You could see the fag lighting up. Creeped me and Sophia out.'

Lucas' heart was beating faster now, and he felt a sense of excitement. This was more like it!

'Thank you both. I am really sorry about what happened. You've been incredibly helpful. If you think of anything else, please let us know.' Lucas handed over his card. 'DC Hancock will get someone to take your details and drop you back home.'

Together, he and Chloe started trudging back towards the car for the second time today. As they walked past the pathologists and forensic team, sliding Sophia into the back of an ambulance, he looked once more at the little stone wall and woodland beyond. Little people in white suits were scouring the opening to the woodland. He wandered over to them, dragging a somewhat irritated Chloe with him.

'Hey guys,' he bellowed, and one of the white suits turned to face him. A hairy man, whom Lucas knew as Darren, waved back.

'DI Miller, how are we? Congratulations on the promotion, well deserved,' he said, and Lucas could feel Chloe physically tense next to him.

'Ah, yes, thanks. As well as can be expected, given the circumstances,'

'Aye, it's all a bit shit this, isn't it?' said Darren, placing his gloved hands on his hips. 'Not found much, but for a few empty cans and fags, etc. The usual detritus, really.'

'There's a ginger bloke been seen hanging about here. We're going to take an interest in him. Seen smoking, selling drugs and wearing one of the hi-vis jackets the staff were given,' said Lucas.

'Oh, well, you might be interested in this then,' and Darren sifted through a grey box on the floor full of plastic bags. He pulled one out and showed it to Lucas. It contained a dirty orange high-vis jacket. Lucas turned it over in his hand, and

43

the world stopped briefly. There it was. On the lower back part of the jacket was a small red blood stain. Lucas's heart skipped another beat. They had something.

44

Lucas woke up at around 4 am, sweating. He'd dreamt he was in a tent, the same tent where the young girl's body had been discovered. A knife was in his hand, and he'd had her tied up. He'd stabbed her and cut her over and over and over. Blood pumping, splashing everywhere. He'd slipped in it, his face smeared as he kept stabbing and stabbing. Music was pumping in the background, the bass reverberating through him as he was filled with a feeling of euphoria, the sense of being in total control; the power was incredible. It felt so good.

And then he'd woken up, terrified, drenched in sweat. He couldn't get back to sleep after that, so he'd left Chloe in the bed, showered, dressed and headed into the station to get a head start. He'd left a note, hoping she didn't mind that he hadn't woken her.

He arrived at about ten past six to find the office eerily quiet. Only a couple of other people were milling about, drinking coffee and looking at computer screens.

Coffee was a good idea, so he re-boiled the kettle and made himself a cheap instant coffee, which tasted like rats piss, and sat at his desk. There was a folder on it, which contained all the information they had on the person behind their mysterious Twitter handle. They'd put together a profile, but there was little to go on. It was the usual stuff. The person had set up the account in 2010 and they'd used an email address from a Gmail account that matched the handle. There were no clues to their identity. They'd sent no message, never tweeted, and hadn't done anything other than follow six of the seven victims and a host of British news outlets. None of the IP addresses they'd traced had yielded anything, and they couldn't pinpoint the account owner's exact location because of a sophisticated VPN. They didn't have the power or the resources to hack into Gmail or learn more about the person behind the account. It was frustrating. He'd have a chat with Carmichael. They'd need more people working on it, and he'd want to have a word with the digital forensics department and see what they could come up with.

Chloe arrived a few hours later in a similar state of dishevelment to the previous morning.

'Good morning,' she said, yawning and stretching up at the ceiling.

'Good morning. I hope you don't mind that I didn't want to wake you. I had a shit night's sleep,'

'Don't worry about it. You look shattered. Do you want me to get you a coffee?'

'I need something stronger than the muck I've just had from the tin. I'll get us something from the canteen.'

'No, it's OK, I'm up, I'll get it.' She left her jacket over the back of the chair and walked to the door. She had a pleasant walk, and her tight professional trousers today did a lot for her. Lucas wasn't a bad-looking bloke, but he could never see why someone like Chloe would go for someone like him. She returned a few minutes later with steaming cups of coffee, which tasted worlds apart from whatever the fuck he'd drunk earlier. Chloe put the coffee on the desk and started talking.

'I've tracked down a few people in neighbouring tents to Sophia. Bloody arduous work, actually; people don't get specific spaces for these things. They get an allocated field, but hundreds of people are in each field. However, a group of girls I spoke to recalled a creepy red-headed bloke trying to sell them drugs. Sounds like it's our man.'

'Oh wow. Good work. We still need to find out his name; do we know who he is?'

'We don't have a name, no. She didn't recognise him, and I don't know if he's connected, but there's something about it. I've contacted the organisers of the festival to see if he was genuinely employed or not. They might have something on him.' She took a sip of coffee, and as she did so, the phone on Lucas's desk buzzed, and then a little notification popped up on the screen. A text from Dr Cross, blunt, direct and typical of the bloke.

Bothering?

He groaned loudly. This was not something he wanted to do.
'You still up for coming with me to the autopsy?'

* * *

Dr Cross had expected Lucas to drag his heels in a bit and make an issue of coming to the show, so he wasn't ready when he and Chloe arrived promptly.

'Lucas, you made it. How wonderful.'

'Oh fuck off, Cross, you know I hate these things.'

'I do, but you might learn something from watching me,' he smirked. 'You look knackered. Is everything OK?'

'Yeah, just not sleeping. Come on, let's get this sodding thing over with.'

'I just need to change, but you can wait in there. I'll ask Emily to set up the room and fetch the stiff so we can get started as soon as possible.'

They moved into the viewing gallery and waited for Dr Cross to change. A girl was on the other side of the partition, setting everything up. One of the new mortuary assistants, he guessed. She was exceedingly pretty, thought Lucas, with her deep caramel complexion, endless legs, and long dark hair, which she'd tied up. She hummed to herself as she got out the nasty-looking selection of blades and pointy things.

'Nice, is she?'

Lucas's head nearly fell off because of the speed at which he swivelled it around to face Chloe. 'Huh, oh, no, I was er...'

'Perving?' She didn't look impressed, not at all, in fact.

'No, I just hadn't seen her before, is all,' he stuttered, his palms becoming greasy.

'Bit young for you anyway,' she said, her voice bitter, like she was trying to swallow a lemon.

'Don't be silly, I wasn't...'

'Yeah, save it, Lucas. I don't care.' As he was thinking of the ensuing argument, something which was slowly becoming a bit too frequent for his liking, Dr Cross emerged to get on with the autopsy. Probably for the best, he didn't have a leg to stand on. He'd been perving, got caught, and was now embarrassed and defensive. He'd have to make it up to Chloe later.

There was a certain irony and discomfort in watching someone get sliced apart whilst sitting next to women who almost certainly wanted to do the same to you. The young assistant, who'd now introduced herself as Emily, was taking notes and occasionally asking Dr Cross questions about the process. He also seemed to be enjoying her company. Lucas felt somewhat unwell throughout most of the dissection, but the part where he took an electric saw opened the top of the skull and removed her brain nearly made him go. However, it was just about worthwhile in the end, as they confirmed that it was likely the same killer. She was stabbed six times in the abdomen, perforating both the small and large intestines. The bladder had been removed as suspected, along with half of the left ureter, which had snapped as it was pulled out. Asphyxiation was once again suggested by petechiae around the mouth and eyes, as well as clear ligature marks on the neck and a fractured hyoid bone. Dr Cross couldn't be sure if Sophia had been raped, although it was likely from evidence of some lubricant inside the vagina that she may well have been sexually active that weekend. They sent some toxicology samples away yesterday, directly from the scene, and these returned findings consistent with intoxication from multiple substances. She had a very high blood alcohol content but also traces of ketamine, cocaine, procaine and something called levamisole. This was a drug used for worming sheep but was commonly used to cut cocaine and ketamine, apparently, and Dr Cross certainly didn't seem shocked or perturbed by its presence. But what had clinched it for Lucas was the discovery of some hair under her fingernails, which appeared to have been torn from someone's head. They were bright ginger.

Lucas took this bit of information back to the team, who weren't as excited as he was, unfortunately.

'OK, but does the DNA match the samples found on the other bodies? I mean, she might have just got laid with some ginger nut before she was killed,' said DS Khan.

'True, but she tore it out, and our bloke was noted for being offensively ginger. So I think it's safe to say it's suspicious.'

Nobody else seemed to think that this lead was as monumentally vital as he did. They all accepted that the mysterious red-headed man was a person of interest and a good lead, but they all seemed prepared for it to be a dead end. They were jaded, thought Lucas, who had a different outlook.

'OK, well, it's a start,' he said, sounding a bit like the boss he was supposed to be. 'I want you to chase up the organisers. Chloe has already been in contact. We need to find this bloke, and it's a matter of urgency.'

'They emailed back about 30 minutes ago, Lucas, ' Chloe said suddenly from behind her desk. I'm going through the ID cards now.' She was clearly still hostile towards him. He'd tried apologising, and he'd tried reassuring her that she was all he wanted. But nothing was diffusing the situation. He leaned over her shoulder to see the PDF file she was searching through, and she shifted away from him deliberately. It contained all the documentation for people employed at the festival, including their ID card photo. She scrolled past person after person, nobody meeting their description, until... there.

Bright red hair, glowing almost. You'd have recognised it even if the picture was black and white. Thomas Mitchel, thirty-nine years old. He looked older, with a wrinkled forehead and hollowed-out eyes. It had an address underneath. Lucas squeezed Chloe's shoulders, and she tensed immediately.

'Brilliant work! Let's go.'

45

Thomas Mitchel was the true embodiment of 'ugly as fuck'. Nasty hollow eyes, crusty, dry skin. His breath reeked of something rotten, which was possibly his teeth, half of which were missing, and the other half were brown stumps. They had picked him up while renovating one of the swanky bars near the canal where Thomas Mitchel was working as a construction apprentice, a job that should have been beneath him on paper. He may look and sound thick, but that resulted from years of sniffing glue or whatever it was he did. He'd got himself some A-levels and had even started a degree in English Literature at the University of Central Lancashire. That was years ago now.

They'd taken him back to the station under protest from Mitchel and his boss. Lucas was now sitting opposite him in his favourite, uncomfortably hot, claustrophobic interview room three, dazzled by the sheer repellent nature of his face. His voice wasn't any better, as he was from Manchester for a start. He was on his own, no solicitor. Legally, he didn't have to have one, as it was technically a voluntary interview. They may have dragged him from work but hadn't arrested him. Of course, if the idiot requested one, they'd have to stop, but until then, he was fair game. It was time to warm him up; there's no need to press the record button just yet.

'What's wrong with having a part-time job, mate?' he said, his voice nasally like he had a horrible cold.

'Nothing. Working as a litter picker for Leeds Fest is a noble thing to do, Thomas. Or are we talking about you selling class-A drugs cut with brick dust and worming tablets to young girls? Which part-time job are we talking about here?' Lucas wasn't in the mood to mess about.

'Woah, calm down, mate. I don't know what you're talking about. I've never done drugs myself.'

'You were kicked out of university for selling weed on campus. Your nose is ready to collapse, and I can see the track marks up your arms,' said Lucas without blinking.

'Ah, yes. Well. Fair enough, pal, you got me. But I wasn't selling drugs at the festival.'

'Fair enough. If you say so. The problem is, we have your DNA on a high-visibility jacket we found caked in drugs, we have witnesses to you selling said drugs, and we have CCTV footage of you selling them.' Very little of this was true, and he was in breach of the law by saying this. But he reasoned Thomas Mitchel was too raddled by drugs to know this, and it might scare him into telling them something useful. It looked like it was working because he had gone paler and his smug expression had dropped considerably.

'I didn't know they had CCTV there. It's a field...' he said.

'On the telegraph poles' lied Lucas. He could see the cogs turning in Mitchel's skull. They dropped into place one by one, and he began to sing.

'OK, so yeah, I sold some drugs. Bit of money. I didn't hurt anyone.'

'We have a dead body,' said Lucas grimly.

'Hang on now, I... I.. don't know anything about a dead body!' there was a palpable panic in his voice now. This was the time to pounce. Lucas turned on the tape recorder.

'Thomas Mitchel, you are being interviewed regarding the recent discovery of a body in Bramham Park on Monday 26th August.'

'I didn't kill anybody!'

'Do you know this woman?' Lucas swivelled a picture of Sophia Sidorova and passed it across the table. She looked lovely in the picture, smiling and laughing. It had been taken on a recent holiday, and her mother had given it to them when they'd gone to break the news. He hated that part of the job and had hoped to shift it to someone else when he made DI, but he'd ended up being there, anyway. It was an anguished, hopeless wail that the mothers did that really got to him.

In all fairness to Mitchel, he genuinely looked at the picture, unlike many guests Lucas had at this table. His eyes widened as he stared into her eyes, and his head drooped.

'Yeah,' he muttered.

'And how do you know her?'

'I don't know her, really. But we had sex at the festival,' he mumbled. Lucas hadn't been expecting this revelation and was rather knocked off his stride. He was thinking he might admit to selling her drugs at most. To say that Sophia could have done better was such a significant overstatement that it was almost funny. Except it wasn't because she was dead.

'In what world, Thomas Mitchel, do you want me to believe that she willingly had sex with you?'

'Er... she wanted some more ketamine, but she didn't have any money. We got talking, she's studying English at –'

'Did she pay you for drugs with sex, Thomas?' interrupted Lucas.

'No, she –'

'Come on,' interrupted Lucas again. This time, rather than argue, Thomas Mitchel stared at the ground. Lucas let him sit in silence for a few seconds.

'Yes. OK. I'm not proud, but I said I'd give it to her for... er... a go,' he shrugged as if this was common, which, unfortunately, it probably was. It would also explain Sophia's likely recent sexual intercourse that Dr Cross had told them about.

'Right, and what time was this?'

'I don't know, do I? Probably about two in the morning?'

'OK, and how long after this did you kill her?' said Lucas casually.

'No, I didn't do that. She was fine when I left. Like, she was high from drugs but not dead,' he shifted uncomfortably in his seat and pulled at his shirt collar.

'Right, so you popped into her tent, gave her some drugs, had sex with her with your silly little high-vis jacket on, and left. Is that what we're saying?' sneered Lucas.

'Yeah. Except, I didn't have the jacket on. I'd given that to the man in the woods,' said Mitchel, stopping Lucas dead in his tracks.

'Man in the woods?'

'Yeah, I don't know who he was. Tall man. I thought he would buy some gear, but he wanted my jacket. He was there when I... you know... went into her tent. He'll tell you I didn't kill her.' He finished the sentence slightly excitedly. Lucas's mind was whizzing.

'Tell me more about him; what did he look like and sound like?' he said hurriedly.

'I didn't really talk to him. He was tall, and he was white.' Mitchel finished with another vague shrug. Lucas quickly began to lose faith in this story as he thought about it.

'Sounds like a load of bollocks, Thomas,' he said. 'You sold her the ket, raped her and killed her, didn't you?'

'No! It's just like I said. Ask that tall man, and he'll back me up.'

'I don't believe there is a tall man, Thomas,' said Lucas.

'There is!' said Mitchel. 'Where's my solicitor?'

Bugger.

* * *

'Water's Edge Reaper' Investigation Continues After Release of Suspect
Simon Davies, Crime Correspondent

The police investigation into the ongoing 'Water's Edge Reaper' case continues, despite the release of a suspect who was arrested in connection with the latest murder.

The body of Sophia Sidorova, 17, was found in her tent at the Leeds Festival on August 26th. She had been stabbed multiple times, and her body was left for her friends to find.

Police arrested a 39-year-old man, Thomas Mitchel, on suspi-

cion of murder. Mitchel is an electrical apprentice previously known to police for a string of petty crimes. He was supposedly volunteering at the festival, but multiple eyewitnesses say he was selling drugs to festival-goers.

The 'Water's Edge Reaper' has been killing young women in the Leeds area for the past five years and is one of the most high-profile serial killer cases in the UK. The case has attracted national attention, and it has left the community living in fear that he will not stop at the seven women he has already killed. Police have been unable to catch him and are appealing for any information.

2023

46

Even by Yorkshire's standards, it was bitterly cold today. Lucas felt slightly smug as he drove in, clutching his heated steering wheel. This feeling vanished when he slipped on a patch of ice as he stepped out of the car and slammed his cut hand down on the pavement. It was only witnessed by a handful of fellow coppers who laughed at him, not with him.

When he got to his desk, the gash on his hand was actively throbbing, and rubbing it wasn't helping. He was searching through his pockets for the blister pack when DS Kim Sterling flashed him one of her smiles, and his mood improved immeasurably. Lucas thought everyone looked better when they smiled, but it's even better when you think they're genuinely pleased to see you. She got up from her desk and worked her way around to his.

'How are you? After yesterday?' she asked kindly.

'I'm OK, thanks. A bit of a shock. You don't expect just to watch someone die like that.'

'I can't imagine. My granny had one of those do-not-resuscitate things when she went to the hospital. I think it was the best thing my dad did for her. Horrible way to go.'

'Yeah, it wasn't nice. It was the smell... Sorry,' he paused and caught DS Sterling's eye. She wasn't judging him. 'Plus, I think she had a lot more to tell us. All we know is he's tall and balding, which could be half the male population, frankly. It's half the blokes in this station, for fuck's sake.'

'Neither of which fit PC Johnson, you'll notice,' said Carmichael, who had suddenly appeared behind the pair of them, causing Lucas to jump slightly and Kim to actually exclaim.

'Oh ya fuck!'

'Pardon DS Sterling?' said Carmichael, an evil grin creeping across her face.

'I'm so sorry I... I..' spluttered Kim, but Carmichael started laughing. Even she looked better when she smiled. 'Lighten up, Sterling, I'm taking the piss. We need a word, though; where's that Professor-psychologist-profiler or whatever the fuck he is? Just seen an email asking us to cover his salary whilst he's up here, so he better be fucking working.'

'I'll ring him and get him to come in if you like?'

'I would like. Thanks.' Carmichael put a spidery hand on Lucas's shoulder and lent closer to his ear, whispering in a mock sinister fashion. 'We have nothing to charge PC Johnson with other than having a shit ginger mullet and no hard evidence at all. And I don't know about you, but I don't think Amelia Watson was trying to describe him, do you?'

'Er... no, I don't, boss,'

'Good, now get him released.' she straightened up and patted him on the shoulder, 'We'll keep a beady eye on him until the DNA from under Miss Watson's fingernails and on the handle of that knife are back, but I'm confident it's not him in the meantime.'

'Yes, boss,' he said, feeling a strange sense of irritation in the pit of his stomach. This was supposed to be his case now; why was she still getting involved? No, stop it, Lucas.

'Thanks,' and she was gone, a strongly scented perfume lingering behind her.

The rest of the morning was taken up with sorting out the slight mess that was PC Johnson. Despite her thorny demeanour, Carmichael had a lot of experience in these sorts of cases and was very good at it. She may not have been especially gentle, but she was kind and supportive. She always made it sound like she had faith in him without ever really saying it, so maybe he should push that irritated feeling back down. There was still that niggling feeling in the back of his mind... that could, of course, just be an act to get him to do what she wanted? Either way, PC Johnson was released and was told not to return to work until the following month, pending an internal investigation. The entire team was gathered and briefed that there would be no hard evidence, so the investigation would now be targeted at finding a man fitting Amelia Watson's very limited description.

'Tall and balding? Fucking hell, Miller, that could be half the bloody city. That's genuinely most of the blokes down my local rugby club,' chimed in DC Green. It didn't surprise Lucas to find out the bloke played rugby. Somehow, he looked the type.

'Yeah, I know. But we're still considering someone with inside knowledge of the investigation, given that note in Amelia's flat.'

'May not be that closely linked though, boss, could equally be a journo, or just some random bloke who heard from his mate down the pub. You and I both know, just because we hadn't released her identity, she'd been named on Twitter,' said DI Khan.

'A fair point, Sadiq' Lucas rubbed his face in his hands. 'Kim, where's that profiler of yours?'

'He's set himself up in one of the spare rooms round the back; he's got some stuff to show you when you're ready,' she replied cheerfully.

'Well, that'll be now, then. You can come with me, please,' said Lucas, pointing at her. DI Sadiq Khan had a face like a bulldog licking piss off a nettle. DS Sterling just beamed.

Lucas took out his phone, but there was no message from Em. Was she still sulking? He was too tired to think about it anymore, but knew he should ring her. Things might have heated the other night, but surely it was still just some silly little tiff, not their first or last. Perhaps he'd try to catch her later when she'd calmed down.

The room which Professor Hawthorne had commandeered was a small one. A long table sat in the middle, and the chairs, which should have been scattered around it, were piled up against the back wall. The rest of the walls were adorned with whiteboards, and the window was covered in paper, stopping any passers-by from looking in. He'd constructed a timeline; images of all twelve victims and their respective crime scenes were plastered along the whiteboards. There were also pictures of Jacob Murray and another of a hideously ugly man with aggressive ginger hair. Thomas Mitchel. Seeing his face made Lucas's shoulders tense.

'Ah, the infamous DCI Miller, come in, come in,' said the Professor, who was standing in the centre of the room, grinning. 'And Kimberly, a pleasure to see you as always.'

'Professor,' she said along with some strange little curtsy.

'Excellent, well, sit down, sit down.' He pulled a chair from under the desk and waited for Lucas and Kim to follow suit. Lucas had doubts, but there was something very charming about him in a strange, eccentric sort of way. He'd give him that. 'Now, I've only spent a few days looking at the case, and there are some things you've done well.'

'Oh, er... thank you,' he said, smirking sideways at Kim.

'But there are some things I think you've missed!'

'Right,' said Lucas a little more quietly. The Professor stood up and walked over to the timeline before turning and spreading his arms dramatically.

'What do you notice?'

'Huh? It's a time-line?'

'A fine deduction, DCI Miller, but I hoped we could expand on that somewhat. Describe the timeline.'

Kim put her hand up slowly, her finger pointing to the ceiling. 'DS Sterling?'

'So as far as we know, the murders started with Jessica Murray in 2011, and he kills another girl pretty much at a rate of one a year. Except, now he's escalating and has killed two in the space of three months.'

'The time between murders is random; we've run the numbers. They don't fall on important dates or follow the lunar cycle or anything like that?' said Lucas.

'Right, right, so what are you missing?' said Professor Hawthorne excitedly.

'He takes a break between 2016 and 2020. About two and a half years without a murder,' said Kim.

'Does he, though? Is that what you would expect our killer to do? He never breaks his MO; he's roughly consistent. Why would he take a break?' said Professor Hawthorne with a knowing grin.

'We've looked into this before,' said Lucas, a little exasperated. 'We have been through all the reported murders in the area, and we've put out alerts to other police forces in case he moved out of the area. Nobody that fits this type has been found. A body with missing organs and a fucking poem rammed inside them would trigger an alert, I can assure you.'

'Oh, could it be someone who was in prison during that time?' suggested Kim keenly.

'It could, but I think it's more likely that DCI Miller has placed his trust in some weak junior officers.' Lucas just looked at him, perplexed.

'The PC tasked with this sent out alerts to every police force… In England. They didn't look in Ireland, Scotland or Wales.'

'For fuck's sake,' groaned Lucas. 'But this story has gone bloody international; surely they'd have come to us if they thought he was killing there.'

'They did. I have spoken to a DI, Scott Williams, in Swansea, South Wales. They have at least three unsolved cases, which they think are similar enough to interest us, all between 2016 and 2020. He sent a case file to Detective Superintendent Carmichael on each occasion. Her response has been… blinkered,' he said diplomatically.

'That doesn't make sense,' said Kim, but Lucas didn't speak. He had nothing to say, so he sat and seethed silently for a moment. 'Why wouldn't she entertain the idea that the 'Reaper' was out of the area?'

'You'll have to ask her that. But I think a nice little trip to South Wales is in order. They have some lovely beaches' he rubbed his hands together gleefully.

'Show me,' said Lucas.

'DCI Miller?'

'Show me the case files. If Carmichael has ignored these, she'll have had a good reason. I want to see them; they're probably bollocks.'

'I don't have the full case files, but I have the summary sheets that were sent to her,' said Professor Hawthorne, moving over to the table, grabbing a bundle of papers and dropping some of them on the table.

'Look at that. Young women were abducted, stabbed repeatedly, strangled and tied up. Same story here and here,' he finished, dropping the remaining paper on the desk.

'There's no mention of missing organs. This doesn't fit.'

'Right, I can explain that,' said Professor Hawthorne, bouncing around on the balls of his feet. He moved over to the back wall where he'd printed *'In Shadows Deep'* on an A0 sheet of paper. The first seven couplets are heart, lung, spleen, liver, colon, kidney, and bladder. All are taken in order. But for Hannah George, victim number seven, he skips some verses and rips out her pancreas. He missed three verses, and we have three potential cases in Wales.'

'Coincidence, we haven't found anyone with their...' Lucas squinted at the board. 'gallbladder, appendix or thyroid torn out.'

'No, not torn out. DS Sterling, do you know anyone without a gallbladder?' said Professor Hawthorn.

'What? No...oh, well. Actually, my mum had hers removed a few years ago. Gallstones.' she shrugged.

'And I, myself, gave up my appendix when I was only twelve years old,' said Professor Hawthorne, rubbing his eyes as if he was crying. 'Thyroids are frequently removed for lumps, hyperactivity, and cancer.'

'Where are you going with this?' said Lucas.

'Carys Williams, late 2016. You've just seen her case notes. Had a cholecystectomy eight months before she died.' He paused, and as the penny dropped, a coldness washed over Lucas. 'Oliva Thomas was found dead in a field near her home in early 2018. She underwent an appendicectomy at the age of sixteen for appendicitis.'

'Let me guess, the thyroid was surgically removed from the last one?' Lucas said, putting his head in his hands.

'Right, you are. Clara Jones underwent a total thyroidectomy three months before she died.'

'I don't know whether to hit you or kiss you right now,' mumbled Lucas through his fingers. DS Sterling was looking aghast at the Professor. This had been a massive oversight; how had Carmichael or someone else not picked up on this?

'I need to speak to Carmichael,' he blurted quickly, getting up, not looking at either of the others. He took the summary sheets with him and silently and calmly walked from the room. He was boiling over inside, however composed he may have looked. Why the hell had this not been investigated properly? Why hadn't he even been told about this? He was DI when this was being discussed and wasn't privy to any of it. This was potentially an utter travesty. He'd worked with Carmichael for twelve years. She wasn't the easiest person, but he had so much respect for the woman. But right now, given this and her desire to keep control of the investigation, he was losing faith rapidly. Lucas kept walking past his desk; he needed her to see his face when he asked about this. He knocked and opened her office door without waiting for her to answer.

'Carmichael' he said bluntly.

'Oh, DCI Miller, come in, ' she smiled; he didn't. 'How can I help? You look like you need a shit. What's wrong?'

'We've had an interesting chat with Professor Hawthorne.' he said, not taking a seat.

'Right, and what does the magic-psychic think then?' She teased, not registering quite how angry Lucas was. 'Do we need some lucky heather? Has he rolled some bones? Well, what do the tea leaves–'

'He's pointed out the two-and-a-half-year hiatus the killer appears to have taken after 2016. What have we done to investigate this?' interrupted Lucas abruptly. He'd likely pay for that.

'Everyone knows about the gap, and you know what we did to investigate it; you were DI. What point are you trying to make, Miller? Spit it out,' she said, finally registering Lucas's tone.

'Did you know that we've had reports of similar killings in Wales? Three, during that window. And that you ignored them!' Lucas raised his voice and waved the papers at her. She looked startled, but only for a second. Her face relaxed, and she sat back in her chair, her arms behind her head.

'Ah, that. Yes, I did know. But they differ from our case. They are similar, but not nearly the same. No missing organs. I received assurances.'

'OK, well, let's look at it again then,' continued Lucas.

'I don't have the time; I have already reviewed the cases and deemed it not worth our effort.'

'Carys Williams, 19, was tortured, stabbed three times in the abdomen, strangled with a rope, and she'd had her gallbladder removed eight months prior. How is that not worth investigating?'

'Different ligature type, different blade. The killer took no organs. None of the other victims have been targeted after an operation, Miller. There was no poem left either. The Welsh had a suspect, the girl's boyfriend. Plus, she's a university student, not a prossie.'

'Ours aren't all prostitutes, we know that?' said Lucas incredulously.

'Most have been. Look, I have considered the Welsh cases, and there were many differences. I deemed them separate from our investigation. If you disagree, be my guest. You and that ruddy psychic can waste your time down there for a few days, but just know that the rest of us will be up here working on the case!' She threw her hands down on the desk and stood up, almost squaring up to Lucas.

'OK, if that's your professional opinion,' snapped Lucas.

'It is,' she replied curtly, pouting her lips together. His hands were shaking. He was furious. Potentially, he'd been made to look like a complete dickhead in front of his entire team. Why on earth had this not been discussed with him at the time? In fact;

'Why on earth had this not been discussed with me at the time? I was DI on the case!'

'Were you though, Miller? I seem to remember you being fairly sodding absent. You were fixated on that ginger fella who topped himself. I'm the only one who didn't blame that on you, but Christ, Lucas. Do not have a go at me for this. I thought I was doing the right thing, and I will stand by that until you bring me evidence to the contrary. Now fuck off to Wales if you like. I hope the weather's shit.'

2017

47

Just under eight months had passed since Lucas had arrested Thomas Mitchel, although if you were to look at the sunken bags under his eyes, you would assume it had been much longer. His life was falling apart, and it had done so spectacularly.

They'd kept hold of Mitchel for a few days, and at one point, they thought they might just get enough evidence for the CPS to press charges. A trace of his hair and DNA was found under her fingernails, but this was no help, given he'd already admitted to sleeping with her. Although there had been no witnesses, he had essentially placed himself at the crime scene with an alibi it was going to be tough to disprove. Unfortunately, the blood on the high visibility jacket didn't match Sophia's DNA, but it matched his, and he wasn't giving a sensible reason for it being there.

'I don't know, I might have bitten my lip or something?' said Mitchel. Was this the best he could muster? Lucas thought Sophia might have caught him in the struggle. No other DNA profiles had been found inside the jacket, which didn't give any credibility to the mysterious 'tall man' theory that he kept referring to. However, the most significant problem which Lucas faced was that Mitchel's DNA didn't match any samples from any of the previous crime scenes. Searching his laptop had yielded very little either; apart from some fairly basic VPN software — otherwise, nothing.

No charges were brought, and Thomas Mitchel had walked free. Whilst everyone was annoyed, most accepted it was likely that he was telling the truth. Carmichael wanted to focus on finding this 'tall man'. Lucas, however, had made himself somewhat unpopular within the team because, despite what his boss might think, he was still adamant that Mitchel was involved. It was hindering the rest of the investigation.

'Look, Miller, we've looked into it, OK? We've followed up with him, and there's nothing there; it's just a dead end. We have a job to do, and it won't happen unless you bloody focus,' said Carmichael.

'I don't get it. Why the hell isn't he still a suspect?'

'Everyone's a suspect, Miller, but we need evidence that will stick. Just because he's ginger and has no soul does not make him a murderer.'

'But he was there. He shagged her minutes before she was killed! If he didn't do it, he must have bloody well seen who did! I don't understand why he's not being more helpful,'

'Because he's a fat Manc with a bad attitude, not a serial killer. It doesn't add up,' said DS Khan from across the desk.

'He studied English Lit. He's got knowledge of poetry. What about his laptop? He's got the VPN, trying to cover his tracks!'

'He's got half a degree, and any twat can read poetry. It's hardly conclusive,' said Carmichael.

'But the VPN!'

'Yeah, he's probably watching weird porn, mate, or illegally streaming Premier League football. Hardly criminal,' said Khan, shrugging.

The frustration at work was building, and the enjoyment he used to find in his job was fading. He repeatedly went home angry and frustrated, meaning he was now opening a bottle of wine a night rather than a week, as he might have previously. He'd never really been one of a beer after work or a glass of wine. But something about the way this case was now heading had inspired him to take up mild alcohol excess as a hobby. He'd tried explaining to Chloe why Mitchel had to be involved. Unfortunately, she wasn't on his side either. In fact, she was firmly in the opposite camp, as with many things these days. He knew she could be right; he could see the evidence, or lack of evidence. And yet, he couldn't let it go.

Unfortunately, he was being egged on by the national press. They'd got hold of Mitchel's name and photograph from somewhere and had it plastered all over the front pages. He'd lost his job and half of his friends because who wanted to be associated with a serial killer?

The worst part of the whole ordeal was that it was at least partly responsible for the regular arguments between him and Chloe. Their relationship was rocky, to put things lightly. He was always angry, never focused, and neglected Chloe and Rachel. They'd been bickering for weeks, and now they were having proper fights. The sort of fights where you don't speak to each other for the entire day. They argued the night before, so he'd slept in the spare room on a bed, which was significantly less comfortable.

'We're just trying to help Lucas. But you have to listen.

We're the police; we work with the evidence, and the evidence just isn't there! For the last fucking time, he didn't bloody do it!' Chloe yelled, folding some laundry on the bed.

'Oh, for fuck's sake!'

'No, stop, you've got to think about this. You're letting your personal feelings cloud your judgement.'

'My personal feelings? What the fuck are you talking about?'

'You feel like a failure; you've not caught the bloody 'Water's pissing Edge Reaper? Is that it? It's not all about you, Lucas; we're a team. *We* haven't caught him yet. I agree Mitchel was the most likely lead we'd had in years, but you're barking up the wrong tree! Just drop it, please!'

'I'm going out,' he said, dramatically flapping his arms above his head.

'If you're going to drive to his house and stare through the bloody window again?' she said furiously.

'Oh fuck off Chloe, I don't need this!'

'Me fuck off? No, you fuck off, Lucas, and you know what? Maybe you should stay somewhere else for a while. I'm not going to let you talk to me like that.'

'Whatever, I don't care,' he muttered petulantly.

'Just leave!' She screamed as he walked out without a second look.

He got into his car and left with a screech of his tyres. After driving for over twenty-five minutes, he pulled up on the curb and turned the engine off. His pulse was still thumping away in his neck, following the argument, and he tried taking long, hard breaths to calm himself. He was outside 19 Belmont Avenue, the residence of Mr Thomas Mitchel. He didn't know what he was doing here. It had been a mistake to come. This was the third time he'd visited to sit outside and observe. He knew it wasn't healthy, but as long as it didn't become a habit, there was nothing wrong with keeping an eye on the creep, was there?

* * *

Another six months had passed, and Lucas was now touching ten visits to Belmont Avenue. It was becoming a habit. He would park up at the end of the street, turn his lights off, and wait. Occasionally, Thomas Mitchel would come out. Most of the time, Lucas was waiting for something that wouldn't happen.

Chloe hadn't kicked him out, although that was probably more to do with Luna than anything else. He'd stayed in the station for a few nights, and she'd kept the dog for fairly obvious reasons. Luna may have been his, but Chloe was very fond of her and didn't want her or Rachel caught up in anything. Long story short, they'd reconciled, and he was back in the house again. That being said, there was significant tension, and their relationship was straining. With all the late nights and his moody demeanour, he wasn't far away from being accused of having an affair. He wasn't; he was working on the Thomas Mitchel 'lead'. But he doth protest too much, as far as Chloe was concerned, and she was getting nervous about him. He didn't think they'd fallen out of love, just that things had gone stale and mouldy. It was his fault, and he knew it.

His reputation at the station was fading just as fast as his faltering love life, given the lack of progress on the Reaper case and his well-known fixation on pinning something on Mitchel. In truth, as the months rolled on further, he'd stopped driving over to the house as much because he had Luna to look after and dumping her on Chloe wasn't fair. Luna was his anchor at the moment. Her massive eyes, wet snout, and waggy tail were pretty much the only reason he still bothered getting up on a morning.

The one positive from all of this was there hadn't been any more murders. The killer was in the middle of his most prolonged dry patch since they'd found Jessica Murray seven years ago. Leeds was a big city, and people got murdered as an almost daily occurrence. Lucas wasn't being assigned any more cases, though; his sole job was to catch the most notorious serial killer the UK had seen in years. And he was failing it. There had been other murders, some similar enough to briefly involve the team.

'No, I don't think it's the same person,' said Dr Cooper, who was at least six months pregnant and looked it. Clutching her belly as she moved across the room, getting her beautiful assistant, Emily, to help her with the autopsy. Emily was the main reason to go to the morgue as far as Lucas was concerned, even if it was only for a bit of an ogle.

'The ligature marks are from an item of clothing, a jumper perhaps? Something made of a thick fibre, like wool. Your man uses a rope. I know there's a massive wound to the abdomen, but the gallbladder and appendix are both still there. Plus, he's secreted on her thigh. Bloody gross if you ask me, sodding hate the secretors. Keep your bodily fluids to yourself, thank you very much.' She smiled nicely at him and completely missed the irony as she lifted her bump over the lip of the mortuary trolly and rested it there. 'You'll get there. He'll make a mistake, and you'll catch him.'

'Thanks, Dr Cooper. I appreciate the help.'

'Not at all. In fact, do you want me to go back over all the reports from the seven victims? See if a fresh pair of eyes can find anything we've previously missed?'

'No, no, don't worry about it. You've got more than enough on your plate' he pointed at her tummy, and they both laughed.

'Seriously, please don't. It's a very kind offer, but you have a baby to prepare for. Enjoy it.'

'Will do, and thank you, Lucas,' and he received another big grin, which was then made obsolete when Emily gave him a little wink from over her shoulder and mouthed 'Caught him yet?'

Emily was waiting by the main entrance as he headed out, blowing on some little black box. Smoke or steam erupted from her nose like a dragon and curled around her head. As attractive as she was physically, neither smoking nor vaping did anything for him at all.

'Hi Lucas,' she said, eyes bright.

'Hi Emily, how are you getting on?

'This and that, enjoying myself a little more these last few weeks.

'That bloke of yours still being an arse?' he said, hoping it would remain subtle and not sinister.

'Oh, I've kicked him into touch; I don't need that sort of negativity; I'm better than that,' she said, taking another drag of her little vape.

'Definitely, I'm sure you could get anyone you wanted.'

'You reckon? Even a senior detective like yourself?' she

giggled.

Lucas felt very warm suddenly, and his brain stopped for a split second. He must have looked like he'd had a stroke or something before he regained his cool.

'You wouldn't want a senior detective. We're all grumpy and are never home. Just ask DS Wilson.'

Emily smirked back at him, a devilish little glint in her eye, 'Fair enough, but don't make the mistake of thinking me and DS Wilson are the same; we're not,'

'Oh, I wouldn't begin to presume what you're like, Emily.'

'Hmm, that's a shame.'

'Why?'

'Because it sounds like you want me to show you rather than tell you.' Thankfully, his phone rang loudly in his pocket, breaking the prickling tension. He didn't know what to say, but he got away with laughing and answering it.

Emily gave him one final penetrating smile, waved and walked away. Her hips didn't usually move as nicely as that, did they?

2019

48

Lucas couldn't sleep; it was too warm, his mind was talking to itself, and his bloody dog insisted on sleeping on top of him rather than on her side of the bed. Despite being small for a spaniel, Luna didn't half make a racket as she suckled and whimpered in her sleep. Chloe was in the other room, and he could hear her snoring softly through the paper-thin walls of the house. Sometimes, you need to break the cycle, so he got a glass of water from the kitchen. As the cold water hit the back of his throat, he looked down at the kitchen table, where yesterday's newspaper lay open on page nine.

Water's Edge Reaper Investigation Stalls as Murders Cease
Simon Davies, Crime Correspondent

Nearly three years have passed since the last murder attributed to the infamous Water's Edge Reaper, and the police investigation into the case has stalled. The reaper has been active in West Yorkshire since 2011 and is one of the most high-profile serial killer cases in the UK. The case has attracted national attention, and it has left the north of England living in fear, with seven innocent women slain to date. Despite the wealth of resources available, police have been unable to catch the killer so far.

Suspects have been at a premium, although most recently, police arrested Thomas Mitchel in 2016 on suspicion of murder in connection with the latest victim, Sophia Sidorova. Mitchel was released without charge following days of questioning. However, DI Lucas Miller of the West Yorkshire Major Crime Unit says he 'remains a suspect' in the case.

There may be some substance to the claims against Thomas Mitchel since his arrest; there have been no reported murders attributed to The Water's Edge Reaper in nearly three years. This has raised several questions. Is it possible that the killer has stopped killing? Or is the killer simply lying low and waiting to strike again? Could the attention on Thomas Mitchel be preventing him from continuing his reign of terror? Whilst some believe that Mitchel may be responsible for the murders, others believe that the Water's Edge Reaper is someone else entirely, and that Mitchel is simply a scapegoat.

Police say that they are still investigating the case with all available resources and are still appealing to the public for information. However, the fact the case has gone cold is a significant concern for the community.

Expert Opinion

Dr Ben Daniels, a criminal psychologist, believes that there are many reasons why the murders may have stopped.

'One possibility is that the killer has been caught,' Daniels said.

'Another possibility is that the killer has died. However, it is also possible that the killer has simply taken a break. One possibility is that the killer has changed their lifestyle,' Daniels said. 'Another possibility is that the killer is experiencing some kind of mental or emotional trauma. It is important to remember that serial killers are human beings and that they are capable of change. However, it is also important to remember that serial killers are often very dangerous individuals,' Dr Daniels said. 'If the Reaper has simply taken a break, then they may strike again in the future.'

Community Concern

The fact that the Reaper has not killed anyone in nearly three years has given some people hope that the horrors are over; however, there is still a sense of fear and anxiety pulsing through most of the community. 'I still worry about the Water's Edge Reaper,' said one local resident. 'I know that the killer may have stopped killing, but I also know that they may be simply lying low.'

Another local resident said that they are concerned about the impact the case has on the community. 'The murders have made everyone feel unsafe,' said the resident. 'I'm worried about the impact that it's having on our children and our female residents.'

The police are urging the community to be vigilant and to report any suspicious activity to the police immediately.

The Water's Edge Reaper case is a reminder that serial killers are a genuine threat to public safety. It is essential to be aware of the danger and to take steps to protect yourself and your loved ones.

The idea was in his head now. Bloody Thomas Mitchel, he just couldn't shake this niggling feeling that the bloke was involved. A lack of solid evidence was a problem, but there were still unanswered questions, and the timeline made him a plausible suspect. Balls to this, he thought, and despite his better judgement, he decided to scratch that itch. He pulled on some jogging bottoms and an old jumper, grabbed his keys, and drove to Belmont Avenue. It was just for a nose and something to do... right?

It didn't take him long, not at this time of night when the roads were clear. Leeds was such a big city that the constant traffic took a lot of enjoyment out of driving, but the quiet emptiness of the early morning streets gave Lucas a strange sense of freedom.

He arrived on Belmont Avenue and parked up as silently as he could. Pulling the handbrake, he noticed Mitchel's car was gone, which was unusual. The bloke was basically a hermit now that the media had wrecked his life. Lucas had contributed to that as well, of course. That was probably why the killings had stopped, he thought. Either way, there was no point in staying to stare at an empty driveway, so he decided to head home.

He was just turning the key in the ignition when a pair of bright headlights emerged from a side street up ahead. As he watched, his hand hovering about the ignition, the headlights turned and came down the road. Lucas remained still, almost frozen. As they got closer, he realised it was indeed the crappy little fifteen-year-old VW Polo which belonged to Mitchel. The car continued down the road slowly and pulled into the drive in one clean movement. He parked at a crooked angle on the drive, and the car lights went out; the engine turned off, and a shabby, ginger man got out. His horrible, greasy hair even looked an angry shade of red in the amber streetlights.

There was a click of the passenger side door, and an icy feeling took hold of Lucas as he felt the blood in his veins stop flowing. Someone else was getting out of the passenger seat. A woman. A young woman, probably in her early twenties. She was brunette and quite pretty, with large, innocent eyes and angular features. She wasn't very tall, barely over five feet, although she wore aggressively tall high heels to compensate. The ankles in these heels were covered in fishnet tights, which crept up a pair of scrawny legs before ducking under tight jean shorts that didn't cover her bony bottom. It was a sweeping judgement and not one that he was proud of, but... she looked like a working girl.

He watched as Mitchel put his arm around the girl, steered her towards his front door, took out a key, and let them both inside. He looked back fleetingly at the street, causing Lucas to drop behind his steering wheel to avoid being seen. The door closed with an audible click of the Yale lock. Lucas's heart was beating firmly in his chest, the throbbing going as far as his ears. She was trapped in there with him!

He put his hand on the door handle of his car and... paused. Was he being stupid? There wasn't enough evidence that this man was their killer... was there? Perhaps he thought there was, but very few people agreed. It was more of a gut feeling... a powerful gut feeling. She might be a girlfriend, a willing partner, or paid company. Either way, what reason did he have to suspect that she was in danger? Other than the detective's intuition that Lucas had lived with for the last two years. Although, he thought to himself, it was an intuition that had led him and his team to the arrest of Jacob Murray, the discovery of '*In Shadows Deep*,' and the Twitter handle.

It needed to be more; no judge would grant him a warrant based on this. He couldn't call it in; everyone already thought he was obsessed, and he couldn't reveal he was loitering outside the man's house under cover of darkness. Chloe would blow her lid when he told her where he was again. If he were wrong, his reputation would be ruined. He should leave. Just turn the key, start the car and drive. Do it, Lucas.

In that moment, though, logic didn't win. His mind was made up. He couldn't worry about his reputation; if this was his killer, she was in danger. He opened his car door and snuck across the road, illuminated in orange from the ageing, flickering street lights, stopping beneath the main living room window. It was dark inside, but the hall light was on. He couldn't see much other than shadows moving about on the other side of the frosted glass door panels. It looked like she was going upstairs as the two dark shapes disappeared from view.

'Shit,' he muttered out loud. His words dissipated into nothingness like swirls of steamy breath. What did he do now? Did he wait? Did he force entry? He checked his phone: 01:12. Maybe he'd give them till twenty past? No, half past? Yes, if he'd not heard anything by then, he would knock on the door and disturb them.

He stayed crouched by the side of the house. Why, whenever you needed to hide, did you always immediately need a piss? He held it, hopping from foot to foot, waiting for the feeling to subside and for confirmation this lady was safe.

It felt like the longest twenty minutes of his life, but eventually, his phone showed 01:30. He sighed audibly. It was now or never. As he stood, the cartilage in his knees clicking, there was a strangled scream from within the house. It was only brief. But then, only silence. He'd definitely heard that, hadn't he?

He flinched. There it was again, for sure, this time. Lucas sprinted around the house, and just as he got to the door, it opened, and the young woman came flying out of it straight into his arms, knocking them both to the ground. She was bleeding heavily from her mouth, her lip had burst, and there was a cut to her eyebrow. She was sobbing, tears streaming down her face.

'Help me!' she squealed through the blood which was pouring from her mouth. Lucas pulled himself out from underneath her, himself now covered in her blood, and looked back into the house, but there was nothing—just blackness in the hallway.

'What happened? Where is he?' he panted, quickly. She just sobbed back at him, unable to form any sensible words.

'Is he still in there?' He was gripping her shoulders firmly and ducking his head down to her level so he could look her in the eyes. She nodded quickly and continued sobbing but managed to squeak out the words 'bedroom'. He took out the keys to his car, walked her over and placed her in the passenger seat where she sat, shivering and sobbing.

'Wait here'

'No, please, don't go!' she whimpered, but more loudly this time, making Lucas flinch and look around to ensure they hadn't been watched. He tried to hush her as best he could.

'I need to see what's happened. It's okay. I'm a police officer. What's your name?'

'A... Amelia.'

'OK, Amelia, my name is DI Lucas Miller. Please wait here, and I'll be back in a second. You are safe, I promise you. Hold this to your mouth.' He put a comforting hand on her shoulder, feeling the bony prominence of her skinny collar bone, and passed her an old jumper from the car's back seat. She took it as he closed the door, locking her inside before returning to the house. The door was still ajar, so he removed his shoes and walked in. He didn't want to leave big muddy footprints everywhere. The living room light was off, but there was a soft glow from the bedroom upstairs. Being careful to touch as little as possible, he made his way up the stairs and nudged open the bedroom door with his elbow.

Thomas Mitchel was lying on the bed, naked, a thicket of ginger pubes covering a shrivelled and pathetic-looking penis. He was pale white and gasping slowly. Lucas walked over and stood over him. The weak and vulnerable face that Lucas had spent so long pursuing was clutching his neck as dark, thick blood oozed out from between his fingers. Lucas could smell it as it coated the man's skin and the bedsheets beneath. He was gasping slowly but harshly, his beady little eyes looking into Lucas's. Time seemed to stand still. He'd only had about five interactions with this man, but he felt he knew him inside out. The evil, grotesque things that this man had done. Probably.

'P... please,' croaked the dying man.

'Why did you hit her, Thomas?' Adrenaline was flowing

through him and his mind was racing, almost like he was having an out-of-body experience. Like he was watching another Lucas, stood there whilst he floated overhead. The light was fading in his eyes, and Lucas needed to act fast to save him. But he didn't. He just stood. Images of the victims flashed through his mind's eye, most notably Sophia in her tent, caked in blood, her bladder torn from her pelvis. Her wounds had been the same deep colour as the viscous scarlet that was teeming through the pale fingers as it emanated from two large gashes in Thomas Mitchel's neck. This man could well be responsible for the deaths of many innocent women.

'I...' gasped Mitchel, visibly getting paler and greyer as Lucas stood there.

'Did you do it? Did you kill those girls? Did you kill Sophia? said Lucas, his voice monotone and so much calmer than he felt. The man was really struggling now; blood was everywhere, and he was ghostly pale, almost translucent. His eyes were rolling back in his head sporadically, and his lips were turning purple. He needed help, but Lucas didn't move. Instead, he thought of his mother and the man who must have killed her. He was never found or punished, but if someone had stood over him like this... Lucas would have wanted him dead.

'Talk to me!'

'I... did...not....ki...' gasped the man, expiring in front of Lucas. He was fading. He took one breath in, then one slow breath out and then... nothing. His pupils relaxed to neutral, the grip on his neck loosened, and his hand slipped down slightly in the blood.

Lucas looked around the floor and saw a small flick knife,

blood streaked across the blade. The handle had the Swiss army logo and a small engraving of the letters *TM*. Lucas reached down and picked up the knife between the folds of his jumper. It didn't take a detective to work out what had happened here. The knife was engraved, and it obviously wasn't hers, so it had likely been within easy reach. Perhaps Mitchel planned to use it on her? Either way, she must have been defending herself when she'd struck him in the neck with the blade. She was going to find herself in hot water over this, no doubt, killing a man in his own home. Even if they could get her off, she was in for a traumatic few months and a court battle. All for doing the world a favour and removing this waste of semen from the gene pool.

A dark idea had flashed into his mind. He should ignore it, but equally, this man was evil. Lucas wasn't sure he'd made a conscious decision but found himself acting, again, watching from above in his out-of-body state. Swiftly and without considering the consequences, he made two minor superficial cuts around the left side of the neck wound. Hesitation marks. He'd just about attended enough autopsies to know that these were a common finding in suicides. He headed into the bathroom, found a flannel and wiped the blade clean before placing it in the right hand of Mitchel, covering it in his fingerprints and some blood. Then he dropped it on the floor, just off the side of the bed. There was a mirror on the desk, which he carefully moved across so it looked as though Mitchel had been using it.

He left carefully, closing the front door behind him, which locked with a clunk. When he returned to the car, he was pleased to find the girl, Amelia, still there waiting for him and didn't appear to have moved a muscle. She was holding the jumper to her mouth, still sobbing. He got in the driver's side and looked over at her.

'I'm sorry,' she sobbed.

'I can keep a secret if you can?'

2023

49

'I win, I win!!' said DS Sterling, a little too loudly, given they were in public. Lucas just laughed and handed her his cards, but Professor Hawthorne tutted and scowled from behind his book. It was a long train journey from Leeds to Carmarthen, and there were only so many times you could play snap. They were at least travelling 1st class at the pleasure of the West Yorkshire Police Force. Superintendent Carmichael had essentially rinsed her hands of this aspect of the investigation; such was her conviction that there was nothing to be found in Wales.

The cards were put away, and they settled down to get some rest, as they still had another three or four hours left. They'd changed at Manchester only an hour ago and were on a run-down, ill-equipped, two-carriage pile of shit headed to Cardiff for their last change. There weren't even plug sockets; it was like being in the third world, thought Lucas.

There was nothing else to do now except for staring out the windows as the Welsh countryside whizzed by.

It didn't take long before Lucas felt his eyes becoming heavy and begin to droop. The rhythmic thump of the track underneath him lulled him to sleep, helped in part by the two pregabalin he'd chucked back half an hour ago. His mind drifted, meandering through his brain, but it came to rest in the same place it usually did these days. The investigation. How could he not have known about the Welsh cases? How had no one in the station known about the cases? Had everyone just forgotten about it? Simon Davies at the Yorkshire Post was using him as a media punchbag, but it was difficult to argue that this whole enquiry wasn't a complete mess.

He was woken with a jolt, and his head snapped up, the world quickly returning into focus. Kim was still asleep, her mouth lolling open and her head resting on his shoulder. He didn't rush to move her head; he just let it rest there, her soft hair rubbing against his neck. It was pretty comforting, actually. But then he saw a text from Em on his phone, and a strange pang of guilt flooded him, so he gently slipped his shoulder out from under her head and checked the messages properly.

'How's the journey going? Bored yet? x'

They had sort of kissed and made up after their blazing row the other day. Things were still a little frosty, and she hadn't technically apologised to Luna yet, but they were amicable. She'd stayed over last night, and they'd at least sorted the physical side of things with a bit of ferocious make-up sex.

'well, this place is miles away lol! What are you doing? Anything interesting on the table? x'

No reply. Lucas checked his phone sporadically as they

changed at Cardiff Central and began the last leg of their journey through Swansea and out to West Wales. They pulled into Carmarthen station, and there was undoubtedly a feeling that this was a place far removed from Leeds. Whereas the train station back home was huge, modern and busy, this was small, quaint, and the only people around were a handful of passengers and a dishevelled man in an orange, massively oversized, high visibility jacket who was collecting the tickets.

'Right, we have a car waiting for us. The police station isn't far, about a ten minute drive, and we're staying in a nice B&B just across the road, so it should be convenient,' said Kim.

'You've booked a proper hotel?' He'd assumed they'd be in something cheap and nasty.

'No, the West Yorkshire Police Force has; they've been very generous, considering it's a bit of a wild goose chase' She flashed a very naughty little grin, demonstrating again that all thirty-two of those teeth were utterly identical, something which Lucas now found oddly attractive.

They disembarked from the train and found that there was indeed a car waiting for them. Unfortunately, it was a fifteen-year-old Nissan Micra, which would barely have been big enough to fit Luna in. Somehow, they rammed the luggage and themselves inside, with Professor Hawthorne folded in half. Not that he grumbled. He remained engrossed in his notes, barely speaking to them. After apologising profusely for the disastrous hire car, Kim took the wheel, and they set off into the miserable Welsh scenery.

It had rained the entire journey and continued to do so as they drove through the countryside surrounded by a simple

49

pallet of green and grey. Lucas felt a bit like they'd landed on a familiar alien planet. Everything looked the same, but different. They drove down a winding country road; the rain hammering the windscreen, the wipers at full speed. Lucas felt his mind wandering again. He was thinking of Em, how she felt, the smell of her hair, her soft white skin. No, Em was black. DS Sterling was white, though. He shook his head and thought about what Carmichael had said to him. Fixated. Maybe he was. Perhaps that's why he didn't know about the Welsh cases. Possibly, he'd just missed them. But, if that was the case, he might need a new fixation to solve this. Just what had been happening in Wales?

50

They pulled into the tiny car park of a small, reasonably neat but outdated building called 'The Juicy Pheasant Hotel'. The yellow AA plaque gave it four stars, so expectations were reasonably high.

They went to check in and dropped their bags off before heading to the police station to meet the detective there. Lucas had nipped to the loo, but when he returned, Kim was already holding a pair of keys. She gave one to Professor Hawthorne, who thanked her graciously, before turning to Lucas, her gigantic eyes staring straight into his.

'It was cheaper to get a double room, and I didn't think you'd mind sharing with me?' she said casually, now flicking a curl of hair around her finger.

'Oh, er...' stuttered Lucas, who went a disturbing shade of pink, his ears about to melt. Em was going to kill him; she'd skin him alive. 'Yeah, but I might be on the floor if that's OK?' His throat was constricting and he could not maintain eye contact.

'Oh,' she said, looking down at the floor meekly. 'I thought maybe we could share the bed, you know, cuddle a little...' she put her hand on his forearm gently, looking deeply into his eyes again, not letting him look away, 'and then you could undress me and...' she suddenly snorted and burst into a fit of laughter, her knees buckling. She punched him on the shoulder. 'Oh, I can't keep it up! I'm taking the piss, you gigantic wet wipe. Em would kill you. Plus, you look like you snore.' She produced a third room key from her pocket and wafted it at him.

'You absolute twat, Kim,' said Lucas, as a wave of relief washed through him, followed by a sense of embarrassment at how pink he'd gone and how gullible he'd been. Although, as he dwelled on it, there was also a strange disappointment that she was only joking. They quickly dumped their bags, sprayed deodorant on their smelly bits, and got straight out.

A few minutes' drive further down the road, they arrived at the police station. Now that they were finally getting on with doing some investigating, Professor Hawthorne had perked up again. It was a large brown block, not particularly pretty, and had too many windows. There were no signs on the front to identify what it was, but a board to the left of the double doors stated it was the headquarters for the Dyfed Powys Police Station. How the fuck were you supposed to pronounce that? He was surprised it was this big; he was expecting something far smaller.

They walked up the stairs, and a few people walked past and smiled at them before appearing in the reception area. A short woman sat behind the counter typing quickly and didn't look up.

'Hi, we're looking for a...' he checked the email on his phone quickly, '...DI Williams' said Lucas after clearing his throat a little.

'Which one? We have four here,' she said, still not breaking eye contact with her computer screen.

'Oh, right? DI Scott Williams?'

'Scott's office is through the double doors and second on the right. Are you the lot from England? He's expecting you.' She finally looked up, forced a brief smile and immediately returned to her computer screen. Lucas didn't feel very welcome suddenly.

They followed her directions and soon found themselves outside a rather lovely oak door with a sign which read;

DI Scott Williams, Serious Crime.

As opposed to the light-hearted crime, thought Lucas.

They knocked and entered to find a man sitting behind a desk, his head in a book. He looked up, beaming,

'Hello, Professor Hawthorne?' He stood up immediately and thrust a hand at the Professor, who enthusiastically shook it. 'And I presume DCI Miller and DS Sterling? Lovely to meet you.' He practically dived across his desk and offered a hand to the other. Lucas was impressed. Scott was a good foot shorter than him and built like a twig, but the enthusiasm was infectious. A stark contrast to the dour receptionist. 'Please, sit. You've had a long journey.'

'Thank you,' said Kim, as they all sat and introduced themselves properly. 'How's it going down here, then?'

'Not too bad. We're a bit quiet, although we've had a couple of these 'one punch' killers from lads scrapping on a night out recently. Terrible stuff. But nothing like you guys have going on in mind; we don't tend to get this sort of thing out here. There's not much to do for a detective. Anyway, tell me how the case is going. I've seen the news, that girl you found alive? How is she doing?'

'She's dead actually, died in hospital a few days ago,' said Lucas, somewhat more bluntly than he'd intended. He got a sudden flashback to the nurse breaking her ribs with each compression during the CPR. The crunch. The smell.

'Ah, shit. Sorry, I should have read up before you got here,'

'It's OK, we're here for your suspected 'Water's Edge' killings, anyway; see if they can drive our investigation forward a bit.'

'Yes, yes, of course. Direct, I like it.'

'So, show me what you have.'

'Right, we have three victims, all here in Carmarthenshire. I correlated with a Wales-wide search but nothing, so I think it's just these three,' he said, swivelling some small files around on the desk. 'We have a small population but a fairly large geographical area to cover. There's about forty miles between each of the girls. But we have Carys Williams, Olivia Thomas and Clara Jones. Carys was found on the 3rd of February 2017, Olivia on the 16th of June 2018, and Clara Jones on the 19th of February 2019. About a year before, we all went into lockdown. All were stabbed multiple times, tied up, tortured, and asphyxiated. We have photos.' He produced a bundle of pictures from another file, and Lucas felt his pulse quicken and his arm throb. He could see that Kim and Professor Hawthorne were also looking pretty keen.

'Jesus. Exactly the same,' said Kim. Professor Hawthorne peered closely at the pictures and made a satisfied humming sort of noise.

'Yup, almost identical. Except for the obvious,' said Lucas.

'No missing organs?' said DI Williams. 'I know. That was why your boss rejected it.'

'We have a solution to that,' said Lucas, gesturing to Professor Hawthorne, who stepped forward to explain how each girl had the correct organ removed during recent surgery. DI Williams listened with rapt attention, his mouth slowly dropping as he understood.

'Very clever. That's genius.'

'Us or him?' said Lucas.

'Both'

'So no one was convicted of these?'

'Nope. I had my suspicions for one of them, but it's hard to prove, and we couldn't link anyone directly to one killing, let alone all three,' said DI Williams.

'Who were your prime suspects?' said Lucas, passing the photos back to the DI.

'On the record, we didn't have any. The scenes are clean forensically, with absolutely nothing to go on. No fingerprints, no blood, not even a black and curly pube. Fucking nothing.' he leant back in his chair, rubbing his face in his hands, evidently still frustrated. 'Off the record, I've always thought he was your man. *The Reaper.* I tried contacting your boss, Patricia Carmichael, or whatever her name is. She rejected me outright, said I was talking bollocks. She'd discussed it with the person she discusses these things with and dismissed it. I disagreed, of course, but I couldn't get anyone else here to believe me, and the pathology reports are fairly inconclusive. So, where do you go from there? They get shelved and remain unsolved.'

'Are you sure they started in 2017?' said Professor Hawthorne suddenly, making DS Sterling flinch slightly.

'Oh yeah, we've been through every murder for ten years before 2017 and nothing which fits the MO like this. And then after Clara in 2019, we've not seen anything similar since.'

'OK. And can we take a look at the other files?' said Lucas.

'Yes, I'll arrange it with the archive department. We can go now if you like. Or are you hungry? It's nearly two; dunno about you three, but I'm starving. Want a bit of lunch first?' said DI Williams, clapping his hands together greedily.

'We ate on the train,' lied Lucas. In reality, he had no idea if the others had eaten. Based on the angry look on DS Sterling's face, she hadn't.

'Right, let's go,' said a somewhat disappointed-looking DI Williams.

They spent the rest of the afternoon in the archives, poring over the complete case files for the other three girls. He couldn't help but feel a strange sense of kinship with the Welsh detective; they all believed the same thing, that there was a connection between these three murders and the ones in Leeds. It was also good to have a break from his team. The dynamic had changed, and he didn't feel as confident around them anymore. DS Sterling was different; she was on his wavelength, and despite being weird, Professor Hawthorne seemed to have the best interests of the case at heart as well.

When 6 pm came, DI Williams was keen to go. 'Look, you guys are welcome to stay, but I have a wife and a cat, both of which are going to be properly pissed off at me if I don't get back home sharpish. Why don't you return to the hotel, have a few drinks and relax? You guys must be exhausted. Come back in the morning. Meet me at the station at nine?'

'Sure, I'll see you in the morning,' said Professor Hawthorne, answering for the rest of them. The bloke was in his own little world. 'I'd like to see the scenes if that is alright?'

'What, all three?'

'Yes, if that's OK?' said Professor Hawthorne, smiling inanely in his odd way.

'Right, there's about eighty miles between them. They're spread out across the bloody county.'

'Ah right, shall we make it 7.30 am then?'

'Right.' DI Williams looked like he was chewing on a wasp, but swiftly swallowed it. He had invited them down, after all. Lucas gave him a look which said 'let me talk to him' and DI Williams departed. Lucas didn't want to waste his time yomping across Wales, staring at soggy fields.

As he left, Lucas checked his phone. Em had yet to reply to him. He'd been texting her pretty much all day, and there were always long gaps between her replies. Was she mad at him again? Maybe. He decided against texting her and instead rang her. It rang and rang. No answer. However, within a few minutes, a text arrived, and his phone buzzed violently.

'Sorry, I'm out with Laura from work. Speak tomorrow OK? Hope it's going well down in Wales! x'

Something definitely wasn't right, but he put his phone away, headed back to the hotel with the other two, and tried to shift it from his mind. They convened in DS Sterling's room, ordered an Indian takeaway, and discussed what they'd found.

'Three more murders, the same as the ones we already knew about. I feel like it's only added to our problems and done nothing to help,' said Lucas as he bit down on a samosa with a scrunched-up look on his face.

'No, no, DCI Miller, this is great stuff,' said Professor Hawthorne, taking a chip and dipping it into his curry. The Welsh seemed to love chips with their curry, and none of them were complaining.

'I'm with Lucas on this one,' said Kim, sipping from a glass of gin, which was bigger than her head.

'Thanks, Kim.'

'No, you're thinking about it incorrectly!'

'What other way is there to think about it, Prof? The team here in Wales is as clueless as we are. They have no new fingerprints, witnesses, no tyre tracks, no CCTV, no murder weapons and no person of interest. They're actually behind us. The last properly good lead we had, genuinely, was when we realised that he was selecting his victims via Twitter. And that stopped soon enough, as you well know. Since then, everything else has been shit.' Lucas finished his rant and took a breath and a massive swig from his bottle of Cobra beer.

'I just found you a murder weapon,' said Professor Hawthorne, shrugging.

'Ah well, yeah, OK. I'll give you that. Any chance you think this could be linked to PC Johnson and make my life easier?'

'No. I don't think it's him. Look, these murders fit the MO, but not in their entirety. There are subtle differences; it's almost as though they're trying to avoid them being connected to those in Leeds but want them to be linkable at the same time. It's strange. I've not encountered this before. That fact is very singular and something we need to understand. Get some sleep, and we'll try again in the morning.' And with that, he just got up and left, leaving the other two with the remaining curry and drinks.

'What an odd man,' said Kim, taking a rather large gulp from her gin and giggling.

51

They were up early the next morning, but there was nothing bright about it. There was a heaviness to the deep, pitch black of the early morning as DI Williams drove them up to a tiny village called Harford. DS Sterling's head was rubbing against the window as she repeatedly nodded off.

Professor Hawthorne's strong desire to visit all three of the crime scenes this morning had been tempered by Lucas a little, and they'd just about convinced him that wasn't necessary, although he was sulking a little in the back seat. They could see from the crime scene photos that the first two were just fields. They were open, exposed, and barren. This was entirely unlike any of the ones in Leeds, which is why Professor Hawthorne wanted to go, of course. However, these crimes were six years ago; nothing of interest would have survived in those conditions. As a compromise, they'd settled for letting him take the case notes with him; he was now studying intently in the back of the car with a childish pout.

Lucas's mother used to say that reading in the car would make him 'queasy', which it inevitably did because she'd put it in his head, and now he was expecting it. Not this time, however, Lucas was distracted and wasn't concerned about feeling queasy. Em was definitely off in her messages and it was gnawing away at him, like the sharp, electric feeling that would occasionally shoot through that scar on his left forearm. The blister pack in his front pocket was one tablet down once again this morning.

'Morning, how's the head? Lots of drinks with Laura? x'

'Mornin, yeah lol. You OK? x'

'Yeah, just drivin to some poxy little village. Where did you go then? x'

'Just out, nothing interesting x'

'Oh, no worries then. Everything OK? x'

'Yeah fine x'

Marvellous, great conversation there, Em. She was being funny with him. Was that because of their argument the other night, or was it because he was with DS Sterling, maybe? He glanced back in the mirror and saw her sleeping against the window, mouth wide open, catching flies. She was disarmingly pretty, even like that. No, stop it. He tried to park the thoughts ruminating around his head and get on with the task at hand.

When they arrived at the Harford crime scene, there was no formal car park, so DI Williams parked on the side of the road, as close to the crumbly stone wall as he could. Lucas had to climb over the centre console and gear stick to get out, which would have been unfortunate had he slipped. Once out, DI Williams began a brief tour of the scene. They stood at the entrance to a thin cycle track that meandered down the slope to a small stream. It was a popular dog-walking area for locals, and was very idyllic, at least when there weren't dead bodies to be found.

'Clara Jones was twenty-six years old and lived ten minutes away in the village,' said DI Williams, pointing over the crest of the little hill behind them. 'She had a small child, a two-year-old boy, Rufus. She was reported missing by her fiancé, a bloke called Geraint Morgan. Alibi checked out on him. He initially assumed she'd just gone out for a jog; she was a runner, you see and had gone missing before. Not like properly missing, just, you know, gone a few hours longer than expected. She'd always turned up later, but she hadn't come home this time. After thirty-six hours, we launched a full search and found her here.'

DI Williams led them along the track, past a large, gnarled tree with a large divot underneath a twisting, thick root. A small stream trickled away down the slope from the tree, not dissimilar to the 'Water's Edge' area in Emmet Woods. DI Williams was pointing into the depths of the divot, and Lucas could see the decaying body of a young woman in his mind's eye. Not so idyllic.

'Who found her?' asked Professor Hawthorne, looking up only briefly from the file in his hands.

'A lady called Mrs Grace Doyle, sweet thing. She had been walking her dog, one of the tiny fluffy white things. I don't know the breed. Anyway, she wasn't found for a while, not until the next morning. Her body was completely covered with leaves and stuff. They'd blown off the tree the previous night.'

'Jesus, that's horrific,' said Kim.

'It was. That's why I don't want a dog; I don't want to run the risk of finding a corpse. Anyway, we've had nothing like this since,' said DI Williams, shrugging. 'I'd made the link already, but this confirmed it for me, and I tried contacting your Carmichael woman, but she all but told me to fuck off.'

'Where is Mrs Doyle now?' asked Lucas, grimacing with embarrassment. How Carmichael had ignored this was puzzling him. What was going on?

'Oh, she still lives just over there, ' he pointed over his shoulder at a small farmhouse about two hundred meters up the road, sitting on a small ridge in the hilly backdrop. 'We've interviewed her a few times, nothing exhilarating, unfortunately. You've got the files' he nodded at Professor Hawthorne, who ignored him as he was still engrossed in the little folder.

They walked further up the track and stopped at the point where they'd found her.

'Had the crime scene been disturbed before you got here?' said Professor Hawthorne suddenly.

'Well, we've no way of knowing if it had been touched at all. We know it wasn't tampered with after we arrived, and we were first on the scene after Mrs Doyle. As far as we know, it's likely to have been intact; she certainly didn't go rummaging around.'

'But I thought it was a popular site with dog walkers?' said Kim.

'It was. Still is, in fact. But the weather was appalling, so nobody was out and about other than Mrs Doyle. She's hard as balls, though, in fairness.'

'Right,' she said, contemplating something in her head. Lucas stood still, looking around him. It was a lovely spot. A quiet place to run. Not that he could ever see himself getting up at the crack of dawn to run.

'Do you run, Prof?' said Lucas, turning to face the Professor, who was slightly back from the rest of them.

'Er... no. I used to swim a lot, but that was when I was in university. Haven't been near a pool since.' His eyes flicked back down, and he continued to study the folder with great interest.

'Me either,' said Kim.

'Right.' Lucas continued walking along the track, which was pretty much flat and straight. He couldn't see any obvious cover for someone dragging a body up to where she was found. It may have been less exposed than the other scenes in deepest Wales, but it was still more exposed than anything they'd encountered in Leeds.

'Do you get much tourism here?' asked Lucas, surveying the landscape.

'Basically none; it's a bit of a hidden gem, really.'

'He must have been confident. This is so exposed. So open, you could easily be seen if you weren't careful.' Silence from the rest of the party as they watched him think. 'He must have known the area. He must be from somewhere round here?'

'The thought had occurred to us, DCI Miller.' said DI Williams, smirking, 'But we've interviewed pretty much the entire village, those where the other girls were found, and nothing. Not a scrap. Which is why I tried getting your boss Carmichael to take a look.'

'Yes, well, we're here now and –'

Professor Hawthorne suddenly slammed the folder shut with a little clap. They all turned to look at him, smiling in his eccentric little way.

'I want to speak to Mrs Doyle, please. I need to ask her about the car.'

* * *

Mrs Doyle placed an ornate-looking teapot on the table before them. It was white, with fancy gold trim. Steam rose from the spout, and the reassuring smell of English breakfast tea filled her little kitchen. Or was it Welsh breakfast tea here? Lucas and DS Sterling sat across from the frail old lady as she tucked her skirt under herself and sat down. Professor Hawthorne was leaning against the worktop, staring intently at Mrs Doyle, whilst DI Williams was standing hunched in the corner, looking irritated. He'd pointed out three times that they'd already interviewed this woman, but Professor Hawthorne insisted.

'Thanks for the tea, Mrs Doyle,' said Kim, taking a steaming mug from her and blowing on the top to cool it.

'Oh, call me Grace, please!' she replied in a shrill Welsh accent, which Lucas was finding hard to get his ears around.

'OK, Grace, thanks for agreeing to talk to us.'

'No problem at all, happy to help. But I think I've told the other policemen everything I know.' She continued to pour the tea into some mugs that matched the teapot.

'Well, you never know we might –'

'Tell us about the car, please,' said Professor Hawthorne abruptly. Lucas's face was not doing a good job of hiding his irritation. However, Mrs Doyle barely flinched and despite the sudden, almost aggressive manner of the question, she obliged to address it.

'What car, sorry?'

'The one parked on the road. You mentioned it in 2019. The day before you found Clara.'

'Oh yes, well, I'm not sure it's relevant. I only noticed it because the fool who parked it had done it on a blind corner. I nearly hit it coming back from the village. Especially when the weather was so rotten,' she tutted, handing out the mugs one by one.

'Thanks. What time was this?' said Professor Hawthorne, who didn't appear to be blinking any more.

'Oh, I can't remember. Not late, I think I'd been to the supermarket or something. So I guess four, maybe five in the evening?'

'Describe the car, please.' He was getting more blunt and direct with every second. Lucas was feeling slightly awkward about all this now.

'It was four years ago. How am I supposed to describe it?' She paused briefly, holding the last mug of tea, only a centimetre from Kim, who wasn't sure if she should take it. Mrs Doyle was a little nettled, and Lucas was on her side. Professor Hawthorne was pushing this point harder than seemed necessary.

'Was it a big car or a small one? Like a hatchback or four-by-four?'

'Small it was. And quite old and battered, I think, there were dents in it. I guess that's why they felt safe parking it where they did.'

'Colour?'

'Er… dark. I don't know, black or blue or something. It may have been grey. It was raining cats and dogs, and I didn't see it until late. So it was something hard to see.' she shrugged. Bless her for being so helpful, thought Lucas; he'd have told Professor Hawthorne to do one if it were him.

'OK, could it have been this car?' Professor Hawthorne pulled a few large photographs from the folder and showed them to Mrs Doyle. She picked them up and studied them for a moment before saying,

'It was years ago, but I think that might be the car. Look, you can see the big dent in the back of it' she pointed at a little point towards the edge of the picture. Lucas took it from Mrs Doyle and looked at it carefully. Kim had got up from her and put a hand on his shoulder to peer over. The touch caught Lucas slightly off guard, and a weird energy grabbed him.

The picture he was looking at was a mid-distance shot of a field surrounded by police tape. The dreaded white tent was in the middle of it, the telltale signal that something grizzly had been discovered. To the side of the field was a small car park for dog walkers and the like. Two cars were parked in it; one was a police car, and the other was an old, black Rover-25 hatchback. It had seen better days; there were multiple dents in it, and one hubcap had come off. Lucas looked up, still puzzled, at Professor Hawthorne, who had turned to DI Williams.

'Who does that car belong to?'

'I don't know'

'Was it ever investigated? Is it known to belong to one of

your team?'

'Oh, I'm not sure.' DI Williams had gone a little pink now. 'Why is this relevant?'

'Because team. This car was photographed at the crime scene of one murder in 2018 and was then spotted by Grace the day before the discovery of another body some forty miles away a year later. To me, that seems suspicious,' concluded Professor Hawthorne, sporting a wide grin of excitement.

Lucas was looking at him; his irritation was evaporating rapidly, and he began to marvel at the tall, odd southerner who had already added so much to the investigation. That was genius, he thought. They had a lead.

2019

52

Lucas was taking a considerable risk, but couldn't think of a safe alternative. He looked into his rearview mirror as he drove away and saw Amelia heading through the hospital doors into the emergency department. Her phone number was scribbled on some scrap paper in the drinks holder, and they'd agreed to meet tomorrow, but she needed medical attention tonight. He was relying on her having as much to lose as he did, although she probably didn't. She just seemed trustworthy, and he was stupid.

Her top lip had almost completely burst open and was hanging on by a strand, revealing the yellowish teeth and gums behind. Mitchel had refused to pay her, apparently, and she always took money upfront before anything sexual would take place. He'd insisted she start without payment. She tried to leave, but he'd hit her repeatedly and grabbed her throat. She'd panicked, reached for the nearest thing she could find, which was the knife on his bedside table, and stabbed him in the neck with it. It seemed reasonable, as far as Lucas was concerned, anyway. This girl was tiny, barely over five feet, and weighing less than fifty kilograms. She desperately needed a good plate of fish and chips. The bravery that must have been required for her to put herself in a room with a bloke like Mitchel was… well… was it bravery? Desperation was probably a better description.

He drove home as carefully as possible, keen not to draw attention to himself. Parking on the drive, he snuck in through the back door, desperately avoiding waking Chloe or Rachel. Luna came to see him, silently wagging her tail and holding a tiny, stripy, woollen jumper in her mouth. She was cold and wanted him to put the jumper on for her, an adorable trait she'd picked up from somewhere. As she poked her snout through the neck hole and lifted her paws so he could slide them in, he knew she wouldn't grass him up at least. Luna was the most trusting creature he knew.

He pulled a plastic bag from under the sink and threw all his clothes in it before forcing himself into a scolding shower in the downstairs bathroom. After quickly drying himself with the dog's towel, which also went into the bag, he stashed it in the corner where Chloe wouldn't spot it, and crept back up to his bed. She didn't stir once.

Sleep was impossible. It felt like he had so many questions whirring around his head, but he already knew exactly what he'd done and how he would deal with it. He lay there for what felt like hours until his alarm rang at 6 am. He cancelled it once he was sure it had woken Chloe in the other room and lay there for a few more minutes. With great difficulty, he got up and made a show of running to the bathroom, careful to make as much noise as possible. Once there, he got to his knees and rammed his fingers as far down his throat as he could manage, making himself vomit violently into the bowl.

'Are you OK?' Chloe had appeared behind him, looking bleary-eyed with her hair in a tangled nest above her head.

52

'Not really. I've felt rough all night. Must have picked something up; I don't think I've eaten anything dodgy,' he said before retching again and letting loose another colossal pile of yellowy sick that splattered loudly on the ceramic. Gross. Chloe wrinkled her nose but was kind enough not to comment further as she went downstairs to get him some paracetamol and coffee.

Lucas looked at his reflection in the mirror and saw two tired, bloodshot eyes looking back at him. He splashed his face with cold water before heading back into bed. Chloe had somehow gotten ready quickly and came to see him before she did the school run and went to work.

'You OK?' she said, stroking his hair.

'Yeah, sorry, I think I have a bug. I'm going to get some more sleep, then hopefully go in later.'

'Don't bother coming in today; the team will cope without you. It's not exactly rammed at the moment. Reapers gone cold, and that home invasion case is pretty cut and dry.'

'Step-dad?'

'Yup, reckon so. If the CPS gives us the nod, we'll get him charged today. I'll let you know. I'll be home about five-thirty. Call me if you need anything. Love you.'

'Love you too,' he said. It was probably true; he did love her, but he was testing the boundaries of whether she loved him; he could feel the tension in her voice, even though she was trying to hide it.

He waited until she had left, gave it half an hour just to be sure, and then got up. He retrieved the bag of clothes from where he'd stashed it and went into the garden. They had an incinerator for burning confidential waste, so he popped the clothes in and set fire to them with some long matches and two-stroke petrol. They burned well, and with it, evidence that he'd just covered up the death of The Water's Edge Reaper. Probably.

53

Amelia sat on the edge of her bed in her tiny, poky little bedsit with a cooling pot noodle in her hands. Her bed was unmade, but she wasn't working today. She wouldn't be able to work for a few weeks, given the damage that had been done to her lip. Nobody would want fellatio from a stitched lip... well... someone probably would, but Amelia didn't want to do it. The doctors wanted to know how it happened, but she didn't tell them. She didn't want to get into trouble, and she didn't want the friendly police officer to get in trouble. She'd killed someone; even if it had been in self-defence, she'd still done it, and they'd throw the book at her. Life had always thrown her under the bus, and she was sure this would be no different.

She had a small television in the corner of her room, a gift from her mother some years ago. The last decent thing she'd done. The ITV News was on, and a lady was talking to the camera, but it felt as if she was speaking directly with Amelia.

'... And we can go live to crime correspondent Simon Davies, who's on Belmont Avenue now. Simon, what can you tell us?'

A tall, not unattractive man appeared on screen wearing a light blue shirt with a blazer and cleanly pressed trousers. Someone had made an effort. He might have been balding, but he pulled it off because of his lovely eyes, thought Amelia.

'Thank you, Sharon. Yes, I'm outside the house of Thomas Mitchel, the forty-one-year-old man who was at the centre of one of the biggest manhunts in recent memory. Although released not long after his initial arrest, he was at the top of the list of 'Water's Edge Reaper' suspects for many years, but today, he's made national headlines for a very different reason.'

Amelia dropped the pot noodle. It spilt over the floor, the remaining liquid soaking the bottom of her bed and the carpet beneath, adding to the collection of suspicious stains. She was gazing at the figure on the screen, her fragile little heart beating like a hummingbird.

'It's understood that a family member called in early this morning after becoming worried about Mr Mitchel following some worrying text messages sent from his phone last night. He was discovered in his bedroom in what appears to be an apparent suicide. Police are said not to be looking for anyone else in connection with the death at present. Whilst it is far too early to know for certain, his friends and family have reportedly told the police that he had been distraught and depressed since being released from custody and had made previous attempts to take his own life.'

Amelia didn't listen to anything that came next. They weren't looking for anyone else! Her palms were slippery, and she felt sweat running down her back. The sense of relief that flooded through her was palpable. She'd spent all night thinking about what would happen when the police discovered what she'd done. Would they believe she was a murderer? The kind officer seemed to understand what happened, but what if he decided to tell someone?

She went to the bathroom and ran to the sink with cold water before splashing her face. She took a deep breath and looked in the mirror. Her lip was full, swollen, and a horrible shade of purple. Several little white stitches lined the edge of the laceration, which stretched almost as far as her nose. Her pale green eyes were both bruised and bloodshot.

Suddenly, there was a knock at the door. She froze. There was another knock, slightly more frantic this time. She edged back into the main room of her bedsit and grabbed the TV remote, turning it off just as the anchor told them about some virus spreading through China. She stood in silence; the hummingbird in her chest was in overdrive. She crept slowly to the door and placed her eye against the peephole.

She let out a small sigh of relief and unlocked the door to reveal the friendly police officer. She poked the side of her face around the door, keeping the rest of herself hidden. He looked at her lip, which was even worse than last night.

'How you doing?' he said.

'Fine. How did you find me?'

'I'm a detective,' he smiled. He had a friendly smile, although his eyes were very close together, like a ferret, and the swept-back fringe was a few years out of fashion. After beckoning him inside, he sat on the edge of her bed, whilst she shut the door. She didn't lock it, which was her habit. She didn't want to appear rude or scared, even if he seemed trustworthy. He'd not reported her, even though he knew what she'd done. She'd killed a man, a horrible man, but all the same, Detective Miller hadn't told anyone.

'How's the lip?' he asked, looking carefully at the stitches on her face.

'Better, I guess. I think I'll be OK. They said it's not too bad, and it will heal.' she sat on the edge of the bed, leaving a space between them. A horrible thought suddenly went through her mind.

'Are you here to arrest me?'

He simply smiled back. 'No, not at all. I'm in as much shit as you if this gets out. I just wanted to check you were OK; you were attacked after all?'

'Ah. I'm OK. Not the first time, I can handle myself.'

'Clearly.'

'Oh no, I usually just run or threaten to call their wife. That's the first time I've... look, it was an accident. I didn't know what I'd grabbed when I hit him...'

'I understand,' he said, leaning backward and resting his shoulders against the wall.

'I didn't go to stab him. I was trying to get him to let go of my throat.'

'I get it. Honestly, don't worry' he smiled again. It was a very reassuring smile, and she liked it.

'So what happens now, then? How long until they do the autopsy? You think they will work out that I stabbed him?'

'I'm fairly certain that they won't. The cause of death will be blood loss from the wound to his neck, and there will be a knife with his fingerprints on it in his hand. As far as anyone is concerned, Thomas Mitchel took his own life. And it's not like he didn't try before, is it? His mother has openly said he'd made previous attempts.'

'So... I'm safe then?' she said hopefully, her eyes lighting up a little.

53

'Yes, I think so. We are both safe,' he said, reaching out and squeezing her knee like a father might do to his daughter. She looked at his hand on her leg momentarily and then put her hand on top of it. She looked up at his eyes and smiled. He removed his hand and stood up. He looked a little awkward.

'Look, I'm sorry for intruding on your morning. I'll go; we don't need to see each other again; we must keep our mouths shut. I think you should also look for another job for what it's worth. Something safer.'

'I can't do anything else,' she said glumly, 'and I'd like to see you again, actually. No people are kind to me.' Lucas thought for a moment. She was sweet, this innocent girl. She'd got caught up in the wrong stuff. It wasn't really her fault.

'I'll take you for a coffee next week,' he said with another warm smile. 'We can talk about your job prospects.'

'OK,' she beamed, although what sort of job he thought she'd be doing, she didn't know. But from that moment on, she had a friend.

54

Lucas stretched his hands above his head, leaning back in his desk chair. It had been one hell of a week. Sleep was becoming a rare commodity, as he was being kept awake by grim visions of Thomas Mitchel gasping and begging for his life. Of course, the bloke was evil, and he was better off dead. But thinking that, believing that, and watching the light fade from his eyes were very different things. Despite what he'd told Amelia, he was still worried that he would get found out. He'd got rid of the evidence, of course, but forensic science was moving on at such a pace that he had to assume they would find traces of him somewhere if they looked. After all, he knew how it worked; it wouldn't be that difficult.

It was Friday evening, and he was getting ready to pick up Chloe and take her for dinner. They'd been out several times this week, but she hadn't questioned him more about his behaviour. She hadn't asked him much about anything. She was becoming more and more distant with every passing month. He had started to wonder if it was fizzling out, and as much as he loved and cared for her, he wasn't sure he would fight for it. It had never been the same since they lost the pregnancy. There was a distance between them that was daunting, and he didn't have the energy to undertake the inevitable expedition to the other side.

They sat in the restaurant, not talking. She was on her phone, and he was looking around at the decor, his mind wandering. The niggling feeling in the back of his mind was becoming more and more prominent and distracting. He made a mental note to speak to the investigating officer on the Mitchel suicide in the morning. He'd deliberately kept his distance until now not to link himself to the case. However, he was in danger of having the opposite effect, as people were now surprised he wasn't taking more of an interest, given his well-documented obsession with the bloke. So, the following morning, he went to see DI Heywood.

'Why aren't you on this one?' he said, looking over his coffee at Lucas.

'You know why. I'm the last person who should be on the case. I was the first to say he was guilty,'

'Yes, but you're always banging on about how you can read people, and you had a feeling about him. Just surprised you weren't all over his death.' Lucas couldn't deny that he'd been vocal about Thomas Mitchel's guilt. He'd been almost unbearable since the moment he'd been released.

'Yeah, well, I'm just disappointed we'll never get to interview him properly,' he said with a shrug. 'I'm interested, though. How's the case going? What are you thinking?'

'I assumed it was because you were guilty,' said DI Heywood with a smirk, and Lucas's arsehole nearly fell open.

'Guilty?' he said, an enormous lump of puke readying itself at the top of his stomach, a wave of icy terror drenching him.

'Yeah, well, you hounded him unmercifully. Between you and that journalist, Davies, you probably drove him to this.'

DI Heywood was being very blunt. He usually was, but this was extreme, even for him. Lucas looked suitably pink, although not for the reason the DI Heywood suspected.

'Suicide then?' said Lucas, trying to move the conversation on, a new sense of relief slithering over him.

'I mean, yeah. Looks that way. Blokes sliced his neck open with his own penknife. The door was locked, no evidence of forced entry. He's got good reason to as well. I need to see what pathology says, but to me, it's pretty open and shut.

'Ah, cheers then.' He was thinking he'd probably head down to the morgue and see what the creepies had to say about it.

'Tell you what, though, Miller. You're going to look a right twat if there's another murder, ey?'

'Yeah, guess so.' It was a fair point. He really hoped that he was right about Mitchel.

He left DI Heywood to his own devices and headed across the city to the morgue. He found the pathologist, Dr Cooper, lurking in the main dissecting room, weighing an organ of some sort. Possibly a liver?

'Hello, DI Miller,' she said, her kind eyes meeting his. She was quite a hefty, strong, and imposing woman, but there was something motherly about her.

'Morning Dr Cooper, how are you? Kids OK?'

'Ahh, surviving, which is more than this poor chap,' she said, lifting the liver off the scales and back into a bucket. 'Kids are well, although Marcus is acting strange. I think he fancies someone in his class.' She laughed, making the spleen she'd just picked up jiggle like a jelly. Lucas couldn't look at it without it feeling a little odd.

'You come down to see Em?' she smirked.

'Huh, Em? Oh no,' he went pink, 'Why would I do that?'

'No idea,' she replied with a wink. Lucas just ploughed on.

'I came down to see if you'd done the autopsy on Thomas Mitchel yet?'

'I have. We did him a few days ago, actually. I thought you might be down sooner. Looking to see if we found a heart? Or a stomach full of prostitute?' Dr Cooper had an especially dark sense of humour.

'Something like that. Was it definitely suicide then?

'Feeling guilty, are we? But yes, I think so. The scene fits. He was naked, as they often are, and he'd done it in front of the mirror. He had attempted to avoid interruption, and there were a couple of hesitation marks around the wound. There's form as well, lots of scarring to the inside of his groin and wrists. There was also a fair amount of alcohol and cocaine in his system, which would fit with someone trying to build up the courage to off themselves.'

'Ah, great,' said Lucas, trying not to look as relieved as he felt.

'I don't blame you for what it's worth,' she said. 'Some guys are going to. They'll say that you pushed him to this. But I think you had good reason to suspect him and were investigating it properly. Dan thinks the same, but he'll never tell you that.'

'Thanks, Doc, I appreciate the support. I might need that if we don't get anywhere with the case soon. I still need to prove that it was Mitchel.'

'Well, if there is anything I can do to help, let me know. In fact...' she reached into the bucket and pulled out a large, pale, salmon-coloured organ covered in deep blue veins. 'pop down anytime you want and pick my brains!'

She was still cackling in the background as Lucas left the dissection room and headed back towards the incident room. As he rounded the corner, he bumped, quite literally, into Emily West, the mortuary assistant. She nearly fell over and grabbed him by the arm to stop herself from tumbling.

'Fuck sorry!' he said, grabbing her waist to stop her from hitting the deck. Once she was righted, he immediately let go, but she lingered slightly and gave his biceps a subtle squeeze.

'No, it was me. I'm so clumsy. Sorry. So... What are you doing here?' she asked him, her eyes running up and down his body.

'Oh, I was just chatting with the pathologist,' he said, hoping he wasn't going pink.

'You have time for a coffee?' she asked, her eyes hopeful.

'No, sorry, not really. I'm on a case and need to get back to the team. But thanks.' He headed off up the corridor and could feel her watching him. Just before he turned the corner, he chanced a peek back at her, but she'd turned and was walking away. She had a nice arse, he thought as he left.

2023

55

As was always the way, the journey back felt significantly quicker than the journey down. Trees and fields flashed by, but Lucas and Kim furiously made phone calls to the team in the Leeds incident room. Professor Hawthorne continued studying the case notes he'd brought with him and the copies of the Welsh ones he'd insisted were made before they'd left.

'Yeah, Sadiq, it's a black Rover-25. Yeah, *BD03 TDS*. No, B for bravo. Yes. I need to know who it's registered to and everything about them. We're going to come straight back to the office when we arrive,' he checked his watch. 'It should be about 2 pm.'

Once again, DI Sadiq 'Mayor' Khan had been understandably irritated that DS Sterling was accompanying Lucas to Wales. The thing was, though, they didn't particularly get on. It wasn't just a clash of personalities, either. DI Khan had been quite vocal in blaming Lucas and his 'witch-hunt,' as he called it, for the suicide of Thomas Mitchel. That being said, he was professional and did still appreciate the need to kiss arse and be present during the vital steps of this investigation, and being denied the opportunity to do this, especially to a DS, was offending him. Not that Lucas cared much; he'd much rather spend the time with DS Sterling, even if he thought it might be the reason for Ems's strange and distant affect.

They returned to the incident room without issue, except for Professor Hawthorne, losing his ticket. He was so direct and firm with the attendant; however, they let him through to avoid a problem. As they walked through the doors to the inquiry room, Lucas was confronted by a rather pissed-off Detective Superintendent Carmichael.

'My office. Now,' she barked. Lucas followed her, feeling the anger building in his shoulders. Was she really about to find some way of being annoyed with him? He'd just found them another three cases and a lead.

As they entered her office, Lucas opened his mouth to speak, 'Boss, I - ' She silenced him with a wave of her wrist, a small gold watch jangling about. She turned and faced him, stood behind her chair, and leaned over it, thinking for a second.

'So. I was wrong, was I?'

'Er... well, it appears they're linked. Certainly, we need to investigate it more closely than before,'

'Grow some fucking balls, Miller.'

'OK. Yeah, you were wrong!' He surprised himself with how forcefully he said that.

'That's better. Just because I'm more senior than you, taller than you, and a woman, it doesn't mean I can't be wrong; you should tell me. Just do it privately, not in front of the team. Half of them fear me, and the other half probably fancy me; I don't want to ruin that.' She winked at him and then laughed. It reminded him of a cartoon witch, the way it cackled up and down, before it became a cough, which made

Lucas wonder if she'd started smoking again.

'Anyway, you were right. Sort of,' she said once she'd finished hacking up a lung.

'What do you mean, sort of?'

'DNA came back from that knife and from the fingernails. They match each other, but nothing on the system. We have both PC Johnson's DNA and his fingerprint on record. He wasn't holding that knife, and Amelia hadn't pulled his hair out. It's not him.'

'Ah, right. Well, OK. You win that one, then.'

'Call it a draw, but seriously. Well done on following up with Wales. It's all a bit shit, and I'm going to get my hairless arse handed to me, but at least we're on the same page. The press is going to have a field day. It's a miracle that bastard Davies hasn't already turned up with his ink and quill, the little prat. Get back out there and brief the team. I'll join you in a moment. I need to lick my wounds.'

Lucas headed back out of her office along the connecting corridor. As he was about halfway, a short, wobbly man with a ginger mullet stepped out of the evidence locker and straight into his path.

'Fuck!' said Lucas, trying to dodge him, knocking his arm and causing the usual pain to race across his scar.

'Ah, sorry, mate. Oh, it's you.' PC Andrew Johnson was looking at Lucas as if he was something that he'd stepped in. The look of disdain was intense, and Lucas might have wilted on another day, but not when he was feeling as positive as he was right now.

'PC Johnson, I thought you were on leave pending our investigation?' said Lucas, regaining his composure. It was cruel, but he didn't feel like telling the bloke the DNA had cleared him. Not just yet.

'I am. But I needed to collect some stuff and drop off access cards,'

'From the evidence room?' Lucas nodded at the door behind PC Johnson.

'Yes, actually, they needed to deactivate my card.'

'Right, OK. Well, look, no hard feelings, but - '

'Don't be a cunt, sir. I have hard feelings. You've ruined my career.' he turned and strode off, leaving Lucas to stand there. He thought about calling him back, but there was no point, and he didn't know what to say. He'd have to let him cool off.

Lucas re-joined the team in the main room; they were all buzzing with the information that there were some fresh cases, evidence and the realisation that there could be another lead. It was nice to have something positive banded around the room. What with the brief physical description from Amelia, the discovery of the murder weapon, knowing there was a Welsh link and now the car, the net was finally closing.

Lucas stood by the window overlooking the car park as everyone was leaving. The tiny figure of a petite, delightfully pretty woman with supple dark skin was heading to her car, long black hair flowing out behind her. What had she been doing at the station? He picked up his phone and dialled Em. He watched her get her phone out of her bag, look at it, and then put it back. Fucking marvellous. She got into the car, and he saw her engine start, but she wasn't leaving yet. He tried again.

'Hello?' Ems's voice floated through his speaker.

'Em, hi, are you OK?'

'Yes, why?'

'Oh, just you hadn't replied to my text was all, just checking everything was alright. I'm back in Leeds if you want to get some tea tonight?' he said with a degree of trepidation.

'Oh Lucas, I can't tonight, sorry. I'm going to be staying late. Maybe tomorrow night?' Lucas's heart sank in his chest. Right.

'Yeah, sure, tomorrow night sounds good. Your place?'

'Huh, yeah, sure, could you text me tomorrow about it?'

'Yeah, will do, see you.' She hung up. A few seconds passed as Lucas stared out the window at her car. Maybe she was getting something from it, and she really was staying late? But then she set off, down the ramp and out of the car park. Maybe she was driving back to the morgue? Perhaps she wasn't lying to him. No, he had no idea why, but she was lying. He could feel it.

A few hours later, still somewhat dejected, he trudged out of the station and round to his own car, parked on the corner of the multi-story, out of the way. As he got to it, he noticed his boot was slightly ajar. The light on his rearview mirror flashed aggressively, meaning the alarm had been tripped at some point. He walked around and lifted the lid of the boot. Empty. It had been empty when he left it, though, so there was nothing to steal. However, as he went to close it, he spotted the glint of something shiny in the periphery of his vision. Silver and dangling with menace, a necklace was hanging from the bottom of the parcel shelf. It was small and dainty with a moon-shaped locket attached. He picked it up and turned it over in his hand. It was very lightweight. He clicked the locket open, saw the picture inside, and immediately dropped it. Shit, shit, shit! He knew

55

who this belonged to. Inside was a picture of three people: Jacob Murray, his wife Sandra, and their innocent little girl Jessica. This was Jessica's missing locket from twelve years ago.

What the fuck was it doing in his boot?

56

Lucas was frozen to the spot. What did he do? Of course, his gut instinct was to call it in and get forensics here now. But he hesitated. This was a set-up. The only person who could have that necklace was the killer, and they'd chosen to put it in his boot for a reason. Was it a warning? Were they trying to frame him? Were they playing with him? He remembered what Carmichael had said when he was interviewing PC Johnson. *It is possible to pin it on him...* That would be ridiculous, wouldn't it? Wouldn't it?

He made a snap decision, probably the wrong one, but he made it all the same. Closing the boot firmly, he got in and drove, his wheels spinning as he set off. He pulled onto the main road, his heart beating in his chest and the pain in his arm raging. This was a mistake, he knew it, but self-preservation was strange, and logic had no place here. He clicked the hands-free on his car and called the one person on earth he truly trusted right now.

'Kim, hi, it's Lucas' he was trying to remain calm, but spoke quickly.

'Oh hi, everything OK?' she said, clearly noting the sense of urgency as well.

'No, not really; I really need your help. Can you meet me at mine in twenty minutes?'

'What's the matter?'

'I'll tell you when we meet. Is that OK?'

A pause, she was thinking. 'Yeah, I'll be there in a quarter of an hour,' and she put the phone down. Lucas took two pills from his blister pack and charged home as quickly as possible.

* * *

She was waiting outside the house when he got there, arms folded and looking puzzled. He parked up quickly, and they met on the doorstep.

'What's going on?' she said, her eyes slanting downwards with concern.

'Inside, and I'll explain.' He ushered her inside and into the living room. She wasn't wearing her uniform for a change. She wore professional tight white trousers and a nice pink blouse. It suited her, but now wasn't the time for ogling.

'Someone has broken into my car whilst we were in Wales.'

'Right, OK. So, report it? What did they take? Nothing important? Shit, Lucas, have they taken any case files?'

'No, nothing. They took nothing. But they left this in the boot. Don't touch it.' He held out a tissue, inside of which was the necklace.

'What is it?' she said, looking even more confused than before. He clicked open the moon pendant and showed her it more closely. She was perplexed for only a second more, and then her eyes widened with disbelief.

'Is that... Jessica Murray's missing necklace?'

'Yup, I think so.'

'Fuck Lucas. We have to call Carmichael and hand it in. Why the hell are you bringing it to me?' She looked terrified now.

'Because I trust you. And it is more complex than telling Carmichael. Someone is trying to put me in the spotlight.'

'No, they're playing with you, Lucas; why would anyone think you were suspicious?'

'There have been other things.'

'Like what, Lucas? You're paranoid. What is wrong with you?'

'Carmichael said it to me!' I've been on the case from the very start, and I live where most of the victims are coming from. I knew Amelia –

'What? Are you taking this piss? You knew her!'

'Yeah, I knew her before she was killed. I helped her with some stuff, but I knew her.' he tried to continue, but Kim cut him off,

'As in knew her, or *knew* her?' Her eyes narrowed.

'I didn't sleep with her, nothing like that. But look, the pen they found inside her; I do actually have one of those. He turned and pointed to the mantelpiece where the pen was in its little glass jar. Except it wasn't.

'Oh shit,' he darted across the room to the glass jar. He dropped to his knees and scoured the floor. No, it was definitely missing.

'Fuck, fuck! I think it might have been my pen!' he said, yet more panic filling his voice as he put his head in his hands.

'How the hell would they get your pen, Lucas? You've probably just misplaced it. Has anyone been here?'

'No, I've not had any intruders. I don't think it's just me, Luna... and Em. You don't think?' he said, his mind racing at a thousand miles per hour.

'No, she's an airhead mortuary assistant Lucas, no offence, but she doesn't exactly fit the pissing profile. Stop being daft and calm down. We need to think this through. That is definitely her necklace, right? Your pen is missing. OK, let's say you are a target. Are you in any danger? Has someone got it in for you?' Kim was counting the questions off with her fingers.

'They only seem to kill young women. I don't think they want to kill me. I think they're trying to incriminate me,' said Lucas, still thinking as rapidly as possible.

'But why? Is it personal? Or is it simply because you're running the operation?'

'I don't know. PC Johnson bloody hates me, though I'll tell you that.'

'Do you trust Carmichael?'

'Yes, I think so. I don't know, though; I still don't like the way she handled the Welsh cases. But yeah, I think I trust her. Maybe? Fuck, I don't know!'

'We need to tell someone about the necklace. We can't just keep it hidden.'

'I've told you?'

'I'm just a bloody DS, Lucas! I don't count. Nobody even noticed when I took a year off with sodding breast cancer. Nobody cares what I have to say. Seriously, what fucking use am I, Lucas?' she flapped, exasperated again.

'You've been the most valuable person on the team, Kim,

and I trust you.'

She bit her tongue for a second; she was a little taken aback by his sudden trust in her. 'OK, look, I won't tell Carmichael. But I think you should. If you don't handle it right, this could cost us both our jobs.'

Lucas turned and looked away from her for a moment. He stared at the empty glass on the mantelpiece where the pen should be. He was thinking about how Em had lied to him over the phone. She'd been here the whole time he was in Wales, and she had a key; she was supposed to feed Luna while he was away. Now he doubted whether she'd have even done that, but Luna looked well-fed when he returned. But then he remembered PC Johnson coming out of the evidence room earlier, looking sheepish. Something wasn't adding up about any of this.

'Look, OK. I'll tell Carmichael. She's going to go fucking spare with me. If this falls in on my head... Do you believe me?'

'Don't be stupid, Lucas, you're a class copper and a class bloke. Of course, I believe you. You're not a killer. With everything you've been through, you're the last person I'd expect it from.'

There was a ringing erupting from his pocket suddenly. He scooped his phone out of his pocket, hands still quivering from all the adrenaline pumping through his veins.

'DCI Miller'

'Hi boss, it's DC Green. Can you talk quickly?'

'Not really a good time, Green. Can it wait until tomorrow?'

'Er... well, it's just we've identified the owner of the car in Wales, sir.'

'Right, OK, anyone of interest?' said Lucas, trying to sound normal desperately. It was a force of habit to be interested in these things.

'Belongs to a Mrs Susan Davies,' said DC Green dramatically.

'Should I know who that is?'

'Well, yeah, it's the mother of Simon Davies. That bloody journalist who keeps pestering us,' said DC Green. Time froze. The journalist?

'Fuck. Bring him in, now!'

'On it, boss.'

He looked at Kim, stood there, hands on her hips, staring back at him with genuine concern. 'I'll tell Carmichael about the necklace, but we're speaking to Simon Davies first.'

2020

57

It had been three long years since the last body was discovered, yet the whispers of a serial killer still hung over the city of Leeds like a giant, pulsating aneurysm, ready to burst at any moment. Not that people were whispering to each other in person these days; it was all over conference calls or through surgical masks at socially distanced events. They were in the midst of a pandemic, and it was making the investigation even more difficult than usual.

Despite the challenges, Lucas was determined to catch his man. Although, perhaps they already had? In his mind, Thomas Mitchel was the guilty party, and he was currently rotting six feet under. The evidence was weak, but there was enough there for Lucas to honestly believe he had been the man they were looking for, although even Lucas might admit that he had an ulterior motive for wanting to pin it on Mitchel. Guilt would sometimes bubble up inside him when he thought about what he and Amelia had done that night. But it would all be justified once he could prove it.

He sat in his dimly lit home office, staring at the grainy CCTV footage on his laptop screen. Resources at work were now being slowly allocated to other crimes, so he was working on the case in his spare time. The Reaper case was still comfortably the most significant project the department had running and vast numbers of officers were working day and night. But they'd taken the foot off the gas, just a little, it must be said.

The footage on Lucas's laptop screen showed Vicky Turner, victim number five, walking down a deserted street on the night of her death. The next morning, she'd been found behind the big Tesco in Bradford, throat cut, bowels removed, and tied to a large industrial bin. Vicky wasn't a sex worker; she wasn't a student; she wasn't anything typical. Simply a woman walking home at night alone.

Lucas sighed and rubbed his eyes, which were dry and beginning to form crusty sleep, but couldn't give up for the sake of the victims and their families. He looked back at the screen and watched Vicky, with her pixie haircut and over-large earrings, saunter down the road, unaware that this would be her last few hours on earth. That was it, though; there was nothing else of use on the tape. No cars, no mysterious hooded man following her. No creep lurking in the bushes. Nothing. Within five minutes of walking off the screen, she'd been kidnapped before being tortured, tied to a bin, and left to rot. The poem left inside her abdominal cavity was as cold and callous as all the others.

The colon, a labyrinthine cave, where shadows dwell and whispers rave,
A passage dark, where secrets slide, in its depths, they silently hide.

There was a creek on the stairs, and his door slid open. Chloe poked her head in, her hair messy and a little greasy. No make-up, as usual these days. No effort at all, thought Lucas.

'You're still up'. This was a statement, not a question, but Lucas answered it anyway.

'Yeah,'

'I'm going to bed now,' she said, another statement, not a question. He didn't reply.

'I love you,' she added, but it felt forced.

'You too,' he said, not looking up from the screen. She watched him for a moment longer and then quietly closed the door. Lucas sighed and rubbed his eyes again. He was tired, but sleep was almost worse than being awake at the moment.

The footage played over and over. The same thing happened every time. Vicky would walk down the street and disappear out of sight. Nothing changed. There was no sign of anyone, apart from the odd passer-by. No cars. Nothing.

Lucas leaned forward, resting his elbows on the desk and his head in his hands. He could feel the tears stinging the back of his eyes, and he tried to fight them back. There it was, the guilt bubbling up again.

The strain on his relationship with Chloe was immense and unsustainable. He'd been working increasingly hard lately and had barely seen her in weeks. They hadn't had sex in months. The fact that he still couldn't let go of this case and move on was making things worse, and he knew it. He knew he should probably give up and walk away. But he couldn't. He just couldn't. They needed some time apart, but the lockdown meant they were in a 'bubble' together, so that was an impossibility. They'd been sleeping in separate rooms for nearly a year now. She was on her own, but he at least had Luna, who was curled up on his feet under the desk. Chloe would just have to put up with him being in the office at all hours. Rachel knew there was a problem. She'd really taken to Lucas and treated him as a father, but these days she gave him a wide berth and stuck to Chloe like glue. He wasn't her real dad, though, and right now, he had no intention of being.

He got up, unceremoniously shaking the furry creature off his feet, and walked over to the window. There was a thick, oppressive darkness to the garden, so he couldn't see much past the reflection of himself. He looked terrible. He hadn't shaved in days, and his face was drawn and pale. The bags under his eyes were heavy and dark, and his hair was wild and unkempt. He looked like a vagrant, not a police officer. He looked, he hated to say it, like his father. A drunk, sad old man, Lucas had almost stopped visiting. There was enough guilt left in him to think he should go around and at least check he was still alive.

He returned to the desk and picked up the picture of Chloe, Rachel, and himself that they'd taken whilst on holiday a few years ago. It was a special picture. They all looked so happy and content; the sun shone, and they were at their best. He remembered that day. It was the last day of their holiday in Pembroke. They'd been to the beach, played in the sea and had a barbecue. They'd sat outside their glamping pod in little pop-up chairs and talked about nothing important but enjoying the company and the view. Chloe and Rachel had made mocktails, and they'd drunk them all night until they fell asleep on the grass. It was one of the best nights of Lucas's life. It might have also been one of the last times he remembered being happy.

The tears flowed, and he buried his face in his hands as he sobbed. The guilt of what he had done was too much, the pressure of the case too great. His relationship with Chloe was in tatters; it may as well be the eighth victim of the so-called 'Water's Edge Reaper'.

He wiped his eyes and took a deep breath, knowing he needed to get some sleep. He closed the laptop lid and headed out of the office and onto the landing. Lucas made his way through the dark house and crept over to Chloe's bedroom door. She was already asleep, snoring softly. He watched her momentarily and felt another pang of guilt for how he'd treated her. He loved her; really, he did. She was a good person and didn't deserve to be treated like this. She deserved better. He thought briefly that he could undress quietly and slip into the bed beside her, but she stirred slightly, and Lucas backed out of the room. He kept going across the hallway and into the spare bedroom, where he tucked himself in bed and had a restless, horrible night's sleep filled with nightmares.

* * *

'Anyone volunteering to follow up with this witness? I hear she's quite good-looking if that changes anything?'

Lucas was sitting in the incident room wearing his blue surgical mask, properly covering his nose and mouth, unlike DC Green, whose mask was practically underneath his chin. They were all sitting at desks spaced two meters apart, trying not to cough. A couple of PCs were off with the dreaded virus, and the new DS Sadiq Khan had already got it reasonably badly. They all knew people who'd ended up in hospital with it, but thankfully, nobody from their unit had died. A receptionist in the Bradford unit had sadly passed away a few weeks ago, and a few of them had lost grandparents. It was bleak and a significant distraction from the case.

The other distraction was the pile of additional cases that was increasing in size rapidly. The size of the 'Reaper' case had meant it had been his singular focus for a few years, but now, with no movement since 2017, he was being given a much greater number of supplementary cases. Currently, he needed someone to interview the wife of a bartender who, it appeared, had spiked the drinks of men and attempted to rape them in the wine cellar. Challenging thing to do during COVID, so he was probably going to get a more extensive sentence for breaking lockdown rules than he was for the rapes, thought Lucas.

He looked around at the gathered officers, waiting for one of them to answer his question. It made a pleasant change to look around at them rather than just be faced with black squares when they refused to turn their webcams on for the conference call.

'Well?'

'Go on then, boss,' said DC Green, somewhat reluctantly.

'Good lad, this is a good one; it might be worth something. You OK to go on your own?'

'I'll manage,' said DC Green, who began coughing violently, using neither his hand nor his mask to cover his mouth.

'Are you sure you're OK?' said Lucas, watching him with concern.

'Fine, sir, fine, just need to get out there and crack on.'

'OK. Well, I will keep my distance from you for the next few days. You sound like dogshit, mate.' The phone rang in the corner of the room, and PC Evans got up reluctantly.

'Right,' said Lucas, 'That's that. Everyone's something to be getting on with - '

'Sir!' shouted PC Evans from across the room. But Lucas ignored her, as usual, when the constables started shouting out.

' - so let's crack on. Something will present itself -'

'Sir!' she shouted again, and Lucas stopped, irritated.

'What? Don't interrupt me. I'm distributing roles.'

'Sorry, sir,' she gasped. 'But it's DI Heywood'

'Right, so what?'

'He's at a crime scene, a young woman stabbed to death,' she said, her shoulders dropping with the scolding she was receiving.

'OK, sounds standard. I've got enough on my plate with these rapes and the murders up at Black Horse Farm. Can't he manage his own scenes?'

'Someone's cut out her pancreas. They've got another poem,' she said, and the blood in Lucas's veins froze instantly. No. This couldn't be happening. He couldn't speak, just sat there, mouth open behind the mask, staring at the PC holding the phone to her shoulder.

This couldn't be happening. But it was.

2021

58

Lucas had always believed in the power of resilience, a trait hammered into him not just by the rigours of his job but by the loss of his mother when he was still so young. That resilience was being tested right now. With its bustling streets and hidden shadows, the city of Leeds had become the backdrop for his apparent abject failure and had lost the charm that had drawn him back ten years ago. Now, he just viewed it as a cesspit and a less-than-subtle reminder of how this case seemed to echo his mother's unsolved murder. There was no standard way to process a situation like this.

His greying hair, thin face and bony shoulders demonstrated the physical cost this investigation had on him. Still, the personal cost cast a much longer and more damaging shadow over Lucas' psyche. Given the melting pot of emotions ripping him apart inside, finding himself standing at the doorstep of his father's home was a recipe for disaster. The pandemic had transformed visiting a loved one into a gauntlet of risks and precautions, but for Lucas, the virus was the least of his concerns.

Three months had passed since he'd last seen his father, three months during which the gap between them had only widened, filled with silence, resentment, and the unspoken grief of a shared loss.

As he raised his hand to knock, Lucas couldn't help but wonder what awaited him on the other side of the door. The last encounter had ended in a slagging match between them. Harsh words and unresolved anger, a pattern that had become familiar over the years. Yet, even as he prepared himself for another confrontation, Lucas couldn't shake the feeling that this visit was a necessary step, not just for familial duty but for the slim chance of bridging the vast emotional distance that had come to define their relationship.

The door swung open, and Lucas's gaze swept over the living room, noting piles of discarded bottles, empty food packets and unopened letters. His father stood there, crooked and barely supporting his weight on the door frame. Christ, he was pissed, even by his impressive standards. It was pathetic, really. He seemed to shrink against the vast emptiness of his decaying little flat. The air was heavy with the scent of stale alcohol, smoke, and regret.

'Lucas,' his father grumbled, the name sounding like an afterthought as he turned away, signalling for his son to follow. The awkwardness of their greeting, devoid of any warmth or connection, hung between them as Lucas stepped inside, the door closing with a dull thud.

The conversation started with trivialities, an uncomfortable dance around the elephant in the room. Lucas hated the way his father's hands trembled, the grip on his drink both a lifeline and a chain. As the minutes ticked by, the tension mounted, an inevitable build-up to the confrontation both men knew was coming.

It was his father who broke first, his words slurred but

sharp, sliding through the pretence of civility. 'You're just like them, aren't you? All these years, what do you have to show for it? My wife, your mother, murdered, and now more women dying. What are you doing about it, Lucas? Fuck all. That's what.' he took a large swig from the bottle.

The accusation stung, a direct hit to Lucas's deepest insecurities. He had dedicated his life to solving cases just like his mother's, yet the killer remained at large, mocking his efforts. He caught sight of himself reflected in his father's disappointed eyes.

The argument escalated quickly, fuelled by years of pent-up frustration and grief. Lucas tried to explain the complexities of the investigation, the dead ends and false leads that had plagued their efforts, but his words fell on deaf ears. His father saw only the failures, not the relentless pursuit of justice.

'You think I don't know what it's like?' Lucas shot back, his voice rising in anger. 'Every day, I see the faces of those families, the same pain and loss we felt. I'm doing everything I can. At least I'm not just drinking myself into an early grave like a sad, defeated old man!'

'Oh fuck off, Lucas, it's just not enough, is it?' his father countered, his voice laced with bitterness. 'Other families are suffering because you can't catch a damn killer. You're a fucking disappointment, son.'

The words hit Lucas like a physical punch, the accusation of failing not just as a detective but as a son, cutting deeper than any knife. He felt the anger rising in him as he retorted,

'And you're a father worth looking up to, are you? You're a waste of fucking space. Mum would be so embarrassed. She'd have fucking walked out, you piece of shit!'

The bottle flew past his head before he had a chance to react, smashing into the wall behind him, glass exploding and sticky rum painting the ceiling and floor. Lucas saw red. He leapt across the room, meeting his father head-on, who was swinging blindly for him. Punches were thrown. Most were missed, a clumsy tussle fuelled by alcohol and rage. His father was weaker than Lucas, but a nastier fighter. He was pulling hair and digging his nails in, drawing blood. Lucas pushed him away and delivered a powerful uppercut which connected with his father's jaw, lifting him off the floor and hitting the table under the window.

A large photograph of Lucas's mother perched precariously on the table's edge was sent crashing to the ground. The glass shattered, scattering sharp shards across the floor and under the coffee table. His father was back on his feet, charging straight for him. He caught Lucas in the midriff, knocking him backwards. Lucas stretched out his left hand to break the fall, but one of the glass shards sliced deep into his flesh. He could feel the glass scraping against his exposed bone as the muscle ripped from its tendon. The pain was immediate and intense, searing through him in a way he'd not experienced before. He didn't scream. He didn't yell out at all. The shock was instantaneous. He glanced down at his arm to see a colossal gash splayed open from his mid-forearm to the wrist. Blood dripped onto the floor initially, mingling with the fragments of glass, but then an arterial pulse squirted out, covering the floor. Shit, thought Lucas, this wasn't good. The fight ceased for a moment, and both men were stunned into silence by the sudden turn of events.

Lucas stared at the wound on his arm; the blood still hosing from the severed artery in his wrist was covering the photograph of his mother, now lying face-down amidst the debris.

His father's voice, now laced with concern, broke the silence. 'Lucas, let me—'

'No,' Lucas interjected, the pain sharpening his resolve. 'Call a fucking ambulance, now!' He took his belt off as quickly as he could and wrapped it around his arm, just below the elbow. He tightened it with his teeth and wrapped a jumper over the huge slice in his arm, which seemed to stem the blood flow for now. He was feeling dizzy now, either from shock or blood loss. 'This... This isn't solving anything,' he panted.

His father, clearly shaken, grabbed the phone, dialling for an ambulance. 'What do I tell them, Lucas?' his voice quivering. Was it nerves, or was it the drink? Lucas gritted his teeth, trying not to lose focus.

'Tell them... I was attacked by a dog.'

'A dog, right,' his father replied, his tone empty, as the 999 operator picked up. As the call was made, Lucas was struggling to keep his wits. He could feel his body going into shock. He could sense the blood pumping into his jumper. It was becoming heavier, the fibres soaking up the claret. His breathing was laboured, a struggle to get the oxygen needed.

The journey to the hospital was a blur; the ambulance crew had asked him a lot of questions and had managed to stop the bleeding. His mind was racing, a mix of anger and regret. He had never wanted things to end like this.

As the doors opened, he was rushed into the trauma unit. They were moving him, talking to him. But their voices were drowned out. He couldn't make out their words. Then the room went black.

2022

59

EMAIL: DI.LMiller3@westyorkshire.police.uk
Subject: Departmental Update

Dear Senior Detectives,

Welcome to the monthly unit update. As usual, we aim to provide you with news on the ongoing investigations into operation 'Water's Edge,' as well as a few less high-profile cases that are equally important.

Water's Edge

The investigation into the serial killings in Leeds, Bradford and the surrounding areas is still ongoing. We feel we are making progress and are confident that we will eventually catch the person responsible.

In the past week, we have interviewed several new witnesses and have collected additional evidence. We are currently analysing this new information and hope it will lead us to a breakthrough.

I understand that this case is a top priority for all of us, and I want to assure you that we are working tirelessly to solve it. We are committed to bringing the individual involved to justice and keeping the public safe.

Other Case notes

In addition, we are also investigating many other crimes. Notable highlights include:

- *A burglary spree in Yeadon, Leeds*
- *A series of car thefts in Broomfields, Bradford*
- *A drug trafficking ring in Wakefield*

We are making good progress in all these cases and are confident that we will make arrests soon.

Social News

I am pleased to announce that Karen's birthday party last week was a success. Everyone had a great time, and Karen was delighted with the turnout.

I am also sad to announce that DC Kimberly Sterling has had to take a leave of absence because of a recent diagnosis of breast cancer. Kimberly is a valuable team member, and we will all miss her. I know you will join me in wishing her a full and speedy recovery.

If you have any questions or concerns, please do not hesitate to contact me.

Sincerely,

Detective Chief Constable Raymond Thatcher

West Yorkshire Police

Lucas moved the email across into his deleted folder. Every update for the last eleven years has read the same. We're nearly there; we'll catch him soon. He couldn't help but feel it was hopeless. Still, at least he wasn't DC Sterling. Her entire future condensed down to a footnote at the bottom of an internal email. She'd been a very useful member of the team recently. He wasn't going to visit her; that would be creepy, but he'd try to be kind to her if she returned.

* * *

The night had settled over Leeds like a shroud, casting long shadows that danced with malice. DI Lucas Miller parked his unmarked police car near the desolate alley, the muted hum of the engine fading away. The pre-dawn light was breaking, casting an unearthly glow over the scene, accentuated by the flashing police lights. The rain had left everything slick and glistening, adding an extra layer of dread to the atmosphere.

As he stepped out, the biting chill of the early morning air cut through his coat, and his breath hung in the frigid darkness. He pulled on his gloves with great difficulty, as he was yet to regain full use of the fingers in his left hand. The surgeons had done an unbelievable job of preserving function, given he'd sliced through a branch of his medial nerve and his radial artery. Weak movement, some numbness and a hideous scar were a small price to pay. The electric shooting pains that came on sporadically were becoming increasingly difficult to manage, but he shifted it to the back of his mind as best he could.

He made his way towards the cordoned-off area, eyes scanning the scene. A small crowd of onlookers had gathered behind the police tape, their faces pale and drawn. Lucas could hear their hushed whispers as he passed by. As he approached the scene, his heart felt heavy with anticipation of what lay ahead, although this had become an all too familiar notion.

The dim glow of street lights fell upon a 2013 Ford Fiesta, its once vibrant 'Copper Pulse' paint now dull in the eerie ambience. The car sat in the dark alley between two competing Indian takeaways; its windows were fogged, obscuring the gruesome contents. He could hear the faint patter of rain on the car's roof, beating rhythmically.

Lucas was met by the stern faces of the uniformed officers. They stood at a distance, their breath forming white clouds in the cold air. One of them was PC Andrew Johnson, the fat little man with the ginger mullet, who had been tasked with guarding the scene.

'Morning, sir,' he said with a nod.

'Morning, Johnson,' Lucas replied, his voice tight with dread and determination. He approached the car, his footsteps echoing softly on the wet pavement.

The car's engine was still running, emitting a soft hum, and the headlights glowed a soft white, creating shadows behind the forensic team working around the scene. As he approached, Lucas could see a silhouette through the foggy, opaque windscreen. It was of a woman slumped in the passenger seat, her head resting to the side at an unsettling angle.

He walked around the side, where the door was propped open. He leaned in over the head of one of the forensic sperm and took in the horror. The woman's clothing was dishevelled, soaked in thick crimson. The surrounding seat was still dripping in blood, which was pooling in the footwell. He could see a small, red footprint on the brake pedal and bloody fingerprints on the steering wheel and across the horn. Arterial spatter had been sprayed across the window and roof and had even landed on the rear windscreen.

She had been stabbed repeatedly in the chest, where there was a mass of stab wounds, and her throat had been savagely cut from ear to ear. But that wasn't all. It never was. Her abdomen was open with a huge horizontal wound that was so deep that Lucas thought he saw the glint of her spine.

The dashboard clock read 04:37. The call was made at 02:24 by a woman living above one of the takeaways. She'd heard the scream and called 999. People might have walked past her whilst she was being attacked, thought Lucas, and by the time anyone came to help her, she was dead, and the killer had escaped. He turned away from the car, unable to look anymore. He wasn't so squeamish these days, he just didn't want to see more evidence of his own failings.

'Secure the scene. No one in or out until we've gathered all the evidence.' Lucas didn't even know why he bothered; the instruction was so hollow and obvious, but frankly, he didn't know what else to say.

The forensics team continued to work methodically, documenting every horrifying detail, collecting fibres, taking fingerprints and scrutinising the surrounding area for any signs of the perpetrator's presence. The blue and white tape cordoned off the area as if trying to shield the world from the horrific sight within, but each sharp flash of the forensic camera suddenly highlighted the revulsion of the growing number of on-lookers.

His phone buzzed in his pocket as he received a text. It took him a few seconds to find the energy to reach into his pocket and look at the message. It was from Chloe.

'I want you gone by the weekend. Fucking gone. I'll burn anything you leave. Do not try to contact me or Rachel.'

He blinked at the words, none of them a surprise to him. He didn't reply. What was the point? He returned his gaze to the silhouette in the car as the team worked around her. He'd said everything he could to Chloe, and there was no saving the relationship; it was probably in a worse state than the lady in the car.

She'd accused him of cheating. He'd denied it, of course; they were just friends, nothing in it. But how hard should you protest when, frankly, he wanted out anyway? Things just weren't right, and it was becoming toxic. They'd been arguing almost daily for months now, and he'd been looking for any excuse he could find to stay away from the house. Work had been a saving grace since Chloe had left the team. She'd been head-hunted by the Missing Persons division and had finally made the step up to DI, which there was no doubt she'd deserved. But this left Lucas on his own again.

No partner on the team meant he was in the office twenty-four-seven, which had become a defence mechanism, an excuse not to go home. But now he'd lost her, and he had no one else to blame. He'd ignored her, neglected her, pushed her away. He'd been so consumed by trying to get his man that he hadn't noticed he'd destroyed his relationship.

His phone buzzed again, but it was ringing this time. He pulled it back out of his pocket, hoping it wasn't Chloe looking to tear another chunk off him, but it wasn't. It was DCI Carmichael.

'Lucas, what's the story?'

'Young woman, stabbed, throat cut, something from the abdomen taken. Could be the uterus. Usual story. She's in a car this time, on the passenger side. Running the reg plate suggests we've found Rebecca King. She's a local hotshot lawyer and definitely not a prostitute. I think the car might be her daughter's though, judging by the 'L' plates on the back. This is comfortably the most public one we've had. It's a bit of a change to the MO, but it's him,'

'Fuck my arse. Right, OK. Why does that name ring a bell to me?'

'She's worked on a few cases we've been involved in. She was part of the defence team for Jacob Murray.'

'Coincidence?'

'At this stage? Yeah, it has to be,'

'What does Dan think?' she muttered down the phone.

'Dr Cross? I haven't seen him yet; it was the minion taking photos and scooping up blood and cum from the seats. I think the lanky bastard is around here somewhere, though. I'll find him.'

'Don't worry, I'll ring him. I want to know what he thinks

about all this. He stops for a break and now we've had another three dead women in two years. We need to be sure we're not dealing with a copycat.'

'We're not. Both Cross and Cooper said it themselves with the last woman, Grace. It's the same bloke.'

'True'

'I think a copycat is worse anyway, boss. I'd rather just one person was doing this; we don't need to be looking for a second person,' Lucas replied.

'That's true,' she said again, not giving much away as per usual. 'I'm going to call Dan now. Get hold of the family liaison. We need a formal identification, and the family must be informed.'

'Will do, boss; talk soon,' he said, putting the phone back in his pocket.

He took a few steps back, away from the car, and took a deep breath of fresh air. The morning sun was slowly breaking the sky, and the smell of the rain had subsided. Lucas thought about the woman in the car and wondered what her story was. What were her family and friends like? Did she have any pets? Had she enjoyed her job? He could ask all these questions, but she was no longer there to answer. She was gone, and there was nothing he could do about it. He could only hope he would catch him before he got to another one.

Lucas had spent the last eleven years chasing this maniac around Yorkshire, but he had nothing to show for it other than a lifetime of guilt and mistakes. He had no leads, no evidence, no suspects. He didn't even know what the man looked like. There was no CCTV, no fingerprints, no witnesses, and no DNA match. Lucas had nothing to go on, and it was eating him up inside.

The killer was so brazen now that he knew that Lucas would be powerless to stop him, and he was right. He was a shadow, a myth, a ghost. A man that they could only ever guess at what he looked like or where he might be. A man who taunted Lucas at every opportunity, always out of reach. A man that Lucas knew he couldn't let go, but a man who was slowly destroying him.

Lucas stepped back over to the car and peered in again, trying to imagine how scared the girl must have been as she was being attacked, knowing that her life was about to end. Did she know that her womb would be torn out? He wondered if she knew her attacker or if it was just a random assault. Did she know why she was picked?

'DI Miller, you will want to see this,' came a slow drawl behind him. It was Dr Cross, who Lucas presumed had just appeared out of the ground like some sort of imp. He handed him a little plastic bag with a bit of brown paper inside, that familiar swirly writing shining through.

Her uterus, a cradle of night, where creation stirs in moonlight's blight,
A sacred chamber, veiled in mist, where life's first dawn and twilight kissed.

Lucas grimaced as he handed it back.

'Dr Cross, how are you?'

'Very well, thank you. I have just come off the phone with Pat; I have reassured her that this poor woman has fallen victim to the same man who has seen off your other nine women.'

'Ah, yeah, I told her it looked the same.'

'She wanted a professional opinion, I think,' he smirked. Lucas looked up at him and considered what he would say next. Unfortunately, he was in a foul mood.

'Fuck off Dan. If she found you that impressive, she'd have let you screw her by now.' Dr Cross looked startled for a millisecond before composing himself again.

'I was only teasing you, Lucas. You're stressed, I understand, but you might be careful. I know for a fact that she is looking at being made the new superintendent within the next six months, which means they'll need a new DCI. I hear they're considering you, I assume, because of desperation. You don't have many friends left in the unit; believe it or not, I am still one of them. You can be an excellent detective when you focus. Don't go burning bridges.' he cracked another condescending smile. Lucas didn't reply; he just maintained eye contact and didn't blink. He was right, of course.

Dr Cross turned to leave, but just before he left, he turned back to face Lucas and leaned over to whisper in his ear.

'Oh, and by the way. She has.' He patted Lucas on the shoulder and walked away, leaving him slightly dumbfounded and with a rather nasty image in his head.

2023

60

Lucas and DS Sterling raced back to the station as quickly as possible without using the blue lights. They returned to the inquiry room to find a flurry of activity. Given it was nearly nine at night, quite a few officers had chosen to come in. Maybe it was because it was a positive lead, or perhaps it was because everyone had been waiting a lifetime to see Detective Superintendent Carmichael rip *'Senior Crime Correspondent'* Simon Davies a new arsehole. Either way, it was busy tonight.

Simon Davies was sat in the interview room, looking rather pissed off. He'd clearly been dragged away from the dinner table, or something similar, because he was still wearing a white shirt and black waistcoat. It was a nice enough outfit, but the creases suggested it had been worn for a few days. He'd only been left in the room alone long enough to help himself to the shitty coffee. Lucas was in an upstairs room watching him on the monitor, and it was clear Davies was getting more agitated with every second.

'How long will you let him stew?' asked Carmichael, appearing next to him from thin air. Lucas jumped slightly, sloshing himself with his own crap coffee. 'Bit twitchy tonight, are we, Miller?'

'Sorry, no, just didn't hear you coming.'

'Criminals never do.'

'I'll give him five more minutes. Is his solicitor here yet?'

'Outside, having his cavity searched. Or his briefcase, one of the two. I'm coming in with you. I know you're desperately trying to get a smelly finger from DS Sterling, but she's not qualified for this. You get me instead.'

'I don't want a smelly finger from you, boss,' said Lucas, winking at her, trying to give the impression everything was normal.

'Good. Keep it that way.' she walked towards the door, paused, and looked over her shoulder. 'But what about a blow job?'

Lucas nearly choked to death on his coffee as the entire molten contents rushed into his lungs. Carmichael was cackling to herself as she left the room, and Lucas tried to regain his composure. She was a weird one, Carmichael. A slight pang of guilt hit him. He really should have just told her about the necklace; of course, she would have believed him, wouldn't she? He'd almost certainly made everything much worse now.

He checked his watch. Now or never. He headed out onto the corridor and down towards the interview rooms on the ground floor, just along from the main reception. They were all identical and numbered. He'd picked number three again. It was the least comfortable and the nastiest one to be inside.

Simon Davies was looking at him as he strode in, shortly followed by Detective Superintendent Carmichael and the beige solicitor they'd dragged in for him. He had that typical look that you get from suspects. He was trying desperately to look calm, innocent, and not like he was filling his trousers.

Lucas could see straight through it.

'Thank you for coming in at such short notice, Mr Davies; please accept our apologies. We will be recording this conversation. Is that OK?' started Carmichael. She hadn't even sat down at this point; she was so eager to get at him. Lucas pulled his chair out and seated himself whilst Simon Davies shifted uncomfortably in his.

'Can't I just go home, and you can come to my house tomorrow?' His eyes were pinned to the desk.

'Not tonight, sorry. We've already started the recording,' said Carmichael, her eyes glinting and quite a nasty grin forming. She leaned across and hit the button. A faint buzz and a few beats of silence before she spoke suddenly. 'This is Detective Superintendent Patricia Carmichael and Detective Chief Inspector Lucas Miller, interviewing Mr Simon Davies' She was leaning forward and speaking directly into the microphone. 'You are Simon Davies. Is that correct?'

'Yes,'

'Do you know why you're here?'

'Not entirely. One of your lot called and asked me to come in for a chat, nothing else.'

'We wanted to talk to you about the recent spate of murders in West Yorkshire. You've been particularly interested in these recently, haven't you, Mr Davies?'

'I'm a journalist. And they're not recent; they've been on the go for twelve years. My readers want to know why you've not caught anyone yet?' he said, beginning to find a tiny burst of confidence from somewhere.

'And how many murders have there been in those twelve years?'

'Pardon?'

60

'How many murders have there been? You're the expert. You've written all your articles. I seem to remember you're forensically trained, is that correct?' she said, consulting her note in front of her.

'I... well. No. Sort of. I have a master's degree in Forensic Medicine, but it was broad; I'm not forensically trained as such, just for my writing. To make it more readable and accurate.' He gave a weak smile at the end of all that. Lucas liked it when they rambled; it was a sign you had them rattled.

'OK, well, we've established you understand forensics very well. But how many murders have there been? Come on, you know this, Mr Davies. It's a starter for ten.'

'Twelve confirmed,' said Davies, deciding he was better off playing Carmichael's games.

'And do you believe there are any unconfirmed?'

'How the hell should I know? You're the police.'

'Come on, entertain us. Do you think there are murders we're missing?'

'Where are you going with this?' said Simon Davies, looking more puzzled than ever. Lucas opened a folder and took out a few documents, including the picture of the second Welsh crime scene where Olivia had lost her life. He slid it over to Davies.

'Take a look at that. Tell me what you think.'

'It's a field,' said Davies, flipping the picture back and pushing it towards Lucas.

'Brilliant, outstanding work. Look harder,' said Lucas, simply pushing the picture back at him.

'What am I supposed to be seeing?'

'That little tent is covering the body of Olivia Thomas. She was murdered in a very similar style to the twelve murders you've just highlighted. She lived in deepest, darkest Wales. In the corner, there is a car. Recognise it?' The journalist took the picture again and squinted at it. A flicker of recognition flashed across his face briefly, but was gone as quickly as it came. He continued to stare at the picture.

'It's an old car,' he said simply.

'What make?'

'How the hell should I know?' But he took a further look. 'I think it might be an old Rover.'

'Indeed, it is. It matches perfectly to an eyewitness report of the same vehicle at the scene of a second murder, a year later, and over forty miles away.'

'Right. What's the point in all this?' said Davies, turning to his solicitor for support, who looked as helpful as a pedal-powered wheelchair.

'You ever driven a car like this, Simon?' said Carmichael. He froze slightly, trying to think of the best way out.

'Probably, I'm not sure.'

'Well, Simon, I suspect you have driven this car, as it's your mother's car, isn't it?'

He licked his lips. He was visibly drying up and shrivelling before them.

'I don't... I don't know. She has a similar car, but I don't know if it's the same one.'

'Well, it has her number plate on it, buddy, so best guess, it probably is,' said Carmichael.

'Right. Yes. Well, she's an old lady, I don't think-'

'We're not suspecting your mother, Simon; we're suspecting you. You have intimate knowledge of the case, and you've been following it from the start. You're forensically able and the link between Leeds and Wales. What do you think?' said Lucas.

'I am Welsh; you know I went to Cardiff Uni. My name's Davies, for god's sake!'

'Ey, but what in the name of sweet baby Jesus were you doing at two different murders?' said Carmichael. Davies struggled to stay calm, and his eyes darted everywhere, trying to avoid looking at them.

'You were stalking, weren't you?' said Lucas.

'No. No, of course not.'

'Yes. Yes, you were. You were stalking them, and then when you saw your chance, you killed them. You're sick, Simon. Sick.' spat Lucas. He'd typically get a bollocking from Carmichael for speaking to a suspect like this, but she was even more riled up than he was tonight.

'No! I was at home visiting my mother, and I heard about the Olivia Thomas murder and thought it sounded similar to the ones in Leeds, so I went to check it out. I was convinced it wasn't linked, so I left it. I've no idea about the second one. Maybe your witness is wrong? I don't even know when it was!'

Lucas flicked the top of the folder. '27th December 2019'

Simon Davies' eyes suddenly lit up at this point. 'December? I can prove it wasn't me; I was skiing in France with friends for New Year's! It wasn't me.'

'You better hope you can. Interview paused.' said Carmichael, who got up aggressively, grabbed Lucas by the shoulder, and strode from the room together. Once outside, she clicked her fingers at a young, terrified, tiny PC standing by the door.

'You! Find out if this alibi is true. He claims to have been in

France on the 27th of December 2019; I want to see passport records and witness confirmation. I want to see his bloody bikini body on the fucking beach.' She growled these words through gritted teeth. She had one hand on the door frame, the other on her hip, and she leant forward, piercing the floor with her eyes. She was so terrifying like this, Lucas didn't have the heart to point out that he wouldn't have his bikini body out on the ski slopes. Carmichael flicked her head up and rounded on Lucas.

'We need to go through each crime with him. I want alibis for all of it. If there's a crack, we'll find it.'

'Yes, boss,' he said, 'I'll grab the case notes now and get started'. Lucas bolted back to the office, grabbed some of his condensed notes on each crime, and strode back into the room with Simon Davies, oozing menacing confidence.

'Right then, Mr Davies, let's start at the beginning' He swivelled a photograph of Jessica Murray round and pushed it across the desk. Simon Davies took it and peeked at it. He considered himself for a second before speaking.

'Jessica Murray was sixteen at the time of her death. Originally thought to be her rapist father, but you couldn't get a conviction.' He had a look of hostility about him. His shoulders were straighter than they had been, and he was making more eye contact. Maybe Lucas didn't frighten him as much as Superintendent Carmichael did? The look of loathing intensified as he continued talking. 'She was found naked, hanging from a tree, and had her throat cut. Her clothes and jewellery had been taken. Your boss, Carmichael, was one of the first detectives on the scene. I remember trying to get a statement from her. She was very rude.'

'And you were the first journalist there, I understand. How

did you find out about it so quickly?' He was dangling the fruit before Simon, hoping he'd take the bait and incriminate himself.

'Word travels on the grapevine. It's my job.'

'Alternatively, you knew we would find her there because you dumped her after you killed her,' replied Lucas. 'We've got your DNA now; when we get a match with the crime scene samples, what do you think the headlines would be?'

Simon Davies smirked and leaned forward; his confidence appeared to be growing. 'How about, *'Fanciful Copper Frames Journalist*? Still, maybe I should be pleased you're only stitching me up; you drove poor Mr Mitchel to suicide. Assuming you believe he killed himself?' There was a sickly, self-righteous look on his face.

Lucas held his gaze for a moment before shuffling the documents in front of him. He selected the folder on Amber Smith, the second victim, and continued to quiz the journalist further. Simon Davies remained relatively calm throughout, dodging questions and continually trying to turn it around and suggest foul play by Lucas. They were well over an hour into the interview when Carmichael returned. She opened the door, striding over the threshold.

'DCI Miller, a quick word.' Lucas stood up from behind the table, but as he did so, the pocket of his trousers caught on the arm of the chair. There was a little tinkling as something metallic hit the floor. The necklace had fallen from Lucas's pocket, and he quickly stooped down to pick it up before anyone noticed. But they had noticed. Carmichael had a mild look of confusion, but Simon Davies was positively beaming.

'I recognise that necklace, DCI Miller. That's Jessica's missing necklace.' The menace in his voice was palpable.

'No, it's..'

'We ran a front-page picture of that for a week. It's her necklace!'

'No...'

'We are in deep shit, detective, aren't we?' drawled Simon Davies as he took a picture of Jessica Murray from the table and handed it to Carmichael, who took it instinctively. She analysed it intently before speaking, her eyes never leaving the picture, not even blinking.

'Show me'

'Boss, look - ' pleaded Lucas, the blood pumping in his ears, his palms dripping with sweat and his mouth drying to a crisp.

'Empty your pockets. Now!' hissed Carmichael, the fury evident both in her voice and across her face, which was still pointed at the photograph. With quivering hands, Lucas produced the necklace from his trouser pocket. Carmichael's eyes flicked to the locket and then back to the picture. She did this at least two more times before Lucas turned his gaze to the carpet.

Nobody said anything for a few seconds. The clock in the room ticked loudly, and the breath in Lucas's lungs caught in his neck. Finally, he dared a glance at Superintendent Carmichael and wished he hadn't. She was looking at him in a way he'd never seen before, which was absolutely horrid. Anger, disappointment and genuine fear all communicated with her penetrating eyes, sharp eyebrows and the severely thin curl to her upper lip.

The silence was broken by the agonisingly arrogant tone of Simon Davies. 'Are you the killer, DCI Miller?' Lucas didn't respond. All the air inside him had dried up. He was transfixed on the spot, waiting for Carmichael to make a move. Surely, she'd believe him.

She took her eyes off him briefly to turn to Simon Davies. 'Wait here,' she growled at him. Without looking at Lucas, she turned and strode from the room, outrage visibly pulsating in her whole demeanour. Lucas followed, still clutching the necklace which bounced in his hand.

She didn't say a word to him or even acknowledge that he was following her until they got to her office. She opened the door and allowed him to follow her in. He closed the door behind him. This was it, he thought. He'd get suspended, and he'd get kicked off the case. Everything he'd worked towards was gone. Because he was too fucking stupid just to call this in when he could. At the very least, he needed to keep DS Sterling out of the firing line. Superintendent Carmichael finally let out a breath; although she could have been breathing fire, the way her shoulders were hunched and the flash of red that was so apparent in her eyes.

'Explain. Fast.'

'Someone broke into my car this evening, and the boot was open. The necklace was in it; I didn't get a chance to tell you because I got the call about him,' he spoke as quickly and confidently as he could, desperate for her to believe him. He felt like crying; everything he'd ever worked towards was about to come crashing down around him. He was going to let down his mother. 'Please, you have to believe me. I'm not a killer.'

'Oh, don't be fucking dense, Lucas. Obviously, I don't think you're a bloody killer, but why are you withholding evidence from me?' She was seething, the words escaping through a clenched jaw. 'What I am worried about with you is that you were planning on planting that necklace?'

'What! I'd never d-'

'Well, what am I supposed to think? When that necklace comes out of your pocket? Why did you have it on you? Were you planning on incriminating Simon Davies?' she yelled at him, her arms spread wide in exasperation.

'No! I just didn't know how to tell you about it,' he implored, his hands together as if praying. 'But I think Simon is involved! He was very quick to point the finger at me, and someone is setting me up, planting this in my car!' He thrust the necklace into the air dramatically.

Carmichael scoffed and turned away from him, arms straight, leaning on the desk. 'Well, you're making it incredibly easy, you fool! How the fuck are we supposed to keep Davies now? His solicitor is probably concocting a way of accusing you of falsifying evidence as we speak. You've fucked this. Stay here whilst I sort this bloody mess and consider what to do with you.'

She straightened herself up and strode from the room, slamming the door so hard that the picture on the wall fell off, the frame cracking on the floor, leaving Lucas alone with the dark thoughts ruminating around his brain and pulsing pain in his arm—time for another pill.

61

Lucas had been alone, surrounded by the heavy silence of Carmichael's office, for over an hour. He'd taken another two of his pregabalin, but his pulse was still racing. He wasn't sure what was happening, but he knew that whatever he did next, his career would never be the same. The clock ticked vociferously behind him, but Lucas couldn't hear it; he was too preoccupied with the thoughts of failure and regret which were screaming at him. The shame was one thing; his ruined career was another, but the real crux of it was simple. Someone was going to get away with murder. At this moment, his best guess was that it might well be Simon Davies. A knock at the door should have startled him, but his mind was too distracted, his senses dulled.

'Come in,' said a croaky voice that didn't sound like his own. The door opened, and DS Sterling walked in. She looked genuinely concerned for him.

'You alright, mate?'

'Fine. I'm fine.' he didn't lift his head and look her in the eye. It felt too heavy.

'They're releasing him,' she said bluntly. 'His alibi checked out and we've not got the DNA result yet. We won't do for a couple of days. We can't hold him on circumstantial evidence alone, especially when his solicitor is kicking off about you.'

Lucas put his head in his hands, somehow feeling even worse. 'Fuck. Fuck.' was all he could manage.

'Look, don't worry, it's OK. We'll get him. Carmichael doesn't exactly believe him, and he will be under surveillance of sorts.' Lucas finally lifted his head, a faint look of hope in his eyes, which were struggling to focus.

'Yeah, but not from me,' he said flatly, the defeatist nature of his words apparent. The telltale click-clack of the Superintendent's high heels reverberated in the corridor outside as she approached the office door. Lucas took a big intake of breath, preparing himself for the oncoming battering. The door opened, and Carmichael strode in, eyeing DS Sterling as she did so.

'Out.' She ordered. Kim gave Lucas a sympathetic smile before exiting the office and closing the door behind her. The silence hung in the air like a foul smell, and Lucas didn't dare break it, not wishing to antagonise his superior any further. Eventually, after what felt like an eternity, Carmichael spoke. Her words were firm, but her voice was softer than earlier.

'You are not to continue investigating the case. I'm putting you on administrative leave. I'll speak with the press office; they can deal with the Davies angle, and you can concentrate on getting yourself out of this mess.'

Lucas looked up at her and met her gaze. He saw no sympathy there, no hint that she thought he was innocent. She was protecting herself.

'We will review the CCTV in the carpark to see if we can identify anyone that might have broken into your car.'

'So you believe me?' he murmured.

'Of course I do. But you're a fucking idiot for not calling it straight in and for then taking the bastard necklace into an interview with a suspect. I cannot have stupidity like that in this case, not with it already being the shame of the West Yorkshire Police Force and under intense media scrutiny,' she said, folding and unfolding her arms. She couldn't get comfortable either and was troubled. 'You will go home. Do not come in tomorrow, and I will ring you with a plan of how we're going to play this.' The authority in her voice was impressive.

He got up from the chair he'd been rooted to for the last hour and a half and went to leave. A wave of dizziness struck him and a sickness began bubbling in the pit of his stomach. Had he taken one too many pills? He glanced fleetingly over his shoulder at Carmichael, who was picking some fluff off her jacket.

'I am sorry,' he croaked. She didn't reply. She just grunted and continued to pick at the fluff, so he continued out the door, dizzy, deflated and feeling especially small and stupid. He walked through the station's corridors, trying to maintain his balance, keep his head down and not meet the eyes of any other officers.

He made it to the seat of his car before he finally burst into tears. It had been building since he'd left the interview room. The stress, the anger, the guilt and the self-loathing all came flooding out of him in a wave of ugly tears, snot and saliva. What could he do? This was dreadful, and it would only get worse. He'd always had a career path, what with being fast-tracked and destined for the top. He'd got complacent, arrogant, in fact. But now that his career looked so precarious, he realised just how important it was to him. The memory of his mother dominated his thoughts. All he'd wanted to do was stop other people from losing their mothers as he had or to get the closure he'd never received. In a career spanning twelve years, he'd failed by every metric.

It probably wasn't a good idea for him to be alone whilst feeling this way, so he pulled his phone from his pocket and went to his contacts. Kim Sterling's name was highlighted, and he hovered over it, ready to call her. Why? Hadn't he screwed this up enough? Hadn't he already risked her career as well with his stupidity? He couldn't do it to her. He flicked down and called 'Emily West' instead. It rang and rang and rang. No answer. Great, even Em was still off with him.

Suddenly, there was a buzz from the phone, and I clicked it open. There was a text from Em;

'Soz, can't answer right now. Call me tomorrow? xx'

Oh great, she was definitely off; in fact, she was almost certainly cheating on him. The lying about her friend Laura and staying late at work. Just what he needed to improve his mood. Although, the more he looked at that text message, the less it looked like Em sent it. She never said '*soz*,' and they rarely sent two kisses to each other. Was someone else texting for her? It was probably her new bloke, thought Lucas, slamming the phone down on the passenger seat. Another relationship he'd fucked up. He could add Em to the pile with Chloe.

But then another thought slid into his mind. If someone was framing him, if someone had it in for Lucas, might it not make sense to target his girlfriend? He was being foolish,

61

overthinking everything. That was a bit of a leap; it made much more sense that she was cheating... Maybe he should check? If she was OK, he could confront her and get it over and done with.

Gripping the wheel tightly, making his knuckles white, he stayed rooted, his mind racing, trying to go through all the permeations of him just turning up unannounced at her house. He switched the car on, still unsure of what he would do. He probably shouldn't be driving right now, given he was still dizzy. Four or five pregabalin was too many. Fuck it. At this point, what did he have to lose? He slipped the car into drive, and his electric Volvo slipped silently out of the car park, turned right, and headed for Emily West's house.

62

There was a mist in the air tonight, which provided a heavy, domineering feeling of foreboding to the evening. Halos and lines were forming around the sparkling city lights and his vision had become tunnelled. The drive had taken just under twenty minutes so far, and Lucas had already changed his mind three times. The dizziness and the slow palpitations in the chest were getting worse, and he was struggling to drive, but he continued regardless.

He had the radio on as usual, although he wasn't listening to the music, which faded into the background. It was replaced by the evening news bulletin, which pulled his attention somewhat. The male presenter's voice crackled with scepticism as they began;

'Good evening, listeners. In the ongoing saga of the 'Water's Edge Reaper,' the police made yet another arrest, only to release the suspect a mere three hours afterwards. Police say that the man, described as being in his fifties, will remain anonymous. However, sources suggest he was not previously known to the investigation and that the evidence against him was fragile. One has to wonder, is this yet another case of the West Yorkshire Police clutching at

62

straws?'

The presenter's tone was dismissive, their doubts obvious as they continued, 'It's been almost thirteen years since the 'Water's Edge Reaper' first struck in 2011, and years of investigation and many more victims, the police seem no closer to a resolution with many continuing to question their methods and their ability to catch this elusive murderer.

In other news, we turn our attention to the ongoing conflict in Israel and Gaza, where tensions remain high. Rockets continue to rain down, and the world watches as this violent chapter in history unfolds...'

The problem for Lucas was that he tended to agree with the news reporter. Heads would have to roll again soon, and he'd just placed his neck firmly on the chopping block.

After what felt like an age, he finally pulled up in the driveway of his girlfriend's semi-detached house, parking in front of her car and blocking her in. He parked closer than he'd intended and fumbled with the handbrake. Em's car was the only other car in the drive. The lights were on inside the living room, and his heart was pounding with slow, strong beats. He was a wreck, and the last thing he wanted to do was cause a scene, but if he was going to end this, he wanted to do it decisively. After stepping from the car, he strode carefully towards the door before taking a deep breath, wiping the sweat off his palms and pressing the doorbell. He heard the familiar tune reverberating deep within her house. Nobody came to the door. He peered in through the frosted glass but couldn't see any shadows. He pressed the bell again and heard the tune inside the house again. But once more, there was no movement from inside.

The obvious crossed his mind, and he stepped back and

walked around the back of the house, looking up at Ems' bedroom window. It was dark, and there was probably nobody in the bedroom. Hopefully.

He decided that he'd try one more time and then leave it. Returning to the front door, he pressed the doorbell and again listened to the tune. Nothing. He turned to go, but out of sheer frustration, he struck his hand out and knocked the door handle down. It clicked open. Em was not the sort of person to leave the door unlocked, even if she was in the house. Lucas was momentarily paralysed before his police training kicked in and he nudged the door open, standing on the threshold.

She had a traditional hallway with a Victorian-pattern tiled floor. A radiator ran up against the left-hand wall and had some pictures and ornaments balanced on top, just underneath a large mirror that adorned the space above.

'Hello?' he called out, stepping into the hallway. His voice was weak with a strange, echo-like quality he'd not noticed before.

'Em?' There was no reply. He stepped forward and looked around. A few pairs of her shoes were lined up at the foot of the stairs, and the coat rack was hung with several coloured coats. This wasn't a sign of a break-in, but Em was definitely not here. Where was she then?

He stepped forward towards the kitchen, which was at the back of the house. The door was closed, and the lights were off, but he reached his hand out anyway, pushing the door open and turning the light on. An empty room. The kettle was switched off, but still relatively warm. There were two plates and two glasses by the sink and a small pot with remnants of a pasta dish in it. So she'd had a late meal with someone and left? But then why was her car on the drive, and why was the front door unlocked? The person who'd eaten from the second plate must have driven, considered Lucas. Or maybe she was in the bath and couldn't hear him? The hairs on the back of his neck pricked up. It made no sense. Something was off; he could feel it. He left the kitchen, leaving the light on, and headed towards the living room, turning the door handle.

He entered the room silently, and the hairs on his neck remained stood to attention. It smelt nasty, with a stale odour of sweat clinging to the air. His eyes took a moment to adjust to the dim light, but he first noticed the TV, which was on. It was tuned into a news channel detailing the arrest and subsequent release of a suspect in the 'Water's Edge Reaper' case. He couldn't escape it. It was everywhere.

His eyes adjusted enough to make out the coffee table in the centre of the room. It had two cups on it, one-half full and with a rim of lipstick around the rim, the other drained empty. He retreated into the hallway and up the stairs. He checked each bedroom and the bathroom, but there was nothing. Her toothbrush was still in its little holder, and her overnight bag was in the closet. Em wouldn't be staying with someone else without them.

He opened his phone and went to the 'Find My Friend' app that he and Em had set up some time ago. She'd turned it off recently whilst they'd been fighting, but it was worth checking. It took a second to load, but then her little icon appeared on the map. She'd turned it back on. He clicked on her icon, and it started loading. The little icon span and span before finally spitting out her location on a map. According to this, she was in a Chinese takeaway twenty minutes from here. She hated Chinese food, though; why would she be there? He prodded his phone again, which brought up the street view feature. There was a flat above the takeaway; maybe she was in there? Lucas was very much aware that the balance of probability was she was in there with a new man, but he still had the niggling feeling that this wasn't everything it seemed, although he clearly wasn't thinking straight tonight.

    He left the house, returned to his car and drove towards the takeaway. The niggling feeling had won.

63

The rain was coming down in large, heavy droplets that were steady and unrelenting. It wasn't quite torrential, but it was enough to make the windscreen wipers squeak a little. The thumping on the bonnet had a cleansing, calming effect on Lucas, who felt much better for having a clear focus. Perhaps the effects of the pregabalin overdose were also wearing off?

The feeling was short-lived. He didn't know what he was expecting as he approached the Chinese takeaway, but an almost overwhelming sense of dread and apprehension gripped his chest. His mind was working overtime, jumping to the worst-case scenario. Assuming that Em was in danger, the knock-on effect could be to put Lucas even more firmly in the spotlight. But who would want to target him? Who was involved in this case, and who would be interested in his personal life? Based on the recent evidence, Simon Davies was an obvious answer, but this felt more personal. Could he have missed someone?

He'd arrived and parked up on the pavement, practically abandoning the vehicle. The takeaway was on a main road, surrounded by a somewhat eclectic mixture of shops, including a kebab shop and newsagents. Lights were on inside, but there was no sign of life. The rain had stopped, but there was still a strong breeze whipping up the leaves and litter, making the street look even more run down than, in truth, it probably was. He stepped out of the car and walked to the door, finding a small sign hanging above it; *'Lords of China'*.

He pushed the door open, and the little bell chimed. A Chinese woman dressed in black trousers and a white apron stepped out of the kitchen, looking at him with a bland expression.

'What you want? Order or collection?.' she said, a noticeable Leeds inflection slightly permeating through her thick Chinese accent. He pulled his ID from his pocket.

'Neither, I'm not here to eat. I'm investigating the whereabouts of a friend of mine who may be in danger. I believe she's here, or at least she was recently.'

She looked at him and raised her eyebrows.'Who?'

'A young woman, black with long hair. I think she's in the flat upstairs. I need to see inside the flat'.

She looked confused and slightly angry as she waved her hands at him. 'No, no flat upstairs is mine. Family in there now.'

Lucas marched towards her, angry and more threatening than he should have been, shouting, 'No, I can track her phone. She's here, and I need to see her. Open the flat, I'm a police officer!'

She crossed her hands and pouted, almost comically. 'No, she not there. Maybe she in basement?' Lucas was about to argue back before he processed what she'd said. The basement didn't sound great. He paused and tried to keep his voice more calm this time.

'What's in the basement?'

She uncrossed her arms and shrugged. 'Flat, a man. He give me rent for many years. He has lots of girls. Maybe yours one of girls?'

Those hairs on the back of Lucas's neck stood on end again, and a chill seeped down his spine. He thought the odds that this was someone whom Em was cheating on him were diminishing, and the longer this went on, the more he feared for her safety.

'I need to see the basement. Please. Do you have a key?'

She stepped back and raised her hand to him, 'OK, OK. I let you check. I take you to basement, is all. Not upstairs. Family eating.'

She gestured for him to follow her as she stepped through a curtain, out the back and into a small courtyard.

'Basement through there,' she said, pointing to a wooden door with a metal grille over the top of it. It looked like it belonged to a prison or an abandoned building. It had the same eery feel to it.

'You open it. Stiff,' she instructed, standing back slightly. Adrenaline was roaring through his veins, and he was becoming hyper-aware and weary of everything. She took a set of keys from her apron and fumbled with the locks.

She turned to him, 'Sorry, we only go down if he shout. He not here much, only stay for one day sometime, when he bring girls.'

Lucas did not like the sound of this. The locks clunked, and the door creaked open, revealing a set of stairs which led downwards into the gloom. There was a light switch on the wall, and Lucas flicked it on. A single bare bulb illuminated the stairs with a pulsating copper filament, and a smell hit him hard. He recognised the scent. It was formaldehyde.

'When did you last see this man?' he said, not breaking eye contact with the bottom of the stairs.

'Today, he come and go.' she shrugged her shoulders at him again. 'I go now, customer waiting. You say when leaving so I can lock, huh?' She turned and left abruptly, muttering something in Cantonese or Mandarin under her breath, which he didn't understand. He watched her walk back inside, then looked back down into the stairwell. Fuck, this wasn't good. He needed to look, but he would openly admit that he was petrified of what he would find down there. However, the thought of Em in trouble was enough to push him down those stairs, so he took a deep breath, steeled himself, and descended into the basement.

The stairs creaked with each step, and the stench got stronger. At the bottom was another door with a metal grille, exactly the same as the first. This time, he didn't wait; he twisted the handle and pulled the door open.

The light was off, so he wafted his hand to the side of the entrance to find a switch, but his hands couldn't locate one. He took his phone out and put the torch on, casting a broad white light into the gloom. He was in a small corridor with a carpeted floor. It was a brown, well-worn thing with a faded pattern that he couldn't make out. His eyes darted around the poorly illuminated darkness and picked out a door on the left, a door at the far end, and a door on the right. The right-hand door was open, and a metal toilet bowl was sitting behind it. It was gleaming, and the reflection of his torchlight was almost blinding. He could see bottles of chemicals by the side of it, and the whiff of formaldehyde hit his nostrils again, more potent this time. The door on the left was also slightly ajar, and he noticed a small room through the crack. It looked like an office, with a desk with a little pink box on it and a small couch against the opposite wall. Lucas strained his eyes, the torchlight cutting through the dimness.

His brain ticked over, and he suddenly recognised the little pink box. It was Em's mobile phone! She was here. Or she had been. He could hear his own pulse as he edged further into the basement flat, and the walls, he noticed, were covered in newspaper. The front-page headlines after the discovery of each of the women, the conviction of Jacob Murray and the suicide of Thomas Mitchel.

He continued yet further into the basement flat and moved towards the end door, which was closed. It was made of a thick wood and was heavily reinforced. Someone was trying to prevent anything from getting in... or out. A small hole had been drilled into the centre of the door, the size of a golf ball. He crept forward and pressed his face up to the hole, cupping his hands to the sides of his face, and peered in. Darkness, nothing other than blackness. He re-arranged his hands to put the torch to the base of the hole and look over it. The light only half illuminated the room, but enough for him to make out a figure strapped to something, possibly a chair, in the middle of the room. He heard a gasp and a gurgling, and the figure moved its head.

'Em, is that you?' he whispered through the hole, hoping it wasn't. He heard another sound, like a moan or a cry—a sound of anguish!

'Em, it's me, it's Lucas. I'm here! I'm here! I'm going to get you out,' he said, still hushed; he didn't know if they were alone. His heart rate was unrelenting in his ear, his mouth becoming more dry, and he wasn't thinking straight. Perhaps it was the adrenaline, or the pregabalin wasn't out of his system after all? He moved away from the door and stood to the side.

He reached forward, his hand shaking, and grabbed the handle, twisting it and pushing the door. It wouldn't move. It was locked.

'Fuck,' he muttered and stepped back even further. He didn't have much choice; there was no way of doing this silently, and he didn't have time to call this in. He slammed his foot hard against the door. The wood splintered, and it buckled, but it held. He kicked again, this time putting his full weight into the kick. The door flew open, bouncing off the wall, making a loud clattering which echoed around the black room. The figure in the chair barely twitched or turned its head. He was in the main living space of the basement flat, although it didn't feel homely as there was no dining room table or sofa. A large steel shelving unit propped against the right-hand wall was covered in large glass jars, each containing a preserved organ floating in green liquid. His eyes were initially drawn to the heart, but the colon was difficult to ignore.

There was a solid metal chair in the middle of the room, occupied by a slim figure who was naked and shivering. Even in this light, she clearly had dark skin and long black hair matted with blood. It was Em. She was covered in cuts, bruises and shining scarlet blood. He could hear her quiet but sharp breaths as she was struggling to get air into her lungs. Her legs and feet were wrapped in a dense plastic sheet, and her hands were tied to the arms of the chair with thick rope, her fingers splayed out like a fan. As he looked, he realised that each of her fingers had long metal nails protruding up through the nail bed, keeping her hands in place. Her mouth was wide open, and a ball gag had been secured to her mouth. Her watery dark eyes were fixed on him, just the light from his phone reflecting back, giving her a haunted look. They were pleading for him to do something. He stood, frozen. He wanted to scream and cry. His girlfriend was being tortured. He wanted to smash everything in this room, but his body wouldn't react. He was paralysed, staring at the broken woman in front of him. Fucking do something!

Then the moment was shattered. He heard a noise from the stairs. It was the sound of a door being slammed shut. He pivoted, and the light from his phone cast shadows through the open door, but he saw no movement. Time to act and do it fast. Move your legs! He turned again to Em, finally darting to her side. He tried to undo the straps, but they were too tight, so he reached up to the back of her head and flicked the buckle of the ball gag, releasing it from her mouth. She gasped once and then screamed,

'Behind!'

Without warning, his head exploded with pain and a flash of stars and lights. He was sent tumbling to his left with such a force he lost all bearings of the room. Someone had smashed him over the head with something extremely solid. Everything was spinning, the pain was immeasurable, and he felt a visceral nausea which went through him. He grabbed the side of the wall to steady himself as his phone soared through the air, landing in the corner with the torch facing upwards. His vision swam back into focus, and he was met with a sight so horrible his stomach nearly dropped out. A tall figure, face hidden in the shadows and wearing blood-soaked brown leather overalls, was standing behind Em, their hand clamped over her mouth to keep her silent. In their other hand was a very long, very sharp knife, which was held to her throat.

'No! Please, leave her alone!' shouted Lucas through the blood in his mouth and the pain in his head.

There was no pause, like in the movies. No hesitation, no long speech and no prolonged build-up of tension. They just did it with terrifying ease. The blade slid across her throat, and blood hosed out, spraying the chair, her bare chest, and Lucas's face. It was warm and reeked of iron and meat in the way only blood could. Em shook in her chair briefly, seizing violently and gurgling loudly as the blood kept pumping. Their other hand was still gripping her mouth, but she couldn't scream now, anyway. The hand slid up and began pulling her hair, wrenching her face out of the shadows and into the light. Lucas could not move. At all. He wasn't breathing. He could only watch in horror as she drained of blood and the light in her eyes vanished. The blood was still gushing; he could hear it spilling onto the floor and pooling all around him. The figure dropped the knife on the floor with a clang and finally let Em's head roll forward.

They moved swiftly past her body and grabbed the shell-shocked Lucas by the hair, punching him in the nose. He felt it break; the crunch echoing around the small flat, but he was numb to the pain. As he lay on the floor coughing up yet more blood, a piercing bright light filled the room from the central bulb with a high-pitched ring. The figure walked back over to Lucas, taking no care to avoid the gallons of deep red blood which coated the floor.

Their sticky footsteps echoed as they moved, and they

63

grabbed Lucas by the hair once more, jerking his head back so they were eye to eye. Lucas's heart stopped, and his eyes widened.

'You?' he gasped.

'Yes, DCI Miller. Me.'

64

DS Sterling yawned heavily and blinked repeatedly as she made a morning cup of tea. She put the water in first and the milk in second. Anything else was strange, as far as she was concerned. She was wearing her Lilo and Stitch pyjamas, her hair wild and tangled. She popped a Tamoxifen tablet and slowly sipped her cup of tea. Despite getting in a lot of trouble with Carmichael yesterday, Lucas hadn't dropped her in it, which he could have done, given she also hadn't told Carmichael about the necklace, even if she had encouraged him to.

As she stirred her tea, she thought he'd looked so deflated and upset when he left yesterday. She really liked him, not necessarily as anything more than a friend; she couldn't quite figure that out yet. But he was an excellent character, and his intentions were always solid. They had fun together, and she respected him as a detective. She picked up her phone and found Instagram already open, so she doom-scrolled through it for a moment, aimlessly trying to wake herself up.

When she zoned back in, she dialled Lucas to ensure he was alright. There was no answer, but he was strong; he'd be OK. She downed her tea and returned upstairs to continue getting ready, trying to shift his plight from her mind.

She was back in the station by half-seven, and the place was quiet. Lucas's computer was switched off, his chair tucked under the desk, and there was no half-drunk coffee by his keyboard. It was a bit jarring, given he always arrived early and had been sitting at that desk when she arrived almost every day for the last few years. To think that it might be some time before she saw him there again gave her a weird, hollow feeling.

She sat, logged onto her computer and waited for it to boot up so she could start digging into the CCTV footage from the car park. Carmichael had asked if there was footage to suggest who might have broken into Lucas's car, and she'd volunteered for the job. She found the files, downloaded them, and settled down to watch them. There were twenty-eight hours of footage spread across two cameras. Christ, she was glad it was only a tiny car park. She sped up the video, watching the cars in the corner where Lucas had parked. Nothing of interest showed up, and she got bored and frustrated after barely half an hour. As procrastination, she'd messaged Professor Hawthorne to find out if he was getting anywhere, and she got a rather strange reply;

'This case is nebulous. I am hunting, but not finding. Come and help me when you can. Prof.'

Even though he was the most effective accelerant to touch the case in many years, Kim couldn't help but think the bloke was bizarre. His results were speaking for themselves, but there was something about him that she didn't get. He can't have many friends, she thought.

'Morning,' said a voice. Kim jumped slightly, her attention diverting from the video to Carmichael, who had snuck up and stood behind her, peering at the screen. 'Anything?' There was a hint of excitement in her tone.

'No, not yet. I was going to take a better look after the briefing this morning,' Kim said, swivelling around in her chair.

Carmichael smiled grimly. 'Ahh, yes. Well, we don't have a briefing this morning. We're leaving it till later in the day. I want to give you and the other guys a chance to verify a few of that prick's alibis. I don't know what it is, but journalists give me the creeps.' She looked a bit distracted for a moment, like she was holding something back. Kim could see the conflict on her face before she gulped and said, 'I also need you to look into Lucas. Something's not adding up about this. Despite Lucas having tried to fuck things up, I do still fancy Davies for this, but he's unfortunately put himself in the frame.'

Kim's mouth dropped open slightly in disbelief. 'Lucas has nothing to do with it! He's dedicated his career to solving the—'

'Yes, yes, yes, I know,' interrupted Carmichael, waving an irritated hand and looking away sheepishly. 'Look, DS Sterling, I don't want him to be involved, but he's got the opportunity, and we've found him with the missing necklace. We need, at the very least, for appearance's sake, to exclude him.' She didn't look happy at all; her brow furrowed, and the muscles in her neck were twitching slightly.

Kim tensed as she was about to reply with something aggressively defensive, but thought better of it.

64

'Have you spoken to him yet, boss?'

Carmichael looked pretty annoyed by this question, the wrinkles in her forehead suddenly becoming even more prominent. 'No, I tried calling him last night and again this morning, but the bloke is still stropping because I've stood him down. You let me worry about DCI Miller; I want you to find who broke into his car and help the others with the alibis.' She nodded again. That was that, then. It was almost as if she'd had a conversation with a wall.

Carmichael walked away, and Kim was left to her own devices. Lucas probably wasn't just stropping because he'd been stood down; he was likely distraught that someone he'd worked with for years and respected was now questioning if he'd spent the last twelve years moonlighting as a serial killer.

She turned back to her computer and continued sifting through the monotonous pixelated footage from the staff car park. She trusted Lucas; he'd been good to her, and frankly, the bare minimum she could do right now was to prove his innocence. Assuming he was innocent. Please be innocent.

The morning went by at a snail's pace, and the car park footage yielded no results. She checked the ticker at the bottom to find she was twenty hours and thirty-seven minutes in. Christ alive, she still had to spend another hour of her life staring at this screen. Besides the occasional person walking by, nobody was caught near his car. Perhaps it had been in his boot for much longer, and he'd just not seen it?

There wasn't a great deal of success with the alibis either. She was still waiting on confirmation from the home office that Simon Davies had been out of the country skiing, and the two organisations she'd contacted to get CCTV confirming his whereabouts had both written back to say the requested footage had unfortunately since been deleted. She asked DC Green to continue sifting through the car park footage, and he agreed enthusiastically. He'd learn.

It was now twenty-to-one, and Kim had taken a break for some lunch. Her chicken and stuffing sandwich overflowed with the PomBear crisps she'd rammed inside it as she rang Lucas again, but once more, there was no answer. Something didn't feel right; Lucas would always answer the phone, even if he were upset.

She grabbed her bag from her chair and headed to her car. The weather had taken a turn whilst she'd been inside, so the wind chill caught her by surprise, stinging her face a little. She hurried over to her car, started the engine, and immediately blasted the heaters. She put the handbrake down and paused with her foot hovering over the accelerator. Was she being stupid? What did she have to worry about? He wasn't in any danger, was he? Except from himself maybe, he was married to the job and being kicked off the case would not do his mental health any good. Nor was being accused of murder. Fine, she was sure he would be OK, but equally sure he could do with a friend right now, so she pressed her foot down and headed away from the station.

She pulled up outside his flat about twenty minutes later and saw that his car was missing. Maybe he wasn't moping about then. Perhaps he'd gone to the gym or to see a friend? She parked up, walked across to the door and rang the bell, regardless. Just to be sure. No answer. She stepped back and surveyed the building. His flat was on the ground floor, and all the windows and doors were shut. Everything was in order. She peered through a few windows, but there was nothing to see. It looked as though he had simply just gone out. Right, time to stop being silly; she'd wasted enough time here, and he'd be fine. Hopefully.

As she turned, she saw a figure across the street staring at the block of flats. It was a man dressed from head to toe in black jogging bottoms and a hoodie. He had a snood pulled up over the lower half of his face, but it failed to cover his sad little eyes and flash of ginger mullet. As soon as he saw her looking, he turned and sprinted away as fast as his chubby legs would carry him.

DS Sterling didn't give chase because she didn't need to. She knew exactly who that was and considered him a harmless waste of space. As she got back in her car and returned to the station, she made a mental note to tell Carmichael. Why was PC Andrew Johnson hanging about Lucas's flat looking suspicious?

65

Simon Davies was walking down the street, hands in his pockets, collar turned against the bitter chill. He'd written more than enough articles about other suspects, named them where there had been limited evidence, never really giving a toss about the consequences. His name hadn't even been published as they'd kept it out of the media as a favour from his friends in high places. However, everyone walking past him looked at him like they knew it was him. He was the one they'd arrested, and he was the one who'd been killing all those women. Their eyes were boring into him, burning a hole in the back of his head. He felt guilty, and he couldn't stand it. He just needed to get back.

The whole twenty-four hours since he'd been released from custody had been spent inside his flat with the curtains closed, hiding in the dark like some freak. He couldn't bring himself to go outside, couldn't stand to look another human being in the eye. He'd spent every waking moment drinking himself into a stupor, his mind a mess of thoughts, questions, and paranoia. But now he was hungry, and the fresh air might do him good, although he regretted not ordering the food to his house.

He arrived at his favourite takeaway, 'Lords of China', it said across the door. It was hardly a royal banquet, but it would do for now. He needed his energy; he had work to do when he got back.

* * *

Lucas felt like shit. There was a slight draft on his skin, and a shiver ran through his body. He was cold. Absolutely frozen raw. He was naked, hungry, and his head hurt like a bitch. Oddly, the only thing not hurting was his arm. He couldn't move. His feet were bare and had been duct-taped together, but his hands were tied to the arms of the chair so that they were stretched out in front of him. The duct tape had also been wound around and around his torso, restricting his breathing somewhat, so he had to take short, shallow breaths. The breathless feeling was exacerbated by the additional tape that was loosely covering his mouth and the blindfold that had been used to hide his eyes.

He lifted his head gently, feeling the blood drain from his skull, and the room seemed to tilt. The smell of iron and formaldehyde was stronger than ever, pooling in the pit of his stomach and making him nauseated. It was almost too much, but he just about managed to keep himself from vomiting. He tried to take a few deep and painful breaths through his nose and out of his mouth, but his nose was broken and congested with congealed blood.

This was bad. Scratch that, this was fucking awful. He couldn't understand how things had gone so wrong. He didn't know if he was even still in the basement, if he'd been moved, or indeed how much time had passed. The sight of Ems's throat opening up, the blood spraying from the wound like a fountain, was burnt onto the inside of his eyelids. His head was swimming with confusion and questions. How had he not seen this coming? He tried piecing together the last twelve years, and the answers started floating into view like pieces of a puzzle. There was no 'eureka' moment, but the signs had been there. He just hadn't seen them. His tongue was swelling in his mouth, his saliva tasting metallic and artificial. He knew he had to get free, but his restraints were so tight. He started to shuffle his feet and wiggle his toes, trying to loosen the tape, or at least work some feeling into them. The tape had been wound around them multiple times, and the pressure on his wrists was agonising. He tried to twist his hands to free them, but nothing worked. Unless someone came to his rescue, there was no way he was getting out of this one.

As he sat in the darkness, terrified, it was all he could do to ruminate on that bloody poem and recite it repeatedly in his head...

In shadows deep, where whispers talk, I walk a path, alone I stalk....

66

It was getting late now, and DCI Carmichael was finally getting to the end of what had been a truly shite day. Lucas hadn't answered his phone despite the fact that she'd been calling him incessantly throughout the day. She was well aware that he might be highly pissed off or embarrassed, but it was very out of character to not even answer or message back, even if it was just to tell her to fuck off.

It was now about five in the evening, and she was supposed to have had the team briefing over an hour ago, but she'd delayed it. Her head was thumping from stress and dehydration; she never drank enough water, but she couldn't recall having had a drop all day. She sat at her desk, staring at the phone, willing it to ring. What if the stupid prick had done something to himself? As little DS Sterling had pointed out, he was devoted to the job and could be very volatile at times.

'Boss, it's me. Any news on Lucas?' Speak of the devil. DS Sterling's voice sounded worried as she poked her head around the door. Carmichael hated it when people said she looked good for her age. It was such a backhanded compliment. It could be paraphrased as 'You don't look appealing, but at your age, I'd expect you to look worse'.

And yet, as DS Sterling stood in the doorway, nervously peering into the room, Superintendent Carmichael became a hypocrite as she thought DS Sterling looked great for someone who'd just had cancer.

'I told you, I'm worrying about DCI Miller, not you,' said Carmichael, although her voice quivered slightly.

'Right. Never mind then,' muttered DS Sterling, and she made to leave, but Carmichael sighed.

'No, nothing. I've been trying all day. Arsehole isn't answering his phone. I assume you've been over his house?' She still didn't sound as commanding as usual; she was uncomfortable.

'I did. He wasn't there, but I tell you who was, though. Andrew Johnson,' announced DS Sterling.

'As in PC Andrew Johnson? What was that saggy little ball sack doing there?' said Carmichael, looking away in mild contemplation.

'Dunno, but he ran when I saw him,' replied DS Sterling.

'He's too spineless to do anything, I think. Do you agree? Of course you do. I'm your boss.'

DS Sterling's forehead became corrugated, and her expression sombre, 'I do agree, yeah, but this doesn't sound like Lucas. I've called him as well, several times. I think he's in trouble. We shouldn't rule out PC Johnson just yet.'

'Fine. You can get someone to find Johnson. Do you think DCI Miller could be avoiding us?' said Carmichael, although the expression on her face answered the question for them.

'He might be avoiding you,' said DS Sterling bravely. 'I don't see why he'd be avoiding me, though?'

'You're special, are you? Let me guess, has he slipped you a length and all?' said Carmichael childishly.

'No, we're friends,' said DS Sterling, blushing a bit. 'But I thought you of all people would trust him, Superintendent?' she continued curtly. Carmichael raised her eyebrows in surprise. She wasn't used to being spoken to like that by anyone, let alone a meagre detective sergeant.

'He's made himself untrustworthy by withholding evidence and taking that sodding locket into an interview with a key suspect, as you well know. What am I supposed to do? My hands are tied here. But putting that aside, I agree with you. His absence is troubling. Get someone to track down Johnson, but in the meantime...' She made a gesture for DS Sterling to sit at her desk. Reaching across, she picked up her phone and punched in a number. She sat, now not saying anything to DS Sterling, the phone wedged between her right ear and shoulder. She was fidgeting with the curly phone wire when someone answered;

'Hello, missing persons. Jayne speaking.'

'Hi Jayne, it's Pat Carmichael. I need to speak to DI Chloe Wilson urgently, please. I need to report a missing person.'

67

Exclusive Interview: Jacob Murray Breaks Silence on Shocking Police Allegations

By Simon Davies, Senior Crime Correspondent

In an unprecedented twist of fate, Jacob Murray, a man whose life has been shrouded in a decade of darkness, is now breaking his silence on the explosive allegations that have shaken the very foundation of the criminal justice system. Murray, 58, convicted of a heinous crime that shook the nation, is nearing the end of a 15-year sentence, but he refuses to go quietly into the night.

12 years ago, the world recoiled at the horrifying accusations that a father had committed both the rape and murder of his daughter. While Murray's murder conviction was eventually overturned, with arguments over the initial frailty of the evidence, the scars of those tumultuous years still run deep. Now, a clandestine source with inside knowledge of the case has come forward with a revelation that could rock the entire police force: a recent attempt by a police officer to frame an innocent man for the murders by planting crucial evidence.

In an exclusive, heavily guarded interview within the prison's concrete walls, Jacob Murray vented his anger and determination to expose the alleged corruption within the police department. His eyes blazed with the fire of a man who has endured years of wrongful incarceration.

'I've fought every day to prove my innocence,' Murray declared, the lines on his face a testament to the hardship he's endured. 'And now, it seems there was a calculated effort to keep me imprisoned for a crime I did not commit. I won't rest until justice is served.'

The shocking revelation centres around an unidentified police officer who, according to the source, recently planted a crucial piece of evidence—a necklace that once belonged to Murray's deceased daughter, missing for nearly 13 years—on another individual. If substantiated, these claims could potentially expose a grave miscarriage of justice.

The accused police officer remains anonymous, but our sources suggest they may reside in a senior position within the West Yorkshire Police Force, casting a shadow of suspicion over the entire validity of this investigation. With Murray's public outcry, the nation is left questioning the accountability of those entrusted to uphold the law and ensure justice.

As the allegations reverberate through the media, the nation watches in disbelief and anger, waiting for answers and action. Jacob Murray's relentless quest for truth and justice, while counting down the days to his release, threatens to unearth a scandal that may forever change how we perceive those sworn to protect and serve. The fate of Murray and the officer, shrouded in a cloud of controversy, hangs in the balance, with the nation demanding transparency and accountability from the institutions designed to safeguard our society.

By now, everyone in the department had read the article online and had an opinion on it. Carmichael was standing by the board in the centre of the inquiry room, pen in hand. There was a large picture of Lucas in the centre of the board, where they usually put suspects. The picture was a blown-up version of the deeply unflattering one he had on his ID badge. Of course, he looked like a murderer in it; everyone did. She was facing the room of PCs, DCs, and a DI or two. DI Chloe Wilson was amongst them, arms folded in irritation, but her brown furrowed with worry. She was still remarkably pretty; her soft features and light brown hair remained unchanged, but her ponytail was tighter and more professional, and she didn't smile as much these days. She was standing next to DS Sterling, who looked equally thrilled to be there.

Carmichael was the one to break the silence with a sudden exclamation. 'This is a fucking disgrace. How on earth has he been able to publish this article under our bloody surveillance?' Silence from the crowd. 'That wasn't a rhetorical fucking question!' She was staring around the room, breathing fire like a dragon. Nobody dared answer. 'This could completely unravel our entire investigation and could cost the lives of many future victims! DC Martin and DC Thomas, you were both tasked with watching this slimy cunt. Therefore, you will both leave this room now and wait for me out there. I need a very strong word with the pair of you.'

Everyone watched as the two officers got up and sheepishly walked from their desks to the large double doors at the side of the room, like children in a classroom. Their footsteps echoed in the tense silence of the room.

Superintendent Carmichael continued, 'We have to find our missing DCI Miller. There is absolutely no way we can get away without investigating this after that bloody article. Some of you will think he has questions to answer, and some will be worried about his safety. Either way. Fucking find him. Right. Any news from your lot, Wilson?' she said, her voice remaining strong and filled with fury.

Chloe had been waiting for Carmichael to call her name and confidently stepped forward. 'The last thing we've got is his car travelling west on York Road about 11 pm two nights ago, but we lost him fairly quickly as the cameras failed.'

'Failed?'

'Yes... I know. I'm not impressed either.'

'Why's he on York Road? That's nowhere near his house?' said Kim from behind her.

'No idea, but it's a common route into the city centre,' said Chloe.

'Yeah, but not from his place or the station. He should be coming from Headingly.' said DS Sterling, pointing to a large map of the city plastered to one of the other boards down the side of the room.

'Had he been to visit someone?' suggested one of the PCs from the back of the room.

'I think he was shagging that mortuary girl, but can't imagine he was in the mood for some strange last night,' muttered Carmichael. She had been standing fixated on the picture of Lucas, which was in the centre of the board, but had now turned around and looked directly at Kim.

'You're strangely close to him. Did you know anything about this?

Kim shook her head. 'No, not really. I knew they'd had a thing, but I think it was on the rocks; Lucas seemed very distracted when we went to Wales. He told me she was properly off with him.'

'So he was with her?' said Chloe, a slight pang of disappointment in her voice. 'bloody knew it.'

'Well, after you left him, why not?' said Kim, a glinting, razor-sharp edge to her tone.

'I left him because he was a cheating twat with this Em girl that you've just confirmed he was humping! Good riddance, as far as I'm concerned! But I don't care; he can do what he wants.' A little rose-coloured tint to Chloe's ears developed, and she adopted a defensive body position with her arms crossed and her shoulders hunched. 'You seem jealous, it wasn't you?'

'Me? What are you talking about?' DS Sterling's ears were also burning up, although more of a coral colour or fuchsia.

'Alright, alright, we all want to shag DCI Miller,' interrupted Carmichael with some force, 'but none of us are going to if we don't find him.' Chloe and Kim began to pout but refrained from sniping further at one another. Chloe returned to pacing the room, and Kim started randomly flicking through the nearest case file, not taking anything in. There was a silence in the room again.

DI Khan's phone buzzed and made a strange, tinkling noise. It took him a second to react and a few seconds more to retrieve it from his pocket whilst everyone stared at him.

'Khan. Yeah, go for it.' there was a high-pitched squeaking

coming from his phone as whoever was on the end of it talked. 'OK, how sure are you? Fine, I'll pass the message on. Good work.' He clicked the screen on his phone to hang up before announcing to the group.

'That was DC Green. He's completed the analysis of the car park CCTV footage. Our favourite mortuary tart, Emily West, you know, the chick that DCI Miller was sleeping with. She's the only person who goes near DCI Miller's car. DC Green thinks she opens the boot at least, although we can't see what she does.'

'That doesn't make sense. OK, if he was shagging her, maybe he gave her a key? And how the hell would she get the necklace? said Carmichael, rubbing the back of her neck in frustration.

'And why would he want her going through his boot?' said Khan. 'Did she have a motive to frame him?'

'He was worried she was having an affair, but I still can't see how she'd have access to the necklace or any reason to plant it. I think this is a red herring,' said Kim.

'Or perhaps he is involved, and they were working together? She could help him with the forensic side of things?' offered DI Khan excitedly, making Kim's blood boil.

'She might not have known what she was planting. Someone else might have put her up to it?' Chloe muttered.

'It's all... nebulous,' said Kim to herself, but Khan overheard.

'That's a very long word for you, isn't it? I know you fancy him, but personally, the way I see it is this. The only person we have more than subjective evidence against is DCI Miller, boss; I think we have to bring him back in and talk to him.'

'Oh, this is complete bollocks,' said Kim, a little louder

than she'd meant to.

The response from Carmichael was immediate. 'Bollocks or not, sergeant, you're not running the investigation.' She paused and looked around. Her eyes flicked from DS Sterling across to DI Khan.

'I agree with you, DI Khan; we must find and bring him in. DS Sterling, you are not a DI, so restrain yourself. If you won't assist us, I'd kindly ask you to leave the enquiry room. Now.'

Everyone turned to look at Kim. She looked at them all, disappointed in them. Admittedly, DCI Miller wasn't flushed with friends on the force, but the speed at which these supposed teammates had dumped him, especially on such flimsy evidence, was shocking. She unfolded her arms and locked eyes with Carmichael. Decision made.

'Fine,' and with that, she headed out of the inquiry room and made a path for the only place she thought there was anyone with any sense; Professor Hawthorne's adopted office.

68

An hour had passed since she'd been dismissed from the inquiry room. She knew they still hadn't found Lucas, as she could hear the chatter filtering through the paper-thin office walls. Three of them stood in the large office Professor Hawthorne had commandeered. The walls had been covered from top to bottom in pictures, notes and cuttings, forming an eccentric mind map. Professor Hawthorne was the only one who stood up; Kim was sitting by a table next to the window looking out nervously, whilst DC Green sat on a chair in the middle of the room, hands on hips, admiring the decorations. He'd snuck in timidly, about ten minutes after Kim, and admitted that he'd thought she was right and wanted to help. Pretty brave for a constable.

'DCI Miller has always treated me well, and I've told my mum I'd like to be as good a copper as him. The least I can do now is defend him,' he'd said. They needed all the help they could get, thought Kim.

She was gazing out of the window, but she shifted, deep in thought, becoming perfectly still with her head in her hands. All fifteen case files covered the table in front of her. Despite being nearly ten o'clock in the evening, nobody had any intention of going home.

'How are you feeling, DS Sterling? You've had quite the day,' asked Professor Hawthorne.

'Honestly, I feel fine. I'm a bit tired, but other than that, I'm fine,' she said, snapping a bit, which was a sure sign that she wasn't fine. Professor Hawthorne nodded anyway, accepting her answer. DC Green looked at her, concerned, but he didn't know what to say, so he said nothing.

Professor Hawthorne gestured to the files. 'Have you found any correlation, DS Sterling?'

She let her hands fall from her face, and the lack of concentration in her eyes was immediately apparent. 'No. Have you developed this profile of yours yet, Prof?' she said bluntly.

'Not yet, but it's developing. I've only got a small part of the jigsaw, as it were.' He picked up his woollen brown jumper from where it had been lying over a chair, put it on and then went over to where a massive map of Leeds was spread over most of the back wall. He stopped just in front of it and peered at the paper. It was a very shabby map covered in tears and holes, but he hadn't bothered to get it changed. The whole of Yorkshire was extended before him, and he studied it for a minute before putting a hand out. His long, delicate fingers brushed the area to the west, between Leeds and Bradford. He took his hand away from the map and began to pace the room, hands behind his waist and his head bowed, giving him the posture of a kiwi bird. It was a very peculiar habit of his and something he did when he was brooding.

'We've identified several things from this killer that give us an indication of their motives. Although these motives aren't the driving force, I don't think, just something which may be interesting to them. In all honesty, it is impossible to get a completely clear image of their mind. The things that make us different, the things we fear or don't, make it difficult. They're what stops us from understanding completely.'

'What the fuck are you talking about' said DC Green, staring up at Professor Hawthorne like he was a freak. Professor Hawthorne didn't stop to acknowledge him; he simply continued pacing for a few seconds before continuing to talk.

'But there are still several things I think are pretty important. For example, it is essential to note that the victims have been taken from a narrow age range and single gender. Our killer appears to be selecting these women for specific reasons. Not by chance, but then what is the reason? Given that there are no secretions to be found, I would argue that there are no proper signs that our killer has taken sexual gratification or pleasure from their suffering, which is relatively unusual, indeed, if they're a male. But despite there being a selection process, these victims appear to have been taken because of opportunity rather than intention. There is no normal pattern.'

'That makes no sense. The murders are too clean and careful. They show some planning and some control. Plus, early in the investigation, it was thought he was selecting them through Twitter or X or whatever the fuck they're calling it now. Surely that's not random?' Interrupted DC Green, who was finding his voice and liked an argument.

'The victims are chosen randomly, constable, but there is some planning behind them, just not in the selection. Our killer is meticulous in their disposal, and we haven't found anything that might even give us a fibre. Until Amelia, the mistake,' replied Professor Hawthorne thoughtfully.

'But they've all been killed in roughly the same way, except maybe Sophia at the festival and Rebecca in her car.,' said DC Green. 'The rest are taken from the street. It's not a home invasion-type scenario, I'll give you that, but I'd say that was some level of intention. How else would you be able to get close enough to gut these girls and not leave a trace? There would need to be some planning. It would be tough to pull this off consistently with a snap decision at the last moment; it's too risky and would take a lot of control and luck. Plus, where is he taking them to torture them? And how is he selecting the dumping sites and transporting them?' DC Green finally took a breath. He was quite invested in his theory.

Professor Hawthorne let a smile pass across his face as he nodded to show he understood DC Green's viewpoint. 'A valid argument constable, but if the killer had got the victim to come to their location, there would be something to be found there. No, our killer is extremely good at planning the act of the murder, but they don't have a plan as to *when* they will do it. This is the reason there are no fibres. They use disposable tools and don't always go through with it when they intend to. Something was missing from the victims, or something not quite right, that caused them to abort; it's why they've not killed as often as we would have thought, given the level of planning. They haven't escalated in the same way you might normally see. The cooling-off periods have remained consistent. They're not escalating or weren't until a few months ago.' He stopped again, strolled around the desk where DS Sterling was sitting, and placed a hand on her shoulder. She'd been listening to them quietly, but looked up at him now that he was touching her. 'Miss Sterling, you're a killer. A clever killer. Violent, but with cunning and self-restraint. When you are on the streets looking for victims, what are you looking for?'

She thought momentarily before slowly saying, 'Someone you think you can control. I'd be looking for someone who wouldn't fight back or would be less likely to. A drunk, for instance, someone who is mentally or physically vulnerable, maybe?'

Professor Hawthorne nodded gently and smiled at her. 'Good. What our killer has is an expert knowledge of human psychology and a very acute awareness of their victims. This knowledge allows them to select who they believe they can most easily target and control with no need for a plan. Just the knowledge and understanding to ensure it goes how they want it to, without making it too easy on themselves. It's not a matter of taking what is there. It is a case of selecting something which suits you. I don't think they need to kill. I think they want to. They can wait if the timing isn't right.' He looked at the wall as if trying to read the vast amounts of information written all over it in one go. He placed a hand on his head, trying to think.

'Should we be writing all this down?' said DC Green.

Professor Hawthorne lifted his head and walked over to an A3 paper easel in the corner. He dragged it into view and rolled the first sheet over the top of the easel to reveal a fresh sheet of cheap, thin, off-white office paper.

'It is clear in my head, but I will make it easier for you to visualise,' he said with such a jarringly condescending tone that neither DC Green nor Kim knew if he was joking.

'Based on the information we have and statistical probability, the best profile I have so far is this.' He looked around to ensure he had a captive audience, which he did. 'The victims have all been young females and only one of them hasn't been white. Therefore, our killer is statistically going to be a white male. Given they've been committing these crimes for at least twelve years, and most serial killers start in their late twenties, he's likely to be around forty years old.' He drew a 'mind map' on the board as he spoke. It was a big, empty central circle, but each key point had its own line and associated bubble from the middle.

'So far, so obvious. The only connection between the victims is the randomness. There is deliberately no obvious connection that can be drawn between our victims, although I will grant you that the majority have been sex workers, but not all. I think that is just a by-product of the fact these women are more likely to be in his selectable cohort. Peter Sutcliffe claimed god told him to kill prostitutes, but I don't think this man has anything against sex workers per se.'

He moved away from the drawing board, leaving a series of circles and lines scattered across its surface, and walked towards the map. 'He's going to be local to the area, based on the geography of the scenes, but he knows Wales. Maybe he grew up there?'

This was a rhetorical question, but Kim heard DC Green mutter 'Davies' under his breath. Professor Hawthorne didn't hear, though, and ploughed on.

'From the description Amelia gave us, we know he's tall and balding, not especially helpful, but it's there, and we shouldn't completely ignore it. I have already mentioned that he is not a secreter. He does not ejaculate at the scenes and likely does not take sexual pleasure from doing this. He may well have done this during the torture, but some DNA might have been found on at least one body, so I think this is probably not the case. An alternative argument would be presumably some level of sexual dysfunction, but I believe this is less likely. The way they're killed is exact. There's a certain amount of pleasure being derived from the torture and killing itself rather than from who the victim is.' Professor Hawthorne moved closer to the map; he seemed to be studying the geography again. Although he was talking to the room, something about his tone meant it felt like he was talking to himself.

'Maybe he just doesn't have the time to... you know...' DC Green made a wanking motion with his hand and looked slightly uncomfortably at Professor Hawthorne, who didn't actually look at him. He must have had eyes on the back of his head, though, as he tutted.

'No, this person plans his attacks, like I said. He'd factor in time for masturbation if it were required.'

'I still think he could do it when he's torturing them?' offered Kim.

'He could. But I feel he'd likely want to disgrace his victims by covering them with his seed. We know he doesn't from the forensic reports, and the fact he doesn't is, I think, important.'

'Maybe he has a wife who humiliates him or someone who left him?' Kim said.

'Possible, but I think it's unlikely he has a wife or girlfriend. Your suggestion that maybe someone left him when he was younger is sensible. It may explain why he gets his pleasure from stabbing and pain rather than a more typical sexual experience.'

Professor Hawthorne took another step closer to the map. He was almost standing with his nose pressed against the wall now. 'The cleanliness of these kills shows a level of planning and extremely high intelligence. I suspect he has a high IQ, perhaps a genius level. His job is likely to reflect this as well; it'll be a profession or vocation which requires hard work, acumen and a large degree of judgement and decision-making. He is very precise with their method, and this person has at least some awareness of police procedure and basic forensics. They understand that the body and scene they leave behind can be their downfall, and they are careful to avoid this.'

Professor Hawthorne pointed to the map and continued his monologue. 'When I think of this kind of planning, I also think of someone with a knowledge of city geography. They know which parts of the city will go unseen by cameras, which streets are dark at night, which areas have the highest foot and road traffic levels, and which don't. I saw this pattern with a taxi driver who branched out to murder once.'

'How many taxi drivers have an IQ of a hundred and forty-five, though?' scoffed DC Green, which earned him a disapproving look from Kim.

'I agree,' said Professor Hawthorne. 'This isn't the work of your local cabbie. But the killer knows the city remarkably well. The choice of location for disposal of the bodies is a very carefully considered decision. I don't think this person will take their victim home. I think they'll take them to an abandoned or deserted area which holds some meaning or value for them. It could be that it's where the first victim died or that they lived in that place before it was condemned.

I think they'll try to ensure that no cameras can capture the killing. But they also don't mind dumping them in more heavily trafficked areas. It is like a game of cat and mouse. They're confident, and I think they feel invincible. These are areas where they feel comfortable dumping bodies. They'll know they can avoid the cameras there as well.' Professor Hawthorne continued his walk around the office, completing a full lap and stopping again at the wall with the map.

'How is he getting them there, though? I mean, they've all been abducted, so how's he transporting them and disposing of the evidence?' asked Kim.

Professor Hawthorne didn't reply immediately; he stared intently at the map and didn't appear to be paying any attention to either of his audience members. It wasn't until DC Green made a coughing noise and said 'Oi Prof' that Professor Hawthorne seemed to remember where he was.

'Sorry,' he said as he looked over at the pair of them.

'How is he transporting the bodies?'

'Yes, yes. This person has a vehicle of some description. A van or truck would be good, but I think this person will have something which can be hidden, discreet and nondescript, inconspicuous, designed to blend in, not draw attention.'

'All well and good, Prof, but some of this is obvious and not helpful. How the fuck are we supposed to locate a 'discreet van?' said DC Green, getting slightly flustered.

'You're not. Their van is not how we're going to catch them,' said Professor Hawthorne, who had now taken to staring at the copied case files that were laid out across the desk. 'They've stayed one step ahead of you throughout all this, meaning I believe he has insight into the investigation, in one way or another. Possibly directly or possibly through another source. You might be looking for the spouse or partner of someone in the investigation.'

'So it's likely to be an inside job?' said DC Green.

'Possible. This person is intelligent and has some level of control and insight. They may well be connected to the investigation or police department in some capacity. He could be a former police officer or someone in a related profession.'

'I saw PC Andrew Johnson hanging around Lucas's house earlier,' said Kim thoughtfully.

'Not to be rude, but as I understand it, he's short, fat, not bald and has been a PC for fifteen years now, with not a hint of progression. I think we can assume he does not have a high IQ because he was hiding outside the house of a missing detective. I think we can discount him,' said Professor Hawthorne scornfully.

DC Green was looking at the mind map and groaning. 'This profile matches DCI Miller, doesn't it?'

'I can see the connection, DC Green, but I don't think it is him. What we've got so far also pertains to that journalist you arrested, possibly. But we're not there yet.' Professor Hawthorne looked again at the map. It had drawn him back for some reason. What was he looking for?

'The dumping sites have been deliberately chosen. They're designed to have a particular effect on those who find the corpses. I believe they knowingly placed them in locations with an emotional and cultural connection; perhaps they were hiding spots during his childhood or where he used to play. Maybe he dumped a childhood pet there or got bullied himself. Something in those dump sites will have a particular meaning and value to the killer. But you must understand that they also serve as a message; it's like he's marking out his territory. It's like he's claiming the entire city for himself.'

Kim thought this sounded slightly mad, but then she looked at Professor Hawthorne and thought she understood where he was coming from. If you are a predator in your own right, why wouldn't you want to claim and control your territory? It is just that most people don't tend to see it this way.

'I can't understand what's so special about where the bodies have been found,' said DC Green with an exasperated sigh.

'Look at them,' said Professor Hawthorne. 'Each one was found in a unique area which would have some emotional value for them but would also mean something to someone else. Some of the dump sites were even repeated. It's like a map. He's sending messages through this map to somebody. They're taunting someone with their knowledge. But the problem with that is that this will probably make it harder for you to find him.'

'I'm not sure I'm following all this?' said DC Green. Professor Hawthorne looked up to the ceiling, appeared to be lost in thought, and then looked down again to DC Green.

'Because this person is sending the police on a wild goose chase, looking for answers that aren't there.' Professor Hawthorne stared at the map for a few minutes. The ensuing silence seemed to hang in the room like a lead balloon.

Eventually, DC Green coughed, prompting Professor Hawthorne to look over him as if he was suddenly aware he had an audience again. Kim didn't know whether to be offended by how easily and frequently Professor Hawthorne appeared to forget they existed.

'Normally, you could look at the dump sites, draw a circle around them, and your killer would be in the centre of that circle.' He drew on the map as he talked. A close-to-perfect circle emerged. 'I think if you try that here, you will fail because, look, it's too neat a circle. No, you're looking at something else entirely. This is deliberately and precisely random and intriguing. A forced pattern. That is the meaning. The answer will be in those folders' said Professor Hawthorne, pointing to the case notes on the table.

'We need to look for other ways in which this case has been engineered from the start. There will be patterns of manipulation. That is what is going to lead us to our individual. They're controlling the investigation. They control the officers. This is a game.'

He then stood up and stared at the folders as if he had x-ray vision, which he did not. He drew a sharp breath through his nose and then walked towards the door, opened it and walked through without another word. DC Green and Kim looked at one another in shock. DC Green had gone as far as opening his mouth and then closing it again in response to his unexpected disappearance. Kim was dumbfounded and confused. She needed to think about whatever Professor Hawthorne had just said, so she looked back down at the case reports on her desk. DC Green stood up and rolled his eyes at her, indicating he also found Professor Hawthorne confusing.

'Fucking odd bloke. Right, I'm going to get a cuppa. Do you want anything?'

69

The community's fear and suspicion were palpable, a thick fog of distrust that seemed to cloud every interaction. No one spoke to him directly, but their sidelong glances and hushed tones were enough to confirm his worst fears. He was no longer one of them; he was the other, the outsider, the accused.

As he waited for his order, Simon Davies' gaze fell on the array of community notices pinned beside the counter — missing pets, local events, and a small poster appealing for information on the very crimes he was accused of. His heart sank further. Was this what his life had become? A cycle of suspicion and guilt, where even the mundane act of picking up dinner felt like an exercise in evasion?

He collected his food with a mumbled thanks, barely meeting the eyes of the server, and stepped back into the night. He'd ordered enough for two people, although he hadn't decided if he would eat it all himself yet.

The city seemed different now, every shadow a potential accuser, every passing car a potential judge. He wasn't haunted just by the eyes of those who passed him, but by the thoughts that chased him through the dimly lit streets of Leeds. Each step felt heavier than the last, each breath a reminder of the freedom he barely grasped. The irony of his situation was not lost on him; a journalist who once thrived on exposing truths was now submerged in a narrative he couldn't escape, his own story a headline he could never publish. Talking to Jacob Murray hadn't helped either. Getting that story out was supposed to be cathartic, but he felt no better, no worse.

He arrived home and stood there, deafened by the silence of his flat. The path would be arduous, fraught with uncertainty and danger, but he had no choice. The alternative was a life spent in the shadows, forever marked by accusations. With that resolve, he began plotting his next move, aware that each step forward was a step into the unknown, a gamble with stakes higher than he'd ever imagined.

* * *

In the suffocating darkness, with the chilling draft as his only companion, Lucas's hope and positivity died. The hours dragged on, or perhaps they were minutes that felt like centuries. Lucas's senses were finally sharpening in the darkness, making him more aware of his impending fate. The smell of iron and formaldehyde that had once threatened to overwhelm him seemed to fade into the background, replaced by the scent of damp earth and mould. It was as if the basement was alive, breathing slowly and rhythmically, in sync with his laboured breaths.

The silence was oppressive, broken only by the occasional

drip of water from an unseen leak. Each drop echoed in the vast emptiness, and Lucas wondered if he'd ever see the light again, if he'd ever feel the sun on his skin or breathe fresh air without the stench of death clinging to it.

His thoughts turned to Ems, to the horrifying moment that had led him here. Guilt gnawed at him, its sharp teeth digging deep into his conscience. Could he have prevented it? Was there a moment, a decision, that could have altered their course? The questions circled in his mind, relentless and unyielding. He needed to escape.

Slowly, painstakingly, he rocked his chair, shifting his weight back and forth, trying to tip it over. It was a gamble—the fall could injure him further, but it could also be his only chance. Sweat mixed with blood on his brow, each movement a Herculean effort.

Finally, with a desperate lunge, the chair toppled, crashing to the cold concrete floor. The impact sent waves of pain through Lucas's body, but it also brought a rush of adrenaline. He writhed on the ground, the chair still attached at the back, making it difficult to move. The sharp edges of the broken chair dug into his skin, but Lucas barely noticed, his focus entirely on freeing himself from the remaining restraints. His fingers, though numb and swollen, worked tirelessly, pulling at the duct tape with a frantic energy. The surrounding darkness seemed to pulse with his heartbeat, every thud echoing off the unseen walls, amplifying his sense of desperation.

The damp, earthy smell of the basement mingled with the iron tang of his own blood, creating a metallic perfume that filled his nostrils with every laboured breath. Despite the pain, Lucas felt a surge of hope as the last of the tape gave way, freeing his legs from their bindings. He was about to attempt to stand when the faintest sound stopped him dead: the creak of a door slowly opening.

Lucas froze, every sense suddenly heightened. The oppressive silence of the basement was shattered by the soft, deliberate footsteps of someone descending the stairs. His heart pounded in his chest, a frantic drumbeat in the quiet. He lay still, barely daring to breathe, as the footsteps drew nearer. Then there was silence.

Lucas felt the presence of another in the room with him and could sense the shift in the air, which smelt sickly sweet suddenly. The sense of being watched was overwhelming, a tangible weight upon him. He strained his ears, trying to detect any movement, any hint of what was to come.

A voice, cold and devoid of emotion, broke the silence. 'I see you've made quite a mess.' The words dripping with a sinister amusement that sent shivers down Lucas's spine.

So close.

70

They were working in relative silence, permeated infrequently by someone letting out a sigh or shifting in their seats. DS Sterling was flicking through all the case reports page by page. She was skim-reading; there was too much information to delve into the details. Maybe something would jump out at her she hadn't noticed before. She kept Professor Hawthorne's somewhat mystic profile in mind: intelligent, professional, and someone who could manipulate them for twelve years. Lucas was becoming a more likely candidate, but she couldn't let thoughts like that lay roots in her mind. She had to believe that he was one of the good guys. She'd spent a lot of time with him over the last few months, and she'd seen nothing that made her think he was anything but a dedicated officer.

Each case report was pretty brief, a little synopsis of where the body was found and who found it. There was a report from the scene of the crime team regarding the evidence, or lack thereof, and a small paragraph about the victim, if they'd been identified. There were autopsy reports and grizzly photographs, which Kim had become desensitised to. This was not why she became a police officer. She wanted to prevent these kinds of things from happening to people. The images of these girls tied up, wounds gaping and organs missing, were so deeply ingrained in her mind now she wondered if she'd ever be able to forget them.

'Why does he take the organs?' she said out loud, the first time any of them had spoken in nearly half an hour.

'Cos he's a freak,' said DC Green. 'Probably eats them or something.'

'A good question, DS Sterling.' said Professor Hawthorne, ignoring DC Green. 'Why do you think he takes the organs? What does he do with them? Why does he feel the need to take them when he's done such a thorough job of covering his tracks? And then consider the snippets of the poem. That is risky, leaving a clue. He is otherwise risk-averse.'

'Well,' said Kim, 'I'm assuming it's a keepsake, like a trophy or something. It's typical of serial killers to take trophies, isn't it? Like a lock of hair or some other belongings. But we know he takes their jewellery, so maybe DC Green's, right? Maybe he does eat them?'

'Thank you! Or maybe he puts them on his mantelpiece!' said DC Green sarcastically.

'Interesting theory, DS Sterling,' said Professor Hawthorne, once again ignoring DC Green. 'It is my view that he takes the organs for a number of reasons. Firstly, to assert control and dominance over his victims. By removing something so intimate and vital, he not only dehumanises them, but also claims a part of them as his own. This act could serve to satisfy a pathological need for power and possession.'

Professor Hawthorne paced slowly, hands clasped behind his back, eyes narrowed in thought. 'Secondly, the specific organs he takes may hold symbolic significance. It's possible that he's not just a serial killer but also someone deeply engrossed in some form of ritualistic behaviour. This aligns with the poetic snippets left at the scenes. They're not just clues but messages, part of a narrative he's constructing. He is mocking you.'

Kim nodded, absorbing his words. 'So, he sees himself as an artist or a storyteller of sorts. Using their organs and the poems to craft a story only he fully understands?'

'Exactly. And this narrative is key to unravelling his identity. Each organ, each poem, is a piece of the puzzle. If we can decode the symbolism, the pattern, we might predict his next move or, better yet, identify him.'

After a moment of contemplation, Kim said, 'What if the choice of organ is related to what he perceives as their sins or flaws? Maybe he believes he's cleansing them or punishing them for something.'

'That's a possibility. Many killers operate under a delusion of moral superiority or a mission. This could be his distorted way of interacting with his victims even after their death.'

'So, we're looking for a deluded, organ-obsessed poet with a god complex. Great, that narrows it down.' DC Green, who had been quietly listening, chimed in, and despite the pressure of the discussion, Sterling couldn't help but smirk at Green's comment.

'Let's not forget the poems,' Sterling added, her tone becoming severe again. 'They're not just taunts; they're part of his signature. There has to be a reason he chose this poem and these particular lines. Maybe they give us insight into his motives or his background?'

'Indeed,' Professor Hawthorne agreed. 'The literary aspect could be key. It suggests a level of education, or at least a strong interest in literature. It's an unusual combination with the brutality of his crimes, but it's a tangible aspect of his identity.'

'So, what does it mean?' asked DC Green.

'Well,' Professor Hawthorne paused, adjusting his glasses as he peered closer at the poem plastered to the back wall. 'This poem isn't just an eclectic collection of verses. It's methodical and deliberate. Each stanza, each organ mentioned, carries a weight beyond the literal. It's as if the killer is following a narrative or a doctrine through the very essence of his victims.'

DS Sterling leaned forward, her eyes following Professor Hawthorne's in scanning the poem again. 'It's almost as if each organ he takes is part of a larger ritual. It's a disgusting poem; that's not an accident.'

DC Green frowned, 'But why poetry? Why go through all the trouble to leave something so… cryptic?'

'Because,' Hawthorne interjected, 'for him, it's not just about the act of killing. It's about sending a message, albeit a twisted one. This poem, these organs—they're his way of communicating. Of asserting his identity.'

The room fell into a contemplative silence, which lingered for a few beats. It was broken crudely by DC Green. 'And what about the fact he sometimes shoves things inside the victims? Ramming a pen into Amelia's vagina was a step up in what he had been doing.'

'I am less sure about that, I must admit. I'm not sure what was different about Amelia Watson. Why did she get special treatment?'

'DCI Miller knew her; he had a personal relationship with her,' said Kim grimly through gritted teeth

'Possibly. I'm not sure, but it wasn't an accident. He is playing a game of cat and mouse, and everything is deliberate. But I am not sure, I must concede.'

'I can't see DCI Miller doing anything like this,' said DC Green, shifting uncomfortably in his seat again. 'Why would he?'

'I don't think he has either,' said Professor Hawthorne.

'Me neither,' said Kim quickly,

'But that being said, you must not hold it against the superintendent and the others for having some suspicions. There is enough here to investigate; from a physiological perspective, he has the background.'

'What do you mean by that?' said DC Green, confused.

'Ah, I'm not sure-' started Kim, who saw where he was going with this. It was too late, and she couldn't interrupt him.

'The murder of his mother when he was a child,' said Professor Hawthorne simply.

'What?' replied DC Green, a look of shock spreading over his face.

'As I understand it, she was murdered when he was a young boy. Aged six or seven, I think. The suspect was never caught. That's quite some burden to have as a child. To have a distinguished career investigating the murder of women, that is odd, I must admit. There is something worth studying about that young man.'

'That doesn't make him a killer,' said Kim.

'No, of course not. But it's something to think about. I don't know him very well, but from what I can see, he's a complex fellow. I'd be surprised if there weren't more to the story than meets the eye. He must be troubled by her death, yet he can encounter it daily. Is it cathartic or a self-punishment, do you think?'

'I don't know. There are those pills he takes for the pain in his arm; they must help,' muttered Kim. He was right; Lucas's desire to work on something so traumatic to himself was not normal. Maybe there was more to this.

'Pregabalin. I saw the packet in Wales. Good for anxiety and neuropathic pain. Not on a prescription, I'm assuming, given how coy he was being. The plot thickens,' said Professor Hawthorne.

This chat was making Kim feel nauseated, if she was honest. She couldn't help but think again about all the young girls and vulnerable women out on the street working alone with little protection. It would only take a moment for the wrong guy to walk into their lives and for them to end up as another statistic, another face staring up from the cold metallic table in a mortuary. As she scanned through all the files, she couldn't see any patterns that might point to someone in the investigation. She didn't recognise any unusual names that kept reappearing in each of the reports, just the obvious ones like Lucas and Carmichael, although that meant nothing. Maybe their killer did not work inside the department? Perhaps they'd worked at the department in the past but weren't part of the team anymore?

Professor Hawthorne and DC Green were still in the room, chatting and reviewing theories, but Kim was blinkered with concentration. There was so much information and many words and phrases to read and absorb, but it felt like they had so little to work with. She had a few vague theories that might match up with significant work and refinement, but that could also be her overthinking. Professor Hawthorne was right, and she couldn't start looking for a connection between the killer and someone in the investigation. There just wasn't anything that succinctly linked all this together. This killer had done an incredible job of making himself seem completely untouchable. The thought of someone who could kill women in the city and get away with it for twelve years was more than she could take.

But then... she noticed something. A name where it shouldn't be. What was that doing there? Her heart started beating a little faster as she sifted through the files, looking for a different report. Her heart rate increased yet further. The name was also there, sitting on the paper, glinting in black ink. She laid out all the reports, and she could now feel her pulse beating in her neck and hear the beating in her ears.

'Fuck!' she stood up so suddenly that DC Green leapt from his seat, and Professor Hawthorne looked round with a marginally panicked expression.

'I've found the link!' she shouted, her voice quivering. The others rushed round to see what she was talking about. She stood there and pointed at the report in front of them.

'Right?' said DC Green, who clearly didn't understand. She ignored him and pointed at the same name on every report in front of them. All fifteen victims were splayed across the table as she tapped each report. DC Green still looked confused, but Professor Hawthorne let out a little gasp.

'Oh. Well done,' he whispered.

'I don't get it. He should be on all the reports, shouldn't he?' said DC Green.

'No. He should be on twelve of them. He shouldn't be on the Welsh reports. Why would he be on the Welsh reports? He had three years off, around the time I was off with my cancer. He must have transferred to Wales. But for the killings to follow him, that can't be a coincidence,' said Kim, failing to hide the excitement in her voice. 'He fits the physical profile, is wicked smart, has intermate knowledge of the cases and has done right from the very start. Who else is better placed to manipulate this investigation? You said it yourself, Professor: the killer is highly intelligent and likely to be professional. It's obvious from the verses he has a profound obsession with human anatomy; he steals organs, for fucks sake! Who do we know who is tall, bald, professional, anatomically trained, forensically aware and has intimate knowledge of the case?

'Oh fuck me,' exclaimed DC Green, the dawning of realisation appearing on his face. Kim strode over to the easel. She took the big black pen and drew lines from each bubble on Professor Hawthorne's mind map to a new circle just off the centre. Inside the circle, she wrote the name of the person who had appeared as lead author on all fifteen autopsy reports. Even the ones in Wales that he had no right to be performing. She wrote the name;

Dr Daniel Cross.

71

It was Baltic. Utterly bone-chillingly cold, Lucas was shivering uncontrollably. His feet were numb, his nose and lips had gone blue, and he couldn't feel his fingers. He was so hungry, although he didn't know how he would eat since the bastard had knocked half of his teeth out. How much time had passed? It could have been minutes, hours, or even days since he'd watched him open up Em's throat like a tin can.

He heard a door open to the left of him. A searing white light flooded the room, and Lucas was temporarily blinded. He'd been in here long enough that his eyes had fully adjusted to the darkness, and the sudden illumination was painful. There was a pause, and he heard footsteps approach him. A tall, balding figure appeared before him, stooping to his level. Dr Cross had often tried to make Lucas feel small; even now, he couldn't help himself. He had a look in his eye, a dullness that Lucas had never noticed before.

'Lucas, my old friend.' his tone was sickeningly patronising, even by his usual standard, and his enjoyment was palpable. Lucas stared at him, unable to say anything; his tongue remained swollen and painful. He desperately wanted to spit at the bastard, but his mouth was too dry. 'You have really put a spanner in the works, detective, haven't you?' His smile was wide and menacing.

Cross didn't break eye contact with those dark, dull orbs deep within his skull. Lucas just continued to stare back and shiver. He could feel the pain in his hands, the blood barely flowing into his fingers. It felt like the tips were stabbed with pins and needles, a sensation spreading backwards proximally. The electric pain that so usually troubled him in the left arm was amplified tenfold. He tried to flex his fingers, but it wasn't working. Dr Cross looked down at him and laughed his big, loud, booming laugh.

'Want one of these?' sneered Dr Cross, dangling the blister pack he'd removed from Lucas's pocket. The answer was yes. He did want one and probably needed one. But he couldn't give him the satisfaction, so he didn't reply; he just blinked and tried to maintain the air of strength that was so close to deserting him.

Dr Cross smiled, pocketed the pills and picked up a large pair of bolt cutters resting against the wall. He held them and opened and closed the blades with discernible menace. They made a sickening clicking sound reverberating around Lucas's ear canals. He reached forward and pulled Lucas's head up by the chin. The feeling in his face was slowly returning, and the throbbing pain in his tongue was intensifying. Dr Cross held his head still with his left hand and put the blades of the bolt cutters around Lucas's right index finger, resting it there gently. Lucas tensed.

'I was hoping to see you go down for my crimes. That would have been such a lovely ending to this chapter. But you've disrupted that plan, waltzing in here. Bravo. I am genuinely impressed you've found me, I'll have to admit, even if it was pure dumb luck. However, I think I can still hang this round your neck.' He grinned broadly, creating deep wrinkles of shadow across his waxy skin.

Without warning, he snapped the bolt cutters shut, making an ugly crunch as the small bones split, and a small spurt of blood erupted into the air, falling to the floor with a patter. The anguished scream masked the softened arterial spray, hitting the floor with soft thuds as Lucas yelled out in pain, his voice croaky and hoarse. He was crying, great salty tears running down his cheeks. He tried desperately to shift his gaze to Dr Cross, whose face was blank and expressionless. The remnants of his finger were hanging loose, held on by a few strands only. Dr Cross twisted the cutters, bending the finger at a sickening angle until it came free and fell to the floor. Lucas yelped and tried to kick his feet as the immense pain raced through him.

The doctor repeated the action with the next finger and the next. The agony was excruciating. When he'd finished, Lucas was left with a few bloody stumps; the rest were bent, mangled, or twisted beyond recognition. Blood was pouring out onto the floor, looking black, almost, and it had that consistency of engine oil. That familiar stench of iron was burning in his throat. His remaining fingers had turned a ghostly grey, and his entire hand tingled. The pain was incredible, like fire burning up his arm.

'You'll want these back, I suppose,' said Dr Cross, smirking. He reached into his pocket and pulled out four teeth. Each was in a clear plastic bag, and he noticed that his front left molar had a massive crack down the side. It was the tooth he'd cracked on the playground when he was eleven. His dad had taken him to the emergency dentist, but had seemed annoyed with him the whole time. His mum wouldn't have blamed him. All the teeth in the bag were covered in blood, and the redness had run down the plastic, leaving little droplets and streaks at the bottom.

'Don't worry, I can fiddle with your dental records, I can fiddle with your DNA sample, I can fiddle with the autopsy results. I can design this however I want.' With that, he threw the bags to the floor and walked out, laughing to himself.

Lucas's heart was racing. He was dizzy, trying not to vomit. The pain in his hand was like nothing he'd ever experienced. His chest was heavy and sore, his legs had turned to jelly. He was going to die. He knew he was going to die. All he could think about was the memory of his mum, who he'd let down, the families of those Dr Cross had murdered and his dog, Luna. She'd be waiting for him, curled up in her little basket, warming her little pink belly. She probably had one of his shoes. But then another thought entered his head... Thomas Mitchel had been innocent.

'Somebody help!' he croaked, his voice still broken and strained as he shifted the guilt from his mind. There was a familiar laugh from the corner of the room behind Lucas. Dr Cross had reappeared. There was the sound of metal on metal, as if someone was sharpening a blade.

'There's nobody here. It's just you and me. Nobody is coming.'

He was right. It was just him and Lucas alone. Nobody knew where he was and he was totally fucked.

72

DS Sterling, Professor Hawthorne, and DC Green burst into the inquiry room, finding it a hive of activity. Every member of the West Yorkshire Police Force appeared to be present, and there was barely space to move. Whilst they were undoubtedly working hard, they were all working under the pretence that Lucas Miller might be a murderer. Some genuinely believed it, some wanted it to be true, but many were simply following commands. Kim marched over directly to Superintendent Carmichael, who was deep in conversation with DI Chloe Wilson and DI Khan.

'So we've scoured all the CCTV and ANPR from the ten miles surrounding his house, and we've got more footage of him around Headingly. I think it's clear he had gone to see Emily West, but they seem to vanish after that. We don't know where she is either. There are black spots across the city, which we have to assume he's in. There is an alert across Leeds on all CCTV cameras and ANPR to trace his car. We're extending that to Bradford, Humberside, and North Yorkshire as well,' said Chloe as the rest of the group looked on. Kim was losing her cool with every stride forward, and she began on the offensive, shouting at Chloe.

'You spent four years living with the man. Do you really think he's capable of murder? Was he out killing behind your back? Should we be looking at you as an accomplice, eh?' she snarled at Chloe, who flinched and looked somewhat taken aback.

'DS Sterling, I thought you'd left?'

'No, I've been working on trying to find the actual perpetrator. I believe Lucas is in danger!'

'What are you talking about?' said DI Khan, folding his arms and rolling his eyes.

'Dr Daniel Cross, we need to find him.'

'The pathologist? What the fuck has he got to do with it?' said DI Khan, laughing.

'That is an exceptionally bold accusation. Explain this, now,' said Superintendent Carmichael with a withering look so severe that Kim lost her flow for a split second. She regained it quickly, however, and launched into an explanation of what they had discovered. How Dr Cross had performed every single autopsy on the case, how he had access to everything from the beginning, and how he fit Professor Hawthorne's profile to a tee. DI Khan had tried to interrupt occasionally but was quickly silenced by Carmichael, who did not break eye contact with Kim. She just listened, as did DI Chloe Wilson.

'Where is he? I think he should be allowed to reply to these far-fetched accusations,' said DI Khan as Kim finished, his face even more punchable than usual. Carmichael didn't silence him this time; she just stared at Kim, her eyes boring into her.

'Well, we're not sure,' said Professor Hawthorne, 'That's what we were coming to ask you. He's not in his office.

Please send someone round to his house. This should be done properly and quickly.'

There was an awkward silence as Superintendent Carmichael, DI Wilson, DI Khan, and several others looked at each other quizzically.

Finally, Carmichael spoke. 'You are not running this investigation, Professor. Neither is the Metropolitan police. We are. I am. And as far as I can tell, you only have some subjective reasoning. There is no actual evidence. The only thing that ties him to these crimes is a profile generated by you, some crackpot from down south.' Carmichael shot a filthy look at Professor Hawthorne, who smiled obliviously back. DI Khan mimicked his boss with an equally scathing stare before she continued, 'That profile could be several people, including DCI Miller and Simon Davies. The only two pieces of physical evidence we have point towards DCI Miller. What reason do I have to fetch Dan?'

'Two pieces of evidence?' interjected DC Green. DI Khan smirked. That horrible smirk when someone knows something you don't.

'Well, yes. We have Jessica Murray's necklace, found in his boot and on his person. Perhaps he was trying to plant it on Simon Davies. But then we've just had word from the lab. On the pen found inside Amelia, well under the lid, they found a significant amount of DCI Miller's DNA. It was his pen.'

The blood in Kim's veins ran cold. Fuck. That was pretty hard evidence. But then, a memory formed in her mind from the other night when he met her at his house to tell her about the necklace.

'He mentioned that someone had stolen his pen to me the

other day; the only person who had been in his house was Emily West. She's also missing, and I think she's involved. She works with Dr Cross. Surely it isn't much of a leap to think he might be using her? DCI Miller isn't a killer. Come on!' Kim was speaking calmly, trying to make herself sound sensible and considered. Inside, she was screaming and panicking. The looks on the others' faces told her everything. Certainly, Superintendent Carmichael and DI Khan simply did not believe her. Chloe was staring at the floor and looking more embarrassed than anything else.

'Right. This has all been very illuminating,' Superintendent Carmichael said. 'However, as you can see, we have several officers on the ground looking for DCI Miller. I do not have the resources to run off searching for a well-respected pathologist on the unsubstantiated hunch of a rogue detective sergeant.'

'But the autopsy reports! Why is Dr Cross performing autopsies in Wales?' said a visibly strained Kim.

'He transferred there for three years whilst his father was unwell. We already had Dr Cooper, and that is why Dr Baker was hired temporarily. You should have known this. Lucas knew this,' said Carmichael.

A light bulb suddenly popped in Kim's head, 'He's the person who told you the Wales cases weren't linked, wasn't he? That's why you didn't bother to investigate them properly, right?' Carmichael glowered at Kim but said nothing. Her silence spoke volumes.

'But surely that can't be a coincidence, that the crimes move to Wales at the same time as Dr Cross!'

'Do not shout at a senior officer, DC Green.'

'It's OK, Sadiq, the detective is just passionate,' said

Superintendent Carmichael, calmly finding her voice again. 'But you need something more convincing than this. I will continue to follow the most likely lead, which right now is that DCI Miller is deeply involved in these murders. However, you three can waste your time investigating Dan if you like. Find anything, and you bring it to me. In the meantime, I will actually try to locate Miller. You are dismissed, DS Sterling.'

Kim was about to respond, but a hand on her shoulder from Professor Hawthorne stopped her. He flicked his head slightly to signal that they should leave. She gave a parting look of sheer acid to Superintendent Carmichael before leaving the room and following Professor Hawthorne with a shell-shocked DC Green bringing up the rear. They were halfway down the corridor when there was a shout from behind them.

'Sterling!' she turned to see who had shouted and was surprised when a slightly out-of-breath DI Chloe Wilson jogged up to them. Kim just stared at her, not sure what she wanted. Chloe was flushed as she spoke.

'No. The answer to your question is no. I don't think Lucas is a killer.'

Kim looked stern but softened a bit as she replied, 'Good. I think he is in trouble.'

'I'm worried as well. I'll investigate your pathologist theory.'

'Brilliant, about time.'

'Er, let me remind you that I am a DI and outrank you here, sergeant. So drop the attitude. You're very good, and you may even be right here. But wind your neck in a little, OK?' Chloe was suddenly quite abrasive and Kim's face reddened whilst she avoided eye contact with DC Green, who stifled a laugh.

'Yes, boss, sorry.'

'Right. So, I'll tell you Cross was at work this morning but has left early, and Miss West called in sick. Technically, she emailed in sick, which, according to the other mortuary tech, wasn't really her style. It might be nothing, but it might be something. I'll send an officer over to Cross's house, but in the meantime, I think it would be good to search his office,' said Chloe, slapping her hands together.

'We don't have a warrant?'

'Unofficially then,' she said with a grin.

73

It might have been dark outside, but equally, it might have been blazing sunshine. The windows in the room were boarded up, and Lucas had no concept of how much time had passed. Dr Cross departed and returned periodically, oscillating between inflicting physical and mental torture on Lucas. Right this second, he was sitting across from him, his gaze penetrating. He was wearing one of the paper suits that he frequently sported at a crime scene, and Lucas could see that underneath was his usual civilian shirt and chino combination.

'How did you manage it?' asked Lucas; his voice was feeble, and he had a soft but audible whistle because of the missing teeth. He was still tied to the chair, his fingers all bent at right angles and covered in sweat and sticky blood. The hopelessness of his situation meant that the pain seemed to be dulled as if there was simply no point feeling it.

'How? But that is such a boring question, DCI Miller. I already told you how; just read my reports. Anyone can kill someone. It's quite fun and certainly not very difficult. You should have given it a try.' He spoke calmly and condescendingly as he stood from his chair and walked over to the table in the corner. It was lined with an array of sharp tools, glinting in the murky light. They must have been stolen from the mortuary at some point. 'Especially women. Weak, fragile, and so very accessible. You'd be amazed at how easily women are persuaded, especially if you give them the impression they're making a choice. He picked up a shining silver drill bit, about fifteen centimetres long and about fifteen millimetres thick. He pointed it at Lucas casually and continued. 'Getting away with it is the more challenging part. But then, I'm a leading pathologist working on my own investigation. Do you need me to explain how I manipulated autopsies and steered the investigation?' Dr Cross twirled the drill bit between his fingers like a conductor orchestrating a symphony of fear. 'Manipulation, DCI Miller, is an art form. And I...' he paused, letting the drill catch a ray of dim light, '...am an artist.'

Lucas tried to focus on Dr Cross's face, to read any sign of humanity that might remain, but it was like staring into the abyss. His once keen detective's intuition now seemed as battered and broken as his body.

'You see, it's all about understanding the human condition. We're creatures of habit, predictable. With the right... influence,' he smiled thinly, 'one can create the perfect storm of evidence. Misdirection, false leads, tampered reports. Child's play for someone with my resources.'

He walked back to Lucas, squatting to be eye-level with the detective, their faces mere inches apart. 'But you, detective, you almost had it, didn't you? That nagging feeling. It's what's kept you alive this long. Admirable. But ultimately futile.'

Lucas's mind raced, even as his vision blurred with the

effort. Dr Cross was a ghost, a wraith that flitted through the shadows of their investigations, untouched and unseen. He had been right in front of them all along, hiding in plain sight.

'The women,' Lucas gasped, his throat raw, 'the patterns were too random, no connections. You made sure of it.'

'Exactly!' Dr Cross clapped mockingly. 'Randomness creates confusion and chaos. And in chaos, there is cover.' he stood up and walked back to his collection of tools, and Lucas could hear the clinking of metal, the slide of steel against steel. Dr Cross was selecting his next instrument of torture with the same deliberation one might choose a fine wine. 'It was hardly difficult, given the incompetence in your team,' he continued, his back to Lucas whilst he deliberated at the table. 'Although you did get close once or twice. If I hadn't been in the room when that DC worked out my Twitter page, you might have had me, you know.' He was playing with a particularly violent serrated blade, peering down at the top edge of it as if it were a rifle. He looked like he was reliving a fond memory.

'So I start to think, DCI Miller. The best way to keep myself out of trouble is to get someone else into trouble. Simon Davies, the arsehole who writes for the local fish wrapper, seems a suitable candidate. Or the fat constable with the mullet. He's always guarding the scenes when I arrive. Rude little shit he is, and I'd happily see him do time for this. But it's all... impersonal. I suppose that is the point. But then I saw an opportunity. You.' He turned around and pointed the drill bit he'd picked up again towards Lucas. 'The one who is going to be blamed for all this. The one who will go down in history. Your face will be plastered over every newspaper and

TV screen for months, all while I watch from the sidelines. How perfect is that?'

He walked over to Lucas, drill bit in hand, and stood over him. 'I killed that escort you visited. I began a relationship with your girlfriend. It wasn't difficult, given how absent you were and how easy she was. She stole your pen, and she planted the necklace. Of course, she didn't realise why. She thought it was a bit of an office spat between you and me. Silly tart.' He was now very close to Lucas, so close he could smell the sweet, metallic scent of his breath. Lucas's mouth was dry, but he once again mustered just enough energy to engage Dr Cross. He reasoned that the longer this went on, the more chance he'd have of being found, even if that chance were so slim it was next to non-existent.

'Why?' croaked Lucas.

Dr Cross beamed at him. 'Now that is a much more interesting question...'

74

DC Green returned to see Professor Hawthorne whilst Kim and Chloe travelled across the city to the Leeds General Infirmary, where Dr Cross and his team had their offices and the mortuary itself was housed. They didn't say a word to each other as they drove, a palpable frostiness floating between them, which was yet to defrost, despite Chloe's admittance that she didn't think Lucas was a murderer.

Once they arrived, they headed to the offices at the far end of the basement corridor, which was deadly silent as the main mortuary was closed. In fairness, it was the early hours of the morning, and they'd had to sweet-talk the security guard into letting them in. They walked past the enormous steel doors which took you into the fridges, and a sense of dread washed over Kim as she considered how many dead bodies were lying there, ready for autopsy. They rounded a corner into a slightly longer corridor with a small wooden door at the far end. It was a plain pinewood thing, cheap and with an equally naff handle. There was a small rectangular frosted window around head height to let light in and a small plaque reading 'DR D. CROSS' in gold lettering beneath it. They padded down the corridor, their footsteps muffled on the standard NHS grey carpet that peeled away from the skirting in places.

Kim was uneasy. This corridor seemed darker, like it was closing in, and a million eyes were watching her, ready to leap out and pounce. The frosted windows of other offices skirted in the peripheries of her vision, casting shadows which danced like faces. As the lights flickered, she wasn't sure that she and Chloe were alone. They were creeping towards the door ahead, both too apprehensive to increase the speed.

Nobody was here to stop them or tell them off, but she felt uncomfortable breaking the rules, regardless. She always had, even as a child, and had often been teased for being a goody-two-shoes. The cancer hadn't helped either, as it had knocked her confidence a bit. All those things that she used to say 'happened to someone else,' well, that had happened to her. If that could happen to her, so could anything else, including being caught breaking and entering.

They were within three feet of the door now, and Kim was almost certain they were alone and unobserved in the corridor. The door that led to Dr Cross's office was right beside the dissecting rooms, and there was now no more corridor left before they needed to turn around. Kim couldn't help but wonder if something might come out of that mortuary. She glanced through the tiny glass panel and saw nothing but darkness inside. It was impossible to make anything out, and she decided not to look through the glass further. They had stopped now, and there was a more uncomfortable silence that neither of them wanted to break.

Eventually, Chloe grabbed the door handle to the office and gently pressed down. The handle gave slightly, and as the lock disengaged, Kim turned her head towards the door of the mortuary to watch it, begging it wouldn't open and release the dead. But there was nothing, not a single movement from inside the fridges and no movement from within the office. The door swung open, and they both turned to peer into the darkness. Chloe patted the left side of the door frame a few times until her fingers discovered the cheap plastic light switch. She clicked it, and the room was suddenly illuminated brightly, burning their eyes briefly. A strange smell came from within, mildly sweet, but it wasn't easy to place. There is also something old and musty, but with a very chemical element to it.

The room was quite big for an office, with a long leather-topped mahogany desk diagonally against the far corner of the room. The light on the desk was one of those dated green and gold table lamps, and there was an ornate framed painting of some fruits on the closest wall. There was a bookcase along one wall, housing a collection of textbooks that Dr Cross had written on subjects such as *'Cult Murders'* and the *'Importance of the Eyeball in Death Investigation'*.

'He's a pretentious prick, isn't he?' said Chloe, breaking the silence abruptly, causing Kim to let out a faint but audible gasp.

'Yeah, a right dick.'

They split up to search as quickly as they could. The filing cabinet had all manner of things in it, from stationary to books, to paperwork and even some expensive-looking chocolates, which had a use-by date of November 2007. Kim was going through them systematically, making separate piles of things she'd found that seemed helpful. There wasn't anything specific in here. She felt a slight rush of excitement when she saw an ornate silver fountain pen, which she thought might be similar to the one inside Amelia, but on closer inspection, it was quite different, and she decided not to bother pocketing it.

The desk had been left open, and the computer was on standby. Kim wasn't sure what to do with the computer. There was no doubt if she switched it on, Dr Cross might know that someone had been snooping, but if she didn't, they might miss something valuable. She had to risk it, with Lucas missing and Dr Cross their most likely suspect. It would be OK if they left the office exactly as it was, Kim reasoned, and it was still around four in the morning, so it was unlikely they'd be interrupted. The computer clicked into life with a hum of the internal cooling fans. The login screen appeared with a little picture of Dr Cross wearing a pale blue shirt and looking right back at them, an icy stare that felt quite unsettling, but Kim wasn't about to let it phase her. She picked up the keyboard and started thinking.

'How the hell are we supposed to hack this? Any idea what his password might be?' whispered Kim, still acutely aware that they shouldn't be there and feeling the need to keep as quiet as possible.

'No idea, we'll have to leave it to the forensic techs later,' replied Chloe, not bothering to whisper.

'Wait? I thought the whole point of breaking in here was to find something?'

'Of course it is, but only what we can. I'm not a computer hacker, and neither are you. So stop wasting time and look in the drawers; we need something physical. Hard evidence.' Chloe moved away from the computer to rifle through the bookcase.

Kim shot her a filthy look, which, thankfully, Chloe did not see, and then turned to the first drawer in the desk, which was full of letters and various papers. She started flipping through them. Most of it seemed to be work-related. Indeed, nothing directly linked to any of the crimes. Finding a signed confession would be really helpful right now.

'Oh, nice,' said Chloe from across the room. She was holding up a red, lacy bra.

'Do you think it's his?' said Kim sarcastically as Chloe inspected it. She was checking the label on the back whilst trying not to handle it too much.

'32D, Boux Avenue, expensive. This is a young woman's bra. Oh, here we go, initials,' said Chloe,

'Initials? How young do you think the woman is if she's still writing her name in it?'

'E W. Emily West,' replied Chloe, looking across at Kim. 'Looks like that woman gets about a bit; we should extend the search and look more actively for her. She's definitely involved somehow.'

'Yeah, I think you're right. I've not found anything here, you?'

'Nothing. We need to get out of here before it gets light.'

They put everything back exactly as they had found it and headed for the door, but just as Kim was closing the last drawer, she heard a rattle. There was nothing in that draw that might cause a rattle. Confused, she re-opened it and listened closely, and sure enough, it rattled again. Inside was a collection of papers, files, and some envelopes. She opened and closed it a few more times to locate the rattle coming from the very back of the drawer.

'Would you hurry up? We've got to go!' said Chloe.

'Hang on, I think I've found something.' She tried removing the draw, but it wouldn't budge, as it was fixed. Shoving her hand into the back of the drawer, Kim felt the back panel, which was loose as she touched it. She put some force into it, and it came away, her hand feeling the icy sting of metal behind it.

She brought her hand back out and held it into the light to see what she'd found—a set of keys on a small hoop and a silver ring with a little bumblebee on it.

'Right, come on,' repeated Chloe from the doorway, a little more exasperated now.

'I've found a ring and some keys. They might be important,'

Chloe moved back into the room and looked at the discovery in Kim's hand. Her eyes widened, and she picked up the ring, turning it over in her hand. She pulled it close to her face and tried to read the inscription that surrounded the inside surface.

Hannah, with Love Ma & Pa

'That's Hannah George's ring. She was killed whilst I was off sick, but I remember it from the case files,' said Kim, her voice quickening with excitement. 'This is it. This is the link. Cross is our man! We need to get Carmichael down here to see this!'

'Fuck... No, we need to put it back.'

'What?'

'We know he's our man. We can chase him now in confidence. But we can't use this as evidence because of how we've found it. Put it back, and once we've found him, we can get a warrant and re-find it. Properly.'

Kim was stunned. She looked at the ring and keys in her hand, then at Chloe. Oh bugger! Chloe was right, but she didn't want her to be. She wanted to shout at her for ruining their chance at catching Dr Cross and saving Lucas, but she knew she couldn't. She was right. 'What about the keys?' she said dejectedly.

'Same thing. But take some pictures; we might recognise the lock they fit if we find Cross.'

Kim did as she was told, and the pair hurried back up the corridor, past the bodies in the fridge, back to the car park and towards the station. They weren't taking this to Carmichael, though; she would lose her shit if she found out what they'd done.

They walked past the double doors to the incident room and entered the smaller office occupied by Professor Hawthorne, who was pacing the room as usual, and DC Green, perched on the edge of the desk, making phone calls.

'Anything?' he said, putting the phone to his chest.

'The smoking gun.'

75

The acrid stench of mouldy blood, sweat, and formaldehyde stung the inside of Lucas's nose. His twisted fingers were throbbing intently, and he could see that the tip of one of them was much paler than the rest. His mouth was extraordinarily raw and dry, but it paled insignificance compared to the pain in his left knee. He looked down at his trousers, which were caked in blood, to see a small, bloody hole under his kneecap where the pain was emanating from. The terrifying mechanical screech of an electric drill sliced through the gloom, causing Lucas's head to twitch violently as he looked up instinctively. Dr Cross was changing drill bits to a larger, more aggressive-looking piece.

'I find if you don't make a pilot hole, it's difficult to ensure you get right into the joint capsule,' he drawled in his thick, tar-like voice. As the new piece clicked, he turned and walked calmly back over to where Lucas was tied to his chair. A small stool was placed in front, which Dr Cross sat on. He put the drill tip into the hole in Lucas's knee and paused.

'Please' gasped Lucas. Dr Cross met his eye, but shook his head. He lifted the gag from around Lucas's neck and forced it back into his mouth, ensuring it was tight.

'No, Lucas, you will suffer.' He pressed the trigger and slammed the drill violently through the hole and deep into Lucas's knee. Pain seared through him as the tendons around his knee were ripped, shredded, and torn apart. He screamed, oh he screamed, but the sound barely penetrated the gag, and he knew nobody could hear him. The pitch of the screeching changed as the drill broke through the soft tissues and into a bony or cartilaginous structure. The spinning drill was incomprehensibly hot as it seared through him. After a few seconds, that felt like hours, Dr Cross stopped and withdrew the drill. A pale fluid with streaks of blood and pink marrow oozed from the hole. Dr Cross tapped him on the other knee and stood up again, walking to the doorway where some industrial-looking chemicals sat, which he began mixing with sinister malice.

'You probably think I was abused as a child. Or maybe I was born this way? Or, you might like this one, or maybe I am just plain evil? I'm sure you've heard all of those before. Well, I assure you they are not the case. I am the way I am because I choose to be. I have never been interested in the petty, superficial emotions and weaknesses of others. I never needed to hurt anyone or anything, but I don't feel the desire to save anything, either. I'm not some psychopathic monster who feels nothing but the need to kill. I usually feel the same as you, but I choose to act on my deepest curiosities, elevating me to something... beyond. ' He turned around, shaking a little bottle of some colourless liquid. He stepped over a pool of blood on the floor, positioning himself right next to Lucas and leaning in so his face was only a few inches away. 'I have thought long and hard about why I do what I do and the answer isn't simple, nor would it be satisfying. No matter what I say, it will not live up to your expectations. You could never understand. Nothing else compares once you have tasted the power over life and death. It's intoxicating, detective. Have you ever lost yourself in the moment? I mean, truly lost yourself? I enter a state of such euphoria that you couldn't comprehend it unless you, too, have experienced the wonder. My flesh becomes electric, sensitive to even the lightest breath of air. I can smell pheromones, taste colours and hear blood pumping through someone else's arteries. I am completely compelled. Nothing will hold me back. Holding so much control over a life that does not belong to you is truly liberating. Do you grant them more time or take it from them?'

Lucas couldn't do anything except listen. He'd never seen Dr Cross so animated and enthusiastic about anything in this way. The tip of Lucas's tongue scraped against the rough plastic gag in his mouth, the pain in his hand throbbed unrelentingly, and the deep, gnawing ache of his knee felt so truly excruciating that he thought his soul might have been wrenched out.

'What is interesting, though, is that it could have been you. Little baby Lucas, son of a murdered mother, right? Well, I told you already that we weren't that different. My mother was also killed back in the early winter of 1972. Long before yours was. My mother was dragged from the street after having her head caved in with a rock. Her body was sliced open. I was only four at the time and had to leave my home in Leeds to go live with my father in Wales. Do you think that's why I do it? Do you think I dream of my mother when I cut these women?'

He leant back out of Lucas's face, his expression still blank and calm. It was like he was making a cup of tea, utterly unfazed by the situation. Lucas's mouth had dried up even more. The way Dr Cross talked about his life and the things he'd done, there was a separation, a disconnect, which set everything on a weird kilter.

'Oh, how silly of me; I'm asking you all these questions, and you can't answer them,' said Dr Cross, feigning concern. He reached around the back of Lucas's head and released the gag. Lucas spluttered and dragged all his strength and focus together to try speaking. He might have been gargling razor blades.

'Please. Stop. Why me? I'm not a pr..pr..'

'Prostitute? Problem? Spit it out, detective.' But Lucas couldn't get any more out. 'I don't care if you're a whore, a woman, a man, black, white, or anything else. You're following the trail of breadcrumbs I laid for you to catch the 'Water's Edge Killer'. But if you think these are the only people I've killed... oh no... oh dear, oh dear. I have complete control, and I have done so much more than you think. Other people enjoy a two-week skiing holiday, not me; I'll pop up to Scotland and strangle a couple of ramblers.' he cracked his face into a large, foreboding grin. 'As for being a problem. You are a problem. I made my first mistake with Amelia; it pains me to admit it. But I thought I might worm my way out of it by pinning it on someone else, possibly that journalist or you. She told me you were her friend, and as I've already told you, it wasn't difficult to convince the little tart Emily to cheat on you. Serial killers are notoriously charming. Having your girlfriend turn up dead in your apartment, absolutely caked in your DNA, won't look very good for you, will it? Do you want to watch me take her... what am I on now? Ah, yes.'

He picked up a little brown piece of paper from the table and read it aloud.

> *'Her tongue, a serpent in its cave, tasting sweetness that we crave,*
> *Yet in its folds, a poison lies, speaking truths and speaking lies.'*

'What… Wh… Why poem?' stammered Lucas meekly.

'Ah, now Lucas. That is private. You'll have to work that out for yourself.' Dr Cross replaced the paper and stood up, placing the bottle of chemicals on the table, his gaze fixating on Lucas with a twisted admiration. 'You've been a worthy adversary. Most give up, or they don't come close, but you, you kept coming. It's a shame, really, that it has to end this way. But every story needs its climax. Your body will never be found. I could just kill you and be done with it, but in all honesty, I've actually never liked you. Torturing you for a few hours is a guilty pleasure. I've even taken the day off work for it,' he concluded.

Whatever he was mixing was finished, and Lucas could hear it fizzing slightly. The mixture was becoming lighter; bubbles growing more prominent as they burst and seethed. The smell was foul and burnt the back of his nose. Dr Cross forcefully replaced the gag, bashing against his teeth, returned to the chair, and kneeled in front of Lucas. He pushed his fingers into the wound he had already created in Lucas's knee and then forced in a dirty grey funnel, which hurt as much as Lucas thought it might. He tried to pull away, but it was futile. Dr Cross poured the foul liquid into the wound, and Lucas felt the pain in his knee increase a hundredfold. Lucas began convulsing as the pain tore through his body. His body was shaking and twitching violently, and his eyes rolled into the back of his head. The pain was so intense he vomited pure bile, which sent yet more pain slicing across his neck. It collected in his throat, building up in his nose, blocked in by the gag. He was choking, he couldn't breathe!

Dr Cross stood up and watched him for a few moments before unhooking the gag so vomit could pour from his mouth. He gasped and spluttered as he watched the pathologist turn around and head back to the bench with the shiny instruments and the bottles of acid, ready to find something particularly nasty.

76

'Here, look!' DC Green pointed to a spreadsheet on his laptop on which were columns of bank accounts, transactions and a bunch of other things, which neither Kim nor Chloe fully understood. Both DC Green and Professor Hawthorne appeared to understand, though, as they were as enthralled in the spreadsheet as they had with discovering the ring.

'What am I supposed to be looking at?' said Chloe, squinting at the screen.

'These accounts are associated with a few of Daniel Cross's debit cards, including his current account. The ones we could get emergency access to, anyway. Your lot have been very helpful, DI Wilson. That DC Adams is lovely, by the way,' said DC Green, turning to look at her over his shoulder.

'She has a boyfriend who is significantly bigger than you. So what have you found in these accounts, come on?'

'Ah, right. Er... OK, so if you look here,' continued DC Green, looking ever so slightly crestfallen. 'Every six months, he transfers a fairly significant amount of money, nearly four grand, to a leasehold business, McCormick & Sons. They're based in Glasgow, but have properties all over the country. I think he's renting somewhere, but he's made some effort to keep it off the books. DC Adams is contacting the company to locate it, but obviously, it's only seven in the morning. She'll ring me when she's got something.'

'Good work. Any news on Emily West?'

'Yes,' came a withered reply from Professor Hawthorne, who sat next to DC Green, fiddling with his phone. 'I think, based on what we've seen so far, that it's likely she was having a relationship with Dr Cross, and he was probably manipulating her to get to DCI Miller. It is unlikely that she is still alive,' he concluded bluntly.

Kim groaned, but Chloe just muttered, 'I thought as much. We should track her last known movements and see if anything triangulates with Lucas and Cross.'

'Way ahead of you, boss,' piped up DC Green. 'ANPR on her car from the last two weeks. She makes regular trips from the morgue to Dr Cross's house, which we still need access to. The officer outside reports no movement or sign of either Cross, Lucas or Emily West. The last time her car flagged up was two nights ago, heading miles out of the city towards Ilkley, but it appears to have been a one-way journey. Her phone has a Find My Phone feature, which is now turned off, but we're in contact with the network to find the last location it was broadcast from. No activity on debit cards since she bought a coffee three days ago, but that was from the canteen at the LGI. We spoke to her mum and dad, who are obviously now petrified. They'd not heard from her for a week, but that wasn't uncommon apparently, so they hadn't been concerned.'

'Yeah, this doesn't sound good,' said Chloe, biting her lower lip. 'We need to see inside Cross's house. DS Sterling and I will speak to Carmichael; you two keep going with finding this property and Miss West's phone. I also want you to deep-dive into Dr Daniel Cross. Speak to people from his medical school? Ex-girlfriends, etc? See if my charming DC Adams will help you. Call me as soon as you have anything.'

'Right, boss,' nodded DC Green.

Chloe and Kim left the room and turned back down the corridor to the incident room. It was a hive of activity, but if you stood and took it in, there was no structure. People were flying about, getting in each other's way, and Kim was almost certain there would be people duplicating work. DI Khan stood with his hands on the back of his head, staring at the board to which he'd pinned a big picture of Lucas. It looked like a rudderless ship.

Superintendent Carmichael was in her office, just around the corner. She looked absolutely shattered when they entered, with big saggy bags under her eyes, her face drawn in and gaunt, and her hair looked greasy and less bouncy than usual.

'This better be good, DI Wilson; I am not in the mood for bullshit right now.'

'Superintendent,' Chloe began before sitting opposite Carmichael, while Kim stood by the door. She was going to have to be sparing with the truth. Not something she did often. 'I'm not sure if you know, but we have a team from the forensic accountancy unit working on Daniel Cross's finances. They've been going through his bank records and credit cards, trying to get a trace of where he is. They have traced a lot of cash transfers to a leasehold business in Glasgow. We think he's leasing a property somewhere he's not disclosed.'

'Right. Where?' said Carmichael, somewhat nonplussed.

'We don't know yet, but – '

'What did I say about bullshit, DI Wilson? A doctor has a second property? Whoopty-fucking-do!'

'I haven't finished yet. We've also confirmed that he was having an affair with Emily West and that she has been missing for at least forty-eight hours now, possibly longer. We believe that both her and Lucas are in danger, and finding Daniel Cross is imperative.'

'I do not understand why you are so hung up on Dan. OK, so it's a bit of a coincidence that he's conducted the autopsies in Wales as well, but you're leaping to conclusions. I've always found him to be a very competent pathologist.'

'Why are you so keen to defend him, boss, and so happy to believe that this could be Lucas?'

'Because there is some physical fucking evidence against DCI Miller, that's why, and nothing tangible against Dan!' Her voice was getting louder and louder, and she was swelling like a bullfrog. The door clicked open, and DI Khan walked in, looking equally tired but still maintaining his base level of punchable smugness.

'Boss, still no luck on Miller. He's found somewhere good to hide. I've put out an alert for road checks in and out of the city. Hopefully, it's not too late,' he said, ignoring the two other people in the room.

'You're a fucking numpty Sadiq,' said Kim from the doorway.

'DS Sterling, should you be in here, or should you be skulking about with a tinfoil hat like the rest of the conspiracy theorists?'

But as she was formulating a reply, Superintendent Carmichael spoke. 'Have we checked his dad's place?'

'Yes, he's not – ' began DI Khan,

'He won't be there; he's not taken any time off for four years,' interjected Kim. She hated not being believed. 'He doesn't even take his annual leave. He barely talks about his father, and I don't think they got on at all. I don't believe he'd go to him, not when he's already feeling this shit.'

'Okay, so where is he then?'

'He's bloody well missing. Like we said!'

'OK, OK, calm down the fucking pair of you,' boomed Carmichael, rediscovering her authority for a moment. She rounded on Chloe. 'Give me some proper evidence to back up this theory on Dan now, or I will have you removed from the station for hindering an active investigation!'

There was a pause; the room was silent. Nobody spoke. Everyone was staring at Chloe, and her whole body had tensed. This was it, decision time. Do it right by the book, or risk it all and save Lucas. She didn't make the decision. She didn't have to. Kim made it for her.

'We found Hannah George's ring in his office.' Everyone swivelled and glared at DS Sterling.

'Pardon?' said Carmichael, trying to act calm, but her fist was clenched so tightly her knuckles had gone white.

'We found Hannah George's ring in his office. The eleventh victim.'

'What are you talking about?' said DI Khan, suddenly looking much less smug.

'We found Hannah George's ring in his office,' repeated DS Sterling for a third time, turning to look at DI Khan. 'It was in a hidden compartment in his desk drawer.'

'Why were you in his office?' said Carmichael, her tone icy.

'We broke in; we needed to move the investigation forward,' said Chloe, nodding at Kim.

'How do you know it was hers? You've compromised the investigation,' said DI Khan, still somewhat aghast.

'Small ring, Bumblebee on top, and it was engraved with her name,' said Kim matter-of-factly.

'I am telling you, Daniel Cross is involved. It's him!' said Chloe, her voice rising. 'DS Sterling, DC Green and that professor, they're all right. Please, believe us.'

Carmichael was quiet. Her face was scrunched up and contorted, like a bulldog licking piss off a nettle. A few beats passed, and nobody said anything. 'Show me.' Kim opened her phone and showed her the pictures of the ring and keys from the office. Carmichael didn't speak, but her hands were starting to quiver slightly. 'Dan,' she whispered, the colour draining from her face. She looked even more frail than when they'd entered her office a little over five minutes ago.

'We're waiting for confirmation of the location of this leased property and the last transmitted location of either Lucas's phone, Dr Cross or Emily West. There has been nothing back so far. We will also need to search his house. Can you get us a warrant? said Chloe. Once again, silence. Even DI Khan looked concerned.

'Alright,' said Carmichael eventually, as she sat down with her head in her hands and began to cry.

77

West Yorkshire Police in Pursuit: The Manhunt for Renegade Detective DCI Lucas Miller

By Simon Davies, Senior Crime Correspondent

In a shocking development that has gripped the nation, Detective Chief Inspector (DCI) Lucas Miller, a prominent figure in the West Yorkshire police force, has been declared the prime suspect in the notorious 'Water's Edge Reaper' serial killer case. Miller, who was the lead investigator on the case, is now at the centre of a nationwide manhunt after recent evidence linked him directly to the gruesome crimes that have haunted the region for over a decade.

DCI Lucas Miller, a respected detective with years of experience handling high-profile criminal investigations, had tirelessly worked on the case, vowing to bring the perpetrator to justice. However, the tables turned dramatically when recent forensic evidence unexpectedly linked Miller himself to the crimes. The specifics of the evidence have not been disclosed to the public. Still, officials have confirmed its damning nature, leading to an immediate suspension of Miller from the police force and a warrant for his arrest.

As the news broke, the community and Miller's colleagues were in disbelief. A detective who had been a beacon of hope in the relentless pursuit of a serial killer is now the focus of a criminal investigation that reads like the plot of a crime thriller. The police force has vowed to conduct a thorough and unbiased investigation. Chief Superintendent Patricia Carmichael states, 'We are committed to upholding the law and ensuring that justice is served, regardless of where the investigation leads.'

Authorities have called on the public to report any sightings of Miller but have warned that he should be considered highly dangerous and not approached under any circumstances. As the manhunt continues, the nation's focus remains fixed on the unfolding drama, waiting for answers in a case that has taken a most unexpected and dark turn. The revelations have not only shattered the trust between the public and the police, but have also left a dark cloud over the many victims' families still seeking closure.

The West Yorkshire police, now under intense scrutiny, have pledged to leave no stone unturned in their quest to uncover the truth. As this story develops, one thing is clear: the path to justice in the 'Water's Edge Reaper' case has taken a twist that no one could have predicted.

* * *

Lucas had lost all concepts of time and place. He was aware of his body and the pain it was enduring, but he felt as though he was removed from it. A passenger in his own body. He had no idea how long he'd been there or when his captor would come back. Was it ten minutes? An hour? A day? The thought of another encounter with Dr Cross sent a freezing bolt rippling down his neck. He'd remained conscious through most of the ordeal so far, but he wasn't sure how much longer he could hold on. The pain in Lucas's knee was getting worse. He'd stopped shaking now and regained some control of his body, but he still couldn't move his arms. The smell of the mixture that Dr Cross had poured into his knee was making him want to be sick again.

A sudden noise came from behind him. Someone was coming back! Lucas tried to open his eyes and turn his head, but found it was impossible. He managed to tilt his head slightly and caught sight of a figure. Lucas strained his eyes to see who it was, but the lights were too bright, and the person was visible only in silhouette. A wave of panic washed over Lucas as the figure walked towards him.

'Hello Lucas' came a voice he hadn't heard in years because she was dead.

'Mum?'

'No detective, not quite' The figure swam into focus, and he was once again met with the sight of Dr Cross in white overalls, drenched in blood. He held a chunk of purple flesh in his hand, slightly tapered at one end. Oh christ. It was Em's tongue!

'Where is my mother?' Lucas said. His mouth was so dry and sore, and every syllable felt like a razor blade sliding between his teeth.

'You're losing it, detective.' Dr Cross suddenly slapped Lucas hard across the face with the tongue to sharpen him up. Wet blood splattered everywhere and stung his cheek. 'She's been dead for years'

'What?' Lucas's brain was creaking. He couldn't work out what he meant.

'OK, let's try this another way then.' He reached past a couple of very sharp blades on his table in order to pick up a metal cube with serrated edges. It looked an awful lot like a cheese grater. 'I've never used this before, but my gut instinct tells me, this is really going to hurt.'

He swiftly reached across, replaced Lucas's mouth gag, and bent down, grabbing him by the ankle. Lucas started shaking as he wriggled in a futile attempt to avoid the inevitable. Dr Cross steadied himself and ran the grater down the front of Lucas's shin. The pain was immediate and agonising. It ripped through him as the skin and flesh were shredded again and again. Lucas heard the metal of the grater hit his bone, but Dr Cross didn't stop. He continued to push the grater deeply into his leg and grate quickly but methodically as the raw electric pain of his bone splintering shot through him. Lucas tried to numb it; he tried to escape into the same place as he had when he thought he saw his dead mother, but the pain was too great. It wouldn't allow him to leave his body. He could feel his entire body, not just his leg. It was excruciating. His brain screamed at him to stop struggling, but the adrenaline kicked in again, and he thrashed around in his bindings.

Dr Cross stood back and admired his work. The tissue from Lucas's shin had been scraped away, leaving exposed bone, which had been further grated so that marrow was oozing out.

'Time to do the back...'

78

Chloe clenched her hands on the steering wheel as she peered through the windshield, the rhythmic drizzle painting a blurred canvas of the road ahead. The early morning winter haze across Leeds covered the rush hour traffic and a throng of pedestrians trying to get to work. She was at the helm of the marked police car, lights flashing and siren blaring. She had DS Sterling in the seat next to her and DC Green in the back. Professor Hawthorne felt that fieldwork was unnecessarily dangerous and remained at the station to continue chasing the leasehold company and network providers instead. They were second in the convoy, behind the armed response unit, followed by an unmarked car containing Superintendent Carmichael, DI Khan and a few solid-looking constables.

She checked the clock on the control unit: 08:12. Each passing minute ramped up the tension. What they would find? The police unit stationed outside Dr Cross's house had reported no activity for twenty-four hours, and Kim thought the concept of everyone piling in like this was a waste of time. She'd said as much to Chloe, who agreed.

'We should send a standard unit round the house to search

the place. The rest of us need to be finding this other property.'

'I agree, Sterling, but orders are orders. Carmichael wants us to do it this way. She had a case a few years ago, a similar style raid, and the guy was hauled up in the house with enough supplies and ammunition to take on the Taliban. I think she's worried about a repeat.'

'Fine,' snapped Kim. She didn't mean to be curt, but her concern for Lucas grew by the second. In truth, she was warming to DI Wilson, not that she was prepared to admit that just yet.

'I don't think this is the right way to do this either, but we are at least making progress. Three hours ago, Carmichael wouldn't have entertained the idea of searching for Cross. Plus, DC Adams and my team are on this; there's nothing you'd be doing at the station other than twiddling your thumbs and making cups of tea for Professor Hawthorne.'

Kim couldn't argue with that, so she sat back and closed her eyes. Without warning, there was a buzzing from the back seat. DC Green jumped, bumping his head on the car's roof as he scrambled to pull his phone from his pocket and answer it as fast as possible.

'DC Green. Hi, yeah, you?' Kim rotated in her seat to look at him, but Chloe had to make do with the rearview mirror. His cheeks had flushed with colour, and Kim surmised it must have been DC Adams on the phone.

'Right, right, OK. Brilliant! Can you text me the details?' continued DC Green's one-sided conversation. Kim made a hand gesture suggesting he put it on speaker, but DC Green ignored her and kept listening. 'And what about the phone coordinates? Holy fuck, you're joking? OK, OK, you're a star, thank you. Speak soon.' he hung up and stared at the two women in the car.

'Well fucking go on then?' said Kim, startling DC Green slightly.

'We've got an address, 21b Park View Lane. It's a small basement flat he's been renting for about fifteen years in Headingley.'

Chloe immediately reached for the radio attached to the dashboard, which she clicked and barked into. 'Superintendent, this is DI Wilson over.' A crackle of static was on the line before a voice blasted out of the speaker.

'What do you want? Oh, Over.' Even over the radio, it was obvious Carmichael was still upset.

'We've got an address for the second property owned by Cross, and I think it's a more likely area of concern than his house. 21b Park View Lane, it's about twenty minutes from here. We should divert the team to the new property. Over.' Again, there was a pause. There was some crackling static once more as they waited for a response.

'I am in charge of this investigation, DI Wilson. We are heading to the house as planned. Once the house is clear, we will move on to this new property. Over.'

Chloe slammed her hand down on the wheel in frustration. 'Fuck! This is stupid!' Kim put her head in her hands and groaned loudly. DC Green, however, leant forward so his head was level with his two senior officers.

'DC Adams has also just texted me the last known transmission from Emily West's phone. It's less than a hundred meters from Park View.'

DC Green had barely reached the end of his sentence when Chloe slammed on the brakes and turned the car around, doing a three-point turn in the middle of the busy A-road. Kim had to hold on to the handle above the door to avoid being flung about the car.

'You're fucking mad, you know that!' she shouted as Chloe sped through the traffic and did another exciting manoeuvrer to drive down the oncoming side of the road, narrowly missing a cyclist who was swearing and shouting at them as they passed. Chloe didn't say anything; she was concentrating. She turned the wheel sharply and took a sudden left, leaving the main road and entering a leafy residential street. The houses were all terraced here, with neat front gardens and bay windows.

The radio clicked, and the static returned, followed by Carmichael's voice, which sounded livid. 'Where the holy fuck are you lot going? I gave you a specific order, and we are going to the house!'

Chloe looked at the handset like she was considering just lobbing it out of the window. Instead, she picked it up and spoke as calmly as possible, given she was racing down a residential road. 'Negative boss, we have new information that Emily West's last known location was the same property on Park View Avenue. There is a significant risk to life; I am duty-bound to investigate this as a matter of urgency. I request that your armed response unit follow us, but if not, we will proceed unassisted.' She didn't wait for a response from Carmichael. Instead, she switched off the unit and threw the handset back into the hands of Kim, who fumbled for a moment before eventually placing it in the slot on the centre console.

'We're going to be there in less than ten minutes, so if they're coming, they'd better get a bloody wriggle on,' said

78

Chloe.

DS Kim Sterling nodded. 'For what it's worth, I think you did the right thing.'

'Thank you, Sterling; you can kiss my arse later, though. This might not end well for anyone.'

79

The acrid, rotten smell that usually hung in the room where Lucas was being held had gone. It had been replaced by the pleasant, warming smell of cooking meat. It wasn't the bland chicken smell, more of a porky scent. The little fluid left in Lucas's body made its way to his mouth via the salivary glands. His stomach rumbled, which was odd; given the circumstances, he thought it would have given up on food.

Dr Cross was in the corner, a small propane hob balanced on the table underneath a small frying pan. A sizzling sound accompanied the delicious scent across the room as some strips of meat cooked in the centre of the pan. The noise was amplified by the metal walls and ceiling surrounding them. Lucas struggled to see what was happening, but his head was still too heavy, and he didn't want to give his captor the satisfaction of watching him continue to writhe around like a worm on a hook. He resigned to simply listening and enjoying the smell of frying pork that continued filling his nostrils.

'Smells good, doesn't it? Personally, I have no issue eating this sort of thing, although I'm going to assume you've never tried it?' There was no reply from Lucas, who continued to let his head fall to the side. From this angle, he could see the enormous length of exposed bone and vessels that protruded from his acid-ravaged left knee. It didn't feel like his leg anymore; he'd written it off as lost. The pain had subsided to a dull ache. Lucas couldn't work out if he should be concerned about that or whether he should be grateful.

'Now Lucas, do you want me to season this for you, or would you prefer to do it yourself?' Lucas could feel his consciousness slipping away. He could hear the words, but he couldn't string them together. His eyelids were so heavy that he struggled to remain awake. 'Come on now, Lucas, stay with me.' There was a crack as Dr Cross's slapped him across the face, bringing him around slightly, as the impact sent waves of pain through Lucas's jaw and remaining teeth.

'That's better. I don't want to miss out on our quality time together now, do I?'

'Fuck off,' mumbled Lucas. He could barely get his mouth open to speak. His tongue felt like a dead weight, and his lips were stuck together with dried blood.

'That's not a very nice thing to say to someone, DCI Miller. I've just slaved over the stove cooking this for you; a little gratitude would be appreciated. Now, let's see what you make of this.'

He placed a moderate strip of meat on the end of a fork and dangled it in front of Lucas. It smelt great, and his stomach gave another rumble. He wasn't an idiot; he knew what it was, but equally, it still smelt so appealing. It had been so long since he'd eaten or drunk anything. He was dying. What was the harm? It smelt so good. He opened his mouth, and Dr Cross placed the strip of meat on his tongue. It was a perfect fit, and its heat sent a surge of energy through his body. He chewed, and the juices ran down his chin and the meat down his throat. It tasted amazing! It was tender and soft; the flavours were incredible. He swallowed and waited for some more. Dr Cross laughed and then took another strip, dangling it from the fork and teasing it close to Lucas's mouth. He was drooling now and opened his mouth expectantly like a baby bird waiting to be fed by its mother.

The savoury aroma wafted through the stale air, a cruel reminder of life's simple pleasures that Lucas had been denied. Dr Cross, meanwhile, seemed to savour not just the food but the situation, his presence looming large in the cramped, metallic room.

'As I've already said, we are not so different, you and I,' said Dr Cross, his voice as oily as the meat on the pan. He flipped some strips of meat with a practised wrist. 'We both made choices that led us down paths we never expected to tread.' Lucas's mind was foggy, but he was helpless and could do nothing but focus on the doctor's words. He had always been one to listen and analyse, and his instinct was still intact. 'I was a young man full of ambition once, a keen medical student with a passion for understanding the human mind.' He paused, his gaze distant, as if visualising his past. 'But my mother was murdered, and my desires changed. They were... unconventional. I wanted to be a surgeon initially. I wanted to play god. But I knew I couldn't do it. I couldn't live with the daily temptation to harm my patients. It was clear my heart wasn't in it, so they pushed me out, and I fell into pathology. This has allowed me to continue my work secretly, pursuing the truths others were too afraid to acknowledge.'

Lucas could see it now, the flicker of madness in the

doctor's eyes, the kind that came from being shunned and driven to the edges of sanity by rejection and obsession. He'd done a brilliant job of hiding it until now.

'Unlike you, I wasn't content with upholding the status quo. You see, I wanted to peel back the layers of the psyche, to manipulate the flesh and bone to understand the soul.' He returned to the stove, flipping the meat again, its scent now mixed with a hint of char. The room was silent for a moment, save for the crackling of the propane hob. Lucas tried to process the doctor's words, to find some leverage, some understanding that could be his salvation.

Dr Cross plated the cooked meat with a flourish, then turned to Lucas with a look of expectation. 'And you, a detective, sought truth in your own way, didn't you? But your methods, your laws, they bound you. You never saw the full picture. I, on the other hand, am free from such constraints.'

Lucas felt a pang of anger; his sense of justice was offended. 'You... call this freedom?' he said, his voice raspy and broken. 'Torture? Kidnapping?'

Dr Cross chuckled, a sound devoid of warmth. 'Freedom is a matter of perspective, Lucas. You're bound by your morality, your code. But in this room, I am god. I decide what is right and what is wrong. And right now, I decide whether you eat or starve, whether you live or die. The power is liberating. I am not the only one who feels this way; you can be sure of that. I have disciples.' He held up another strip of meat, the juices glistening in the dull light. 'So, Detective, will you dine with the devil tonight?'

Lucas's hunger was a physical pain like the one in his leg and arms, but his resolve was more robust. He turned his head away, refusing the offering, refusing to give in to the twisted game.

Dr Cross's expression hardened. 'Very well,' he said, the mock sadness gone from his voice. 'But remember, I am merely a product of the society that cast me out. You, the upholder of its laws, you created me.' Dr Cross paused and allowed the silence to build.

But then they heard it. Both of them. The crunch of gravel outside. Dr Cross placed the plate on the table and went to a window hidden behind a blackout curtain, peeking around the edge.

'Oh, bugger.' Lucas could just about hear the sound of voices outside on the drive. Female voices he recognised. Surely not? Was he hallucinating again? Dr Cross moved away from the window, placed the gag back into Lucas's mouth, and turned the lights out. Lucas was plunged into darkness again, and he could only wait.

So that's what he did. He waited.

80

About a mile out, they'd turned off the siren and adopted a stealthier approach. Chloe pulled the car onto the communal gravel drive. There was a small brown, old Rover 25 parked in front of number 21, which was a battered-looking Chinese takeaway.

'That could be the car from Wales, you know?' said Kim as they got out of the car. Chloe grunted to acknowledge what was said and trudged towards the takeaway. It was a small terraced property with the typical features of a 1960s house. It had a brick bottom and wooden slats covering the top half. They'd been painted white at some point, but was now peeling and filthy. The takeaway had metal-framed windows and a sign in the window saying it was closed. As they headed towards the door, DC Green noticed steps down to flat 21b.

'I'll go first.' Despite being quite a solid bloke, he knew these two women could handle themselves significantly better than he could. But he'd been raised old school and felt he should be the protector.

'Go for it,' said Chloe, 'We don't know what's down there.' He gulped and took the steps tentatively. At the bottom was a small wooden door with a metal grill across the top, more peeling paint, and a Yale lock, which looked robust enough.

'Should have brought those keys,'

'These keys?' said Kim from behind him, and she dangled the keys from the draw over his shoulder.

'I thought you put them back?' said Chloe, slightly cross, slightly pleased.

'Well, I put the ring back but... I thought the keys might come in handy.'

'Well, that's highly illegal, completely unadvisable, and absolutely genius,' said Chloe, a big grin appearing. Kim handed the keys to DC Green, who tried them in the lock. The first one didn't fit, but the second gave a satisfying click. He turned it, the lock opened, and the door swung forward.

'Do you smell bacon?' asked DC Green, sniffing the air like a dog. 'Must be the Chinese, it smells nice,'

They pulled their torches out and shone them into the blackness to illuminate a set of metal stairs descending further down into a basement. One by one, they crept down; the stairs creaking slightly as they went. A second door awaited them; this one didn't have a lock, so they pushed it open, revealing a small corridor. Someone was lying on the floor, face down. DC Green turned his torch toward them and moved over to the figure.

'Wait,' hissed Chloe, but DC Green shrugged her off and grabbed the person on the floor. Nothing, they didn't move. It was a woman with long dark hair, smooth black skin which had turned slightly grey and a slender frame. She was freezing cold and rock solid. DC Green turned her over, needing to use both hands and some effort. He glanced at her face in the torchlight, ghostly white eyes with little black spots. They were wide but completely vacant. Her throat was splayed open, and a massive gaping wound with dried blood and an exposed windpipe was staring back at him. Her mouth was open in a silent scream, and even in the half-light, DC Green could see her tongue had been torn out. There were flies circulating, but otherwise, she looked like she'd died recently.

'Emily West,' said DC Green grimly, covering his mouth with the back of his wrist. 'She's dead. We need to call it in and retreat.'

'She's not going to get any less dead, Green, and I already called it in with Carmichael. They know where we are. We're on our own until she grows up. We need to find Lucas!'

They continued further down the corridor, using the narrow beam of torchlight for guidance and entered the room at the end. The door creaked open, and there was a pause as their eyes adjusted to what the beams of light were illuminating. The full horror was revealed, and they couldn't take it all in. Kim's eyes were drawn to the gaunt face, the sunken eyes and the vomit-covered mouth. Chloe was fixed on the mangled hands, with twisted, broken and missing fingers pointing in all directions and the blood crusted to the chair that he was taped to. DC Green's attention was grabbed by the shredded bone protruding out of a swollen, moth-eaten knee. Dark red vessels dangled down to supply the pale foot, twisted round at a right angle.

'Lucas!' shouted Kim, suddenly forgetting where she was. She dashed across the room as his head shot up, eyes wild and bloodshot. From the left came a flash of steel as a huge knife came crashing down, catching her on the upper arm, splitting her skin wide open. She screamed in pain as a spurt of scarlet jetted from the wound. DC Green acted fastest; he lurched forward and tried to throw the assailant to the ground. He landed on top and came face to face with Dr Cross, whose expression remained one of only mild irritation as with considerable force he punched DC Green in the face, who saw stars and fell off.

Cross reached for the blade, but Chloe kicked it towards the wall. Her leg was an easy target for Cross, and he grabbed her ankle hard, pulling her to the floor. She yelped in pain as her shoulder collided with concrete. As she lay there in agony, she heard the clink of metal as a long, pointed tool fell off the table and hit the ground. She grabbed it to defend herself, but Cross wasn't coming for her; instead he grabbed Kim by the hair and pulled her to her feet violently. DC Green flung himself again at Cross, but he bounced off the wiry pathologist.

Chloe jumped to her feet, the pain in her ankle fading as the adrenaline coursed through her. 'Argh!' she screamed as she ran at him, the pointed tool in front like a lance. It struck him in the flank, gliding deeply upward into his chest. He gasped in pain, letting go of Kim, who let go of the tool, and he keeled over to the side with a thud. Chloe and DC Green helped Kim to her feet, and blood was trickling down her face from a deep wound that had the glimmer of bare skull underneath.

As they pulled her up, however, Cross once again rose to his feet, unwilling to die. He left the metal tool in his chest, breathing deeply against it, which must have been agony. Without thinking, Kim grabbed the frying pan next to her and threw it at Cross, who ducked, but just too late, and it caught the top of his head, cutting him but only superficially.

He ran suddenly, directly at Chloe, without fear or hesitation, and barrelled her straight into the wall. Her head cracked against the plasterboard, forming a considerable dent, and Kim was skittled backwards into the long table, scattering the remaining knives and torture tools to the floor.

Cross was on top of Chloe, throttling her with his large hands wrapped tightly around her thin neck. DC Green leaped across and threw a barrage of punches but they were feeble and did little to distract Dr Cross, who was now focused purely on strangling Chloe to death. She resisted, but meekly, the impact against the wall had dazed her. Kim fished around on the floor, and her hands closed around a box cutter or something similar. She grabbed the nearest part of Dr Cross that she could reach, which was his left ankle. Without thought, she sliced deeply through his Achilles tendon and the back of his leg. He screamed in agony, and she could see the muscle contract and ball up at the top of his calf as the tendon gave way with an audible pop. He tried to kick out but failed, and she quickly fumbled for his other ankle and repeated the trick, slashing deeply and repeatedly, almost down to the bone as blood splashed out across her face and into her mouth.

She spat the blood out and rolled away, standing up to face him. The pain in his calves meant that DC Green had finally got the better of Cross, who was forced off Chloe. DC Green helped back to her feet, blood running down the back of her head. The three of them stood, staring at Cross. He was spitting and writhing around in agony. His arm reached up and grabbed the side of Lucas's chair, knocking one of his broken fingers, making it even more angular. He tried to pick himself up but couldn't; his ankles completely gave way as the gashes at the back opened up down to the white bone beneath. He toppled forward, smashing his face into the floor.

'Quick,' panted Kim. 'Cuff him!' DC Green obliged, grabbing his wrists together and placing metal handcuffs tightly around them. Too tightly, in fact, DC Green was hoping to cut off the blood supply if possible.

As DC Green lifted him to his feet, causing him as much pain as possible, Kim spoke through large pants and hot adrenaline-fuelled breaths. 'Dr Daniel Cross, I am arresting you on suspicion of murder. You do not have to say anything, but it may harm your defence if you do not mention when questioned something which you later rely on in court. Anything you do say may be given in evidence...'

The air in the basement was thick with broken tension and the acrid scent of blood and sweat. DC Green pushed Dr Cross against the wall, and he, Chloe and Kim took a moment's pause. It hadn't sunk in. Was it over? As DC Green held Dr Cross, there was no gloating in their victory, only the raw, urgent necessity of what had to be done next.

Chloe, despite the throbbing pain at the back of her head, locked eyes with Kim, who was still pressing her hand against the gash on her arm, trying to stem the flow of blood. They shared a nod. Free Lucas.

Kim, with her operational arm, and Chloe, with her adrenaline-fueled determination, moved towards him. The sight of him made them grimace. His eyes, once bright with keen observation, were now glazed with trauma. Chloe's hand shook as she reached out to untie him, her fingers fumbling with the knots that had held him captive.

'Lucas, it's okay. We've got you,' Chloe said, her voice a

soothing and surprisingly effective tonic. Lucas had barely understood what he had just witnessed. Had they just beaten Dr Cross, or was he hallucinating? His eyes focused on Kim, struggling to free his leg, a flicker of recognition cutting through the haze of his pain.

As the bindings fell away, Chloe carefully cradled Lucas's mangled hands in her own. She winced as she saw the damage's full extent: the broken and missing. She couldn't comprehend the cruelty he had endured. Having finally got his leg free, Kim stood up and wrapped her jacket around Lucas; a makeshift bandage and a shield from the horror.

DC Green pushed Dr Cross gently and watched him fall to the ground, breaking the fall with his nose and jaw. Police brutality, with every justification. Now that Cross was secure, he joined them in extricating Lucas from the flat. He was the least injured and, therefore, took charge of supporting Lucas's weight as they prepared to move him. Lucas's leg, damaged beyond recognition, dragged lifelessly on the floor, the bone still jutting out grotesquely. DC Green grimaced, knowing that shock must be the only thing keeping Lucas conscious.

As they lifted him, Lucas let out a guttural sound, something between a groan and a sob. It was the sound of a man who had faced the unthinkable and emerged broken but not defeated. Kim kept close, her uninjured hand gently brushing Lucas's hair from his forehead. She murmured words of encouragement, her tone belying the fear that gnawed at her. Her other arm hung limp at her side, the blood had soaked through the fabric of her sleeve.

They returned through the corridor, stepping over the body of Em, who lay stiffly on the floor like a fallen mannequin, the horror across her face, but Lucas felt numb to it. He was still hallucinating, wasn't he? Each step was cautious, the fear of Cross regaining consciousness shadowing their every move. But of course, he remained out, a heap of malice handcuffed and dragged along the cold concrete floor.

As they ascended the stairs, the fresh air of the outside world felt like a different universe. The transition from the hellish basement to the quiet night was jarring. Lucas, supported between Green and Chloe, blinked at the dull morning sky, the stars obscured by the polluted glow of the city.

Chloe took a moment to look at Lucas, really look at him. His eyes met hers, and she knew. She'd seen that look before, the lost and empty face he'd worn when she lost the baby years ago. They had saved him, but the journey ahead would be fraught with difficulty. Somehow, he was going to have to rebuild and struggle to heal both physical and mental wounds.

Kim listened intently to the faint noise she could hear in the distance. The sound of police sirens getting louder and louder. She looked past DC Green as he flung Cross into the side of the car, and Chloe, who was gently trying to lower Lucas against the car door. Down the street she could see Carmichael's car charging up towards them, followed by an armed response and an ambulance. She stood, panting, the winter morning cold blasting her face whilst greasy sweat trickled down her neck.

It was over.

81

'WATER'S EDGE REAPER' CAPTURED AFTER 12-YEAR MANHUNT: Dr Daniel Cross, Police Forensic Pathologist, Unmasked as Serial Killer

By Simon Davies, Senior Crime Correspondent

In a harrowing turn of events, a man who was once a trusted forensic pathologist for the West Yorkshire Police has been identified as the notorious serial killer dubbed the 'Water's Edge Reaper'. Dr Daniel Cross (48) has been operating undetected within the police force, terrorising the north of England and Wales for over a decade, with at least 16 women falling victim to his heinous acts since 2011. However, speculation abounds that he may be linked to more unsolved murders across the country, potentially numbering as high as 40 to 50 victims.

The breakthrough in the case came following a daring raid on a flat in Park View Avenue, Leeds, owned by Dr Cross. The well-planned operation not only led to the capture of Britain's most wanted criminal but also uncovered the body of Emily West, a mortuary assistant who had been missing for a number of days.

Additionally, the police arrived just in time to save DCI Lucas Miller from becoming another of Daniel Cross's victims. Miller, who had previously been under suspicion for the murders, is said to be suffering from life-changing injuries inflicted during his captivity. The revelation that the actual perpetrator was a member of their ranks has caused a seismic shock within the West Yorkshire Police, leading to widespread public outrage and calls for accountability at the highest levels.

Detective Superintendent Patricia Carmichael, the officer who once steadfastly defended the integrity of her force's investigation, is now facing intense scrutiny and demands for her resignation. The case's mishandling, particularly the failure to identify Dr Cross as a suspect earlier despite his close involvement in the investigations, raises serious questions about the internal practices and oversight of the West Yorkshire Police. Moreover, disturbing speculation has arisen regarding a potential personal relationship between Superintendent Carmichael and Dr Cross, fuelling concerns that this connection may have clouded her judgement or led to preferential treatment within the investigation.

Public Outcry and Expert Opinions

The capture of Dr Cross has sparked a media frenzy, with journalists and onlookers gathering outside the Leeds courthouse, seeking answers and justice. Amidst the crowd, we spoke to Alice Thompson, a local resident, who expressed her shock: 'It's like those crime shows we watch on TV, but it's real, and it's happened right here. How could they not see what was right under their noses?'

Dr Sarah Jennings, a criminologist at the University of Leeds, provided some insight into the situation: 'The fact that Dr Cross was a forensic pathologist is chilling. It gave him the knowledge and opportunity to cover his tracks expertly. This case will be studied for years as an example of cognitive biases in criminal investigations, such as 'trust bias,' where the credibility of a colleague overshadowed the evidence.'

Embarrassment for West Yorkshire Police

The revelation that the Water's Edge Reaper was, in fact, a respected member of the investigative team has led to a scandal of unprecedented proportions for the West Yorkshire Police. An internal review is underway, with external oversight to ensure transparency and regain public trust.

Detective Superintendent Carmichael has faced the press, stating, 'I understand and share the public's anger and dismay. I will fully cooperate with the ongoing inquiries and am determined to ensure that our force learns from these grave mistakes.'

The Raid and Its Aftermath

The raid that led to Dr Cross's capture was initiated after new evidence linked him to the murders of three women in South Wales, which bore a striking resemblance to those in Yorkshire. Acting on this information, the police moved quickly, uncovering a scene that one officer described as 'a chamber of absolute horror.'

In the flat, the police discovered the deceased Emily West, and the critically injured DCI Miller, who had been leading the investigation until his disappearance. The revelation that Miller had been wrongly suspected adds another layer of complexity and embarrassment to the case.

Detective Sergeant Kim Sterling, who was part of the raid, recounted the moment of discovery: 'Nothing can prepare you for such a scene. It was a mix of relief and horror. Relief that we had finally found our colleague and horror at the realisation of who had been behind these murders all along.'

The Victims and Their Families

The families of the Water's Edge Reaper's victims have expressed feelings of heartbreak over the recent developments. 'It's a bittersweet feeling,' shared Daria Sidorova, whose daughter was one of the Reaper's early victims. 'We're relieved he's been caught, but nothing will bring back our loved ones. The thought that he was there, examining the bodies of those he killed, is unbearable.'

A Community in Healing and a Way Forward

As the north of England and Wales grapples with the aftermath of Dr Cross's heinous crimes, community leaders have organised vigils and support groups for the victims' families and survivors. The focus is on healing and preventing such tragedies in the future.

The West Yorkshire Police have announced a comprehensive review of their investigative procedures, emphasising psycho-

logical screening and monitoring for all officers and forensic staff.

The Water's Edge Reaper case hasn't ended with Dr Daniel Cross's capture, and it leaves a community scarred and a police force in disarray. The road to rebuilding confidence in law enforcement will be long and arduous, with this case serving as a stark reminder of the importance of vigilance, both within and outside the ranks of those sworn to protect us. As the investigation continues and the trial looms, the nation watches, hoping for closure and justice for the victims and their families.

82

Three weeks had passed since Lucas had been rescued from the basement, although it felt like a lot longer. He was waiting for his fourth operation on his hands, and they'd so far saved all but three of his fingers. Attempted revascularisation had worked well for the pale digits, but the little finger on his right and little and ring fingers on the left had quickly failed. The doctors had put horrible squirming leaches on them to stop them from becoming congested, but within days they'd turned black and he'd had to go back to theatre to have them terminalised. The ones he had left wouldn't be great for anything too dexterous, but he could change the TV channel and pick his nose. His left leg was gone; the surgeons didn't even try to save it. The acid had wrecked the knee, all his cartilage had essentially eroded, and there wasn't enough viable tissue from his calf, so he'd had to have an above-knee amputation.

He was sitting in his wheelchair on the rehab ward, looking out of the window over the city of Leeds. The Christmas lights were being taken down from the lampposts. It was getting even colder outside, and the trees were yet to show any signs of regrowth. There were still plenty of reds and browns on the ground, framing the modern array of cars and glass-fronted buildings, which the winter sun was reflecting off, almost blinding him. He didn't mind, though; in fact, he quite liked it.

A gentle knock came at his door, which slid open slowly to reveal DS Kimberly Sterling. She wasn't wearing her uniform, just a simple jeans and thick jumper combination.

'How are you?' she asked gently. Lucas didn't turn around immediately; he carried on looking out over the city, watching the cars go by and the people walking along, utterly oblivious to everything that had happened to him.

'I'm OK, thanks. I'm just contemplating going for a run. How are you?' he said, turning and smiling at her and although she smiled back, he quickly turned to watch the world go by again. Kim took a few steps towards him and then stopped, looking at the back of his head, his messy, unkempt hair. She didn't know what to do or say next and felt awkward.

'Does it hurt?'

'They've got me drugged up to the eyeballs. So no. They're medicating me even more strongly than I'd been doing it myself. Come here. Sit with me and look out this window.' He beckoned her over and patted the bed beside him. She sat down on the bed next to him. His left arm was covered in bandages and was resting in a sling across his body, and he had several bandages on his face and head. 'What's happening in the case? I've read the papers, but I want to know what's really going on. Simon Davies is a shit writer and makes half of it up,' he said, turning to look at her again and smiling. She looked beautiful today; the jumper was a good choice and complimented her eyes.

'Well,' she started, fiddling with a little ball of fluff on her sleeve, 'there's plenty of evidence in that basement. We are going through it all now, but there are going to be more victims. There were drawers of jewellery that didn't belong to any of our girls, and his DNA has already been linked to a couple of unsolved murders in Cornwall and one in Sheffield. It was also on a bag of saline fluid retrieved from the hospital, which had been injected with some drug I can't pronounce, so we know he tampered with it and killed Amelia. Not that he's admitting anything, he's 'no commenting' everything.'

'Any people been strangled in the Scottish highlands?'

'Nothing has come back on that yet, but we'll keep sifting. They're saying he might be one of Britain's worst serial killers, behind Harold Shipman.' She fiddled with the observation chart at the end of his bed.

'Best serial killer. I've never understood why they call them the worst serial killers when they kill loads of people. He was good at it, in all fairness.'

She giggled a bit and then smiled. 'Yeah, I've never thought of it like that'. They both continued to look out of the window for a few moments.

'Have you spoken to Chloe?'

'Yeah, she's popped in a few times. She might come today, actually. I heard you two made quite the team in the end,'

'Well, after I convinced her you weren't a serial killer,' she laughed. 'Are you two... you know...'

'Nope. That's not going to happen. We weren't right for each other. But I want to see her daughter Rachel again, and I'm pleased we're back on speaking terms. She didn't hate me that much if she bothered to come and find me.'

'I don't think she ever hated you.' Again, there was silence for a bit.

'You guys in any trouble?' said Lucas, to break the silence again.

'Trouble?'

'Well, you did disobey a direct order from a superintendent, raid a house unarmed without a warrant, and then attack a man with a variety of knives, cutting his ankles to shreds. I was just wondering how they'd swept that under the carpet?' Lucas had a big grin, exposing his missing teeth.

'Well, Cross isn't speaking. Superintendent Carmichael is resigning, and we ended one of the biggest man-hunts in fifty years. So I think we're OK. Has, er... has Carmichael been to see you?'

'She turned up at the hospital last week, but I refused to see her. I worked with her for twelve years, giving everything to the investigation. And she sided with a bloke she'd been sleeping with. No, I don't need to hear her explanation, if I'm honest. From what Chloe told me, if she'd listened to you from the start, I'd probably still have most of my fingers and my leg.' He turned away from the window to face Kim again. 'You know, I'll never be able to say thank you properly.'

'You'll never need to, Lucas,' she said, placing her hand on his. It was comforting for the pair of them, although neither knew if it was a sign of friendship or something more. They stayed like that for at least ten minutes, watching the world go by.

'Will you be coming back?'

'I doubt I'll be able to, with my missing bits.'

'Don't see why that should stop you,' she replied doggedly. 'You still have your mind.'

Lucas paused and considered what he was about to say.

'It was your mind that solved the case. I ended up in that basement by a combination of chance and stupidity. You were there through hard work and intelligence.'

'I... well...' Kim was flustered; she didn't quite know how to take such a compliment.

'It's too early to say if I'll be back. Right now, I want to get out of here and get back to Luna. I'm sure she's been missing me, but nobody is allowed to bring her for a visit. She's in some kennel, and I know she'll hate it. I want to see her as soon as I can get outside.'

'Ah,' said Kim, a cheeky smile forming. 'She isn't in a kennel, actually.'

'Sorry? Is she OK?' he said, panicked.

'You tell me,' replied Kim as she got up from bed and went to the door. She opened it and waved in DC Green, who was wearing his full police uniform, complete with an overly large high-visibility jacket.

'Sir,' he said, nodding at Lucas. He opened the jacket to reveal a small, black and white spaniel whose tail immediately wagged so furiously when she saw Lucas, that her whole back end moved like a metronome. Even with her arthritis, she was wiggling around desperately trying to get free from DC Green.

'Luna!' shouted Lucas without thinking, tears welling in his eyes. Kim took the animated dog from DC Green, who turned and retook his post outside. She placed her as gently as she could on Lucas's lap. Luna stood up on her little back legs and licked Lucas's face without a moment's hesitation as he sobbed and stroked her back with his free hand.

'She's been staying with me for the last few nights. I thought you'd prefer that,' said Kim. 'Chloe had her for a bit, too; you should know that.'

'Thank you,' blubbered Lucas through fits of tears. He took a big sniff to get some composure back. 'It was something that kept me going, down in that flat. The first thing I'm going to do, the moment I'm able, is take this dog to one of those beaches we saw in Wales. I'll let her pad around on the sand, paddle in the sea, and do whatever she wants. She's never seen the beach, which is a tragedy. I spent all this time married to the job; I couldn't even take Luna to the beach.' Yet more tears were starting to form in the corner of his eye, but he quickly stopped them by blinking.

Kim squeezed his hand and said, 'You know, the chemo unit I was in is about a hundred yards down there. When you get your prosthetic and can walk again, I'd like to show you it,' she said.

'Look, I know you had cancer; I know it was worse than this, but please, just let me have my moment of sickness, will you?' He flashed a playful grin at Kim, who zipped an even cheekier one back.

'No, cancer is the ultimate trump card, Lucas. Your missing leg is nothing compared to my missing tits!' and the pair of them fell about laughing whilst Luna continued to wag her tail and push herself into Lucas's chest.

Chloe stood in the doorway, some flowers in her hand, watching the pair laughing together.

'You can go in if you want,' said DC Green, smiling.

'It's OK, I'll let them finish' She didn't want Lucas back; that ship had sailed, but she wanted him to be happy. So she waited, and she let them have their laugh. It was good to see him smiling, especially with someone as pure as Kim. She watched through the doorway as Kim put her jacket back on and left, but not without one final comforting hand on his shoulder and a little kiss on Luna's forehead. As she came out of the door, Chloe pretended just to be arriving.

'Hi, how is he?'

'Oh, hi,' said Kim, beaming. 'He's in good spirits; it's one of the good days. Especially now he's got his dog. What about you?'

'Me? Getting by. I've got to keep face for Rachel. I still get the headaches, though. Your cuts and bruises seem to have gone?'

'The ones on the outside have.'

'Look, with Superintendent Carmichael stepping down, your complete team will get a reshuffle. I'd understand if you want to hang about and see what comes your way, but we could do with someone like you in Missing Persons. DC Green here has already jumped ship, although I think that was to try shagging DC Adams.'

'Oi!' said DC Green incredulously.

'Thought she had a boyfriend?' smirked Kim.

'No, I only said that because DC Green didn't stand a chance.' she laughed before turning to DC Green. 'But you're a good egg, actually, so I put in a good word for you. I can't help you being ugly, though!'

They all fell about laughing before the two women exchanged a quick hug and said their goodbyes. As Kim walked away, Chloe turned and headed into the room. Lucas turned and gave her a big grin, a pleasant grin. But not the same grin he'd given DS Kimberly Sterling.

Epilogue

The soft, golden light of the sun danced in the sky, reflecting off the gentle waves that lapped at her paws. She raised her snout to the sky, snuffling the air, which ruffled her greying fur and blew with the unfamiliar scent of salt and adventure. Her little foot pads touched the grainy ground, a new sensation to this furry little spaniel. The beach, an expansive world of wonder and mystery, unfolded before her. The vast stretch of sand beckoned, extending far beyond her keenest sense of smell.

With each step, a cascade of delightful textures greeted her. The sand was cool and slightly damp, and she felt a rush of joy she hadn't experienced in years. The sand squished between her toes as she raced back and forth, barking in sheer delight. It felt like the earth whispered secrets through the grains, tales of the ocean's ebb and flow.

In the distance, a symphony of waves roared, a mesmerising melody that piqued Luna's curiosity. She ventured closer, the salty breeze swishing faster, tousling her fur and carrying the enticing scent of fish and seaweed. Her floppy ears perked up, and her head cocked to one side; he wasn't following her. Her human was sitting on a piece of driftwood up by the dune near the top of the beach. She could see him watching her, but he wasn't playing. He didn't play anymore.

With a burst of excitement, she tried to dash towards the

water's edge. Her little legs were stiff with the arthritis, but today, she didn't care. She would bound through the pain as she had never experienced anything like this before. It was truly remarkable.

She turned again to check on her human. He was exactly where she left him. The only thing that could make this new experience better would be if he would just play with her. He was sad; she could see it in his eyes. They weren't as shiny as they used to be. She turned back and looked at the waves. Oh, how she longed to go trotting through them. But he was sad, and she knew how to help him when he was sad.

She wandered back to him, and when she got close enough, she nuzzled her soft snout through his hands and put her little head on his lap. She looked up at him. His eyes were watering now. She felt him take her ear in his hand, as he often did, and begin massaging it. That would cheer him up, she thought.

And it did.

Printed in Great Britain
by Amazon